DEVIL'S GAME

DEVIL'S GAME

JOANNA WYLDE

BERKLEY BOOKS, NEW YORK

THE BERKLEY PUBLISHING GROUP
Published by the Penguin Group
Penguin Group (USA) LLC
375 Hudson Street, New York, New York 10014

USA • Canada • UK • Ireland • Australia • New Zealand • India • South Africa • China

penguin.com

A Penguin Random House Company

This book is an original publication of The Berkley Publishing Group.

Library of Congress Cataloging-in-Publication Data

Wylde, Joanna.
Devil's game / Joanna Wylde.—Berkley trade paperback edition.
pages cm—(Reapers motorcycle club ; 2)
ISBN 978-0-425-27235-0 (paperback)
1. Single mothers—Fiction.   2. Motorcyclists—Fiction.   3. Motorcycle clubs—Fiction.   I. Title.
PS3623.Y544D48   2014
813'.6—dc23   2014006268

PUBLISHING HISTORY
Berkley trade paperback edition / June 2014

PRINTED IN THE UNITED STATES OF AMERICA

10 9 8 7 6 5 4 3 2 1

Cover art by Tony Mauro.
Cover design by George Long.
Interior text design by Kristin del Rosario.

ACKNOWLEDGMENTS

I live in terror of leaving out someone important at the beginning of every book, because so many people have worked together to make *Devil's Game* possible. Special thanks to Cindy Hwang, my editor, and Amy Tannenbaum, my agent, for all your ongoing support. I am also very appreciative of the entire team at Berkley, especially Jessica Brock, who has worked so hard to help me achieve success.

I want to thank my writing friends and beta readers, who give me daily encouragement. These include Kylie Scott, Kim Jones, Renee Carlino, Kim Karr, Katy Evans, Kristin Ashley, Cara Carnes, Raelene, Sali, Hang, and Lori. You ladies are amazing.

Without the support of reading groups, bloggers and super readers (you know who you are), no author would ever reach her audience. I love you Maryse, Jenny, Gitte, Lisa, Giselle, the ladies of the Triple M, the ladies of Kristen Ashley Anonymous, and all the incredible women in my Junkies group. I also want to give a special shout-out to the girls I originally met on Maryse's Facebook page— I'm so honored to have your support as I've built my writing career. I hope you know how much I treasure you in my life!

Finally, I need to thank my family for their endless support. My husband, my kids, my parents, and my brother kick ass. I love you guys so much!

AUTHOR'S NOTE

Devil's Game covers some of the same time period and events in *Reaper's Legacy*, but if you've read other books in the series you'll note that this book is slightly different in tone. I've had several people ask me why, and the only explanation I can offer is that the characters are younger and this is how their story played out. In many ways this is a New Adult book, and the structure reflects that.

A note on motorcycle club culture: One of the most common questions I hear from readers is, "How real is the Reapers MC?" It's difficult to answer because my books are romantic fantasies, and aren't intended to delve into the inner workings of a club or explore the ethical implications of club life. They're meant to entertain, and have been sensationalized to make that happen.

Having said that, as a former journalist, I started the series determined to make it as realistic as possible in terms of culture and language. To that end, *Devil's Game* has been reviewed for accuracy by a woman currently attached to an outlaw club, and the club details are relatively true to life (with a few minor exceptions, where I allowed myself some artistic license). MC culture is diverse and the lives of women living in clubs are relatively undocumented. It has been my privilege to get to know many of these women through my research, and I have come to believe that stereotypes about their existence are often inaccurate and even damaging. Their input on this story has been extremely valuable, and I am deeply appreciative of their ongoing support.

PROLOGUE

"For fuck's sake . . . they're like weasels in heat. I'm gonna puke."

I nodded, agreeing with my sister one hundred percent.

Barfing was the only reasonable response to this shit.

We stood in our dining room, which connected to the kitchen through a pair of pocket doors. Dad had Mom up on the counter, legs wrapped around his waist, his tongue so far down her throat it should've triggered her gag reflex.

"You do realize we're watching you, right?" Kit asked loudly. Dad pulled away and turned his head to glare at us. Mom winked, but she didn't have the grace to blush.

"Take another ten minutes to fix your hair or something," he said. "Then come back down for breakfast."

Kit growled next to me. She had Dad's temper. I wish I did. I always followed the rules, and it kind of sucked. Kit called me a daddy's girl and maybe she was right. But I just really hated pissing him off.

"It's the first day of school and I don't want to be late," she declared. "You can screw each other any time, but this only happens once a year. I'm hungry."

Dad stepped slowly away from Mom, turning toward us and crossing his arms. His faded tats told a hundred stories, and most of my friends were a little nervous around him. His black leather cut, emblazoned with Reapers MC colors, didn't help. Lucky us— we couldn't have a normal dad who worked at a bank or something.

Nope.

Ours had to be the president of a motorcycle club.

According to my best friend Quinn, Dad was a badass motherfucker, and she was right. I knew no matter what happened, he'd always be there for me. Secretly, I liked the fact that the Reapers would back him up. The sight of Dad's tats and patches made me feel sort of safe, but I'd never admit it. None of that made finding him and my mom practically doing it in the kitchen any less disgusting. I mean, I made sandwiches on that counter. Now where was I supposed to make them?

"For once," Kit said, narrowing her eyes, "would you please act like normal parents and just ignore each other during a meal?"

"Sounds boring," Dad muttered, narrowing his eyes right back. Mom and I locked gazes, and she made a face. I hated this part— Dad and Kit could turn anything into a fight. Mom said they were way too similar, and I agreed. She was the oil that kept our family running smoothly, defusing situations before they got out of hand.

"I don't like being bored," he added. "Go do whatever it is girls do in the bathroom for a while, and then you can come back down. My house, my rules."

I grabbed Kit's arm, tugging her away before she fired back at him. She was only twelve and I was fourteen, but she always stood her ground. Sometimes that was a good thing . . . But she needed to learn to choose her battles.

"Just come upstairs," I hissed at her.

"They're too old to be screwing in the kitchen!"

"We're not screwing," Dad said. "But if we were, that wouldn't be any of your business, either, kiddo."

I dug my fingers into Kit's arm, dragging her out of the dining room and up the stairs. I heard Dad laugh in the background, and Mom gave a little squeal.

"They're so disgusting," Kit said, flopping down on my bed. We had our own rooms, but she spent a lot of time in here because it was bigger. It also had a tree branch we could use to sneak out . . . Not that we ever did, but Kit had big plans for high school.

"I know," I replied. "He's right, though. It's his house."

"At least you aren't stuck in dumbass middle school," she said, sighing heavily. "I can't believe you're going to be gone! It's not fair."

"Only one more year and you'll be there, too," I said. Figuring I might as well take advantage of the delay, I studied my hair in the mirror on the waterfall vanity Mom had given me when I turned thirteen. It'd been hers growing up. I'd always loved sitting at it as a little girl, putting on her makeup and pretending to be a princess. "And I'm sure it won't be that great. I mean, freshman year is kind of lame."

"Beats the hell out of eighth grade," she said. "But you won't get to do much anyway. Do you really think Dad'll let you go to any dances?"

"Of course he will," I said, even though I had my doubts. Dad could be . . . intense . . . Kit opened her mouth to say something but then snapped it shut as we heard the roar of Harley pipes coming down the drive.

"What the hell?" I asked, going over to the window. Outside, six of the Reapers were pulling up—at seven thirty on a Tuesday . . . Not good. The guys in the club didn't tend to be morning people.

"Shit," Kit muttered. "Something must be going on."

We looked at each other, and I wondered if she had the same sick feeling in the pit of my stomach I did. "Something going on" could mean anything in our world. Dad didn't generally let club business overlap with family life, but I'd seen enough growing up that I couldn't just pretend things were fine and dandy when a third of the brothers showed up without warning.

"I'm going downstairs," Kit said, her voice grim. I shook my head.

"They won't want us around."

"Fuck that."

We crept down the stairs like junior felons.

I expected to hear hushed voices, to feel the kind of tension in the air that only came when things fell to shit. Instead I heard men laughing and talking in the kitchen. We entered the dining room to find our uncle Duck sitting at the table as my mom brought him a cup of coffee. Dad sat next to him, along with Ruger—the very hot young prospect who'd been with the club about four months. I had to look away before I started babbling or blushing or something.

When I grew up, I was *totally* marrying Ruger.

This was not something I'd be sharing with my father, no matter how much of a daddy's girl I might be. Ruger had graduated from high school a year ago, and Quinn had told me she'd caught him screwing her sister, Nicole, in their living room when her parents were out for the night. I'd pretended to be horrified, but I made her share all the gory details . . . and there were a lot of them. Quinn hadn't run away when she found them. Nope. She stayed hidden and watched the whole thing, which, according to her, wasn't a quickie.

Not even close.

Quinn also said that Ruger had a pierced dick, and that her sister cried for three nights straight because he never called her back afterward. When I was old enough, he'd be calling *me* back. I had big plans for us.

"Morning," Duck said, smiling at me. He wouldn't tell me why they called him Duck, but I always thought he looked more like an old bear. Big and hairy, which would've been intimidating if he hadn't been giving me airplane rides and sneaking me candy for as long as I could remember. "You look beautiful, Em. You're gonna do great in high school."

He glanced over at my dad.

"I still can't believe our girl is old enough for this."

Ugh. I hated it when they did this, especially in front of Ruger. Everyone seemed to think I was a baby, but I was fourteen now. In less than two years I'd be driving. Well, driving legally. I'd been driving on the property for years . . .

"Appreciate you coming out," Dad said to the guys. "Em, grab some breakfast. We're gonna give you a ride to school this morning. I don't want to be late."

My mouth dropped open and I heard Kit make a startled, choking noise.

"We?" I whispered, hoping I'd heard wrong.

"All of us," Dad said, offering me a broad smile that didn't reach his eyes. "You're turning into a young woman. I figured it might not be a bad idea to remind those little pricks at your school who your family is. Go ahead and set things straight from the start."

I actually felt dizzy.

"Daddy, you can't be serious!" Kit burst out. "If all of you guys show up, you'll scare the crap out of the boys! How will Em ever get a date that way?"

Dad's smile turned feral.

"Any boy who can't handle Em's family has no business dating her."

I swallowed. This couldn't be happening. My mom ran her fingers through his hair, and he pulled her down into his lap. They were always like that—all over each other. Still, Mom usually stood up to him when he got crazy protective. Unlike Dad, she had a clue what it meant to be a teenage girl.

"Mom, I thought you were giving me a ride?" I managed to squeak out. She shook her head sadly.

"Sorry, baby. Your father is set on this," she said. "I'm driving Kit and he's taking you, along with your uncle Duck and the brothers."

"Those little pricks at your school need to know who they're dealing with if they fuck you over," Dad added, his voice dark. "I don't want to make things hard for you, but I've been a teenage boy. They think with their cocks, so they need to realize they'll lose those cocks if they don't treat you right. Nothing quite like a show of force to put a kid on notice."

"That's bullshit, Daddy, and you know it," Kit said, coming to my defense. Thank God, because I'd lost the ability to think or move. "And it's sexist! Em can take care of herself. You have no right to humiliate her like this."

"I have every right," he replied, and I knew from his tone that it was all over. "I'm your father, and it's my job to protect you. Not my goal to embarrass you, Em, but I'll do whatever it takes to keep you safe."

"Nobody wants to hurt me," I managed to say.

He snorted.

"They'll want to fuck you, though."

I felt my cheeks turn bright red and I kept my eyes down, terrified to look at Ruger or any of the others.

"You want me to treat you like an adult?" Dad asked. "Pretty hard when just mentioning sex makes you blush. If you can't talk about it, you sure as shit aren't ready to do it. This way nobody will pressure you to, either. Now grab some cereal if you're planning to eat. We'll be leaving soon."

I felt sick. My high school life was over before it even began, and he wanted me to *eat cereal*?

"I'll just have a granola bar," I muttered, glaring at him. Dad shrugged and I saw his hand slide between my mom's legs.

Ugh. My life sucked.

• • •

I usually love riding with my dad.

There's nothing better than sitting behind him—arms wrapped tight around his waist—as we fly down the highway. Kit may have gotten Dad's temper, but I got his passion for the road. I'd been saving for my own bike since I was six years old, and I saw the pride in his eyes every time I begged him to take me with him.

Today, though . . . For the first time in my life, I hated it.

We pulled up to the school in a roar, me and Dad in the lead, followed by six Reapers (including Ruger, who'd probably slept with half the girls there before he graduated). Dad stopped right out in front, in a no-parking zone, and the brothers all backed their rides in next to his, forming a row of gleaming chrome. Any fantasy I might've had about a quick, quiet entrance on my first day was gone.

One of the teachers—a woman who was probably in her midtwenties—stood out on the lawn looking nervous, but as the guys swung off she didn't ask them to move. Nope, she just gaped at us, which would've been funny if I hadn't been fairly sure I was in one of her classes. I recognized her from the open house. Ruger smirked and swaggered over to her. She blushed brightly.

Shit, was there anyone at this school he hadn't had sex with? Maybe I should rethink those wedding plans.

"Okay, well, thanks for the ride," I told my dad pointedly. "You can go now."

"Show me your locker," he said, obviously determined to smash any chance of happiness I might have during the next four years. I looked up at him and gave it everything I had. The puppy eyes, the little-girl lip bite, a hitch in my breath. Usually I could even squeeze out a tear or two, but that took more prep time.

"Daddy, can you just let me go in on my own?" I asked, my voice a quavering whisper. "You made your point."

He shook his head, ruthless.

"Don't even try," he said. "I've seen it all before, and compared to your mother, you're an amateur. I'm coming inside because I want every kid here to understand you belong to the Reapers MC, and they'll be answering to us if they fuck with you."

I don't know why I bothered trying.

Dad was a force of nature—a tidal wave determined to destroy my life. Every eye followed us as we walked through the doors and down the hallway. Quinn caught my gaze and raised her eyebrows dramatically. I shrugged, resigned, and looked for number 1125, which was on the first floor near the boys' locker room.

The locker room where the football team was starting to wander out after an early-morning practice.

Perfect.

My life was fucking perfect.

I looked up to see Quinn's brother, Jason, a junior and one of the team's defensive starters, watching us. I'd always had a crush on him. In fact, I was sort of secretly hoping he'd finally notice me as someone other than his little sister's annoying friend. Seriously—if I wanted a guy like Ruger to call me back, I'd need some practice, right?

"Reed," Dad said casually, jerking his chin toward Jason. "Great season last year. How are things looking so far with the team?"

Jason swallowed, eyes darting between us.

"Um, pretty good," he said. I opened my locker, wishing desperately that I could crawl inside and die. Or at least disappear for the next four years. Sadly, not even a boobless wonder like me could fit in that metal box.

"Glad to hear it," Dad replied. He leaned over and kissed the top of my head, then spoke so loud his voice practically echoed. "Enjoy high school, princess. You let me know if any of these guys give you shit, got it?"

I nodded, praying for death. Something fast, merciful. Aneurysm? Yeah, that'd do it.

"Just go," I whispered.

"I'll see you tonight," he replied, then turned and sauntered down the hallway, the colors on his back a grim reminder to everyone who saw us that my dad was president of the Reapers motorcycle club.

Quinn came up next to me and leaned against the lockers, eyes wide.

"Wow," she said. "Nobody's gonna ask you to homecoming or anything, you get that, right? And you're never, ever gonna get laid."

"I know," I said, miserable. Not that I wanted to get laid—not quite yet.

But it'd be nice to go to homecoming. I sighed.

"I'm gonna die a virgin, Quinn."

She nodded gravely, eyes full of sympathy.

"I think that's a given," she said. "But look on the bright side."

"What's that?"

"Nuns don't have to wear those penguin costumes anymore, so at least you won't have to buy all new clothes."

I looked over at Jason, who was staring at me like I'd grown a second head.

My dad was the meanest parent ever.

Ugh.

EIGHT YEARS AGO
STOCKTON, CALIFORNIA
HUNTER

Natalie wiped off her mouth and looked up at me, her beautiful face sly and calculating. I shoved my softening cock back into my pants and zipped up, pushing forward off the brick wall behind the gas station. Nat rose to her feet, giving me a little smile and biting her lip. I think she was going for playful.

It came off desperate.

"So?" she asked. I raised a brow, questioning.

"So what?"

"Um . . . I was wondering if you could hook me up?"

Fucking typical. Rich bitches.

Not that I should be surprised. In Natalie's world, I'd never be more than a quick fuck with the right connections. That wasn't a problem. In the end, business is business, and Nat had plenty of money.

"Whatcha lookin' for?" I asked, hoping she didn't expect a discount for the blow job. She was okay, but nothing special. She'd been all over me, and who was I to turn down some chick who wanted to suck my cock? Now that she'd swallowed, she'd turned annoying. Before Natalie could answer the question, my phone vibrated.

Kelsey. Shit.

I answered, turning away from Natalie. "Hey, Kels."

"Jim got laid off at the plant today. You need to get home fast, because he's drunk and I'm scared."

My entire body tensed and my vision narrowed. *That cocksucking bastard. If he touches her . . .*

"I'll be there in a few, okay? Stay calm, Kelsey," I told my foster sister. "Try and get out of the house and take off for the park. If that doesn't work, lock yourself in the bathroom. Just hang on—I'm coming for you."

"Okay," she whispered, and I heard Jim's loud, booming voice roar in the background. James Calloway was the foster father from hell, not to mention a complete fucking asshole. I ended the call and glanced over at Natalie, keeping my face blank. I'd learned the hard way to never give away more than I had to.

"I need to get back home," I told her. "Can I have a ride?"

She smiled, trying to play coy and innocent.

"Of course," she said, tracing little circles in the dirt with the toe of those fuck-me shoes she always wore. They'd seemed a hell of a lot sexier half an hour ago. "But before we go . . ."

Shit. I didn't have time for this.

"Give me the fuckin' keys," I said shortly, out of patience. She opened her mouth to protest and I narrowed my eyes, letting them go flat and dead. I'd perfected the look over the years and it never failed. She sucked in a quick breath and dug out her keys, handing them off to me. At six foot three, I knew I was a scary fucker.

Terrifying a girl didn't bother me one bit, either.

I strode around the building to Natalie's cute little Mustang—a sixteenth-birthday present from Daddy. I slid in and the engine turned over with a roar I might've enjoyed at any other time. Natalie jumped into the passenger seat, obviously worried that I'd leave without her.

I would've, too, but I didn't want more attention than necessary. Last time I'd pulled Jim off Kelsey, I promised to kill him if it happened again. Christ, she was only thirteen and had already learned to sleep with a knife. I had a bad feeling things were going to get ugly, and the last thing I needed was a police report about a stolen car.

Five minutes later the Mustang screeched to a halt outside my foster father's decaying ranch house, which was surrounded by a dying lawn and rusting swing set. His own kids were long gone, and I suspected he'd lose the place without the state payments he got for me and Kels. The social workers hadn't noticed that his wife, Autumn, had taken off nearly six months ago. Who could blame her? This was only short term for me. But to stay here, rotting for the rest of your life? Fuck no. I'd have run, too.

Usually I didn't even mind living in his shithole. I liked having my own space. I had the whole basement, although I let Kelsey sleep down there with me. She wasn't comfortable in her own room upstairs. Too close to Jim. Smart kid.

I jumped out of the car and started toward the house.

"Wait!" Natalie called, following me.

"Yeah?" I asked, not slowing. I heard Jim yell something inside and froze, trying to think. What was the best plan of attack? A loud, clanging noise from next door broke my concentration. That old guy must be out in the garage, working on his bikes again . . .

"You said you'd hook me up?" Nat asked, offering a weak smile. *Jesus, is she still here?* I reached into my pocket, pulled out a baggie, and threw it at her. Hard.

"There," I said. "Now get in your fuckin' car and go."

Her mouth opened and closed like a goldfish, and I seriously wondered why I'd let her wrap it around my dick. Then Kelsey's voice tore through the air again, and my vision went red. Making plans was for pussies—that asshole needed to experience pain. I took off toward the back gate, hoping Natalie was happy enough about her freebies to forget anything she'd seen or heard.

Goddammit.

It was locked.

I boosted myself up and over the tall privacy fence, catching a glimpse of Natalie in the process. She wasn't paying me any attention. Nope, bitch was way too busy scrabbling in the dry grass for her goody bag. Kelsey screamed again. I tore around the house, sliding down through a narrow window into the basement.

Jim always kept the doors locked and I wasn't allowed a key. Not that it mattered—I'd yet to find a lock I couldn't pick—but right then I didn't have the time. I ran up the stairs and toward Kelsey's room, freezing in the doorway.

She cowered back on the bed, shirt ripped almost to her waist, exposing the little flesh-colored bra I'd had to buy for her. Fuckin' awkwardest shopping trip of my life. A bright red handprint covered her cheek, and blood was seeping from her bottom lip.

Jim loomed over her, sweaty and reeking of booze, shoulders heaving as he took deep breaths. His pants were already loose, hanging off his flabby, narrow hips, and his skinny dick bobbled like a drunken cobra.

"Leave her alone," I said, letting all the hate constantly boiling inside me show. Jim turned toward me and grunted, his red, bloated nose a rotten tomato in the center of his face.

"Or what?"

"You'll die," said a low voice behind me. Then I heard the unmistakable sound of a gun being cocked.

We all froze as our next-door neighbor walked slowly into the room. He held his pistol casually, more like a TV remote than a weapon. An older guy—probably in his midfifties—and so far as I could tell, he spent most of his time out in his garage, tinkering with motorcycles he fixed up and sold.

In fact, I'd been eyeing his latest project, mentally tallying whether I could afford to buy it.

Burke.

That was his name. No idea if it was first or last. He was badass, too, with a long, graying beard and faded tattoos all over his arms. I knew he was part of a motorcycle club called the Devil's Jacks from the patches on the leather vest he always wore. This was the first chance I'd gotten a good look at it. On one shoulder there was a red and white patch with "Burke" over the word "Original." The other shoulder had a diamond that said "1%" on it. Down below was a long line of smaller patches listing names and dates.

His heavily tanned hand didn't waver as he held the gun, his eyes as cold and dead as my own.

"Kelsey, get your ass out of here," I ordered, keeping my voice steady. I really didn't know Burke for shit, and I had no idea what he planned to do . . . But if I got Kels out safe, I honestly didn't give a fuck.

"Do what the kid says."

Kelsey nodded, eyes wide, sliding off the bed and scuttling along the wall to get out.

"Go down to my room and wait," I told her. "Lock the door and don't open it for anyone but me."

Time hung heavy as she disappeared.

"So whatcha gonna do, shoot me?" Jim slurred, his voice belligerent. Not the brightest man at the best of times, but when he got drunk, things really fell apart.

"Depends," said Burke.

"On what?"

"The kid, here," he replied, jerking his chin toward me. "You want to shoot this asshole, son?"

I glanced over, startled. His face was cold and serious—Burke wasn't joking. Shit.

This was real.

"Think hard," Burke said. "You pull the trigger, you can't go back. But you won't have to worry about him rapin' your sister, either. We can make the body disappear."

Jim's eyes darted between us, wild with terror.

"Don't listen to him," he whispered. "You'll go to jail. Death penalty. He's talking about *murder*."

"Unlikely," Burke told him. "Never cared for you, Calloway. In fact, I don't think one person on earth gives a fuck if you live or die. Your wife is gone, your kids hate you, and according to the papers on your kitchen counter, you got no job. It'll be like you never existed. Couldn't happen to a nicer guy."

"The social workers," Jim gasped in desperation. "The social workers have to come check on the kids. They'll notice."

I couldn't help myself—I started laughing. I hadn't seen my social worker in over a year. If it weren't for the state checks Jim drank up every month, I'd assume they'd lost my file. My foster father's face reddened in rage, and I saw the exact moment his brain turned off and he forgot about the gun.

"I'll kill you, you little shit," he growled. "You think you're so special but you're trash. That little slut of yours is trash, too. Two piles of garbage stinking up my house."

"Probably should decide soon, kid," Burke muttered. "You wanna take him out or not?"

Did I want to kill him? I thought about Kelsey crying, and the time he'd broken my ribs when I refused to hand over a cut of my sales.

Fuckin' A.

I *definitely* wanted to take him out.

"Give me the gun," I said, the words tasting sweet.

Jim lunged toward us and the sudden, cracking echo of a gunshot rang through the room. My foster father screamed and fell to the floor, clutching his shoulder. Bright red blood oozed out between his fingers.

Burke didn't even blink.

He just held his weapon firm, still trained on Jim, and reached around his back to pull a second pistol from his pants. Then he handed it to me.

It fit my hand perfectly.

"You know how to use it?" he asked.

I flipped off the safety and cocked it in answer.

"Finish him off, boy," Burke said, smiling for the first time. Almost like a proud father. "You're already in deep, so you might as well make it count."

I centered the barrel on Jim's chest and fired.

Looking back, the neighborhood had been exactly what we needed that day—nobody in it gave a fuck about each other, because they didn't give a fuck about themselves. All of us were already dying slowly. When Burke and I sped up the process for my foster father that afternoon, the neighbors didn't even notice.

Nobody complained about the shots.

Nobody bothered calling the cops when I carried a hysterically crying Kelsey next door to Burke's house.

They didn't look outside when a cargo van pulled down the alley to stop behind Jim's place. Ten minutes later it left again, carrying a human-shaped package wrapped in black plastic garbage bags.

Jim ceased to exist. So did me and Kelsey.

The next week, we were living in a different town with new birth certificates, courtesy of Burke's cousin and his old lady. He gave me a hell of a deal on that motorcycle, too. I paid him with the wad of cash I found in Jim's wallet. A year later, I celebrated my eighteenth birthday by becoming an official prospect in the Devil's Jacks MC.

Burke couldn't have been more proud if I were his son by blood. In a way, I guess I was.

PART ONE

CHAPTER ONE

FIVE MONTHS AGO
COEUR D'ALENE, IDAHO
HUNTER

"Who the fuck gets a pedicure in February?" Skid asked. "Won't her feet freeze?"

"You don't know any women at all, do you?" I asked, cracking open a Mountain Dew. We'd driven all night to get here from Portland. What I really wanted was sleep, but Burke's orders were clear. Scope out Reese "Picnic" Hayes's daughter and figure out a plan of action. With all the drama that'd happened between our clubs, Burke insisted now was the perfect time to make a move, maybe even rewrite the future for the Devil's Jacks.

Leverage with the Reapers would be critical—maybe even make the difference between a successful takeover of our club or a shallow grave if we failed. Leverage this little bitch was supposed to provide us, apparently. I wasn't entirely sure what the old bastard had planned, but I'd do my part. I always did.

I glanced down at the picture of her taped to the truck's console, then looked at the storefront again. Pretty girl. According to her Facebook page, she was meeting a friend here this morning. I'd spotted her car as soon as we pulled in. Now we waited. I wanted to study her, maybe trail her a little. Get a sense of who she was before making my move. There were so many different ways to play a woman—I found it never paid to make assumptions.

"I know your sister," Skid announced out of nowhere.

I gave him a blank look.

"You asked if I know any women. Does she count? 'Cause her toes are cute as hell, but I don't see her walkin' around in flip-flops in the snow."

"Why the fuck are you lookin' at my sister's toes, cocksucker?"

"I look at a lot more than her toes."

"Don't make me kill you, bro."

He snorted and shrugged. "You could try."

I adjusted my sunglasses, deciding to ignore him. The truck windows were tinted, but I'd still taken a few basic precautions to change my appearance. Hipster beanie, which matched the full beard I'd grown for my last job. Long-sleeved shirt that covered my ink. Even if she saw me, all I needed was a quick shave and change to turn into a different man.

The shop door opened and I sat up as two girls stepped out. There she was.

Emmy Lou Hayes.

"That's our girl," I said, with a jerk of my chin. She was studying her phone and, sure as shit, she wore flip-flops. Bright pink foam thingies threaded through her toes, separating them, and I wondered how the hell she could even walk. Fuckin' crazy. At least the sidewalk was mostly clear of snow. Her brown hair sat on top of her head in one of those messy topknot things girls always seem to have, and she wore tight little jeans and a black leather jacket.

Damn, Em was cute. Way cuter than her sister.

Something fell out of her pocket, and she turned away, leaning down to grab it.

"Nice ass," Skid said. "Very sweet. If you have to fuck her, at least you'll be able to keep your eyes open, unlike that last bitch you did for the club."

I snorted, but he raised a good point. Fucking Em had just jumped up a couple notches on my list of possible ways to manipulate her into helping the Jacks. She glanced down at her phone again, waving good-bye to her friend absently.

Then she walked right off the curb and almost fell on her ass.

Her phone flew across the ground and under a car, like something out of a TV show. Em staggered to one side and then the other, somehow managing to stay on her feet, arms flailing. Skid choked back a laugh, but I just watched, mesmerized, as she finally caught herself. That's when Em looked up and across the parking lot, right into my face. Her expression was startled but fucking gorgeous. She broke into a brilliant smile, offering me a goofy wave.

My cock stiffened and a burst of adrenaline hit me like a punch to the gut. Sticking my dick inside Emmy Hayes had suddenly become a very high priority. It took everything I had not to throw open the truck door and toss the girl over my shoulder before hauling her back home for a long, hard fuck. Instead I sat back and watched.

There's a reason the club calls me Hunter.

She lifted one leg slightly, pointing at her toes and giving a triumphant thumbs-up in my direction before turning away to search for her phone.

"Christ, there's something wrong with that chick," Skid muttered, but I ignored him. Instead I grabbed my phone and dialed Burke, my mind made up.

"Burke, I'm lookin' at her right now."

"You got a plan for me?"

"Gettin' there," I told him. "But whatever direction we take, Emmy Hayes stays my target. Nobody fucks with her but me."

"No shit?"

"No shit."

"Make it work for the club, son, and I could give a fuck. But no matter how much you want the bitch, don't forget where your loyalties lie. Jacks first. Forever."

"Jacks first," I agreed, watching as she dug her phone out of the snow.

This was gonna be fun.

PRESENT DAY
COEUR D'ALENE, IDAHO
EM

"If you don't make a move on Painter tonight, I will personally charter a plane, fly up there, and kick your ass."

"Easy for you to say," I muttered into the phone at my sister. "But you don't get a vote. I'm still pissed at you for not coming home this summer."

"Riiight," she drawled. "Let me see—internship in San Francisco or yet another summer of Dad growling at me . . . Sooo tempting. If you had half a brain, your ass would be down here with me."

I rolled my eyes.

"It's not that easy, Kit."

"Yes," she replied, her voice sharp. "It *is* that easy. Let me walk you through the conversation. 'Dad, I've decided I want a life. Deal with it.' Then get in your car and drive south."

I sighed.

"It's not that easy for *me*," I said, looking over at the Reapers clubhouse. The big, isolated former National Guard Armory was fully lit, a beacon in the summer twilight. The trees surrounding it felt familiar, like old friends. I'd played in them as child—hide-and-seek, pixies . . . oh, and motorcycle clubs. We'd played MC a lot.

Pisser about that—now the boys got to play Reapers for real and I still couldn't land a fucking date.

"I don't like that disappointed look in Dad's eyes," I said, fully aware my voice held a hint of whine. "You know, how they get cold and icy right before he starts punching walls?"

"Jesus, it's like you're still in high school," Kit replied. "So what if he gets pissed off? That's what he does—he gets pissed, he yells, it's over. Yell back, for Chrissake."

"Easy for you to say," I replied. "You're the baby. You can get away with anything. He has all these expectations of me."

"Enough," she snapped. "I'm not going to listen to you feeling all sorry for yourself all night. I'm the youngest, but *you're* the fucking baby. Either shit or get off the pot."

"That's kind of mean," I said, frowning.

"No, that's reality. You're twenty-two years old and still bitching about Daddy not letting you out to play. You want to be his little-girl doll the rest of your life? Fine. That's your choice. But if you do, you don't get to complain about him. Grow a fucking pair already."

Then she hung up on me.

I sat in the car, stunned. Kit never hung up on me. We talked, we fought, we laughed . . . but she always had my back.

Shit.

A loud knock on the window nearly gave me a heart attack. I looked up to see my friend Marie standing outside, arms crossed, face expectant. Must be almost time. I climbed out of the car and she caught me up in a hug.

"You excited?" she asked, eyes shining. "Because you don't *look* excited. You look like someone stole your last M&M. You know, one of the red ones? I always keep those for the end. They taste best."

I stared at her.

"You're weird, you realize that, right?"

She laughed and shrugged.

"I'm okay with it. You didn't answer the question."

"I guess I'm excited," I said, although my little chat with Kit had put a damper on things. "I mean, it's great that Painter's getting his patch . . ."

Marie widened her eyes at me and smirked.

"Don't give me that," she said. "You've got a thing for him. I *know* you've got a thing for him, because you tell me all about it whenever you get drunk."

I shrugged, a smile catching me off guard.

"Okay, so I have a thing for him," I admitted.

"And he definitely has a thing for you," Marie replied. "He's like a puppy whenever he sees you."

I grunted, my smile fading.

By some miracle, I hadn't spilled the story of when I'd cornered Painter last month and made him an offer no red-blooded man should've been able to refuse . . . An offer he'd shot down without a second thought. In fact, I'd tried to seduce him several times over the past year. A year I'd spent watching him, lusting after him, and thinking about what things might be like between us.

I didn't get why he wouldn't sleep with me. I knew the attraction was mutual. Everyone saw it. His eyes followed me around the clubhouse, and when I went out, he menaced anyone who hit on me. Dad wasn't too hot on the thought of me with any guy, but he'd told me that someday he'd like to see me settled with a Reaper.

"I guess we'll find out, won't we?" I asked, grabbing my bag. "Sorry I couldn't come out to help set up. I had a late appointment and really wanted to get her in. I already canceled on her once, so her nails were way overdue for a fill."

"No worries," Marie said, tucking her arm through mine. We started toward the gate to the courtyard, and despite my concerns her mood was contagious. Tonight was a happy night—after more than a year of prospecting, Painter would become the newest full member of the club.

In fact, he probably was already.

I'd just gotten here, but I'd seen this happen my whole life. First the guys would drag him off with some story about this shitty job

DEVIL'S GAME   25

he needed to do, or tell him he'd fucked up something important. They'd scare the crap out of him, and then when he was just about ready to die from a heart attack, they'd surprise him with the new patches for his cut.

Those patches marked him as a Reaper, now and forever.

As for us ladies? It was our job to put together the party, and I was sorry to have missed out on that . . . It might be work, but it was laughter and drinking and joking, too. Made me think of my mom—five years ago we'd buried her, and I never missed her more than on nights like tonight. One of my earliest memories was of playing under the tables in our backyard while she set up for a club party. This was a celebration for Painter, but it was also a gathering of my family. They weren't exactly typical . . . They were mine, though, and I loved them.

Tonight that family was getting bigger.

"I really wish Mom was here," I said. Marie smiled at me, wrapping an arm around my shoulders and hugging me tight. Then she dragged me past Banks, the unfortunate prospect left behind to watch the clubhouse, and we walked into the courtyard.

The guys were late.

It'd been about forty-five minutes—just enough time for me to drink two beers and exchange texts with my friend Liam. I'd never actually met him except online . . . But I knew he wasn't a total serial killer because he was a regular at my friend Cookie's coffee shop in Portland. He posted on her Facebook page all the time.

That's how we'd first started talking, a few months back. He'd comment on one of my posts, then I'd comment on one of his, and then one day he sent me a private message and things took off from there. Now we texted each other all the time. He was funny and interesting and he actually listened to me. Total opposite of Painter, now that I thought of it. It was nice to have a friend who wasn't all tied up in club life—Liam was nice and normal and safe.

ME: Painter isn't here yet. Fingers crossed for me!!!

LIAM: I don't get why you're bothering with this douche. A real
    man doesn't sit around waiting when he meets the right
    woman. He makes a plan to claim her ass

ME: Little Neanderthal, ya think? Someone's grumpy tonight

LIAM: Call it like I see it. I'll bet you a hundred bucks he bails
    on you. Not because you aren't gorgeous, Em, but because
    he's a fucking pussy. Don't you see what's going on here? He
    wants to make your dad happy, not you

ME: Whose side are you on?

LIAM: Yours

I frowned down at the phone. I wasn't quite sure what to say to
that. Liam didn't like Painter, and he could be kind of a jerk about
it. He'd even made a joke once about Dad selling me off for six
goats and some aftermarket Harley parts. It hit a little too close to
home . . .

That didn't mean he was right about Painter, though.

ME: You don't know everything.

LIAM: Never pretended to. But I do know you deserve better
    than a guy who ignores you for a year.

ME: He doesn't ignore me. It's complicated. You should see him
    when we all go out. He's always watching out for me

LIAM: No, he guards you. There's a difference

I frowned. It *was* complicated. Painter had been prospecting,
which meant he wasn't exactly free. But Liam didn't know that—
I hadn't told him about the club for some reason, although he
knew Dad was a biker. I guess I liked having one person in my life
who didn't see me as the president's daughter. Hell, in some ways
Liam was the only person I could really be myself with. Tonight,
though . . .

Tonight he was pissing me off.
Enough.

ME: I have to go

I muted my phone, then shoved it in my pocket. Then I grabbed another beer and wandered toward Marie and the other girls, who were laughing over some story she was telling about her old man, Horse. Good music was playing, and as the alcohol warmed me from the inside out, I felt optimistic, despite Liam. What did he know, anyway?

I fully intended to end the night in Painter's bed.

Or on his bike.

Maybe under a tree?

Hell, I didn't care. Not so long as he finally punched my V card and I got my prize, along with a lovely "thank you" for playing. And yeah, I know it's fucking ridiculous I still had a V card to punch. But Dad wasn't exactly friendly toward my boyfriends. One of his favorite things to do was show them his guns and talk about the types of damage different bullets could do to the human body.

Oh, and then there was that hunting accident. Oops.

For some reason, the men of Coeur d'Alene started avoiding me after *that* one. Now the closest I got to flirting was chatting with Liam, which was pretty pathetic when you considered he lived nearly four hundred miles away.

Tonight, I told myself. *Tonight everything changes.*

The men still weren't back after another half hour, but I didn't just stand around waiting for Painter. Hanging out with my friends kicked ass. Most of them were old ladies, meaning they were attached in some way to one of the guys in the club. Some were like me, though . . . adrift. Maggs, for one. Her man was in prison, so she was on her own.

There weren't any kids at the Armory because things would probably get crazy fast. I could already see a few women clumped on the other side of the courtyard just waiting for the wild times to start. Hangaround types, club sluts, sweetbutts. Some were strippers from The Line, the club's titty bar (and yes, that's what they called it, so don't blame me!), and others were girls who just weren't into settling down. They all had one thing in common, though—they were disposable. I'd grown up with them in the background, and in the past few years I'd woken up to find more than one in our kitchen making breakfast.

Dad was kind of a slut himself these days.

Their group didn't usually mix with ours and we liked it that way. I knew my dad never cheated on my mom, and I knew some of the guys—Marie's man, Horse, for example—could keep it in their pants. But others slept around. We all saw it. I never quite understood why a woman would put up with that, but I figured that other people's relationships weren't really my business.

Now we heard the thunder of bikes pulling up outside and the brothers started coming in. Dad was first, and I saw him glancing around until his eyes found me. His hard face broke into a smile, the same ice-blue eyes I'd inherited from him flashing with pride. The rest of the guys followed him, and then hoots and whistles rang out as Painter walked in, grinning like crazy.

God, he was cute. Short, spiky blond hair, sharp cheekbones . . . His body was lean but strong, and at six feet tall he had a good five inches on me. Didn't hurt that he'd taken off his shirt, wearing his cut over his bare chest.

Yum.

I'd had my arms wrapped tight around that chest more than once when he'd given me a ride home, although it never went past that. *It's a matter of respect for my dad*, I reminded myself. He was the president of the club and Painter knew better than to mess around with me if he wasn't serious. To be fair, prospects didn't really have the time to be serious about anyone.

At least that's what I'd been telling myself.

Prospects were too busy running errands, guarding bikes, and whatever other nasty or degrading jobs the members could think of. All that had changed now. This party was for Painter—he'd earned some fun, and the guys would make sure he got it. I had my own special congratulations to offer, although it might take a few hours to get him alone. I would, though. I was determined.

Tonight was our night.

"How goes it, Emmy Lou?" asked Duck, coming up and pulling me in for a hug. I crinkled my nose. I hated that old nickname, but it was damned hard to get rid of one once it stuck.

"Good," I said. "You got a beer yet? Want me to grab you one?"

"Sure, sweetheart," he muttered, looking across the yard. I saw his eye catch on one of the girls. "Who's that? She with your dad, or just here to party?"

He nodded toward a blonde who'd wrapped herself around my father. My eyes widened. Holy shit, I'd gone to high school with that bitch. In fact, she'd been a fucking freshman when I was a senior. Disgusting. I shrugged, feeling a sense of inevitability about the situation.

"Hell if I know," I muttered. "I stopped keeping track of his whores."

My tone came out uglier than I'd intended, and Duck gave me a sharp look.

"Sounding a little bitter there, Emmy Lou," Duck said. "You aren't in the mood to have fun, maybe you should go home. This isn't a family party and Picnic's free to screw whoever he wants. Not your job to judge."

I sighed, knowing he was right. Dad was definitely free—to the best of my knowledge, he hadn't even had a steady hookup since Mom died. I wasn't in charge of his social life and if I was going to be uptight about sex, I was in the wrong place. I looked over to see two blondes with long legs, short shorts, and cutoff tops wrapping themselves around Painter, taking turns giving him congratulatory kisses.

Oh hell no.

I wasn't leaving him alone with those hos. Tonight was do or die—he'd be mine or I'd be done with him. If I stayed, I might end up in Painter's bed. I might not. But if I left? One of them would be sleeping there for sure.

"What he does is up to him," I muttered. I left Duck to grab a couple of cups, filling one for each of us. I brought it back to him and then stood and watched the crowd.

Everywhere I looked there were couples.

Marie and Horse, Bam Bam and Dancer . . . Ruger and his random skank of the week.

"Holy shit," I burst out, almost spewing my beer.

"What?" Duck asked.

"That's my teacher from cosmetology school over there with Ruger," I muttered. "Oh, she is such a cunt. She failed me three times in a row just because Dad didn't call her back after he fucked her."

Duck snorted out a laugh.

"Good thing you're all graduated, because Ruger won't be calling her back, either."

And just like that, my good mood was back. *Go Ruger!*

"I'm gonna congratulate Painter," I said.

"Have at it," Duck said. "But remember—this is his time to cut loose."

"I know," I replied. "Maybe I can help him celebrate."

Duck's expression clouded.

"Emmy Lou, tonight isn't the night."

"It's never the night," I said, shrugging. Then I chugged my beer. "Don't worry, Duck. You've always taken good care of me, but I've got it covered. I'm an adult."

"Yeah, I know," Duck replied. "I guess when I look at you, I still see you with pigtails and a doll."

I rolled my eyes. Then I tossed my cup in the garbage and headed over to the newest Reaper.

Painter stood next to the bonfire, the two girls still hanging off him. I ignored them completely, because they were just club sluts and I was the president's daughter. They didn't rank compared to me and we all knew it. Painter gave me a slow smile as I walked up, and from the glassy look in his eyes I knew he was already well on his way to shitfaced.

"Hey, Em," he said, reaching out and pulling me into his arms for a hug. Oh, he smelled good. Kind of woodsy and smoky, with an underlying scent of motor oil from the shop. His arms were hard and roped with muscle around me, and his body was hard, too.

Hellfire.

Painter's *dick* was hard. I thought it was my imagination at first. Then he pulled me closer and I felt it again—bigger. Yeah, I know. V card. Little Miss Innocent. But just because I'd never done the deed all the way didn't mean I was ignorant. I knew damned well when a guy's cock was poking my stomach.

Then he let me go and I stepped back, thankful that the sun had set because I knew my face had to be flushed. Painter looked down at me, and something almost magical hung between us. He stared at me like I was the most beautiful girl on earth, the woman he planned to claim as his own.

My dad walked up and slapped his back.

"Congratulations, son," he said. "Proud of you."

Just like that, Painter dropped his arms and turned away, apparently oblivious to our magic. Dad was well and truly cock-blocking me, and it was bullshit.

Wait, did it count as a cock-block if you didn't have a cock?

"You have fun tonight," Dad was telling him. "Tomorrow you rest and recover, because after that we've got work for you."

Painter nodded, running a hand through his hair. One of the

blondes who'd been hanging off him attached herself to my dad, and the other oozed back up to Painter right in front of me. I wanted him to tell her to fuck off. Maybe rip out some of that bleached hair. Instead he wrapped his arms around her and pulled her in for a hard kiss.

Damn it.

Dad's eyes flicked toward me, assessing.

I turned and walked away.

Fuck that shit. I had my pride.

Two hours later I was well and truly drunk.

Maggs and I sat in the old tree house that attached to the children's play structure with a rope bridge. I'd barely made it over the swaying net and wasn't entirely sure I'd be able to get back down without help.

"Life is short," Maggs said suddenly. Her face was sad.

"You thinking about Bolt?" I asked. She nodded.

"Yup," she said. "I think about him every day, but particularly at parties like this. I'm tired of watching everyone else have fun with nothing at home for me but my magic bullet."

I snorted out a little laugh, then forced it down because it wasn't exactly appropriate. I couldn't help it, though.

"Buzzzzzzzz . . ." I hummed with drunken precision. "You go through a lot of batteries? I know I do. Can you make it walk across a table if you turn it on high enough?"

Maggs started giggling, her momentary sadness gone, and then we were both laughing. In fact, we laughed so hard that Maggs rolled off the edge of the platform, falling to the ground with a thud.

"Maggs!" I yelled, jumping up so fast I almost went over myself. "Maggs, are you okay?"

She moaned and turned over, looking up at me with a startled expression on her face. Then she started giggling again. Ruger and

Bam Bam had been sitting near the fire, and Ruger jumped up so fast he dumped the chick on his lap off into the dirt.

I couldn't help it. I burst out cackling so hard my stomach hurt. It wasn't appropriate, I knew that. Maggs could've broken her neck. But the look on her face and the sight of Ruger's 'ho—my former teacher—on the ground were just too funny.

"Okay," I heard a deep voice say, and looked down to see my dad. "Looks like someone needs to head home."

He reached up for me and I jumped down into his arms, just like I had when I was a little girl. Dad caught me easily, still as strong now as he'd been ten years ago. Of course, he was only forty-two, way younger than most of my friends' parents.

"Emmy Lou, you're drunk off your ass," he told me.

"No shit," I replied brightly. "I'm having fun."

"Yeah, but it's about time for you to go home."

"Are you serious?" I asked. "Dad, I think it's great that you're always watching out for me, but I'm not a little kid. There's nothing wrong with me sticking around."

His face softened.

"Sweetheart, this is Painter's night," he said. "His time to celebrate and be free. You shouldn't be here."

"You're talking about him fucking whores, right?" I asked. Dad stiffened.

"It's none of your business, Em," he replied. "He doesn't owe you anything."

"I'm aware," I said grimly.

Dad sighed.

"Banks will give you a ride," he said. "You don't have to leave right this minute, but I want you to stop drinking now and start saying your good-byes. Got me?"

"Yes," I said, and thought about Kit. "You know, I don't have to do everything you say."

That caught him off guard—I saw it in his eyes.

"No, you don't," he admitted, shocking me. "But you have to

do what the club president says on club property. Painter's a Reaper now. You're my daughter, but he's my brother—and tonight is about the brothers."

I wanted to flip him off. Instead I nodded and quietly pulled away from him. He knew I wasn't happy but didn't push. I looked around, finding Maggs still sitting under the tree. Ruger was crouched down next to her, showing her something on his phone. I wandered over to join them.

"This is him," Ruger was saying, flashing a picture. I looked down to see a shot of Ruger, a little boy, and a pretty woman I didn't recognize.

"Your nephew?" I asked. "He's cute."

"Fuckin' adorable," Ruger replied. "That's Sophie—his mom—next to him. They're in Seattle, I need to get over there and check out their new place soon. I saw them earlier this summer but I didn't get much time."

Something in his tone caught me—Ruger sounded almost . . . wistful? No, that wasn't right. Ruger was many things, but never sweet or longing. He'd always taken what he wanted because he could. I leaned over for a closer look and nearly fell on my ass.

Dad was right—I really was pretty drunk.

"Maggs, I'm heading home," I said. "You okay here? Wanna take in a movie or something?"

"I think I'll stick around," she replied. "It's good people-watching. Dancer's got a sitter for the night and she's lit up like a firecracker, so things could get fun."

I laughed. Dancer lit up was something worth seeing, no question. I waved at them vaguely, then wandered around saying good-bye to a few key people.

The one person I didn't see was Painter.

I grabbed my stuff and ducked into the building for a quick pee before leaving. Painter was there in the hallway, leaning against the wall and looking at his phone. This time there weren't any skanks or parents to get in the way. Perfect. I walked over to him and put my hand on his bare chest.

"Hey," I said, looking up at him. His eyes flared, and I saw desire in his face. He wanted me.

"Hey," he said back.

I dragged a finger down the center of his chest slowly, all the way to his stomach. Then I spread my fingers out, brushing the top of his jeans. His breath hissed.

"So are we doing this or not?" I asked him bluntly. "Because I'm tired of waiting."

His eyes darkened and he leaned forward, kissing me very softly on the forehead. A sweet kiss. The kind of kiss you give a little girl at bedtime. Something inside me broke. I'd have said it was my heart, but I didn't feel sad.

Nope. I was fucking pissed.

Painter had been following me around without making a move for a year. I'd go out dancing and he'd scare off guys who tried to buy me a drink. I'd pick up groceries for the club and he'd insist on following me and unloading them. I even caught him checking my tire pressure once. He'd given me rides home more times than I could count.

"You're a pussy tease," I told him. His eyes widened. I dropped my hand lower and gripped his cock firmly through the front of his jeans. Hard as a rock, and good-sized, too. Total waste, so far as I was concerned. "*This* wants me. But either you're too fucking chicken or you want more time to play around. So sorry, but you lose. Eat shit and die, Painter."

I turned and walked back outside, feeling a rush of something . . . almost wild?

It was liberating.

I felt empowered, and looking around the party I realized that no matter how much I loved these people, I needed to branch out. I was more than Picnic's daughter, but none of them seemed to get

that. I'd show them. I'd show all of them, and Painter could spend
the rest of his life screwing his whores. Sooner or later he'd figure out they were shit compared to me, but it'd be too goddamned
late.

I was almost out the gate when I discovered the fatal flaw in my
big exit.

My purse still sat on the bathroom counter. I groaned, wondering if I could risk leaving it. Nope. No fucking way it'd be safe at a
party like this. Nobody from the club would mess with it, but I
didn't trust these random bitches for a minute. I turned and headed
back inside, hoping Painter had taken himself off somewhere. I
didn't want to look at him right now. No matter how empowered
a girl got, there's only so much you can expect of yourself.

No sign of him in the hallway. That was good news. I sighed in
relief as I pushed into the bathroom, then froze.

Painter had some slut pushed down across the counter, ass
pumping as he fucked her from behind. She moaned dramatically
with each stroke. Her disgusting, porno-red lips could've kissed my
handbag sitting next to her on the counter, her face was so close to
it. Neither of them seemed to notice me.

I wanted to run and hide.

Instead I walked calmly over to the counter and reached for my
bag. Painter stopped suddenly, looking down at me with horrified
eyes not a foot away from my face. I let my eyes trail slowly along
the length of his body, from his sculpted chest to the faded jeans he
hadn't even bothered to push down, with pointed disgust. Then I
turned and walked out the door. I heard him yell my name and the
girl squawked in outrage.

I didn't slow down or look back.

I held it together for the ride home. I'd be damned if I'd give that
asshole one more ounce of my energy. He didn't even deserve my
thoughts.

Damn it.

Why had I left my purse there? I'd wanted to be done with Painter, but it didn't need to be so humiliating. I decided that if anyone showed me even one tiny drop of pity, I'd shoot them.

Dad wasn't the only one with a gun.

Banks dropped me off at the house and I stumbled in, still slightly drunk and pissy as hell. Story of my life—things were starting to get good, so naturally something happened to fuck it up. And that "something" was always connected to the Reapers. To be fair, everything in my life was connected to the Reapers, but still . . . I grabbed a pop out of the fridge and climbed the stairs to my room. I pulled off my clothes and then clambered into bed with the TV remote.

My phone dinged with a text message. I considered ignoring it, but habit won out.

> LIAM: How's the party? Hey, I wasn't trying to be an asshole earlier. I just want you to be happy. You deserve good things, Em

I smiled, immediately feeling a little better. Unlike *some people*, Liam had better things to do on a Saturday night than sticking his dick in random skanks—texting me, for one. Of course, I'd never actually met him in person, so maybe he *was* fucking skanks? If so, at least he didn't rub it in my face.

> ME: Tonight was a bust . . . Worst party ever
> LIAM: I take it things didn't work out with Painter?
> ME: Nope. He's screwing some slut as we speak, while I settle in for another night alone. Long story
> LIAM: Fuck that asshole. You're better than him—way too good to settle for some pissant who won't fight for you

I almost started crying. Liam always knew what to say.

ME: Thanks ((hugs))

LIAM: You got my full support, babe, but I draw the line at texting hugs. It's a guy thing. I start doing that shit, the other guys'll confiscate my dick. Can't risk it

I giggled.

ME: Well, I wouldn't want you to lose your favorite toy over a text message.

LIAM: Oh, it's not a toy . . .

ME: I'll take your word on that. What are you up to tonight?

LIAM: Not much. Just hanging out, watching some TV. Thinking about you

ME: :)

LIAM: So please tell me you're ready to ditch his ass now? Permanently?

ME: Definitely. Even if he came after me at this point, I'd be crazy to give him a shot. Hate to admit it, but you were right

LIAM: I'm always right . . . So how about me?

ME: ?

LIAM: How about giving me a shot?

I froze.

I liked Liam. I liked him a lot—I'd even fantasized about him a little, especially when Painter was being a jerk. But that's all it was—a fantasy. Liam was far away, safe. Still, I knew he was hot because Cookie told me. I'd also seen a few pictures online, although his profile was pretty sparse.

ME: You serious?

LIAM: Yeah. I want to meet you

ME: Um . . .

LIAM: No pressure. Think about it. I just wanted you to know

I'm interested. I think about you a lot. You're fucking beautiful, Em, and I'm not just saying that to make you feel good. It's a fact. Funny too

Shit.

Wow. I felt myself flushing and felt all warm. Liam was cute, but I'd never really let myself think of him that way. Not really. Still, it seemed like I could talk to him about anything. He always had time for me and he didn't try to tell me what to do. Of course, it helped that in some ways he wasn't quite real to me.

But this was very real.

ME: Are you sure you're not a sixty-year-old ax murderer?

LIAM: Give me a minute

I waited, feeling a strange sense of excitement. Then my phone pinged again, and a picture came through. Like I said, I'd seen Liam's photos before. There was his profile pic, and a couple of snaps of him at a park.

This was something else, though.

He'd taken it with his phone in what was clearly his bathroom, and holy hotness . . . Liam wore ratty jeans that hung low on his hips, the top button loose and the second in clear danger. No shirt, and his dark brown hair had that sloppy, messy thing going for it. His face was beautiful, almost pretty. Hell, if he didn't have all those tattoos running across his shoulder and down his arm, he could've been in a boy band.

Except nobody in a boy band ever had muscles like those.

He needed a shave, I decided. My eyes dropped back down to his jeans, and I couldn't help but notice a pretty good bulge down there. *Shit, is he . . . ?*

No, I decided. Must just be how the jeans folded. I had a dirty mind.

LIAM: Not an old man . . .
ME: Um
LIAM: Call me

This was a huge step. I wasn't sure how I felt about it. Sure, we'd talked on Facebook and texted each other. A phone call, though . . .

Couldn't hurt, right?

I took a deep breath and a wave of dizziness washed through me. Booze or excitement? Maybe my judgment was off. I wanted to call him, though. I wanted to call him a lot. I scrolled through my contact list and found Liam's phone number. I pressed the green button and listened as the phone rang.

CHAPTER TWO

THREE WEEKS LATER
SPOKANE, WASHINGTON

I fluffed up my boobs, studying my cleavage carefully in the bar's bathroom mirror. I'd worn a black halter corset, which I was now second-guessing.

"I look like a slut," I moaned.

"Walking the line between hot and slutty is tricky," Kimber said, leaning forward to put on more lipstick. She smacked her lips carefully, then ran her tongue over her teeth. "But you're firmly on the hot side tonight. I still think you should be wearing more makeup, though."

I glanced at her, wondering if she was right. I'd only met Kimber a week ago, but she seemed to have her shit together. Sophie called her a sexual bloodhound. Of course, I'd only known *her* a week, too, but she was the mother of Ruger's nephew, so she came with references.

"You look fantastic," Soph said, from the stall behind us. "I wouldn't have let you out of the hotel room if you didn't. How much time before the mysterious and magnificent Liam arrives?"

I glanced down at my phone.

"Looks like I've got maybe half an hour?" I said. "If he's on time."

"I cannot *wait* to check him out," Kimber declared. "If he's hot, can I grab his ass? I need to know if those pictures were real. If they are, you're just lucky I'm married."

"Behave," Sophie said, opening the stall door. She joined us to wash her hands. "I think we need a picture together."

She pulled out her phone and held it up.

"Okay, strike a pose," she said. "I want to see sexy, I want to see passion! This is not a game, ladies."

I started giggling as Kimber crouched, pointing her fingers like a gun at the mirror. Sophie clicked the pic and we all looked at it.

Wow, I did look sort of hot.

"Text that to me?" I asked.

"Me, too," Kimber chimed in. Sophie fiddled with her phone, then mine buzzed in my pocket.

"Serious talk now," I said, looking at them in the mirror. "I know I said I wanted to have sex with Liam, but only if it feels right. Don't be disappointed in me if it doesn't happen."

Sophie wrapped her arm around me.

"Hon, you shouldn't do anything that doesn't feel right."

"Exactly," Kimber said. "Just because he's hot doesn't mean he brushes his teeth. There's all kind of potential deal breakers here. Just remember, if he isn't what you want, there's always another guy. You just need to stay away from the club and you'll start meeting them."

"I still feel weird being here without my dad knowing," I said. "There's been lots of trouble this past year . . . For a long time we were all on lockdown. They almost got Marie, you know. The Devil's Jacks?"

Kimber's eyebrows rose.

"Really? Is that a story I want to hear?"

I frowned.

"I don't know all the details—what I *do* know is that I didn't get to go anywhere without protection for a long time," I answered. "The Jacks and the Reapers have always fought with each other."

"But you're not on lockdown now," Sophie said firmly. "And you haven't been for a while, right? Ruger is crazy controlling about safety for me and Noah, and he didn't say anything about needing protection. We're fine. It's just a night out—no drama, unless getting well and truly fucked counts as drama. Fingers crossed for you on that one, babe."

I thought about Liam's picture and felt a delicious shiver run through me. Fingers crossed for sure . . . I wanted to lick him all over. There were six condoms in my purse, just ready and waiting. Not that I thought we'd need six, but a girl could hope, right?

"I want to dance," Kimber said. "You up for it, ladies?"

"Yeah," Sophie said, but I shook my head.

"I want to grab another drink first," I told them. "It's silly, but I feel really nervous about this."

"Drink up," Kimber said. "But not too much. Don't want to make an ass of yourself and turn him off."

"Oh, shit," I muttered. "Do you think I will? This is so weird and scary . . . I don't want to blow it."

"You have a black corset, tight jeans, fuck-me heels, and a purse full of condoms," Sophie said gravely. "It would take a *lot* to turn him off. This isn't about whether he likes you. It's about whether *you* like *him*—otherwise you'll just keep shopping around."

I hugged her impulsively.

"Thanks," I whispered.

"Any time," she whispered back, squeezing me tight. "Now go out there and get a drink, then come dance for a while. Life is too short to waste time on a guy who isn't right for you, no matter how hot he is. Always remember that."

I considered her words, wondering if she was talking about me or herself. Sophie's situation with Ruger was complicated . . . Sophie let me go and then we walked out of the bathroom and into the bar.

• • •

I sat at a table toward the front of the room, sipping a Sex on the
Beach, loud music pounding through me like a manic heartbeat. It
felt like the clock over the bar must be broken, time moved so
slowly. I kept thinking about the hotel room I'd booked earlier tonight. Kimber and Sophie had one connected to it—safety first,
right? Assuming everything went well, I'd be taking Liam back to
that room in a few hours.

My intentions toward him weren't honorable.

Not even a little bit.

Letting go of my crush on Painter had been hard—good thing I
had Liam to get me through and remind me I had options. Whatever else happened, I owed him for that. I swirled the drink with
my straw, then looked up to see him leaning against the bar.

Shit. SHIT. Liam was here. Early.

I wasn't ready yet. My mojo was all fucked up. It didn't help that
he wasn't smiling. Nope, he was looking at me like a hungry animal. So hungry it was scary, and I actually glanced behind me
because I couldn't believe that look was actually for me.

Then he pushed off the bar and started toward me. I froze, terrified. What had I been thinking, meeting a total stranger in a bar?
I didn't know this man. He was . . . *bigger* than I'd pictured. I
mean, I'd seen pictures but my phone screen was small. "Small"
wasn't a word that applied to this guy. Liam in real life seemed to
take up more space than the people around him. He was sexy, too.
All long, lean muscles that flowed as he crossed the room. His gray
henley covered broad shoulders, and his faded jeans moved like a
part of his body.

He also wore biker boots and a Harley-Davidson belt buckle.

Holy shit, was Liam a biker? He'd never said a thing about that.
What else hadn't he told me? People moved out of his way, the
women eyeing him speculatively and the men uncomfortable meeting his eyes.

Then he stopped in front of me.

"Em," he said, reaching out to catch a strand of my hair. He rolled it between his fingers and smiled. It transformed his face from terrifying and dangerous to outright glorious. His eyes were a rich dark brown, with long lashes, and his hair really needed a trim. I wanted to touch it. "You're prettier in real life than your pictures."

I warmed, feeling what had to be a truly dorky grin take over my face.

"You're taller," I said, projecting my voice over the music.

He leaned forward and kissed my cheek, then slipped into the chair opposite me. I felt myself relax with the distance, until I realized that now I had to face his intense gaze head-on. The pictures hadn't conveyed the power of his eyes—not even close. I had no idea what to say or do, so I took a sip of my drink. He cocked his head, eyes fixed on my lips. I sat there like an idiot, watching him watching me.

"You want something?" a waitress yelled over the music, breaking my Liam-induced trance.

"Yeah," he told her. "I'll take an IPA, whatever you have on tap. You want another?"

I shook my head and the waitress moved on to the next table.

"This is really awkward," I said, giving a nervous laugh.

He held a hand up to his ear. Great. He couldn't hear me.

"This is really awkward," I yelled. "I mean, I know we know each other, but meeting in person is weird."

Liam's mouth cracked in a panty-wetting grin.

"It's different," he said back, voice pitched to carry. "But I like it. It's good to finally be in the same room. Are your friends here?"

"They're dancing," I told him, my voice faltering. Jesus, at this rate I'd end up with a sore throat from trying to talk so loud. "They want to inspect you."

He grimaced.

"Of course they do," he answered. "Sophie and Kimber, right?"

I nodded, impressed that he remembered their names.

"How do you know them?"

"Um, Sophie is . . . hmm, hard to explain," I said, thinking about the Reapers, her weird nonrelationship with Ruger and all the reasons I hadn't told Liam my full situation earlier. I took another sip of my drink, trying to decide what to say. Dad didn't like me talking about the club, but it wasn't exactly a secret that we were in one. Not really . . .

Fuck it. If the club was going to scare Liam off, might as well get it over with.

"You know, there's something I've never told you," I said loudly across the table.

He raised a brow.

"Is this the part where you confess you're actually a man?" he shouted right as the music died. Heads turned and it was just like high school again. Everyone was looking at me. Liam glanced around at our audience, then winked at me. "'Cause if you are, I'm totally into that. Whoever did your boob job is a fuckin' artist."

I burst out laughing as the next song started.

"No," I replied, rolling my eyes. "But there's a reason I haven't dated very much. My dad's part of a motorcycle club. The local president, actually. Anyway, one of the guys in the club has a nephew, and Sophie's the kid's mom."

Liam straightened, his face turning blank. I don't know what I expected . . . Concern, maybe? A snide remark? Somehow the total lack of expression in his eyes was worse.

"What's the matter?" I asked. Damn it, carrying on a conversation in this place was nearly impossible. Had I made a huge mistake? Shit. Would Liam be like all the other guys, too scared of Dad to make a move?

He shook his head.

"Sorry," he said. "Just remembered something I forgot to do earlier. Hey, you want to get out of here?"

"Um, I'm not sure—"

"That came out wrong," he told me, smiling again. Had I been imagining things? "I meant, do you want to go to another bar? Public place, lots of witnesses, but maybe a little quieter? I want to really talk to you and it's kind of hard in here. There's a place down the street I like. Owner is an old friend of mine."

I frowned.

"I don't know," I said. "I don't want to leave Sophie and Kimber."

"We don't have to," he yelled. "No worries."

I smiled, thankful he wasn't going to push me. My phone vibrated in my pocket, and I dug it out to find a text. Several of them, actually, including one from Liam telling me he would be early. It'd come in at the same time Sophie sent the picture. Oops.

> KIMBER: He hre yet? I want to check out his ass. See if its worthy . . . think he'll let me touch? I think we shud make him dance with us!!!!!

I frowned.

"Everything okay?" Liam shouted. I studied his handsome, concerned face and pictured his reaction when Kimber Davis, Sexual Bloodhound, started groping him on the dance floor. I wasn't sure what would be worse—if it bothered him or if he liked it. Either way, it would embarrass the shit out of me.

"Let's hit the other place," I hollered. "You're right, it's too loud in here."

"Text your friends and finish your drink," he said. "Let's go talk for real."

Liam's choice surprised me.

I don't know what I expected, but not some grotty little hole in the wall my dad would've loved. The sign outside said Mick's, and the guy behind the bar looked like a giant pit bull. I'd never been here before, and for good reason.

It wasn't the kind of place you went with your girlfriends.

The room was long and narrow, with a bar along the left wall and rows of high-backed wooden booths with battered tables down the right. Liam held my hand, gently tugging me toward the back. The place wasn't exactly busy, mostly guys who looked rougher than your typical Saturday night club boy. A lot rougher, actually. Hell, they could've been Reapers. Fortunately, I grew up around tough guys and they didn't scare me. I wouldn't want to come in here alone, but I felt safe with Liam.

"Here we go," he said, stopping at the last booth. I slid in, and then he sat down next to me, his long thigh pressing against mine. I could smell his scent, too. Clean and fresh, with just a hint of strong soap.

"Lots of witnesses, but privacy, too," he added.

Sitting so close felt like being a little drunk. My hormones were all happy and I wanted to reach down and grab his leg. Instead I forced myself to make small talk.

"So how long are you in town?" I asked, appreciating the fact that I didn't have to shout.

"Depends," he replied, smiling at me.

"On what?"

"Whether there's a reason to stay."

Oh, I hoped there would be a reason. Despite how nervous he made me, Liam made Painter look like a Ken doll.

"What about work?" I asked, realizing I didn't know what he did for a living. How had we never talked about that?

"It's flexible," he replied. "I guess you'd call me a freelancer. I take on jobs as needed, and it seems to balance out in the end. Have you heard back yet on that aesthetician's program you applied to down in Portland?"

"Not yet," I said, feeling sheepish. I'd been planning on sending my application for two weeks now but kept putting it off because I didn't know how to tell Dad I was considering a move. "I only sent in the paperwork a few days ago. I kept losing different parts of it, and . . ."

My voice trailed off as he reached up to touch my cheek, running the back of his big finger across my skin. Pure fire. I couldn't think. I didn't *want* to think.

And I really, really didn't want to talk about getting my aesthetician's license.

"I'm gonna kiss you," he said. I nodded, and then his lips covered mine.

Fuck small talk.

The kiss started out softly. Liam threaded his fingers into my hair, tracing his tongue over my lips, parting them gently, almost worshipfully. I opened for him, my eyes falling closed as he moved in. I'd been kissed lots of times, despite Dad's reputation for shooting my boyfriends (which was totally unfair—he'd only shot one, and he swore it was an accident). This was a whole different world of kissing.

I lost myself in Liam's lips, drifting along on a wave of sensation that grew as I forgot the room around us. Then his fingers clutched my hair and the kiss hardened. His head slanted across mine, taking instead of asking. My nipples tightened, desperate for more. I reached down and found his thigh. It felt like solid rock. My fingers dug deep into the muscle and he groaned, hips shifting.

Seconds later, he broke free of my mouth and shoved the table across the booth floor, creating more space for us. Then he lifted me to straddle his lap.

"Liam, we can't do this!" I hissed, eyes wide. Sure, people were pretty open around the Armory, but this was a *public bar.* "We'll get thrown out."

"Mick's a friend," he told me, eyes dark and intent. "Don't worry about it."

He leaned forward and nuzzled my breasts, which were conveniently located in front of his face. The corset served them up like a fucking buffet. Shit, were people watching us?

"Jesus, you got good tits," he said, not sounding quite like himself. Rougher somehow. Then he slid a hand down my back and grabbed my ass, crushing me into his hips. I think my womb clenched. Or *something* did. If it wasn't my womb, I had a very confused appendix. Liam grabbed my hair with his other hand and pulled me in for another kiss.

This one went straight past gentle, all hard and deep and full of desperate hunger. I shifted my hips, unconsciously rocking over the rapidly stiffening length of his cock. He responded by pushing up at me, grasping my hips. Eyes closed, I gave in to sensation. Even with all the fabric between us, my clit felt everything and was begging for more. I rocked harder, my desire for him blowing up like a match striking pavement.

Liam's mouth tore away from me.

"Look at me," he commanded, and I did. His eyes were dark pools of hunger, so intense my insides twisted. "Unhook the front of this corset thing you're wearing. I want to see you."

I shook my head, but his fingers dug into my hips, dragging me back and forth across his now-solid cock. Holy shit, that felt good.

"Do it," he ordered. I nodded, forgetting why I'd protested.

I reached for the little hooks down the center of my corset, popping the top half of them open. My breasts spilled out. A small part of my brain screamed that anyone could see us, but when I glanced around, there was nobody. The high walls of the booth gave us total privacy and the tables across from us were empty.

Liam studied me carefully for a moment, then leaned forward and caught my left nipple with his teeth.

I shuddered, terrified that he'd bite me and that he wouldn't, all at once.

No biting, though. Nope. He sucked it in deep, dropping his

body lower on the bench. The hard edge of the table against my back didn't make it easy, but somehow he managed to deepen my back-and-forth slide along the ridge of his erection. If it wasn't for our pants, I'd have him inside me.

Stupid pants.

Liam groaned, then let me go abruptly. He lifted me by my hips and set me down on the bench next to him.

"Are we doing this?" he asked, his voice tight and tense.

I looked at him blankly. My clit wanted to know why we'd stopped, because she was *not* a happy camper about it. Neither were the girls up top. Liam took a deep, ragged breath, eyes intense.

"Are we having sex?" he asked bluntly. "Because if we aren't, I need to go jerk off. Not trying to pressure you, Em, but it's the fuckin' truth."

A wave of lust hit me hard, and I made my decision.

"Let me text my friends," I said breathlessly. "Then we can go back to the hotel."

"You sure?"

"Oh yeah," I whispered. "I'm sure."

I don't know what I expected after that. Maybe a stately exchange of text messages with Sophie and Kimber, followed by all of us walking back to the hotel together. They'd meet him, we'd all laugh, and then when they quietly gave me a thumbs-up, I'd steal him away.

But Liam was a man of action.

He grabbed my hand and pulled me out of the booth, all but dragging me behind him as I clutched my corset closed in shock. To my surprise, we headed toward the back of the bar instead of the front door. Brushing past a muscular guy who slapped Liam on the back, I followed him down a darkened hallway. On our right were some dubious-looking bathrooms. On the left was a door, which Liam opened, pulling me in.

HUNTER

If I've learned one thing in this life, it's that lying to yourself is a waste of time.

This hadn't stopped me from pretending tonight was all about the club, and that Em was just a means to an end. Leverage against the Reapers.

It wouldn't be the first time I fucked a chick for the Devil's Jacks, and God knew taking her wouldn't keep me up nights. I'd done far worse things, and that was a fact. But Christ, Em was gorgeous and even worse, she was funny and cute and I was pretty sure she'd taken over one whole region of my brain. About a week ago, I'd convinced her to send a picture of herself in bed. To hell with porn, that shy little pic of her wearing an old T-shirt did it for me every time.

There was a part of me that had whispered she couldn't possibly be as hot as I remembered, or as sweet as she sounded on the phone. That's what I wanted to believe—no, *needed* to believe.

But I'd taken one look at her in that bar and it was all over.

Now my dick was so hard I thought it might punch through my pants. Seriously. Complete loss of thinking power. I have never wanted to fuck a woman more in my life. And yeah, I'm a douche, but I hadn't planned to actually screw her in Mick's office. That was before I tasted her and realized I'd die if I didn't get inside what I was pretty damned sure was the hottest snatch I'd ever feel clamped around my cock.

I slammed the door shut behind us, the dim glow of a single lamp lighting the little room. Thank Christ there was a couch in here. A longish leather one, and while it probably wasn't the cleanest, it wasn't the worst place I'd screwed a girl.

Em definitely deserved better. I didn't care.

My mouth covered hers, my hands reaching down to grab her ass, hoisting her legs up and around my waist. Her hands dug into my hair and I felt her boobs against my chest and I shit you not—I nearly came. What the hell was it about this chick? Fuck, from the moment I'd first seen her last winter, I'd been obsessed. Talking to her on the phone was just the nail in the coffin, because the worst of it was I actually *liked* her. Burke would laugh his ass off if he could see me now—the coldest bastard in the club was officially pussy whipped.

At least for the moment.

I should've dropped her and taken off running while I still could. Instead I slammed her against the door, thrusting my cock up at her as if I could penetrate her through our clothing if I just tried hard enough. She tugged up my shirt. Then her fingers dug into the muscles of my back, nails scratching me as she dragged them downward.

Lines of sharp pain followed.

Impossibly, my dick got harder. Em looked hot as hell in those tight jeans of hers, but she needed to get them the fuck off before I stroked out. I'd do her hard and fast this first time—no way I could hold out. Fortunately, she was just as worked up as me, so odds were good she'd go off like a firecracker. Then I had every intention of dragging her back to the hotel and showing her just how many different ways I could make her come.

First I needed to free up some of that blood pooled in my lower body for my brain, though. Right now I couldn't even remember how to breathe. I carried her over to the couch, dropping her down, and then covered her, our hips rubbing together in the hottest dry hump in history.

Jesus.

I really was gonna come in my pants.

I kissed her one last time, tasting how hot and sweet her mouth was, then forced myself to pull away.

"Never wanted to be inside anyone half as much as you, Em," I told her, the words rough. Her blue eyes opened wide and her breath caught. Her cheeks flushed a delicate pink and I wanted to wrap her up and carry her off like a caveman or something. I rolled to the side, digging in my pocket for a condom.

"Jeans off, baby," I added. "I can't wait any longer."

"I have to tell you something."

I found the condom and reached for my fly, only half following her words. God*damn* she was hot . . . Boobs popped out, nipples flushed, eyes bright with excitement.

"No," she said. "Seriously, I need to tell you something."

"What?" I asked, wondering what the hell could be higher priority than getting naked. Then it hit me—she was a girl, she needed reassurance. Damned if I knew why, but they all did. "Hey, I didn't just bring you here to screw you, babe. You mean something to me, I swear. But I can't think right now. Can we talk later?"

She looked away and I started to get a sinking feeling. Shit. Something was really wrong. I don't know what bothered me more, the idea of blowing my mission or *not* blowing my wad.

No contest—to hell with the mission. This was about her cunt squeezing my cock.

"I haven't done this before," she said without meeting my eye.

"Fucked on the first date?" I asked her. "This isn't like that, babe. I don't know what you're thinking, but I'm not—"

"Jesus, will you just shut up and listen to me?" she snapped, sitting up and swinging her legs off the couch. "Why does everyone in my life need to be so damn bossy?"

I stared at her, dick throbbing, confused as hell.

"I haven't had sex before," she said abruptly. "And I really like you and I totally want to do this, but I don't want to do it on a dirty couch in a bar. Can you understand that?"

Now *that* caught my attention.

"The fuck? What do you mean, you haven't had sex?"

"I mean I've Never. Had. Sex," she told me, spacing out her words carefully. "True story. You got a problem with that? Because you're looking at me like I've got herpes and that's not working for me."

I stilled, trying to wrap my brain around what she'd said. It was hard, given the lack of circulation. Then it sank in.

Shit. Em was *mine*. All mine. No other asshole had been inside that pretty little cunt—this was fuckin' beautiful. I smiled slowly, running a hand through my hair.

"That kicks ass, babe," I said, sinking down to sit next to her.

"It does?" she asked, her voice small. I pulled her over and onto my lap, running my hands up and down her body. God, she was just tiny. A perfect little package I wanted to lick all over and then take home and hide away from the world.

"Yeah," I said, feeling something like triumph start to build inside me. I wasn't going to share her—not now, not ever. This body was mine. All mine. Best present ever. Fuck if I knew what I'd done to deserve it, but not a chance in hell I'd let her get away.

"I am gonna have so much fun teaching you everything I know," I said, kissing the side of her neck. Shit, she smelled good. My cock wanted inside her now, but somehow my brain had reengaged, and I was not going to fuck this up. If I played things right, she'd fall for me so hard she'd never know what hit her. And I wanted that. I wanted it a lot. Win for me, win for the Jacks, too. Perfect.

Em gave a little laugh.

"You kind of scared me there," she whispered, and damned if she didn't blush a little. So cute. "I mean, it's silly, but things were just moving so fast. It's never been like this for me before."

"Well, we've got some great fuckin' chemistry," I told her. "Damned good thing you spoke up when you did. I promise, I'll make this good for you, babe. Wanna head back to the hotel, or do you need some time first?"

She wrapped her arms around my neck and gave me a soft smile.

"Hotel," she said. "Let's take it slower, though. Okay?"

"No prob."

Silence fell between us as I leaned into her for a soft kiss, tugging at her lower lip. Then a loud knock on the door broke the moment.

"Go away," I yelled.

"Need to talk," Skid said on the other side of the door. "Important, bro. Get out here."

Em frowned up at me.

"I didn't realize you were here with someone," she said.

"Didn't feel like sharing you," I told her, offering a quick grin. My mind had already gone cold and hard, though, switching modes instantly. Skid wasn't an idiot and he didn't fuck around. He wouldn't interrupt if it weren't important.

"Give me five," I told her, settling her on the couch. Sadly, she started hooking up her corset, covering those gorgeous tits. I walked to the door and stepped out.

One look at Skid's face and I knew I was screwed.

"Make it good, asshole."

"We got a situation," he told me. "Kelsey called from our place in Portland. Said some crazy-ass motherfucker burst into the house and started shooting. Grass is down, shot in the chest. Not sure he's gonna make it. Shooter managed to grab Clutch and took off with him. Guess there were some girls who saw the whole thing and now they're talkin' to the cops. Kels was upstairs in your room, came running down with a gun too late. She couldn't do a goddamned thing but watch when he threw Clutch in an SUV and took off."

I felt the world narrow to a pinpoint, my mind running through a thousand calculations. "She get a decent look at the guy?" I asked.

"Yeah," he replied, his eyes growing colder. "Gave her a message, actually. Told her to let us know the truce with the Reapers is dead, and Clutch will be, too. Payback for Gracie."

"We got a name?"

"Called himself Toke."

"I'll call Burke."

"Jesus."

"Em, I need to make a quick phone call," I said, ducking my head back into the office. I smiled at her softly, pretending to be human. Harder to pull off every year. "You okay in here for a minute?"

She looked up at me, her face all innocent and trusting, and I savored the sight. I had a pretty good feeling that I'd never see her like that again. Not after tonight.

"Everything all right?" she asked.

"Yeah," I replied, lying easily. "Just a little misunderstanding back home. I'll get it taken care of and get back to you."

I started to close the door.

"Hey," she said, giving me another soft look. "I like you, Liam Blake."

"I like you, Emmy Hayes," I replied, wishing things were different.

Don't know why I bothered.

Shit happens. Fuckin' weak and stupid to let yourself care.

I went back out into the hallway and called Burke to get my orders.

CHAPTER THREE

EM

Liam stepped out of the room and I shivered, so excited I could hardly exist. This was better than I'd hoped. *He* was better than I'd hoped. So incredibly cute, he made me feel amazing, and best of all? He didn't seem particularly interested in talking about my father.

That last one was a biggie.

I pulled out my phone—I wanted to get back to the room, but I'd promised I wouldn't go alone. I pulled up Sophie's number, my fingers fumbling, although I couldn't decide if it was from the drinks or the excitement.

> **ME:** I want to go back to the hotel. He's defintely THE ONE
> **SOPHIE:** Dont u dare! We have to chck him out frist. Ur NOT follwing the plan
> **ME:** Yu'll meet him in a minut come down to Mick's and we can head from there. We'll wait outside.

I slid my phone into my pocket, then hugged myself, rubbing my arms up and down quickly. I still couldn't quite believe all this was happening. I'd met Liam and he was fantastic. Sexy. Beautiful. Even sweet . . .

More important than that, though—he had an edge. An edge like the guys I'd grown up with, and that was critical. Ultimately, I couldn't be with someone who couldn't handle my MC family. Liam could, I was almost certain of it.

Not that I was stupid—I knew it might not turn into anything.

But it might. Tonight I'd finally get to see for myself what all the fuss was about. Funny, but Painter had actually done me a favor in the end. If he'd gone for it, I might be with him right now instead of Liam. And while I hadn't known Liam all that long, I felt a connection with him that I'd never felt for Painter.

Painter was a fantasy, a dream about what could be. Had I ever even had a real conversation with him? I couldn't remember anything that went past casual. But Liam was *real*. Liam wanted me as much as I wanted him, and while there was no question things were physically intense between us, I knew there was more to it than that. We'd connected from hundreds of miles apart. I could tell him anything and he made me laugh, and the fact that he was hot as hell was just the icing on the cake.

I had a feeling I'd have fallen for Liam if he'd been shorter than me with a gut and a hairy back.

That was a theory I'd have to go without testing, poor me. Liam in person was sexier than I'd ever imagined, and I had a very good imagination. The office door opened and he stepped back in, giving me a burning, intense look that made me wet.

"You're beautiful, Em," he said. "One more kiss, okay?"

Yeah, wasn't gonna argue with that.

He pulled me into his arms and his lips covered mine, tongue sliding deep inside. He was almost brutal in his intensity, burying himself in my mouth.

Then he broke loose.

"Let's go."

"I need to wait for my friends," I said. "I texted them while you were making your call. We're supposed to meet them out front."

"Kimber and Sophie, right?" he asked. "How well do you know them?"

"Um, not that well, actually," I said. "Sophie is sort of weirdly involved with Ruger. It's complicated. Kimber's her friend. They're really nice, and lots of fun. But I don't think either of them really counts as available, if you're thinking of the guy who came with you?"

He shook his head.

"No worries," he said. "Hey, while we wait do you mind running out to my van with me? I want to grab a bag. Toothbrush, that kind of shit."

I felt my cheeks heat up. He needed that stuff because we were spending the night together. *Me.* Spending the night with *him.* Damn. Why couldn't I be all cool instead of dorky?

"Sure," I told him. "We have a couple minutes."

Liam took my hand and walked me down the back hall.

"There's parking out back?" I asked.

"Employees only," he told me. "Mick doesn't mind, though. We go way back."

He opened the back door, popping out the deadbolt so the door couldn't fully close behind us. Then he tugged me toward a black cargo van.

His friend stepped out from behind it. I smiled at him, then looked at Liam, expecting him to introduce us.

He didn't.

The other man moved toward me, his face grim. This wasn't right. Not right at all. Deep inside my head an alarm bell blared, complete with flashing red lights. As long as I could remember, my parents had taught me to trust my instincts, and every instinct I had told me to get the hell out of here.

Liam was up to something. *Fuck*. Too good to be true. Just my luck.

How to do it? The door behind us was still open, but I wasn't sure anyone in that particular bar would help me, even if I made it inside. I glanced down the alley—we were midway through the block and loud music filled the air from a nightclub next door. Screaming would be useless.

I had to get out of this narrow passage and find some witnesses.

I pretended to stumble, then knelt down as if I were fixing my shoe. Instead I undid the straps so I could step out of them when I took off. At least the alley was paved . . . Maybe I wouldn't cut up my feet too bad? I was gonna look like a real dumbass if this was nothing.

Pisser.

"You okay?" Liam asked. I looked up at him and smiled sweetly.

"I'm fine—just need to fix my strap," I told him. Then I took a deep breath, rising slightly into a runner's start, and took off down the alley, my gorgeous fuck-me pumps left behind. I sprinted toward the street, hearing their surprised shouts. Vaguely I heard Liam yell at me to stop. If there wasn't anything hinky going on, I'd look like a crazy woman.

But you know what?

Something wasn't right about the situation. I knew it in my bones, and Dad had pounded it into my head—listen to your gut. He said it'd saved his life more than once. Good enough for me. I heard feet pounding behind me, but I was getting close to the end of the alleyway. I saw people up ahead, walking past. It was noisy outside, between traffic and the loud music. Would they hear me?

I'd just opened my mouth to scream when he tackled me from behind. The ground came toward me and I had a fraction of a second to wonder just how bad the hit would hurt. Then my body twisted and flew up. Somehow I was on my back, on top of Liam, his strong arms wrapping around me like shackles.

His friend caught up to us and pointed what looked like a gun.

I gasped for breath, eyes wide.

Yup.

That was definitely a gun.

At least he didn't have a clear shot with me on top of Liam.

I tried to scream again and a big hand clamped around my mouth. Then I tried biting Liam and used every bit of leverage I could to kick down at him. Unfortunately, it wasn't much.

"Shut the fuck up and stop fighting," he growled in my ear. "If you do what you're told, you won't get hurt."

I didn't bother listening. I just kept kicking and biting as his arms slowly tightened around me, making it harder to breathe.

Then his fingers pinched off my nose and I froze.

"You want to stay awake, princess, you'll stop fighting. Nod your head if you understand."

I was so fucking pissed off. I wanted to kill him, but I'd started seeing spots and I knew I wouldn't hold out much longer. What the hell would they do to me if I lost consciousness? Nothing good.

I nodded.

Liam let my nose go and I sucked in air, the darkness fading away.

"Now I'm gonna get up and we're going over to the van," he said. "I don't have time to argue with you, so if you want to stay awake, you do what I say."

I nodded again.

He sat up, taking me with him.

"Get your ass moving," his friend said, eyes dark and full of something like hate. Not good . . . "Walk over to the van and keep your fucking mouth shut. Hunter might not want you hurt, but I could give a shit—got me?"

I could tell he meant it, so I stood slowly and walked toward the van, considering the implications of his friend calling Liam "Hunter." None of them were good. I tried to stall as long as I could, but it was pointless. Nobody saw us. Nothing.

I stopped next to the van.

"Arms up and on the sides," Liam said, his voice cold. Completely unlike the man I thought I'd known. Christ, I sucked at reading men. First Painter and now this bullshit? I assumed the position, choking back a little laugh. I'd seen this on TV a thousand times. What a fucking cliche. Pathetic.

I heard the back of the van open, then hard hands ran over my body. Liam's hands. I smelled him behind as he thrust his knee between my legs, separating them. He frisked me so thoroughly that for one horrible moment I wondered if he was an undercover cop.

Then his hand stopped on my boob and his breath caught.

Shit. If Liam was a cop, he was definitely a dirty one. That was good news—dirty cops could be bribed. He pushed into me, and I felt the length of his erect cock dig into my ass as he whispered in my ear.

"Sorry, babe. This wasn't the plan."

"Fuck you."

He sighed.

Then he stepped back, taking my hands and pulling them behind my back. Cold metal clicked around my wrists. Suddenly a strip of fabric came down around my face.

"Open your mouth," Liam told me. I shook my head. He pushed forward into me again, and his dick felt even bigger and harder now. Holy shit, this was turning him on.

Kidnapping girls turns him on.

Fuck. FUCK.

"Open. Your. Mouth," he said again, and this time the menace in his voice was unmistakable. His prick nudged me again, and then his hips, shifting, sliding it slowly up the crack of my ass. I felt a whole new level of fear.

Who is this man?

I opened my mouth and the fabric slid inside. He tied it tight around my head, then reached a hand around to my front, pulling me back and into him. My cuffed hands bumped his stomach, my ass cradling his erection.

"What about her friends?" I heard the other guy ask. "Any value there?"

"One's connected to the club," Liam said, his breath warm against my ear. "Same bitch we saw in Seattle with the kid. Not sure how official it is, but Ruger's got something goin' on with her. The other one's just deadweight."

I shivered, hoping to hell Kimber and Sophie didn't come looking for me. Oh God. I'd never forgive myself if I dragged them into this . . . whatever the fuck "this" was.

His hand on my waist lowered, finding the sliver of bare flesh between the bottom of my corset and the top of my jeans. Then his hand dipped into my pocket, lingering with indecent hesitation before pulling out my phone. Liam stepped back. I saw the glow of the screen reflected in the van's darkened window as he called up my message history.

"She told them to meet her out front," he told his friend. "Go inside. Let's give it ten minutes, see if they come looking for her. Might give us an advantage if we can grab one."

"Got it."

I heard the slam of the bar door closing as Liam's accomplice went back in. Strong hands grasped my upper arms, turning me to face him. I stared up into his darkened face with wide eyes, hoping I didn't look as scared and helpless as I felt. He lifted a hand, sliding his fingers into my hair and tightening them.

Liam's other hand found my waist, inching up toward my breast. I thought he'd touch me there, but at the last minute he pulled away until only his fingertips grazed me. He traced upward between my breasts, then caught my chin and tilted my face toward him.

"I think you might be even prettier tied up," he whispered. "Christ, I want to fuck you."

He lowered his head, running his nose along my cheek, scenting me. I shuddered, and not just from fear. Even now—after it was so clear he'd been lying to me all along, although about what I couldn't be certain—I wanted him.

Liam made a strangled noise, then pulled back and jerked my upper arm, dragging me around to the open back of the van. He pushed me in, face forward. I fell, bracing myself to hit hard, but at the last second he caught me, lowering me to the floor on my side.

Then he grabbed my feet and pulled them together. His hands lingered on my ankles, then one slid upward along the back of my thigh. He found the curve of my ass, tracing the line where it met my upper thigh until his fingers cradled my butt cheek. His thumb dipped down between my legs ever so slightly . . . Then he squeezed my flesh hard, almost spasmodically, and I squeaked in surprised pain.

"Sorry," he murmured, rubbing the hurt before returning to business.

I felt rope wrapping tight around my ankles, then Liam leaned forward over me. I glared at him, putting everything I had into sending him the message that I'd be killing him just as soon as I got the chance.

His face was serious and strangely blank, but he reached out and tugged my hair out of my face.

"Fuckin' shame," he said, his voice almost thoughtful. "I doubt you'll believe me, but I'm really sorry about this."

I raised my eyebrows, making it clear he was right—I didn't believe a word he said. Liam sighed, then closed the van doors.

Huh. Shitty, *shitty* first date.

I lay in the dark for what felt like forever, waiting for something to happen. Ideally, this would include the entire Reapers nation bursting through the van doors, but I was mostly just hoping Sophie and Kimber wouldn't get dragged into my shit.

A few minutes later I heard a scuffle and then the back opened again. Sophie flew in, hitting the floor. Liam climbed in after her, cuffing her, gagging her, and tying her up just like me. I stared at her terrified face, torn between guilt that I'd gotten her into this and determination to kill Liam myself. Preferably with my bare hands.

After castrating him.

I heard his friend climb into the front and gun the engine.

"Sorry, girls," Liam said. "Hopefully this won't get too ugly and you'll get to go home soon."

Oh, it would definitely be getting ugly. I promised him that with my eyes.

He ignored me, moving forward to join his friend as the van took off. We didn't drive far, though. After a few minutes they pulled off the road and came to a stop. Then they stepped out and walked around to the back. Liam's friend reached in and grabbed Sophie, sitting her up. He dug into her purse, pulling out her phone.

His sleeve rode up as he did it, and my heart stopped.

There was a *fucking Devil's Jacks tattoo on his arm.*

Shit. *Shit.* SHIT.

This was much worse than I ever imagined. I'd spent my whole life hating the Devil's Jacks. They'd been fighting with the Reapers for twenty years in one way or another. I saw things in a sudden, bright, horribly clear light.

Liam, slowly becoming my friend.

Liam, asking me about my day, talking to me about anything and everything. Liam, always willing to hear me out and encouraging me to share with him.

My good "friend" Liam was a fucking stalker.

A stalker who'd used me to learn about my club, and now he obviously planned to use me against my father. Acid filled my stomach, and for one wretched instant I thought I might vomit and choke myself, because this was the worst thing I could imagine doing.

I'd betrayed my club.

Not knowingly, but that hardly mattered. There would be fresh bodies because of this. Those deaths would be on me and my stupid, impulsive decision to let Liam into my life.

Liam tugged me down and picked me up, carrying me around to the front of the van. He leaned me up against the hood like a spare fence post. I balanced unsteadily, forcing myself to stop glaring at him long enough to look around. We were down by the river, probably near the park somewhere. Above us was one of the high bridges going over the falls, and I realized that if he decided to pitch me over the fence I'd fall a good ten stories before I either smashed on the rocks or drowned.

Would he do it?

Of course he would do it—*he was a fucking Devil's Jack*—but only if he was done using me.

Shit.

"Em, look at me," he said. I glanced at his face to find cold, dead eyes studying me. The eyes of a sociopath.

How could I have been so fucking stupid?

"We're calling your dad," he said. "I'll let you talk to him so you can give him this message. You'll tell him that you're with Hunter, the Devil's Jack he met in Portland. Let him know that we have you and your friend Sophie. Then you'll tell him that we'll kill you if he doesn't do exactly what we say. Got it?"

I nodded. I felt tears start to build in my eyes, but I'd be damned if I'd show him even a hint of weakness. I refused to blink as he pulled out my phone and scrolled through the contacts.

Liam reached up and tugged out my gag, then held the phone to my head. It rang twice.

"Hey, baby, what's up?" I heard my dad ask.

"Daddy, I'm in some trouble," I said quietly.

"Talk to me," he replied, immediately all business.

"I'm here in Spokane with a Devil's Jack named Hunter," I said, focusing all my emotions into one horrible, hate-filled glare at Liam. Too bad I didn't have lasers in my eyes. I was pretty sure I could've cut him in half with that look. "He said to tell you that he has me and Sophie. He's going to kill us if you don't do what he says. He's also a giant fucking pussy, and I think when you catch him, you should let me cut out his balls with a dull spoon before shooting him in the head."

Liam—Hunter? whoever the hell he was—grinned at me, then pulled away the phone as Dad started shouting. He tugged the gag back up and stuffed it into my mouth, then stepped toward the cliff's edge, talking softly just out of earshot.

I wobbled, wondering if there was any point in trying to hop away.

Not really.

Hunter spoke for a moment longer, then turned off the phone and casually pitched it over the fence and into the falls.

He turned back and gave me an evil smile.

"Your daddy's pretty fond of you, Em," he said. "Things are going to work out just fine."

Not for him, they wouldn't.

The van drove forever, and I lost all sense of time as we jolted around in the back. Hunter and Skid—apparently that was the other asshole's name—spoke quietly, making the occasional vague phone call in what had to be some sort of unholy Devil's Jacks kidnapping code.

I couldn't communicate with Sophie, but I did everything in my power to send her a message with my eyes. *You're not alone, our men will rescue us. I'm so damned sorry I brought this down on you.* Something along those lines.

Not sure it sank in.

She was probably thinking about her little boy, Noah, and wondering if she'd ever see him again.

It was a good question. Wish I knew the answer.

The van finally stopped and they dragged us out. We were in front of a house, an older one. Two stories, big porch, and apparently in the middle of nowhere. There were sparse trees off in the distance and gentle hills that kept me from seeing any other houses.

Great.

Hunter carried me into the living room and set me down on the couch gently. Skid dropped Sophie down next to me, and she struggled to sit up.

"Here's the situation," Hunter said. "You're here as leverage. One of the Reapers down in Portland—Toke—made a real bad call tonight. He went to our house and started shooting, no warning, no provocation."

Fuck, I thought, eyes going wide. Toke was definitely a Reaper, but he'd been in the wind for the past week. I felt a burning pain in my side, where the wound he'd given me the weekend before was still healing. He'd cut me with a fucking knife in the middle of a party. Allegedly it was an accident, but Dad wasn't amused. He'd taken off after him shooting.

Now Toke had found a new way to cause damage. Asshole.

"He took a hostage when he left. One of our brothers is down and a second is probably getting tortured to death right now, so you'll have to excuse us for being a little abrupt about this whole thing. Your daddy"—he nodded at me—"is gonna do what it takes to get our guy back for us. That happens, you go home."

I studied Liam, torn between hurt that he'd betrayed me and unspeakable rage toward Toke. I didn't know the details of what had gone down between him and the club. Last weekend there'd been a big meeting, but I didn't have anything to do with that. Not like I was privy to club business—that was a boys' game. But I wasn't stupid, either, and I'd been born a Reaper.

Something had gone very wrong in that meeting for things to get this far out of balance.

I really did want to shoot Toke, I decided. I also wanted to shoot Liam. *No, his name is Hunter*, I reminded myself. *His name is Hunter and you don't know him at all.*

"You're dead, *Liam*," I told him, emphasizing the fake name, making it clear I was onto his shit. He didn't respond. "My dad is going to put you in the ground. Let us go now and I'll try to talk him out of it. Otherwise it'll be too late. I'm serious. He. Will. Kill. You."

This was the simple truth.

"Sorry, babe," he said, and his voice sounded so sincere, so much like the man I'd thought I'd known . . . It cut through me in a way Toke's knife never could. "I get that you're scared and pissed, but I'm not going to let a brother die just because some Reaper had a tantrum."

Don't talk about my club that way, I wanted to growl at him. Goddamned men. Why did their bullshit always have to spill over on me? I narrowed my eyes at him, willing every bit of angry hatred I felt into my words.

"Fuck you."

Hunter (I decided not to call him Liam anymore—Liam was a nice name for a nice guy, and it didn't fit this bastard at all) glanced at his friend, then rubbed a hand over his face. For a minute he looked tired.

Jackass.

I was going to laugh at his funeral.

"Okay, let's go upstairs," Hunter announced. He glanced over at poor Sophie, who had gone pale. My anger faded a little, replaced by guilt. I needed to stop worrying about my hurt feelings and start planning our escape. If we had to wait for Dad to find Toke, we might find ourselves dead in a ditch.

Not that I really thought Hunter would kill me . . . Despite the evidence to the contrary, I just couldn't fathom him truly hurting me. Denial? Probably. Skid was another story. There was something evil in his eyes.

Hunter pulled out a Leatherman and knelt down at my feet. I considered kicking him in the chin but decided that wouldn't do me much good strategically. Pity. Then he cut the rope. Skid pulled out a pistol and cocked it loudly.

"You cause trouble, I'll shoot you," he said, and I realized I'd succeeded in conveying my homicidal intentions clearly. *Yay me!* "Hunter's nice. I'm not."

Strangely enough his words helped me focus—I'd let myself get worked up over my hurt pride, but I couldn't let anger take over my brain. I couldn't afford to do something stupid. Sophie might be a sweetheart, but she wasn't a Reaper and she had no idea what we were up against. I'd have to be the one to get us out of this.

Sobering thought.

Hunter grabbed my arm and pulled me to my feet. Then he tugged me up a flight of stairs off to the side of the living room. Behind us I heard Skid and Sophie following. Hunter opened a door on the right and pulled me in, kicking it shut behind us. I looked around. It was a bedroom.

With a *bed*.

Suddenly the situation took on a new set of implications I hadn't considered before. Liam's whole persona might've been a great, big, fat fake, but he hadn't been faking one thing. I'd definitely felt his dick poking my ass earlier. Either he wore a hell of a prosthetic at all times, or he actually wanted to fuck me. Now he had a nice, comfy bed to do it on.

Shit.

His hands grasped mine, and I heard the click of the lock turning on the cuffs. I wasn't free, though—he held my wrists tight as he pushed me across the room. I refused to move my feet, stalling. He leaned down, speaking softly in my ear.

"Get on the fucking bed, Em."

Warmth bathed my ear and I could *smell* him all around. Because there's something wrong with me, that turned me on.

"That sounds like a bad idea," I said, trying not to sound nervous. I needed to get on the offense, take some control of the situation. "Let's talk about this."

"Talk away," he muttered, bringing my hands around to the front of my body. He stepped forward, taking both of them in one big hand. I felt his heat behind me, his large body dwarfing and surrounding mine.

I also felt his cock again.

No fucking way I could miss that giant thing digging into my lower back. Double shit. I needed a diversion.

"I don't think you realize what's happening," I said quickly. "I know you want to find Toke. I get that—if someone attacked one of our club brothers, I'd be after him, too. But Toke stabbed me last weekend—"

Hunter froze, then I was moving through the air, lifted straight up against his chest as he carried me. He pushed me down, rolled me to my back, and straddled me all in one smooth move, pinning my arms up and over my head.

"What the hell are you doing?" I demanded.

"Explain how he hurt you," he said, his voice grim and his eyes cold. "Now."

I closed my eyes, trying to think.

Oh, I was at this party with all my friends and family, and then this guy I'm supposed to be able to trust got pissy for some reason (that I'm not allowed to know) and he cut me with a big, giant knife. Then my dad tried to shoot him, I got a few stitches, and now we're all pretending it never happened.

Nope, nothing weird about that.

I'd planned to tell him it was an accident if we got far enough for him to find the bandage hiding under my top. Seemed believable enough to me, seeing as most people don't go running around with random knife wounds. Not like it was particularly bad. Sure, it hurt a bit if I pulled at it, but it wasn't exactly deep.

I took a deep breath, trying to figure out the best way to handle this. Toke definitely wasn't my favorite person right now, but he was still a Reaper and this was our private business. I couldn't give Hunter anything to use against the club. On other hand, I needed to keep him on my side, what with the not-wanting-to-end-up-dead-in-a-ditch issue.

"It was an accident," I said slowly, which was sort of true. I was pretty sure Toke had no intention of cutting me, personally, when he'd unsheathed his knife. "We were just fucking around at a party last weekend—"

"Fucking around?" he asked, eyes growing colder, which really shouldn't have been possible, yet he still managed to pull it off. "What's the story between you and Toke?"

"Nothing. Shit, nothing, okay? Although why the hell you would care I can't imagine."

"You have no idea what I care about."

"And I could give a shit," I muttered. "Do you want to hear the details or not?"

"Tell me the fucking details."

"We were at a party," I started again. "It wasn't that late or that crazy, although it was moving in that direction. I went to find my dad and say good night because Sophie and I were heading out. I was walking past a group of guys and then suddenly someone fell against me and his knife caught my rib cage. No big deal."

Hunter dropped his hands to my sides, running his fingers lightly across the corset, searching for the wound. I gritted my teeth when he found it, refusing to acknowledge the twinge of pain. Something must've given it away, because he growled.

Growled.

Like a pissed-off wolf. *No, like a whiny dog,* I told myself firmly. *One of those little yappy ones.* Wolves kicked ass and Hunter didn't. He was a giant, fake asshole.

Then his hands went to the front of the corset and started fumbling with the hooks. This was not okay. I grabbed his wrists, trying to jerk him away, but he ignored me completely. Seriously. He was so much stronger than me that I wasn't sure he even noticed my protests.

"What the fuck are you doing?"

"I need to see it," he said. "You should've said something earlier. I could've hurt you in the bar. Why the hell didn't you tell me when it happened?"

My jaw dropped.

"It's none of your fucking business," I burst out. "None of it is. And don't try telling me you care whether or not I'm hurt."

My breasts popped free as the corset opened. I tried to cover myself, hating the sudden, horrible feeling of vulnerability.

"*You* are my business," he told me, his voice grim. He didn't pause to perv, either. Nope, his touch was impersonal—almost clinical—as he felt around the fresh, white bandage I'd put over it earlier.

"It's not that big," he said, looking almost surprised.

"No shit. I told you it wasn't a big deal. About three inches long, and not even half an inch deep."

"They take you to the hospital?"

"They took care of me," I snapped. "They always take care of me. That's why—if you want to live—you need to let me go and get yourself the hell out of town."

He laughed, sounding almost like the old Liam, and then he turned his attention toward my breasts. I slapped my hands over them, but he caught my wrists and dragged them high over my head again. I struggled but it was pointless. His strength was effortless, and while he might not be bulky with muscles, his lean body was like steel.

"Damn, you're beautiful," he said, the words low and rough. I couldn't quite tell if he was talking to me or himself. It hit me right between my legs, though, and I felt like an idiot because not even learning he'd played me was enough to kill my desire. He leaned down, lowering his body over mine, one knee nudging roughly between my legs. I stiffened, refusing to give, and I think I could've pulled it off if he'd done something obvious like grope at my breasts.

Instead he dropped his head and ran his nose along the line of my collarbone upward, tickling my neck. It was such a light touch, so faint I'd have questioned whether I was imagining it if I couldn't see him so clearly. He took in deep breaths, sighing against my ear.

"And I thought shit was fucked up before," he whispered. "Em,

I know you won't believe this, but I didn't plan this. I never wanted to hurt you."

"Then don't. Let me go before things get worse."

He shook his head slowly, lips brushing my cheek as he did it.

"I can't, sweet girl," he replied, and if I didn't know he was a soulless bastard, I would've called that regret in his voice. "My brother's life is at stake."

My breath caught and for a second I thought I might cry. I didn't want to die. I didn't want anyone in my family dead.

And I didn't want my Liam dead, either. Intellectually I knew "my Liam" had never existed, but I could feel him and smell him all around me. My body refused to believe he'd betrayed us.

Fuck.

"Toke doesn't care about me, so it's not like he's going to turn himself in to save a couple of women," I said carefully. "And the rest of the Reapers can't make it happen. I don't know what's going on, but I do know this—if my dad could find Toke, he'd be dead already. Club business aside, my father would *not* let a man who hurt me live. Period. Kidnapping us isn't going to get your brother back any faster."

Hunter kissed me, catching my mouth and sliding his tongue deep inside. Need exploded through me, curling up from my pelvis through my body like fire, and the world slowed as his hips nestled between mine, spreading me open beneath him. His big, rough hand caught my breast, his callused thumb sliding back and forth across my nipple as the kiss deepened.

Oh shit . . .

I'd love to say I fought valiantly to preserve my virtue, but that just wasn't an option. I don't even have the words to describe how much I'd wanted him earlier that night, but that was nothing compared to this. I was pumped full of adrenaline and anger and fear and so many emotions.

In an instant they all turned to lust.

My hips cradled his as he started slowly rocking into me, our jeans a barrier I suddenly hated. His thumb and tongue played me in time as a slow burn built deep inside. This was different than it'd been at the bar, darker somehow.

Probably because back then I'd had hope.

Now every rock of my hips was a betrayal of my club, my family, the father who'd given everything to take care of me through the years. But I was empty, and the growing ridge of Hunter's erection would fill me perfectly—I knew it as surely as I knew he wasn't real.

He started moving faster, pulling his mouth away from mine and dropping his head down into my neck. He'd let my hands free somewhere along the way, which I discovered when I brought them around his back, tugging at his shirt. Not that I was undressing him, at least not consciously.

I just needed to feel his bare skin under my fingers.

Each movement of his hips scraped the long, strong length of his jeans-clad dick along my core, the rough fabric causing just the right amount of friction mixed with delicious pain. His shirt rubbed at my nipples and I found myself wishing he'd tug and play with them.

Then he gave a long, low groan and things changed.

Before he'd been almost tasting me, and whatever had been between us was almost painful in its restrained intensity. Now the wildness I'd felt from him at the bar, the darkness from the alley, they all came back. His muscles grew tight and his body stiffened. Then his hands came down on either side of my head as he pulled up abruptly.

Now Liam—*no, Hunter*—looked down at me, his eyes still full of that horrible tension I'd seen when I'd told him about Toke. His gaze burned into my face as his hips pinned me down into the mattress. Instinctively, I wrapped my legs around his waist, finding a better angle as he started pumping against my jeans-clad opening.

I think that's when it hit me—I didn't even need to take off my pants.

I was going to come, right here, right now, just from the feel of his cock rubbing me through the fabric, and I gave a little gasping moan of something between horror and incredible, terrible need.

"Please," I whispered as my leg muscles quivered. "Oh, shit . . ."

Hunter bared his teeth at me in what I suppose could be called a smile. But he wasn't smiling. He looked like he wanted to eat me and I felt fear because I knew I'd let him. I'd do anything, so long as he didn't stop moving until it ended and I shattered apart.

"Em," he said, and my name came ragged off his lips. "Em, baby. C'mon, Em. Now."

His hips pressed me deep into the bed then, rotating with rough efficiency. The stimulation was so intense it hurt. But the hurt wasn't a bad thing. Something about it, the way his eyes burned into mine, the way I couldn't have fought him off if I tried . . . my utter helplessness.

Fuck.

I loved it.

I felt my back arch as his hips crushed mine, and then my world exploded and I screamed. It wasn't a pretty, sexy scream, either. It was full of all the rage and anger and hurt and incredible fucking need I felt for him as it burst out of me.

Seconds later his body shuddered and he shouted, punching the mattress right next to my head. Then he collapsed on top of me, panting.

Unreal.

That's when it all hit me and I started laughing.

I'd just had incredible, indescribable sex with the hottest guy I'd ever met—and I was still a fucking virgin.

Jesus. Just like high school.

I couldn't *give* this shit away.

CHAPTER FOUR

HUNTER

I flopped down next to Em, trying to make my brain work again.

I'd come in my pants like a fucking kid.

Yeah. If the brothers saw this, they'd crucify me.

"You're gonna kill me," I muttered, reaching over to tuck a strand of her hair behind one of those perfect little ears. Her crystal-blue eyes looked up at me, dazed, and not entirely homicidal. Damn, I liked that way too much.

Damn, she was pretty. Smelled good, too.

"No, it's Dad who'll kill you," she said quietly. Thoughtfully. Great, because thinking wasn't going to make this any better on her end. "Liam—wait, what the hell is your name, anyway?"

"It's Liam. Hunter is my road name."

A shadow crossed her face.

"Are you really one of them?"

I didn't pretend not to understand.

"Yeah, I'm a Devil's Jack. Nomad. Been my job to keep tabs on you and your sister for a while. Among other things."

"Why?" she asked, her face genuinely confused. "We're not important."

I laughed, wondering how she could be so impossibly naive.

"You're pretty fuckin' important, babe," I told her. "That club loves you, even more than your sister because you stayed in Coeur d'Alene. Half the guys consider you their daughter and the other half want to bang you. All of 'em are scared of your dad. Still can't quite figure out why he's not national president. When Atlas retired last year, we figured he'd step up for sure."

"He's not interested," she said absently. Then she leaned up on one arm, studying me. I kept my eyes on her face, because clearly she'd forgotten that corset thing was wide open and showing off her tits. Not my place to remind her . . . Fortunately, her puffy lips provided a nice distraction. I kept picturing them wrapped around my cock. "Tell me the truth, Liam. Was there ever anything real between us?"

I should tell her it was all real. Tell her it was love at first sight, that we were Romeo and Juliet and I'd defy my club to be her one and only.

But for once I was just fucking sick and tired of lying.

"I have no idea what's between us," I said, not even sure that was true. The first time I'd seen Em, it'd felt like a gut punch. I'd wanted to nail her on the spot. That hadn't changed, but now that I had her laid out on a bed, for some reason making her feel better was more important than sticking my dick in her. Go figure.

"Not sure I know what real is," I said. "But I don't believe in love, babe. I believe in gettin' laid."

"That's the saddest thing I've ever heard."

I shrugged, feeling almost philosophical about the situation. There's a certain freedom in being totally screwed—and that was definitely what this was shaping up to be. Clusterfuck all around.

"Well, I do know I've got come all over my pants, and that's not something that happens every day," I told her. "You're fucking hot, babe. No matter what other stories you tell yourself, don't doubt it for a minute. I can't remember the last time I blew like that. Not sure what it means, but that part's sure as shit real."

"Heh," she said, then rolled onto her back and looked at the ceiling. "Am I gonna end up dead?"

I considered the question seriously, rolling it through my mind. I felt certain about one thing. I'd kill myself before I hurt her—well, hurt her physically. I was relatively sure I'd already done serious damage emotionally. But so long as I needed her making phone calls to Daddy, I couldn't afford to let her feel safe. Those calls needed to motivate him, and that required fear.

Crap.

I didn't like this feeling, I decided. I didn't like feeling at all. Half the guys in the Jacks thought I was some kind of killing machine, and they were probably right. Give me a target, I'd neutralize it. But that usually involved guns or knives . . . or on one very memorable occasion a particularly sharp deer antler. Sometimes you just have to improvise. I tended not to talk to my victims much, let alone try to comfort them.

But for reasons I didn't care to consider, I wanted to make her feel better.

"I don't want anything bad to happen to you," I finally said, compromising. "I'll do everything in my power to keep you safe."

"What about Sophie?"

"I got nothing against her, either. All I want is my brother back. Alive."

Silence fell again. I could almost hear her thinking.

"What would you do for Kit?" I asked her abruptly.

"What do you mean?"

"How far would you go to save her life?"

Would she make the connection? Understand why I had to fight for my brother?

"I'd do anything I had to," she replied softly, and I heard a hint of despair in her voice. Yup, she was starting to get it. Somehow that was even worse. "I'd steal. I'd lie . . . I'd kill. Anything."

Silence fell again, heavy between us. Shit. I pushed up suddenly, rolling off the bed. Her eyes followed me as I walked across the room to the closet, opening it to find my bag and pull out a clean pair of briefs. I thought she gave a little gasp as I slid down my pants and kicked them off, but that could've been wishful thinking. I pulled up the fresh ones, then tugged my shirt over my head.

Her eyes went wide as she watched me come back toward her. I wanted to believe my body impressed her, but hell—she was probably just looking over my tats to decide which one she hated most. I didn't have a back patch with my full club colors on it, but there were a few DJMC symbols here and there.

"You should put on some clothes," she said.

"Need some fuckin' sleep. Might as well get comfortable," I told her, and that part was the truth. Apparently I'd shot all my adrenaline out through my dick, and while a second round would finish things off nicely, I didn't think she was up to it. I leaned down over the bed and swung her up, setting her on her feet. Then I reached for the snap of her jeans, figuring she'd be more comfortable without them, but also pretty sure she wouldn't take them off herself.

That's when she punched me in the stomach, and it wasn't a girly punch, either.

Christ.

It fucking hurt.

Em glared at me, backing away slowly. She had her fists up and was balanced lightly on her toes, clearly ready to defend herself. Cute. But if she was a martial arts specialist of some kind, I hadn't seen any evidence over the past six months.

Jesus, you sound like a fucking stalker, asshole.

I suppose I was.

"Glad you didn't go for my nuts," I commented, taking in the sight of her. Boobs out, pink nipples all hard, teasing me. Shit. Maybe a second round wasn't out of the question?

"Next time I'll rip your *dick* off," she muttered, eyes narrowing. Okay, so round two was definitely out for now. Noted. Still, fearsome Em was fuckin' adorable. Kind of like a really angry baby mouse.

"What were you trying to do, anyway?" she demanded.

"I want to sleep," I told her. "You need sleep, too, and it's more comfortable without jeans. That's it, babe, no big, evil plan to get you out of your clothes. It's gonna be a long haul, you should rest while you can. God knows what'll happen tomorrow."

"My dad's killing you tomorrow," she muttered, but she didn't sound entirely happy about it. Interesting.

"You sound almost sad," I said. "Don't tell me you've decided I should live after all?"

"Fuck you."

"That an invitation?"

She turned away from me and started doing up her corset-thingy, which was a damned shame. Then I caught a glimpse of the bandage and sobered.

"You in any pain?"

"It's fine," she muttered. "You aren't sleeping in here, are you?"

"Yeah," I told her. "Don't worry, I'll share the covers with you."

Em cocked her head at me.

"Why don't you put me in with Sophie?" she asked. "I'll bet she's scared."

"Are you?"

"Am I what?"

"Scared?"

"That's a dick question, under the circumstances," she muttered. "I guess it was all a lie between us, but please don't think that because I was stupid enough to fall for your shit once means I'm actually stupid, okay? I'm not going to talk this out with you and give you more information, or let you play with me for your own entertainment."

Now that was a shame. My cock liked the idea of playing with her quite a bit . . . But she was right—this wasn't a game, we weren't friends, and I shouldn't fuck with her head any more than I had to.

Had to respect her for that.

"Okay, lie down," I told her bluntly. "I'm going to cuff your wrist to the bed. Then I'm going to sleep and so are you. Don't fight with me and I won't play games. This isn't a negotiation."

I saw something cross her face . . . Disappointment? Maybe. Or resignation.

Either way, I knew I'd just broken her a little more.

Like so much that'd happened tonight, I didn't know what to think of that.

An hour later I was still wide awake.

I don't know what I was smoking, thinking I'd fall asleep with Em in my arms. She dropped off pretty quick, which kind of surprised me. I mean, *I* knew she was safe with me—at least physically—but *she* didn't.

She'd refused to take off her clothes, but I still felt every inch of that beautiful body up against mine and it was fantastic. Of course I knew guys with old ladies, and they seemed to enjoy being around them. I'd never understood it, but if it was anything like this, maybe it wasn't so crazy.

I decided to play a little game. I'd lie in the dark, holding her, and pretend she was my old lady for a while. Pretend we lived in a world where I could have something as beautiful as her. That I didn't owe the Jacks everything, or that she wasn't a Reaper.

Then I caught myself, because what the fuck?

Christ, I didn't want an old lady—or at least one like Em, who could think for herself. I'd signed on for someone who'd do what she was told and be thankful for it. That'd been the plan, and now it was blown to shit. If I was gonna pretend, a better fantasy would be rolling her over and screwing her brains out. Nice . . . Imagining myself inside her was fun for a while, but then my cock started getting pretty pissed off that we weren't screwing her brains out for real. Considering I'd only brought a couple changes of clothing with me and I'd already soaked one pair of pants, seemed like a good idea to get some space.

I managed to get out of bed without waking her and headed downstairs to find Skid in the living room, playing Halo. An energy drink sat next to him, right next to a dusting of white powder. Guess I wasn't the only one pulling an all-nighter.

He set down the controller and raised a brow.

"So, what kind of game you playing, bro?" he asked me. "Because something feels off to me. This bitch is your means to an end. That's it, right?"

"I'm aware," I said, my tone dry. "Believe me."

"Just don't forget whose team we're playing for. I heard from Kelsey. Grass is stable. She says it's not as bad as they thought when he first came in."

"No word on Clutch?"

"Nope," he answered.

"Em says Toke's gone rogue. Reapers have lost control of him. If it's the truth, we're fucked."

"Think she's messin' with you?"

I considered the question.

"I think there's a good chance he's off the reservation," I replied. "None of this makes sense. We've got a truce, the Reapers voted on it. Shit with Gracie happened a long time ago—if this was a club hit, I don't think they'd have bothered talking truce in the first place. Retribution's worthless if you don't claim it."

"Asshole couldn't have fucked Burke over better if we'd planned it out with him," Skid said, sighing. "We don't shut this down, it could take him out. All of us fucked then."

I didn't bother responding, because it was the simple truth. We had one shot at revolution in the club. Mason had already given Burke the heads-up—his cancer was spreading. The national president of the Devil's Jacks MC was on his way out. He wouldn't be able to hide it much longer, which meant Burke had to make his move soon or it was all over.

This was our chance to take the Devil's Jacks back, make the club back into what it'd been created to be. A brotherhood of riders. Not a bunch of cheap thugs looking to line their own pockets. We'd hoped for more time to consolidate our position, but if the truce held, we'd have the votes we needed. The charters down south were desperate for help keeping out the cartel—help we couldn't give them if we had to fight a two-front war with the Reapers.

"Hey, bro?" Skid asked.

"What?"

"Call me crazy, but I'm pretty sure even if we manage to pull some kind of peace out of the fire, you won't get to keep your pretty toy upstairs."

"Yeah," I muttered, letting myself fall back into a chair. I scratched my stomach and eyed his can of Monster. I needed some of that shit. "It's fucked."

Silence fell between us.

"That's all you have to say for yourself?" he asked. "'It's fucked'? Where's the big plan? You're the one always thinkin' things through, telling us we need a strategy."

"The plan isn't coming together this time," I said. "Do you still think we can pull it off?"

"Pull off what? Surviving tomorrow? I give us sixty-forty. Feelin' optimistic."

I laughed, because he was probably right. I'd get Em through it, though. No way that pretty girl was gettin' caught in the crossfire. I wasn't quite sure why I felt so strongly about keeping her safe, but I did.

"Tomorrow I'm going to meet with Hayes," I said. "Burke's checking out his story, maybe our sources down south can say whether it's true he doesn't know where Toke is. Based on Em's reaction, I think there's a pretty good chance he's gone rogue."

"How do you know she's not spouting the party line?" Skid said. "I think we've established your dick's doing the thinking when it comes to her."

"You're probably right there," I admitted. "But I believe she's telling the truth. According to her, he's been on the run for a full week. He sliced her up at a party last weekend. She's got a knife wound—*someone* cut her."

That caught Skid's attention.

"Damn," he muttered. "What the hell is going on in that club? Hayes is serious as shit about his girls, no way he'll let that stand."

"Exactly," I replied. "That's why I'm not ready to give up on the truce just yet. If she's telling the truth, they want his head as bad as we do. But what the fuck do I know? She could be setting me up."

Skid laughed.

"There's karma for you . . . You at least get laid up there?"

"I'm not gonna answer that."

Skid started laughing so hard he choked on his drink.

"You fucking pussy," he muttered finally. "She's got your balls in her pocket already. When's the last time you got some ass? Haven't seen any coming out of your room lately."

"I'm not gonna answer that, either."

"You think Princess Emmy's got a bike?" he asked me, an unholy gleam in his eyes.

"No idea."

"Better find out. You'll look cute riding bitch."

I considered tackling him, but it seemed like too much work. I flipped him off instead, then reached for a game controller.

"Wanna play?"

"Sure."

It felt good to zone out, and for a little while I was able to pretend we were back at our house and this was just like any other Friday night. Well, except for being fuckin' sober and having two girls cuffed to the beds upstairs.

Well, except for being fuckin' sober. Heh.

After a while Skid spoke, not bothering to look at me.

"Just remember you can't keep her."

"I know."

"Just checkin', bro."

"No worries. I got my orders."

"Don't forget—Jacks first. You really like her?"

"Jesus. What is this, Oprah?"

"If you give a shit about her at all, you'll hurt her bad. Make her give up on you now. Burke wanted her to fall for you, but with this kidnapping shit nobody'll think twice about her hating your guts after it's over."

I snorted.

"Considering she's cuffed to a bed after being lied to, you really think I need to go out of my way to hurt Em more? Seems like overkill."

"You got scratches on your back, dickwad. They don't look like defensive wounds to me, so no, it's not overkill. You need to hurt her so much she never looks back."

I considered his words and sighed.

"You're probably right."

We played a few minutes more, and then I turned on him and shot his character point-blank. Animated blood spattered the TV screen.

Skid started laughing again.

"You got anger issues, bro. Or maybe just blue balls. Not my fault you're a pussy."

"Eat shit and die."

"Maybe tomorrow. Tonight I'm gonna eat a pizza pocket. You want one?"

I considered the question carefully.

"Yeah, sounds good."

I climbed back upstairs around five in the morning.

Skid had camped out on the couch, still playing games and

bitching that he'd given up a perfectly good bed so Sophie could have her beauty sleep. A bed that had more than enough room for him *and* her . . .

I pointed out that if I couldn't have Em, he couldn't have Sophie.

He pointed out that I could've had Em. I reminded him that Burke wanted peace, which probably wouldn't happen if I screwed Emmy Lou Hayes while she was prisoner handcuffed to a bed frame. We settled the argument by calling each other assholes and glaring at each other for a while, which seemed to do the trick.

Now I found myself back upstairs, looking down at the most beautiful woman I'd ever seen. Before I left this room, I'd make her cry.

I couldn't take my eyes off her.

She'd rolled onto her stomach, kicking off the covers. One leg was cocked to the side, which curved her ass perfectly, nicely set off by the fact that her low-rise jeans didn't quite cover the top of a red thong.

And there, right in the center of her back, was a fuckin' tramp stamp.

I looked closer, trying to figure out what the hell it might be. Some kind of Chinese symbol surrounded by angel wings. Pretty goddamn awful. Cliche as shit.

I loved it.

It made me think of every porno I'd ever watched, and because I'm an evil bastard my dick got so hard I felt my heartbeat pulse through it. I wanted to pull off those jeans and fuck her pussy, then hit her ass. I'd finish up blowing my wad right in the center of that tat.

Shit.

Yeah. She wouldn't be down for that.

I slid into bed with her anyway, because she hadn't been through enough. I tugged her into my body, wrapping my arm around her. Her corset had ridden up, leaving a thin strip of flesh across her stomach. I found myself stroking it, wondering what it would feel like to run my cockhead across that smooth skin. Em squirmed, stretching forward in her sleep. This pushed her ass back into my crotch, which was both the best and worst sensation I'd ever experienced in my life.

Then she stiffened and I heard her breathing change.

"Good morning," I said quietly.

"Crap, this really happened, didn't it?" she asked, and her voice sounded small and soft. She was only a few years younger than me, but that softness reminded me just how different our lives had been. Compared to her, I was an old man.

"Yeah, it really happened," I told her, sniffing her hair. Flowers. "I'll meet with your dad today, see if he's found Toke. Maybe end this whole thing before it gets any worse."

She made a little noise, a sort of hopeless moan that she immediately cut off. Shit. She hadn't faked that. Either Toke really was in the wind, or she knew the Reapers wouldn't give him up, even to save a couple of their women. If the whole club decided to take a stand, probably wasn't much Hayes would be able to do.

I rubbed her stomach again, and she shifted back into me restlessly. Very nice. Skid's warning that I needed to hurt her ran through my head, but maybe I could touch her just a little more, first. I promised myself I wouldn't actually fuck her, which made it okay, right?

It wasn't because I have morals. Hell, it wasn't even because I knew she deserved better. I just wasn't sure I'd be able to give her up once I'd felt that tight cunt squeezing down around my dick. Wars have been fought for less, and now I understood why. But seeing as we'd already fooled around once, I figured a little more playtime wouldn't really change much in the long run . . . In fact, it would make the betrayal even worse. I'd be doing it for her own good.

I slid my fingers under the top button of her jeans.

"What are you doing?" she murmured, her voice sleepy.

"Makin' you feel better."

Em muttered something, but I couldn't tell what it was and she didn't try to stop me when I popped open the button. Then my fingers slid down the zipper and my hand slipped inside.

She was wet already.

Nice.

Had she been dreaming about me? Hell, maybe she'd been dreaming about someone else. If so, I needed to kill the mother-fucker ASAP. She shifted her legs as my fingers found her clit, sliding past it to dip inside and collect some of that sweet moisture. Then I found that sensitive spot again and circled it, teasing.

"I hate you."

"I know you do, babe," I whispered. "If it makes you feel better, you can pretend you have a choice."

"Do I?"

I considered the question.

"We always have a choice," I said finally, and for some crazy reason my foster father's face popped into my head—the way it'd looked right before I'd killed him.

The fuck?

"Are we going to have sex?" she asked, breaking through my twisted thoughts.

"Do you want to?"

It satisfied the hell out of me that she had to think about it. Then she shook her head.

"No, I want someone better than you for my first," she said firmly. Fair enough.

"Let's compromise," I replied. "How 'bout I get you off. I can feel how much you want it."

I circled her clit again for emphasis, and Em shuddered.

"Unlock me and take off your pants," she demanded.

I burst out laughing.

"You're supposed to be a little more subtle about seducing me into letting you go."

"I'm not really good with subtle," she said. "How's this . . . You want to get me off, right?"

"That's the plan."

"Do you want my hand on your dick while you do it?"

I swallowed.

"What do you think?"

"Here's the thing . . ." she whispered. "I won't pretend that getting away from here isn't a high priority. But you can feel for yourself how wet I am for you."

My finger twitched on her clit and she shivered.

"So," she continued. "It's your call—is it worth the risk to find out whether I'm messing with you? I'm sure a big, bad biker man like you is more than capable of defending himself from me. You've already proven how much stronger you are."

She wiggled her butt as she spoke, cradling my cock between those tight cheeks. Hell yeah, it was worth the risk—and you'll be shocked to learn the little head made that particular call. I'm not an idiot—I knew she was playing games with me.

I just didn't care.

I stood up and stripped quickly. Em watched at first, then turned her eyes away as I reached for my briefs. I considered leaving them on to make her more comfortable. Yeah, fuck that. I pulled them down, then crawled across the bed and lay over her, lowering my face down to hers, catching her lips with mine.

I didn't bother with the sweet kisses. My cock had been hard for a hell of a long time and the idea of her touching it was almost more than I could handle. Probably a good thing she still had her clothing on.

Otherwise I might just lose control and push deep inside.

I knew damned well *that* would be a huge mistake for any number of reasons. Not least of these was the fact that most people would consider it rape. Picnic Hayes would probably be among those people and he had enough reason to kill me already.

Fear of her father wasn't why I was determined to hold back, though. Some small, rational part of me didn't want her looking back and rewriting what happened between us, to believe I forced her. Since when did I give a shit about a woman's regrets? I figured it was better not to consider that too carefully.

Em pulled free after a minute and nuzzled my neck.

"Unlock me," she whispered.

Fuck it.

I reached up and unlocked her, bracing myself for an attack. Instead I felt her arms come around me, their delicious warmth tracing along my back toward my ass.

Shit, that felt good.

I kissed down her neck and then started unhooking that god-damned corset. It must've had thirty little fasteners. I'd always thought these things were hot as fuck, but my interest in them was fading fast.

"Let me," she said softly. I looked into her eyes and they were all soft and full of need. "Roll off for a minute, okay?"

I rolled off her and she blushed, then turned away.

"I've already seen your tits, babe."

"It's a lot, Liam," she said softly. "Just give me a sec, okay?"

"Okay," I said, letting my eyes trail down her back. I really loved that little tramp stamp of hers. Tacky as hell, but I'd always been a sucker for them.

Nice to have a target.

"What does your tat say?"

She sighed heavily.

"It's supposed to say 'Forever,'" she said. "My sister and I got them one night not long after our mom died, that's why the angel wings. We wanted it to be a memorial to her. I have to admit, we were a little drunk when we came up with it . . . It was a bad time in our lives. But the guy who did it was a fucking idiot. It actually means 'squirrel.'"

"Shit," I said, trying to hold back a snort of laughter. *Thou shalt not laugh at the naked girl when she's about to touch your cock.* "Well, I guess nobody looking at it would know. How'd you find out?"

"When I went to college," she said. "I did a semester over in Seattle. My roommate was Chinese, so she filled me in."

"That sucks."

"Not as much as my mom dying," she muttered. She seemed to be struggling with the corset, and I was just about to ask her if she was okay when she rolled back and clocked me over the head with a heavy, hardback book.

Well fuck.

Really shouldn't have let my little head do all the thinking.

CHAPTER FIVE

EM

It wasn't the best of weapons.

A gun would've been nice, or a baseball bat. Maybe pepper spray.

Knife?

I knew how to use them all. For the most part, my dad drove me crazy growing up. He was overprotective, overbearing, controlling . . . paranoid. Just paranoid enough to spend a certain amount of time teaching his girls to look at anything and everything as a potential weapon.

Even books.

God bless Stephen King, because the hardback I'd found wedged between the wrought-iron headboard and the wall was fucking huge. It had obviously been back there for a hell of a long time, too. Totally covered with dust.

I didn't feel a moment of guilt as I slammed it down onto Liam's head, just savage satisfaction. I wasn't under any illusion that this was a stellar escape plan. The odds were against me. But if I managed to hit him just right, I might be able to knock him out long enough to cuff him.

Then I'd only have Skid to deal with.

I figured the longer we stayed kidnapped, the more likely it was more Jacks would show up. Waiting for a better shot wasn't worth the risk—at least that was my logic.

The book hit Liam with a satisfying thud, knocking him to the side. I followed it with a smash against the side of his face, which he managed to block with his arm.

Still knocked him off the bed, though.

In an instant I was up and over him, kicking him as hard as I could. I'd aimed for his crotch but he twisted at the last minute, blocking me. Liam sprang back up—rather impressively, I have to admit—and then it was all over. He tackled me against the bed, pinning me down with his full weight. One hand caught both of mine and dragged them high over my body. The other covered my mouth, immobilizing my head so I couldn't head-butt him.

My little rebellion had lasted about thirty seconds.

Crap.

Liam's face was directly above, and I looked up at him, expecting to see anger or betrayal. Instead I saw his eyes dark and intense and hot with need.

Fuck. Fighting with me turned the bastard on.

I needed to start remembering that.

One of his knees pushed between my legs, shoving them apart, and then he was up against my center and shit . . . That felt good. Sometimes I hate myself. On the bright side, I definitely hated him more.

"Next time make sure you have a better plan, babe," he said softly. "This one never had a shot, and you risked pissing me off. You do that to the wrong man and he's gonna really hurt you."

And you won't? I wanted to snap, but he kept my mouth

covered. Then he pushed his hips into me, the heat in his eyes flaring.

"Fuck, you tempt me," he muttered. "You have no idea how much I want to shove my dick into you. No idea at all."

I glared at him hatefully, because the smell of him, the feel of him over me, the adrenaline rushing through me . . . All of it headed straight between my legs. He'd invaded my dreams earlier. When he started touching me and I'd woken up, I'd already been on fire. Now it was worse, which was pretty damned unfair.

"I'm going to let you talk," he said. "But remember, you start screaming, there's nobody to hear you but me and Skid. Oh, and your girl Sophie. She can't do shit to help you, but hearing you yellin' will probably scare the hell out of her. That what you want?"

I shook my head as much as I could, which wasn't much. His hand lifted.

"You're an asshole," I muttered.

"I know, sweetheart," he said. He fumbled with the cuffs, and a few seconds later I found myself with both hands fastened to the top of the bed. Liam sat up, straddling me. I was stupid enough to look down, where I found his cock standing out, hard as a rock.

It was the first time I'd actually seen him.

Wow.

Liam wasn't small. It was long and the tip was all red and angry looking. Just a tiny bit of fluid welled out at the very top, and I licked my lips unconsciously. His breath hissed and I flushed, forcing myself to look up at the ceiling instead.

"You still want me to get you off?" he asked, offering a dark smile. "Seems like the least I can do, under the circumstances."

I flushed more and didn't bother answering his question. I'd like to say this was because it was so crazy, or that I knew he wouldn't listen if I said no. Maybe he wouldn't. But a secret, dirty little part of me kind of wanted it . . .

And yes, the answer to your question is that I am definitely fucking insane. But betrayal and evil ways aside, Liam was hot—

his body called to mine in a way that I couldn't seem to fight. I'd love to say that it disgusted me to see how our fighting turned him on, but that would be pretty damned hypocritical.

It turned me on, too.

Something about how he overpowered me, the way he didn't handle me like I was fragile. Liam wasn't scared to touch me, unlike every other man I'd ever known. His fingers came down over my corset and unhooked it quickly. My boobs spilled out, and he took one in each hand, squeezing them softly, pinching at the nipples. Sensation raced through me and I squirmed. Then he pushed them together, gaze utterly focused.

"I'd love to fuck your tits."

I gasped and he gave a harsh laugh.

"Christ, Em, if that scares you, you definitely don't want to know all the other sick shit I have running through my head. What I'd do with these, if I owned you . . ."

His voice trailed off as he scooted down my body. Then his lips caught my nipple and sucked it in deep. I felt his hand trail down my side, and it slid between us to tug down my jeans.

I was still wet from my dream, not to mention when he'd touched me before. His finger penetrated me smoothly and I moaned. Shit. How did he do that?

This was what people meant by chemistry.

Damn.

Why the hell had I wasted any time chasing after Painter?

Because Painter isn't a fucking kidnapper? the sensible part of my brain pointed out. A second finger slid in and then his thumb started circling my clit. I moaned again, twisting underneath him. He pulled away from my nipple and laid his cheek down between them, giving a low laugh.

"How much do you hate me right now, Emmy girl?" he asked, his voice a whispered taunt.

I didn't dignify it with a reply.

His fingers curled up inside me, pressing against my inner wall as his thumb slid slowly back and forth. I shuddered and my hips bucked. That tight tension that builds up to an orgasm crept through me, his power over me a tangible thing.

Shit, I wanted his cock inside.

"You hate me enough that you want me to stop? Because I'll stop, Em. Just say the word."

He stopped moving, and my hips pressed up at him, begging for more. God. There's something *wrong* with me. Liam laughed again, then started licking his way down my stomach.

"How's that, baby?" he asked, thumb starting to work my clit again. "Feel good being turned on by a Devil's Jack?"

It felt fucking fantastic, but I'd be damned if I'd acknowledge the point. Apparently I didn't need to, because he slid lower, tugging down my jeans and panties enough for his mouth to reach my cleft. He breathed softly on it for a second, then flicked his tongue over my most sensitive spot.

I squealed, my hips bucking. Liam laughed again.

"Tell you what," he said. "You say the word, I'll pull off those pants and throw your legs over my shoulders, show you just how much you've been missing."

I stayed silent. He licked me again, pausing to tug on my clit with gentle suction.

"I hate you," I said, but it came out as less of a declaration and more of a plea.

"Everyone hates me. But not everyone tastes as good as you, sweetheart. What'll it be? We doing this or not?"

I wanted to tell him to fuck off. But a traitorous little voice in my head pointed out that the damage was already done . . . Why not enjoy it? I'd already made a fool of myself and nothing would change that.

"No sex," I said.

"Define 'sex,'" he replied, kissing my mound almost tenderly.

"No sticking your penis inside me."

"I can work with that."

Seconds later my pants were gone. Liam's lips covered my pussy and then I lost track of time. I'd had one other guy go down on me and I'd enjoyed it, but it was nothing compared to this devil's tongue. He alternated between my clit and my lower lips, fingers deep inside me, playing me until I couldn't even breathe, let alone talk. The first orgasm hit me hard and I had to bite the inside of my cheek to keep from screaming.

That's where I expected it to end, but he just kept going until I couldn't tell how much time had passed or even remember how many times I came. Heaven and hell, all rolled together and tied with a bow.

Make that a handcuff.

Then he pulled away with a groan to kneel over me, eyes feral with hunger.

"Roll over."

HUNTER

Em surrounded me . . . Her taste, her smell, those little noises she made when she came. All of it washed through me, driving me crazy. I've never wanted anything more in my entire life than I wanted to shove my cock deep into her cunt. Ride her. *Own* her.

I couldn't do it, though.

Not that I had any illusions—if I survived this little adventure, she'd never talk to me again. But I'd be damned if her first shot at real sex would come handcuffed to a bed in the middle of a club standoff.

But I'm no saint.

Staring down at Em's heart-shaped ass, I knew I'd be pretty happy up inside there, too. Also not gonna happen. Those cheeks, though . . . I could make them work for me. I grabbed her hips and

pulled her up onto her knees. She wavered unsteadily, so I grabbed
a pillow and shoved it under her stomach. Then I ran my cock along
the crack of her rear, savoring the heat.

"No," she said quickly, her voice panicked.

"Relax, babe," I said. "No dick inside, remember? I promised."

She stayed tense, though, as I pushed her ass cheeks together,
cradling my cock between them. When she tensed her muscles, they
got even tighter, so I wasn't about to complain.

Slowly I started sliding my cock in and out, precome seeping
from the head and smoothing my way perfectly.

"That feels incredible," I muttered. She gave a little grunt, like
she'd protest if she had the energy. Fortunately, I'd pretty much
wiped her out already.

I picked up speed with each stroke, her tight heat making my
dick impossibly harder. I stopped thinking, eyes focused on that
Chinese squirrel symbol. Fuckin' crazy girl. I felt my balls tighten
and knew I was close.

Shit, this was like every porn fantasy I'd ever had coming true.

Well, not quite true. Ideally I'd be inside her, but honestly . . .
Her ass cheeks cradling my cock felt better than any pussy I'd ever
fucked. I guess that's what happens when you find the perfect
woman.

"Shit, babe," I whispered. It pulled inside me, the terrible desire.
Her slick heat surrounded me, her legs quivering beneath me. I felt
all powerful and consumed with need.

Then it hit.

My head exploded into lights as my cock blew out. I let her
cheeks go and watched in utter fascination as my come covered her
tattoo.

Christ, Em was a good lay.

I stayed there, running my hands up and down along her sides,
soothing her for long moments. I heard a sniffle, and wondered if
she was crying. Probably.

Then it was time.

I pulled away from her slowly, carefully, treasuring the sight of her lying there. I stood back and pulled on my jeans. Then I dug through the pocket to find my cell phone.

Damn . . .

I don't know what was worse—what I was about to do, or how much I was looking forward to it. I turned it on and opened the camera app, coming up behind her and taking three great shots of her jizz-soaked ass.

"What're you doing?" she murmured softly, stretching. I took action shots the whole time, wishing she'd roll over so I could get those tits.

"Saving the moment," I told her absently. "Want something to show the boys back home. You look like a fuckin' porn star. Think Daddy'll want one of these?"

She tried to sit up but the cuffs caught her. Instead she fell heavily to the side—facing me, thank fuck—and I started taking pics of her tits and that sweet pussy I could just see peeking out between her legs.

Her eyes met mine, full of sudden, horrific comprehension. *This has to happen*, I reminded myself.

Em screamed in wordless rage. Then she raised her legs and kicked the wall, the force of her anger driving the bed a good six inches across the floor. A mirror mounted over the dresser fell to the floor with the crash of shattering glass.

"*You cocksucking bastard!*" she shrieked.

I took one last shot, then turned off my camera. That should do it.

"Consider this a lesson why you shouldn't trust strangers you meet on the Internet," I told her, offering a nasty smile. "I'm gonna go get something to clean up the glass. Be a good girl while I'm gone—unless you want another lesson? I can do worse than pictures, you know."

I opened the door and stepped out quietly. She screamed at me again, the sound tearing through me as I jogged down the stairs.

Skid looked up from the couch and cocked a brow.

"Do I wanna know?" he asked.

I shook my head.

"Naw, just took your advice," I replied. "I hurt her bad. Should be enough to do the trick."

"Right thing to do, brother."

I shrugged.

"Guess so. Fuckin' sucks."

"Yeah, that's why I don't usually follow my own advice," Skid muttered. "Glad you did it, though. Frees her up to find someone else. Get her out of this game."

"Every once in a while, I wonder what life would be like outside the club," I admitted, rubbing a hand through my hair. "You know, if we didn't have all this shit to deal with? If we could just live like normal people."

"Never gonna happen, so might as well forget it," Skid replied. "Hell, you'd be bored off your ass. Can you imagine holding down a regular job? Fuck, what would you even do? I know you're fuckin' great at hunting people down, taking them out—"

"Don't say shit like that, bro."

Skid laughed.

"My bad. You're fuckin' great at whatever it is you do for Burke," he said. "Probably fetching coffee, delivering flowers. Shit like that. But a regular job? You'd be fucked, man. It is what it is."

"Sometimes I hate this."

"Yeah, me, too. But you know what? Sometimes it fuckin' kicks ass, so let's focus on getting through the next day or two. Then we'll head back home and get you laid. She's not the only pussy in the world."

"Don't talk about her like that."

Skid snorted.

"Fuckin' pussy."

"I said don't talk about her like that."

"I was talkin' about you, asshole. Biggest damned pussy in the house."

This time I decided tackling him was worth the effort.

EM

I refused to speak when Hunter finally returned, focusing my gaze exactly two inches above his right shoulder. After a few minutes of one-sided conversation, he gave a frustrated sigh and walked me over to Sophie's room.

She'd been cuffed to a bed just like me, and even in sleep she looked as rough as I felt. Shit. I hoped to hell Skid hadn't decided to teach her the same kind of "lesson" Liam gave me.

"You okay?" I asked, sitting down on the side of the bed. She opened her eyes slowly, face twisting.

"I need the bathroom," she whispered.

I looked over at Liam—no, *Hunter*. I needed to remember that. Liam was the imaginary nice guy. Hunter was the giant douche who'd taken dirty pictures of me.

"Can she go to the fucking bathroom?" I asked, not bothering to hide my hatred.

"Yeah," he replied, his face blank. He walked toward us and I scooted out of the way, glaring at him while he unlocked Sophie's cuffed arm. "C'mon. Both of you."

I grabbed Sophie's hand and pulled her across the hallway and into the bathroom.

"I can't believe how stupid I was," I told her, feeling sick. "I actually invited him to come and meet me. I made it so easy. *Idiot.*"

Sophie used the toilet and then washed up, cupping her hands to get a drink. She seemed so quiet, so subdued. I couldn't understand why she wasn't more pissed. Hell, she *should* be pissed—at *me*. I got her into this shit.

"Do you have any idea what's going to happen to us?" she asked. "Skid scares the crap out of me."

"Did he hurt you?" I demanded, feeling my blood pressure rise.

"No."

"That's good," I muttered. "This is a pretty fucked-up situation. Toke—he's the one who cut me at the party—he's gone off his rocker. This shooting thing makes no sense to me at all, but if it really happened, we're screwed. Nobody knows where Toke is, not even Deke, and he's Toke's president. They've all been looking for him since the party. Cutting me was not okay, and Dad wants to make sure he pays for it."

"Shit," she said, eyes wide. "So your dad couldn't give them this Toke guy, even if he wanted to?"

"I don't think so," I said slowly, wishing I could fix things—for her, if not for me. Hell, Sophie was a mother. What would her little boy do without her? "I mean, he's really protective of me. When Toke hurt me like that, Dad lost it. If Dad could find him, he'd be found already. We're pretty fucked here, Sophie."

"Do you think they'll hurt us?" she asked, her face pale.

I thought about my answer carefully. I didn't want to freak her out, but I wanted to be honest.

"Liam won't," I said, and for some reason I believed it. Maybe because he hadn't raped me? "I mean, he won't hurt me. I don't think he'll hurt you, either."

She cocked her head at me.

"You do realize he was lying all along, right?" she asked. "Just because you liked him doesn't mean you can trust him."

I almost started laughing, because that was rich.

"Oh, I know that. Believe me, I'm well aware that I'm the fuck-wit that got us into this."

"You're not a fuckwit," she said forcefully. "He's a liar and he's good at it. Not your fault that he targeted you."

"You guys okay in there?" Hunter called through the door.

"We're fine," I snapped. "Give us a fucking minute, asshole!"

Christ, I wanted to kill him.

Sophie's eyes widened.

"That was pretty bitchy," she hissed. "Do you think that's smart? Maybe I'm reading the situation wrong here, but don't we want him in a good mood?"

I snorted, thinking about those pictures.

Hunter was such a prick.

"Fuck that. I'm a Reaper and I'll be damned if I'll suck up to some Devil's Jack dickwad."

"Well, I'm not a Reaper," Sophie said, her voice quiet but hard. I looked at her, startled—this was the first real emotion she'd shown. "And I'd just as soon not die here and leave Noah an orphan, so don't piss him off."

That took the wind out of me. Shit, I needed to be *thinking*. I knew it was up to me to get us out of this, and to pull it off I'd need to use my head. Damn. We finished up and left the bathroom. Hunter jerked his head toward Sophie's bedroom. It took everything I had to obey him quietly, but I kept picturing Sophie's boy and reminded myself I had to be smart about this.

"Go lie down on the bed."

We did what he said. Thankfully, he only cuffed one hand each, which was far more comfortable than having both stuck up over my head. I tried to ignore him as he leaned over me, tracing a finger across my cheek.

"I'll bring you some food," he murmured.

"I'm gonna buy a bright red dress to wear to your funeral, *Liam*," I hissed. Shit. I needed to control my tongue . . .

"Yeah?" he asked. "Make sure it's short and shows off your tits."

"I hate you."

"Keep tellin' yourself that," he muttered, then walked out of the room, slamming the door behind him.

I closed my eyes, trying to picture a dress bright and slutty enough to send just the right message as I stood over his coffin. Sophie cleared her throat.

"Don't worry," I muttered. "We'll find our way out of this. We'll escape somehow. Either that or the guys will find us."

I wondered if she believed me.

Probably not. I didn't even believe myself.

CHAPTER SIX

HUNTER

I slapped together two peanut butter sandwiches, feeling strangely guilty because Skid and I had killed all six pizza pockets between us while we played Halo.

That left sandwiches and stale potato chips for the girls.

Why I gave a shit about what Em ate, I didn't know. This wasn't me—I didn't worry about women, or take care of them. Feed them. Okay, so I kept an eye on my sister, but she didn't count. I grabbed a couple handfuls of chips and dropped them on the paper plates next to the sandwiches, then tucked two bottles of water under my arm. Em was so not getting an energy drink. Fuck. Like I needed her more riled up . . .

When I entered the upstairs room, I felt like an even bigger dick because they were obviously hungry.

"You've got ten minutes," I said, unlocking their cuffs. I frowned at Em, then pulled out a chair from the desk, spinning it around to straddle it. Both girls ignored me pointedly, tearing into the food like starving prisoners.

Then again, I guess they were.

"In a minute we're going to call your dad," I said. "Let him know you're alive, and find out if he's made any progress."

No response. My mood grew darker as they finished their food, Em still refusing to look at me.

"Lie down again."

I cuffed Sophie first, then walked around to Em. I leaned over, then felt something touch my back. Fuck, were there spiders in here?

Sophie shrieked and spat a mouthful of blood at me. *The fuck?!*

"Jesus Christ!" I yelled, because I shit you not.

Bitch. Spat. Blood.

"Oh my God, are you all right?" Em screeched at Sophie, nearly taking out my eardrums in the process. "Hunter, you need to get her to a doctor!"

What was going on here? Blood and spit ran down Sophie's chin, confusing the hell out of me. Her eyes were bright with some kind of emotion I couldn't read. Something was off with this situation in a big way. Blood doesn't just shoot out of people.

"I'm tho thorry," she mumbled. "I bith my tongue and ith thcared me."

I looked down at my arm again, which was covered with red spray. Just what I needed.

"You're fucking kidding me," I muttered. "What the fuck's wrong with you? Shit, you got any diseases?"

"No, I don't hath any ditheatheth," Sophie mumbled, her tongue getting in the way. Then she seemed to bite it again. "Owth!"

Good. I hoped the damned thing fell off.

"Drive me fuckin' crazy. I'll get you a piece of ice to suck on. Jesus, that's fucking disgusting."

I left the room, slamming the door behind me.

What next?

• • •

Five minutes later, I scrubbed the blood and spit off my arm while frowning at my reflection in the bathroom mirror. Sophie and Em were up to something. I wasn't sure what. Not that it really mattered . . . It was pretty clear to me by now that I was looking at a complete clusterfuck.

I'd broken Em, or at least I'd tried to. I'd terrorized Sophie, who hadn't done shit to deserve it. We weren't any closer to getting Clutch back, and Burke was fucked when it came to the election if we didn't put a lid on things.

In a few minutes I'd be calling Picnic Hayes. I wasn't sure if I'd be meeting with him to talk business or facing my own execution.

Good times.

I walked down to the kitchen and dug through the freezer, finding an ice cube. Then I wrapped it in a napkin and took it back upstairs, along with a disposable cell phone. I handed Sophie the ice, which she popped into her mouth.

"We're going to call your dad again," I told Em. "I'll let you talk to him for a minute, then I'll see where the situation's headed."

"What about Sophie?" she demanded. "Ruger will want to talk to her."

"Ruger can fuck himself," I said impatiently.

"Pleathe?" Sophie whined, reddish drool sliding down her chin, making her look like a zombie. I don't think she could've looked more disgusting and pathetic if she'd had a full Hollywood makeup team. "My boy—Noah—he'th got a prethcription he needth. Ruger doethn't know where it ith. Let me talk to him for two minuteth. Pleathe."

I studied her, then took a quick look at Em. Both seemed way too eager.

"You're full of shit," I said.

"You want a seven-year-old kid to die?" Em asked, glaring at me. "Not enough to kill two women, now you're gonna take out a little boy, too? You're a hell of a man, Liam."

Jesus Christ. Take a few pictures of the girl naked and covered in fresh come, and she went full bitch.

"Do you never shut up?" I asked. Fucking woman was determined to drive me insane. Still, I considered the request . . . It probably didn't matter. Let Sophie call Ruger—maybe it'd quiet her down. If it gave me two minutes of blood-free peace, that'd be worth the cost of admission right there.

I popped open the phone and hit the number, setting it on speaker. We listened as it rang, and then Ruger answered.

"Yeah?" he asked, his voice tight.

"It's Thophie," Sophie said, her swollen tongue twisting the words. "I'm here with Hunter and Em, they're lithening."

I snapped the phone shut, annoyed. Should I really be surprised she'd try and warn him I was here? Probably not, but I wouldn't let her get away with it, either.

"No fucking games," I growled. "You're done."

Sophie nodded and put the ice back in her mouth. So much for her desperate need to talk to Ruger about medicine for the kid. There was a lot more going on here than I could follow.

Bullshit all the way.

I glanced over at Em, who was still glaring at me. So far as I could tell, she only had the one expression at this point. I don't know why it bothered me so much. I wanted her to hate me, right?

"Calling your dad now," I told her. "Be a good girl, Emmy Lou—or did you need another lesson?"

She flinched and looked away. I smirked at her cruelly, hating myself because I wanted a smile from her so bad. The phone started ringing, and then Hayes's voice came through the speaker.

"Picnic."

"Hey, Daddy," Em said. "We're okay for now."

She glanced up at me, an unspoken question in her eyes—would they stay okay?

"What the fuck's wrong with Sophie?" Picnic asked. "Ruger says she wasn't talking right."

"She bit her tongue," Em said. "Don't worry, she's fine. But you need to get us out of here."

"We know, baby," he said, his voice softening. "We're working on it."

Very touching.

This guy was definitely gonna kill me. I know I would, in his place. Maybe I should've screwed her after all, I thought wryly. If I was going to die over a woman, would be nice to actually collect . . . I studied Em, whose eyes were suspiciously moist.

Well, fuck.

"That's enough, girls," I said, pulling away the phone. I turned and walked out of the room, putting it to my ear.

"Hayes," I said. "We need to talk."

"We're talking," he said, although I heard restrained fury in his voice.

"Em says you don't know where this Toke asshole has gone," I said. "Says he's on his own. That true? You can't control your own men, now?"

"It's complicated," he replied. "But that's the essence of it."

"I don't buy it. I know Em thinks that's the case, but sounds like Reaper games to me. You using your own daughter to play me?"

Picnic sighed.

"I wish to hell I had that much control over the situation. We voted to pull Toke's patch before he grabbed your boy. He's out bad."

Shit . . . Every instinct I had said he was telling the truth.

"I want to save this truce," I said slowly. "I think you do, too. But that can't happen until we have our guy back. And it needs to happen today."

"I want those girls back. Safe. They got fuck-all to do with this."

"We got ourselves a hell of a problem here," I muttered. "I want to meet, talk it out in person. You convince me you're telling the truth, give me something to take to my club. Maybe there's still a

way out of this. The girls'll stay with my brother—they're my safe
passage."

"Where do you want to meet?"

"Spirit Lake," I told him. "Two this afternoon. And Hayes? You
touch me, Sophie and Em are dead. In fact, you better hope I drive
careful, because unless Skid sees me in one piece at the end of this,
he'll take it out on them. He's a mean bastard, doesn't give a shit
that they're women."

Silence stretched between us.

"I hear you," he muttered. "We'll be there and you'll walk away
safe. For now. Someday you're gonna pay for this."

"I'm aware," I said, and I felt a grin tug at my mouth. "Although
I have to admit, you don't scare me half as much as your daughter
does. She's a tough little bitch, isn't she?"

More silence.

"Tryin' to decide how to take that."

"Take it to mean she's not afraid to defend herself," I said, wondering if I'd lost my mind. Burke always said never give out more
information than you need to, and he was right. Yet here I was,
either bragging on Em or bitching about her. Wasn't sure which.
"You did a good job with her. She made me, right before I grabbed
her. Took off running, tough to catch. She's a fighter."

"Fuck you," Picnic said. "I'm gonna kill you."

"Maybe, but it won't be today. Not if you want her back. I'll see
you at two. Bring whoever you want, but don't think you can follow me afterward. If I'm not home on time, Skid will pull the trigger. I'll leave the target up to him. Until then, make sure you've
done everything you can to find Toke. There's more at stake here
than you realize. We aren't careful, we'll start a war that could
destroy both our clubs. The cartel loves shit like this."

"Fuck you," he repeated.

I smiled and hung up the phone.

Em's dad was a tough bastard. As much as I hated to admit it, I
kind of liked him.

EM

Shit.

All other issues aside, being held captive was boring.

I lay in the bed next to Sophie, one hand fastened to the headboard. Thank God for that—no matter what else happened, at least we were together. I felt pretty good about what we'd accomplished during the whole phone call incident. I'd managed to lift Hunter's Leatherman tool from his pocket while Sophie distracted him by spitting blood. Impressive thinking on her part, because it'd been truly disgusting. Then I'd grabbed his wallet when she called Ruger.

Now I had both items hidden under the mattress, ready and waiting for our escape attempt. I wasn't sure what use the wallet would be, but the Leatherman was worth its weight in gold. I was almost positive I could use it to pick the locks on our handcuffs.

Lock picking. Another fun hobby Dad had shared with us girls . . . I also knew how to hot-wire a car, although I only seemed to get it right about half the time.

Naturally, Kit always nailed it on the first try.

Thinking about her almost made me cry. I wanted to see her again so bad . . .

"When do you want to try our escape?" Sophie asked, her voice a whisper. I started to answer, but before anything came out, the door opened. Hunter walked into the room. He came over and stood next to the bed, studying me. To say the silence was uncomfortable was one hell of an understatement.

"I'm gonna go see your dad in a bit," he said, holding my eyes. There was something intimate and scary about his gaze . . . I blushed, and wondered if it all screamed "Guilty!" to poor Sophie. I sure as shit *felt* guilty—it wasn't enough that my stupidity had brought this down on us. No, I'd all but had sex with the enemy, and I have to be honest. I'd have gone all the way if he'd asked me to.

Might as well hand him the keys to the Reapers' clubhouse while I was at it, because that's how loyal I'm not.

Fuck it. No more.

"Em?" he asked, and I blinked, realizing I'd missed something. "What?"

"Roll your hand over so I can get to the lock," he repeated, his voice quiet and firm. "I want to talk to you before I leave."

I did what he said, shooting Sophie a glance. She bit her lip, obviously scared for me. She really, really didn't deserve this situation.

"C'mon," Hunter said, taking my hand and pulling me to my feet. He grasped my upper arm, leading me out the door and across the hallway to his bedroom.

"Have a seat," he said quietly. The only place to sit was the bed, which held such fond memories.

"I'll stand."

"Sit on the fuckin' bed, Em," he growled, and I realized he might be quiet right now, but he was anything but peaceful. I sat. Hunter came and crouched down in front of me, hands resting on my knees, face-to-face. I didn't want him touching me, and it took everything I had not to kick him in the face. I'd already learned, though. No point in attacking unless I had somewhere to go with it.

"I want some information from you," he said. "I've got a meet with your dad in an hour. I need him to tell me the truth about Toke, and I need to make him listen about the truce between the clubs. What can you tell me to make that happen?"

"Are you fucking kidding me?" I asked, raising my brows. "You already used me to screw my club. Fool me once, asshole. I have nothing to say. Nada."

"Babe, I know you believe Toke is out of control," he said, his eyes earnest, boring into mine. I squirmed, uncomfortable with his intensity. "And I think there's a pretty good chance your dad is telling the truth when he says that's the story. But here's the thing . . . Right now, only a few guys in my club know what's happening. We can keep a lid on it for one more day at most. Once the rest find out, we're looking at a war and nothing can prevent it."

"Fuck. You."

He smirked.

"Later, sweetheart. Now try to keep your mind on business for me like a good girl."

"Jesus, you're a perv!"

"Yeah, you're right about that," he replied, grinning. Then his smile faded. "I'm gonna fill you in a little on some shit we don't talk about, okay? That's how fuckin' serious this is. There's two groups in my club. One side—which includes me, Skid, and our brothers in Portland—wants peace with the Reapers. We aren't too happy with the way things have been these past few years. I hate to admit it, but a lot of the Devil's Jacks have lost their way. More interested in money and territory than living free and brotherhood. Our national president is weak, babe. The Jacks have been running loose, and it's time for someone new to take over, clean house. Up until last night, we just about had things lined up to control the next election. Toke fucked that up for us."

I listened, stunned. What was this, some kind of trick?

"I'm telling you this because it's our last chance, babe," he said quietly, obviously reading my thoughts. "This gets out, Burke—that's our guy—loses his shot at the presidency. We bet everything on the truce with the Reapers, on a complete change of direction for the club. There are others who want war, and Toke will give it to them. Mason, our old president, held on as long as he could, trying to give us the time we needed to pull it off. He can't hold on any longer—cancer. Hasn't been able to ride for nearly a month. We don't put this problem to rest—today—it's all over. That means war between the clubs, babe. The cartel will move up from California and we won't be able to stop them. They'll destroy the Jacks and then they'll come after the Reapers."

Wow. This was way bigger than I'd ever imagined, and I wished to hell I knew what to do with it.

"Call my dad and tell him," I whispered, searching his face. "Maybe he can work with you. I don't have anything for you, Hunter. And if I did, I still wouldn't talk. It's not my call to make."

"Not gonna happen," he replied, shaking his head. "Not unless you tell me what side he's on. Is he for peace with the Jacks? What's his agenda?"

"I have no idea," I replied, thankful for once that it was the truth. I couldn't betray my club if I didn't know anything. "Dad doesn't share club business with me."

My words hung heavy between us—Hunter had just shared far too much club business with me. He'd trusted me. Why? Because dead girls can't tell stories?

"Are you going to kill me?" I asked quietly, subdued.

He reached up and cradled my face with his big hand, wiping a thumb across my cheek. Shit, was I crying? Goddammit.

"No, sweetheart," he replied, his expression impossible to read. "By the time you're loose, it'll be over. Worth the risk, if you can give me any information to make this go smoother. I want a way out, babe."

He sounded so sincere. Shit. Why did I keep falling for this? *Remember how he used you and took pictures of you naked? This man is evil!*

"Why did you start talking to me?" I asked, unable to resist. Hell, why not pick at the scab? See if I couldn't make myself hurt just a little more, because I'm masochistic that way . . . "Why the whole fake romance thing? I understand keeping tabs, but I don't see the advantage in getting tangled up with me."

He smiled, but it wasn't a happy smile.

"We wanted peace," he said. "Seriously, that's still what we want. We can handle the cartel on our southern border if we're not fighting with the Reapers up north. If my faction pulls it off, we'll have the votes we need to take the national presidency. That means we can turn the club back in the direction it needs to go."

"But what does that have to do with me?"

"We wanted you to seal the truce," he said, sighing. "Nothing horrible. If you fell for me and I was your old man, that'd be motivation for your dad to push peace between the clubs. He might not be a national officer, but he's a major power broker."

I studied his face, confused.

"Your big plan was I'd become your old lady?" I asked. "How was this supposed to play out long term? What was the exit strategy, or were you just planning to dump me once the cartel was beat back?"

He frowned.

"No," he said. "I planned on you being my old lady."

I shook my head, starting to get pissed off again.

"You said there was nothing real between us," I snapped. "You made it pretty damned clear, actually. You were just playing me the whole time."

"No, I said I wanted to fuck you," he replied. "I hate to crap on all your fairy-tale fantasies, but you don't have to love a woman to make her your property. Hell, I already told you I don't believe in love. But you know what club life is like, you've got good connections. We'd have done okay—more than most couples have going for them. I was lookin' forward to it, to be honest. The fact that you're smart and I like talkin' to you didn't exactly hurt, either."

"And were you ever planning to fill me in on this? Or just romance me and use me?"

He didn't answer.

"I need a minute," I said, overwhelmed. I didn't know what to think. Clearly, Hunter was an even bigger asshole than I'd imagined, which was impressive, considering his track record. I felt him stand up, and then the bed sank next to me and his arm came around my shoulder. I threw it off as water filled my eyes. Shit. I hate crying and the last thing I needed was to show him how much power he had to hurt me.

Unfortunately, my nose betrayed me and I sniffed.

"Fuck," he muttered, and then he grabbed me, pulling me up

and onto his lap as he leaned back against the headboard. His arms came around me and he pressed my head to his chest. I burst into tears. It felt good. Cathartic. Everything had fallen to shit and yet, for reasons I couldn't quite fathom, having him hold me felt good.

Eventually the crying storm died down, and I forced myself to pull it together. So I had a moment of weakness. It happens. Didn't mean I was going to give him any information about my dad or my club. No matter how nice it felt to have his hand rubbing my back softly.

Finally I spoke._____

"So you're seriously telling me you were prepared to be my old man indefinitely, all to get my dad behind this truce?"

"No."

I sat up and turned toward him.

"Could you be more confusing?"

"I was prepared to take you as my old lady so I could fuck you whenever I wanted, keep you around, maybe make something together. I also needed to get your dad behind this truce. Multipurpose plan."

"Are you crazy?"

He shrugged, eyes impossible to read.

"Burke wanted leverage and I wanted you. Have ever since I first saw you. We made a deal and that was the end of it, at least until Toke lost his shit. Now it's all falling apart, which is why I'm heading out to meet your dad in ten minutes. I'm not just trying to save Clutch, I'm trying to save all our asses. I wish to fuck you'd give me something to work with."

I shook my head.

"I don't know anything, Hunter," I said carefully. "But you got one thing right—I know what club life is like. And that's why I'd never tell you shit, even if I knew anything."

He smiled at me. Actually *smiled*, proving my theory that he was batshit insane.

"Fuck, I knew you'd make a good old lady. A woman who knows how to keep her mouth shut."

He leaned forward and brushed his lips against mine, because he hadn't fucked with my head enough already. I tried ignoring him, but he nibbled just right and this wasn't like our other kisses— it wasn't desperate and wild and fueled by adrenaline. Nope, this was just sweet and beautiful and perfect. Here was the Liam I thought I'd known *before* . . . How was this the same guy who'd taken those horrible pictures of me?

I sucked his lower lip into my mouth and he groaned. Then he pulled away and leaned his forehead against mine.

"You really want to catch my dad's attention, take me and Sophie with you," I whispered. "Give us back."

"Then I'll end up dead."

I pulled away.

"Liam, you're gonna end up dead anyway," I whispered. "But if you bring us back, I promise I'll fight for you. Tell them why you did it, explain what's going on."

"We're all dying, babe," he said. "Some faster than others. But I'm not giving up. It doesn't matter if Toke was acting under orders or not, he's still wearing Reaper colors. Your guy started it, and unlike him, we aren't shooting yet. There's still time to save the situation."

I pulled away.

"Take me back to Sophie?"

He sighed.

"Sure."

My talk with Hunter left me confused as hell.

It was shitty to learn he'd plotted out my future without even considering what I wanted. And he still insisted caring had nothing to do with our relationship.

I wasn't sure I believed him, though. In fact, I didn't. He definitely cared about me. I knew it. Maybe not in a romantic, lovey kind of way. But he'd held me while I cried, and that kiss had been sweet and gentle. Not about sex at all. My cynical brain told me it was just one more attempt to get me to soften up and give him information.

But he hadn't asked me for anything after he kissed me.

It felt more like a good-bye.

Shit.

I glanced over at Sophie. We were stuck together on the bed again, each of us cuffed to the top by one hand. She didn't ask me what had happened while I was gone with Liam, which I appreciated. No way I wanted to explain that one.

"He's going to go meet with Dad," I told her.

"Why?"

"I think he's trying to save the situation. I think he actually cares about me, Soph."

She looked at me like I'd gone nuts.

"You can't be serious. He wants to screw you—I get that, he's a guy and you're hot. But a man who cares about a woman doesn't kidnap her."

The roar of a Harley outside the house cut the air, and we heard the sound of someone riding away. Hunter leaving.

"If I get away and Dad finds out I'm safe, he'll kill him for sure."

The thought made me sad. Yes, he was a dick. And he was definitely a liar and a user and worst of all, a Devil's Jack.

That kiss, though . . .

"Don't you dare have second thoughts," Sophie hissed, seeing through me. "This guy is dangerous and we're going to get seriously hurt if we stay here. We're going to escape. In fact, we're going to escape soon."

"I know. I just wish—"

"I don't want to hear it," she snapped, sounding angry with me for the first time. I suppose I had that coming. I was determined, though. I wouldn't fail her again. I'd get us out of here and I'd get her home safe to her boy, no matter what it took. I wasn't just any twenty-two-year-old girl—I was a Reaper's daughter, and Sophie was part of my family through Ruger. She was my sister and my responsibility.

I wasn't going to let anything fuck up this escape, especially not a man.

Not even a really cute one.

We gave it an hour before making our move. I pulled out the little Leatherman multitool I'd stolen from him and picked our locks in under five minutes. Once we were both loose, we snuck over to the window to look outside.

What we saw wasn't encouraging.

The house was in the middle of nowhere. There were scruffy shrubs all around, but nothing big enough to hide a person. The few scraggly pine trees weren't much better. At least there weren't a bunch of bikes parked out there—no reason to believe there was anyone besides Skid in the house. It was better than nothing.

"If he chases us, we don't have a chance," Sophie murmured, looking spooked.

"He won't chase us," I told her firmly. "Here's what we'll do. We're going to sneak downstairs. We'll figure out where he is, then you go out one side of the house and I'll go out the other. I can see a back door from here."

"And if he sees us?"

"Whoever he sees has to slow him down long enough for the other one to get away and find help," I said, holding her gaze. I tried to impress my confidence on her, my belief that she could do what needed to be done. "No matter what it takes. And I'm going to be the one closest to him."

"Why?"

"Because you have a kid. All other issues aside, Noah needs you and nobody needs me."

That was unfortunately the truth, as much as it hurt to say it. Sure, my dad loved me, but I wasn't a mother.

"Your family, the whole club, they all need you!" she protested.

"You know I'm right," I said flatly, thinking of Noah's little face. I'd only met him once, but he was a great kid. A kid who deserved a mother. I'd lost mine in high school and I'd be damned if I'd let it happen to Sophie's boy. "Don't even try to be noble here or something. If only one of us gets out, it's you. Let's not fight about it, okay?"

She nodded, still looking nervous but also more determined.

"Okay, promise me one thing," she said. "You need to seriously try to get away. Don't let yourself get caught or something just because you want to keep Hunter safe."

I scowled at her. I wouldn't do that . . . would I? No. Definitely not. I wasn't stupid enough to throw away our safety just because some asshole kissed me.

Oh wait—that's what got us into this in the first place. Ugghh . . .

"Might as well go now," I said, feeling a little deflated. "I'll keep the knife, unless you know how to use it?"

"You mean to fight?" she asked, looking startled. I bit back a wildly inappropriate laugh. "Um, no. I didn't take knife-fighting class in school. You can keep it."

This time I did laugh.

We crept down the hallway together, pausing at the top of the stairs, my fuck-me heels clutched in my hand. They wouldn't be much good for running, unfortunately. Not to mention the unholy racket they'd make on a wooden floor. At least Sophie had somewhat sensible shoes on, little fake boots with soft soles. I could hear

Skid in the living room, either watching TV or playing video games. Hopefully the latter, since that would be more distracting.

"I'll go down the stairs first," I whispered. "Then I'll wave you on. Be ready to go whatever direction I point you, based on where I see him. If I point back at the bedroom, go up and get yourself back into your handcuffs, okay? If I wave you on, that's it. We'll only get one shot, so don't fuck it up. I'm counting on you to send help for me if I have to distract him."

"I can do it," she whispered back. "Let's both get out, though, okay?"

I nodded at Sophie and started down very slowly. When I reached the bottom, I peeked around the side of the stairwell. Skid sat on the couch, facing away from us. Some sort of loud game filled a giant, flatscreen TV, the sounds of shots echoing around the room.

Perfect.

I touched Sophie's hand. Then I pointed at myself and the front door. That was the route I'd take. I pointed at her and toward the back of the house.

She nodded tightly, her face determined.

Okay. Time to do it.

I held up three fingers and then counted down. Two. One.

Sophie slipped past me, walking quickly through the living room and into the back hallway.

Skid didn't even pause in his shooting.

Holy shit. She'd done it. I decided to wait a few minutes before trying for the front door. Instead I studied it, and that's when the plan started falling apart.

It had three locks, including two deadbolts.

Would I really be able to open those without making any noise? Probably not. Time to change it up . . . I'd wait a little longer and then go to the back.

But not until I was sure Sophie had a good head start.

Unfortunately, Skid turned off the video, set down the controller, and stood, stretching. Then he casually strolled over to the window and looked outside.

Sophie had shit luck, because she ran right past him.

I pulled out the Leatherman, flipped open the knife, and stepped out of the stairwell. Skid grabbed a gun off the coffee table and looked up to see me right as I launched myself toward him. I didn't have any illusions that I could take him. I just needed to buy Sophie enough time to get away.

You know, I think I could've pulled it off if I'd had decent shoes I could run in.

Unfortunately, right as I launched myself toward him, my bare toe caught on my pant leg and I fell down heavily. The knife slid away from me, under the couch. I dropped the heels with a clatter.

Seriously?

Then Skid was standing over me, gun pointed at my head. Well, crap. Dad would definitely be disappointed in this particular performance . . . And Kit? She'd kick Skid's ass just to clear a path to kick mine for being so uncoordinated. The worst part was I hadn't even bought much time for Sophie.

If I survived, I was never wearing high heels again.

I stared up at Skid towering over me, trying to guess my next move. He didn't seem too happy, which was fine with me. I wasn't very happy, either. Somehow, I had to find some way to slow him down or Sophie was toast. I'd love to say that I was utterly selfless in my resolve to sacrifice myself for a friend, but in reality, she was my best shot at a rescue now that I'd been seen.

In the movies, this is where I would have slinked back, fluttered my eyelashes, and used the power of my sexuality to distract him. But frankly, my sexuality hadn't been bringing great things into my life lately. I didn't quite trust my instincts in that arena.

But my teeth? *Those* I trusted.

I pushed off from the stairwell wall with my feet, sliding across the wooden floor toward Skid like a missile, hoping to hell he wouldn't actually shoot. My hands caught his ankle, shoving up his pant leg so I could lock my jaws around his flesh.

"Fuck!" he yelled as my teeth sank in. "You fucking cunt!"

I ignored him, biting down harder. He started kicking at me, and I held on tight, sliding back and forth across the floor as he thrashed his leg. I heard the gun cock but I ignored it. I might be fucked, but Sophie wasn't. Utter determination took over and my brain held one thought, and one thought only.

Keep biting Skid's leg.

That's why I didn't even notice when he pointed his weapon. The loud crack of a gunshot broke through my fog, but I didn't feel any pain.

Huh. Must've missed me.

Blood filled my mouth as I dug deeper, wondering if I could sever his tendon if I tried hard enough. Probably not, I'd need to rip at him to make that happen . . .

That's when he shot again, and this time I definitely felt pain.

Holy shit.

I'd never experienced anything like the trail of fire that ran across my thigh. Agony. At first I couldn't get my jaw to unlock. Then he kicked again and I went flying, slamming into the wall with a scream. I lay there, stunned, watching blood seeping out of my leg.

Wait.

BLOOD WAS LEAKING OUT OF MY LEG.

I slapped my hands down, pressing hard against the wound in my upper thigh. That felt just as fabulous as you might imagine. *Shit. Holy shit. Sweet baby Jesus!*

"You shot me," I whispered, stunned. Why this was such a surprise, I don't know. Skid glared down and shook his head.

"What did you expect, you stupid fucking bitch? You fucking *bit me.* Christ, do you know how dirty a human mouth is? I'll probably get sepsis."

"Oh, I'm so fucking sorry that your ankle hurts," I growled, my vision blurring. "I'd kiss it all better if I wasn't busy *trying to keep the blood inside my body*!"

He raised the gun and pointed it right at me.

"What the fuck Hunter sees in you I cannot imagine," he told me. "But listen up. You got one pass. You fuck with me again, I'll shoot you in the head and tell him you made me do it. I'll sleep like a baby afterward, too. Got me?"

I nodded, remembering a little too late that I shouldn't be pissing off the guy with a gun.

That's when the doorbell rang.

CHAPTER SEVEN

Skid and I looked at each other.

"Keep your fucking mouth closed," he hissed. That sent a surge of hope through me. He wasn't expecting anyone . . . Rescuers? If it was Reapers, great. But what if it was some random person, or a kid? My thoughts started spinning . . . Skid could kill them.

I couldn't just lie here like a lump, bleeding. I had to do something.

"Who's out there?" he yelled.

Nothing.

The doorbell rang again.

"Fuck off!" he yelled, turning toward the door. I lunged at his knees from behind, hoping to knock him down. Miraculously, he crashed to the floor, dropping the gun. We wrestled over it briefly as the doorbell started ringing again, over and over. I was nowhere near as strong as Skid, so it wasn't a huge surprise when he shoved me away and got to his feet. My head hit the wall, sending sickening waves of pain down along my spine.

"You are fucking dead if you make a noise, cunt. I'm through with you," Skid hissed.

He stomped to the door, beyond furious. Then he threw it open and Sophie smashed a wooden chair over his head.

Wow, didn't see *that* coming.

I jumped up as his gun fired, adrenaline killing the pain in my leg and skull. The chair crashed into him again. Skid roared and lunged forward. I knew this was it—either we'd win or we'd die. I attacked him from behind, throwing myself on his back, wrapping my arms around his neck and jerking him backward with my full weight. He staggered as I bit his ear, worrying at it like a dog.

Out of the corner of my eye, I saw Sophie grab another chair and go for his legs.

This definitely wasn't the plan.

No time to worry about that now. Skid screamed as he staggered forward, falling off the porch face-first into the dirt. I rode him down and then Sophie was there, kicking him over and over. He managed to roll to the side, which was a huge mistake, because it gave her a clear shot at his crotch.

She attacked his balls viciously, and his screeching cries of pain filled the air. That didn't slow her down in the least. Over and over she kicked him, her face twisted with hate. He stopped struggling, and I realized he'd passed out.

I don't know if it was from pain or if I'd managed to cut off his air. Sophie grabbed the gun, handing it off to me. I pointed it at Skid's bloodied body, panting.

"Go upstairs and grab the cuffs," I managed to say. "We'll get him tied up and then call for help."

Sophie took off, and I held the gun on him the whole time she was gone, hoping like hell he wouldn't wake up. I was prepared to shoot—but that didn't mean I wanted to . . .

It wasn't because I was scared to kill another human being. Of course, the thought sickened me. But I couldn't stop thinking about my talk with Liam, and everything he'd said about the truce and the cartel. Maybe he'd been lying to me—I certainly wouldn't put it past him . . . But what if he'd been telling the truth? If he was, killing Skid would ruin the peace and sooner or later the cartel would come after the Reapers.

We needed him alive.

Sophie returned with the cuffs. Strangely, she also had a bedsheet and a knife from the kitchen. Together we wrestled Skid's limp body over to the porch pillar and fastened his hands around it.

I felt the tension in my chest loosen, and I looked up at Sophie and grinned.

"You don't listen very well when you're told to run, do you?"

She smirked.

"I guess not," she said. "I heard the shot and knew you were in trouble. I just couldn't leave you—it didn't feel right."

"Thanks," I said. "I think you might've saved my life. Not sure if he would've killed me or not."

She held up the sheet.

"You want me to bandage that leg up for you?" she asked. I looked down at my leg. Sure enough, blood still oozed out, although not much of it at this point. Damned if I hadn't forgotten about it during the fight. God bless adrenaline.

Everything immediately started hurting again.

"Yeah, might be a good idea," I said. "Obviously it's not life threatening, but wow . . . I can't believe I got shot."

She glanced at me and cocked her head.

"Can I ask a crazy question?"

"Sure," I replied. "I think we're past being formal with each other at this point."

"How often does this happen?"

"What do you mean?"

"How often do people get kidnapped, or shot, or whatever? In the club, I mean."

My eyes widened.

"Um, never?" I said. "I mean, I'm sure men have gotten shot. But not anyone in our chapter, at least not that I know of. Not related to the club, at least. One of the brothers, Bagger, died in Afghanistan last year. But seriously, this is not normal shit."

She sighed and used the knife to cut the edge of the sheet. Then she tore it into a long strip and started wrapping my leg.

"Glad to hear that," she murmured, frowning. "But even this is too much. I can't take this. Noah can't have this in his life."

"Well, now isn't the time to try and figure all that out," I said, trying to calm her down. I could see a hint of crazy in her eyes, a delayed reaction now that we were safe. I didn't want her melting down on me, at least not until we got out of here.

"I need to find his phone," I said to distract her. "Got to call Dad, get him out here. For all we know, there's fifty Devil's Jacks on their way."

Sophie shuddered, and then tears filled her eyes. She sniffed and wiped her nose with the back of her hand. I reached out to touch her, but she shrugged me off.

"Sorry," she said. "You better tie the bandage. I don't want to touch it after touching my nose."

I laughed.

"Thanks. That'd be just my luck—I'd survive kidnapping and Skid, only to be taken out by nose cooties."

She smiled at me, and then she started giggling. It had a bit of a hysterical note to it, but I figured she'd earned it.

I found Skid's phone on the coffee table. Thankfully it was his personal phone, not one of the burners I'm sure they kept around for talking business. I turned it on and there was another stroke of luck—Skid didn't have it password protected.

That was stupid of him.

I scrolled through it, looking at his messages. Nothing of interest. Looked like he'd been sexting with some girl named Kelsey the night before. Not club related, though. His email was protected. Oh, and there . . . perfect. Google Maps. I clicked on it and found us. The house was along the Spokane Valley, back in the hills. Maybe half an hour from Coeur d'Alene. Funny, it seemed like we should be farther away—this place felt like a whole different world. Of course, if they'd been using it as a base to spy on the Reapers, it couldn't be too far.

I opened the phone app and started dialing my dad's number.

Then I stopped.

It was just after two p.m., so Hunter was probably still meeting with the club. If I called right now, told them I was safe, would they kill him? My stomach clenched. Whatever else I felt about Hunter, I didn't want him dead. How to protect him? I could wait to call . . . But I had no idea how long the meet would go, and if I waited too long, more Jacks might show up.

What if I warned him?

The thought was so startling that I had to sit down on the couch. If I warned him, he could get away. But would warning him count as betraying the club?

Yes.

Yes, it would. That would absolutely be a betrayal and I should be ashamed of myself for even considering it. But then I thought about his soft, brown hair matted with blood. His body buried in an unmarked grave up in the mountains . . .

I'd warn him for the same reason I was keeping Skid alive, I decided. That wasn't a true betrayal, was it? Dad could always hunt him down later, but for now I should help preserve the peace.

It was enough of an excuse for me to do it. I dialed him quickly, before I changed my mind. There was a scraping noise from the porch, and I looked through the window to see Sophie dragging over a chair to sit on. Would she ever forgive the Reapers for getting her into this? Poor Ruger. He was already in a weird spot with her, and this wouldn't help.

"Skid?" Hunter asked, his voice tense. "I'm in the meet. Just got word, they found Toke. Clutch is alive but he's in rough shape."

"This isn't Skid," I said quietly, heart pounding. "If you want to live, you need to keep your face blank and listen to what I say."

Brief silence.

"I hear you."

"Sophie and I are in charge at the house now. Skid is alive, but he won't stay that way if anyone tries to get us before Dad picks up. If you have any friends you're planning to call, don't. Understand?"

"Yes."

"As soon as I hang up with you, I'm going to take ten minutes to go to the bathroom and clean up some scrapes I have," I continued. "Then I'm calling my dad and telling him everything. If you want to survive, you better be gone before then."

More silence. "Why are you doing this?"

"I don't know," I said. *Crap.* "To keep the peace. Just get out, okay?"

"Okay."

I hung up the phone and walked over to the door, pushing it open.

"I'm going to go clean up in the bathroom for a few. You okay out here?"

She nodded.

"Leave the door open so you can hear me screaming if I need to."

"You got it."

I found a bathroom between the living room and the dining room. When I looked in the mirror, I had to laugh. I looked like a lunatic woman. My hair was all over, I had raccoon eyes, and a bruise was starting to rise on my cheek.

Oh, and Skid's blood had run down my chin and dried there. I thought it added a touch of class.

"Damn, you're sexy," I whispered, giggling. I washed up all my scrapes and found some toothpaste in a drawer. I used my finger to rub it all through my mouth, which still tasted like evil biker ankle. Ten minutes later I pulled on my ridiculous shoes and hobbled out of the house toward Sophie, holding up the phone.

"Dumbass has Google Maps installed," I told her. "I know exactly where we are. I'm calling them to come and get us."

"That's good news," she replied. "He hasn't moved at all. Do you think he has internal injuries?"

I shrugged, because I really didn't care. He was alive. That was good enough.

"If he does, there's nothing we can do about it. We'll let the guys take care of him."

I dialed Dad's number and he answered.

"Picnic."

"Hey, Dad? It's me," I said, trying to hold it together. I realized my hand was shaking. Shock, maybe? My leg felt numb.

"Oh, Emmy," he said, his voice full of relief. "Christ, I can't believe it's you. Are you all right? Fuck, that prick Hunter just left. Lucky bastard."

Yeah, wasn't gonna touch that comment.

"We're okay," I said. "Could use a ride, though."

Dad laughed, incredulous.

"You've been kidnapped and that's what you have to say for yourself? Did you escape? Where are you?"

"I'll send you the map," I told him. "There's just one guy here, Skid. He's a Devil's Jack. We managed to beat him up and now he's handcuffed to the porch."

"Holy shit. Proud of you, girl. Any witnesses I should know about?"

"No, it's all good," I told him. "But you might want to bring the van. We may need some cargo space."

I gave him the directions and hung up. I looked up to find Sophie watching me. She looked a little shocky, I decided, and the gun
trembled in her hand. I'd take over guarding Skid in a minute, but
I had one more thing to do first.

"They'll be here in about twenty minutes," I told her. "They
sounded pretty happy to hear from us."

"Was Hunter with them?" she asked.

I swallowed.

"No. The meet was already over. I guess we missed him by
maybe five minutes. He's got good luck."

Sophie raised a brow and I met her gaze head-on, challenging
her to question my story. She didn't. I stepped off the porch and
dropped the phone on the ground, stomping on it with my spiky
heel. The glass shattered and crunched.

"What the hell?" Sophie demanded. "Why'd you do that?"

"GPS," I said, which wasn't true. I just didn't want my dad to
see that I'd called Hunter. "I don't want the Devil's Jacks tracing us
with it, and we can't leave it here."

"What if we need it again?"

"We won't. Dad and Ruger will find us. Don't worry. By this
time tomorrow it'll be like this never happened. In fact, I don't want
to talk about it and I don't want to think about it. Got me?" I added
pointedly.

"Got you," she said, narrowing her eyes. I waited for her to say
something else, but she didn't. My opinion of her went up another
notch. Whatever else she might not get about MC life, Sophie
seemed to understand sisterhood.

Sometimes sisters need to shut their mouths and drop it.

This was definitely one of those times.

By the time Dad and the other brothers arrived, I was exhausted.

The adrenaline had faded and my entire body was sore and stiff.
The little wrestling match with Skid hadn't helped. Now I stood on

the porch watching my father roll Skid's body over with his foot. I was trying to play it cool, but all I really wanted was to crawl into his arms and sleep for a year. But I wasn't a little girl anymore . . .

"He's been bleeding, but not too bad," I said, rubbing the back of my neck. "Don't know if he's passed out from a head injury or from shock. Sophie kicked his nuts to hell and back."

Dad grunted, then stepped up onto the porch, holding out his hand for the gun I still gripped. I gave it to him and he wrapped an arm around my shoulders, pulling me close.

Suddenly I felt safe again.

I looked down at the brothers filling the yard. Ruger. Horse. Duck . . . Painter. I'd never seen them looking so serious. Bam Bam, a big man who was married to my friend Dancer, studied Skid thoughtfully. My former crush stood next to him, eyes haunted. He looked different somehow. Older. It was attractive, I realized in a distant way. Huh.

"How we gonna play this?" Bam asked. I knew what he was really saying, of course. He wanted to know if they were going to get Skid medical help or put him in the ground. I braced myself and took a deep breath, knowing my work wasn't done quite yet.

"Not in front of the girls," Dad muttered, and I knew the answer. So far as Dad was concerned, Skid was already dead. "Ruger, you and Painter take them, get them safe. Call the medic. He can meet you at the clubhouse. We'll clean up here."

I shook my head.

"Don't kill him. You do that, there's going to be even more fighting."

"This is about the club, Em," my dad said quietly. Translation— *Go home and be a good girl. Let the men do the thinking for you.*

Suddenly I was sick of it.

I'd gotten kidnapped because of their bullshit, and I wasn't even supposed to know why I'd nearly died. I'd gotten myself out of it, no thanks to them, and now I was expected to just nod and smile.

Fuck that.

I popped up on my toes and whispered in Dad's ear.

"Hunter told me about the truce and the cartel. If you kill this guy, we're all going to suffer. I know you're pissed, Dad, but we have to think of the club. Please. Think of me and Kit—I don't want to live in fear."

He stiffened.

I pulled away, looking up at him, begging with my eyes. *Don't let your ego make this decision.*

He shook his head, jaw rigid. Fuck. I crossed my arms and stepped back, my plea turning to a glare. How fucking typical—the king's pride got hurt, so now we all have to go to war? *If anyone gets to make the decision, it should be me and Sophie.*

Dad held my eyes for long seconds, then sighed.

"Okay, we'll take him with us and dump him somewhere he'll be found," he said. "See if you can find something to bandage him up with, Bam."

Relief crashed through me. I wrapped my arms around him, hugging him tight.

"You're doing the right thing, Daddy," I whispered.

"This was club business, baby girl. You shouldn't be worrying about things so much. That's my job."

His words cut through me and I stiffened. I wasn't a fucking baby to be handed a sucker and told to go play.

Wait, where had *that* come from?

Dad wasn't saying anything he hadn't said a thousand times before, but for some reason this time it really pissed me off. *This is what it feels like to be Kit*, I realized, suddenly understanding her need to rebel. Oh, I didn't like this feeling. I didn't like it one bit.

I glanced toward the brothers. Nobody was paying attention to us. Perfect.

"Daddy, I love you, but this stopped being club business when I got kidnapped and cuffed to a bed," I said quietly, making sure my voice didn't carry. "That made it *my* business. I'm still trying to figure out what happened and what it all means, but I have a right to worry about things that might destroy my life."

He frowned at me.

"Let's talk about it later, baby."

Right. I knew that tone. "Later" meant "never."

I sighed, because I'd gotten as far as I would for now. That was okay—this wasn't the kind of conversation you have in front of an audience, anyway. I was determined, though. I wasn't going to just slide back into life as usual.

Everything had changed.

I'd been raised to let the men in my life tell me what to do, and look what that'd gotten me. It'd been so easy to follow Hunter away from my friends and into that alley. I'd been so fucking naive. Blind.

Never again.

From now on, I'd be making my own decisions and Dad would just have to deal with it.

CHAPTER EIGHT

ONE WEEK LATER

I was right.

"We'll talk later" meant "We won't talk about it."

To be fair, Dad wasn't around much in the days following my rescue. He didn't say where he was going, but I assumed he was off dealing with Toke and the Devil's Jacks. I just hoped he hadn't "dealt" with them permanently. Of course, I was expected to stay home and forget all about it.

That shit used to be okay. Not anymore.

Not that I would confront Dad directly or try to push my way into a club meeting to find out the real situation—nope, that wouldn't accomplish anything, anyway. But it did confirm what I'd started to realize the day Sophie and I took down Skid. It was time for one Emmy Lou Hayes to get the hell out of Coeur d'Alene.

I needed to grow up and get a life.

Finding a place to go was the first challenge. I knew I could stay with Kit, but she only had a studio at school in Olympia. I didn't think it was fair to put that kind of pressure on her. Nope, I wanted to find my own path. At least I had money saved . . . One advantage to living with my father was I didn't really have many expenses. I'd already applied to that aesthetician's program in Portland. It was a great school, but I wasn't sure I wanted to risk being in the same city as Hunter. On the other hand, it was a city—not a village. Wasn't like I'd see him around all the time. Hell, I'd probably never run into him at all.

I even knew where he lived, so I could be sure to avoid him.

(Okay, so I'd done a little online stalking of my own by now. I still had his wallet, which I suppose I should've felt guilty over. Instead I used his credit card to order some really cute lingerie. I didn't spend enough to bankrupt him, but it was enough to make him suffer a little. Oh, and I sprang for gift wrapping and overnight delivery, because why not? Just because I'd saved his life didn't mean I'd forgiven him for what he'd done.)

Unfortunately, ordering presents for myself online was the closest I could get to real shopping, because Dad put me on lockdown. And if that weren't bad enough, Painter had appointed himself as my own personal guardian angel while Dad was gone. I couldn't believe I used to crush on that guy—now all I saw when he walked into a room was a vision of him screwing some skank on a bathroom counter. Liam had been right. I *definitely* deserved better. Despite my hostility, Painter insisted on driving me to work every morning and meeting me for lunch. Then he'd drive me home and hang out at the house, spending the night on the couch or in Kit's old bedroom.

To call this awkward was one hell of an understatement.

Thus I took to spending a lot of time in my room. That's where I was on Friday night, exactly one week from the day I'd met Hunter for the first time. I had my TV on and I was playing around online when a private message popped up.

LIAM: Hey Em

I blinked. I'd blocked his ass. How the hell did he get through?

LIAM: Are you there?

I considered the little flashing message alert. Should I answer? What would I say? Direct confrontation, I decided. Call him on his shit, because seeing his message didn't send a little thrill through me at all. No thrills allowed.

ME: How did you contact me? I blocked you.
LIAM: Probably best not to give up all my secrets. How are you?
ME: I'm great. Nobody took naked pictures of me without my consent today.
LIAM: Guess I had that coming. You wearing any of those panties you bought with my card?

I giggled, then managed to cut it off. Didn't need Painter bursting in to check on me. And why was I laughing, anyway? Still . . . I wish I'd seen Hunter's face when he realized I was spending his money.

ME: Yes. I'm wearing a midnight blue pushup bra and matching thong, because I'm getting ready to go out on a date. I like my new man a lot because he doesn't kidnap people.
LIAM: A date? Pretty sure you're stuck at home tonight with Painter. Please tell me you aren't dating him? Hate me all you want, but you really can do better.

My breath caught. How did he know Painter was here?

ME: Are you stalking me again?
LIAM: Just tonight. I need to talk to you. Promise—last time— then I'll leave you alone. You saved my life. Let me share what I know so you can stop worrying. I know your dad hasn't filled you in, but you deserve answers.

I stared at the screen. How fucking stupid did he think I was? I should turn off the computer. But I was also curious . . . After all, I'd betrayed my club for this asshole. Now I wanted to hear what he had to say.

ME: So talk.
LIAM: Not online. Can you come outside?

I froze again. Shit. He couldn't be serious, could he? I glanced at my window, relieved to see that the shade was tightly closed. Someone outside might be able to see that my light was on, but they wouldn't be able to see inside.

ME: Why would I be stupid enough to do that?
LIAM: Because you're curious. Bring a gun if it makes you feel
    better. But come outside and talk to me—I promise it's safe.
    Don't let Painter follow you, though. Last thing we need is
    another standoff.

Like hell I'd talk to him. I closed my computer and set it on the bed, grabbing the TV remote. *Of course* I wasn't going outside. That would be incredibly stupid. I reached down and rubbed my leg lightly over the still-healing gash. Despite all the blood, Skid's bullet hadn't really caused any real damage—just a flesh wound. But even flesh wounds hurt like a bitch. I wondered if Hunter had ever been shot, and had the sudden urge to march out there and demonstrate to him just how painful a graze from a bullet could be.

I had excellent aim.

I flipped through the channels, trying to find a distraction. There was nothing on, of course. Just some creepy reality show about a woman who thought she was a squirrel. *Life with Cara*, or some such shit. My phone buzzed. Another message from Hunter . . .

LIAM: Come outside and see me. It's safe. Remember—I only took you to save a brother's life. I may have scared you, but I wouldn't have actually hurt you. I know I destroyed what we were starting and I understand I can never fix it. Doesn't mean I don't miss you.

I dropped the phone and flopped back on my bed. The clock next to me said it was one in the morning. I should just turn off the light and go to sleep. That was what the old me would've done. But I couldn't stop thinking about what he'd said. We had been starting something—something good. Because despite everything between our clubs, I'd spent hours talking on the phone to this man, sharing jokes and telling stories. We'd laughed together and that hadn't been fake.

Remembering all that pissed me off, too. He'd killed *us*, whatever the hell "us" had been growing into. *He should pay for what he did.* I got up and pulled on a pair of ratty sweatpants. A hoodie and my favorite pink Converse completed the outfit.

Yeah, I know. Sexy.

I had a flash of déjà vu as I tiptoed down the stairs past Painter, who was sleeping on the couch, TV still flickering in the darkness. I stopped off in the dining room, grabbing a tiny pistol from behind a plate in the china cabinet. It was full of stuff my mother had collected—stuff we never used but wouldn't consider throwing away in a million years.

I gave it a quick check, making sure it was loaded (it was) and ready for action (damned straight). Then I tucked it in the pocket of my hoodie right next to my cell, and slipped out the back door. The moon was full, and as I walked away from the house, the night's beauty startled me. There were crickets singing all around, and while the stars were faint in the bright moonlight, they were everywhere.

Keeping my eyes sharp, I looked around carefully. No sign of anyone, but I knew just how sneaky Hunter and Skid could be. My hand tightened on the gun. Now what?

My phone buzzed again.

LIAM: I'm out behind the bunkhouse

I glanced up, spotting the small building nestled back in the trees. Once upon a time it housed workers on the ranch that used to surround us. The land had been divided up and sold off years ago, but the old outbuildings still stood. Kit and I used it as a playhouse, and now it was full of random junk my dad had collected over the years. I fingered the gun again, the slight pain in my leg a constant reminder that this asshole had gotten me shot. Time for payback?

I couldn't quite decide.

HUNTER

I heard Em before I saw her. She stumbled over something in the darkness and started cussing. Cute. Then she peeked around the corner of the building, her face shadowed and unreadable.

"Back here," I called softly. I sat leaning against the wall, holding my hands up so she could see for herself I wasn't up to anything.

For once in my life, I wasn't.

Go figure.

I just wanted to see how she was and make sure she knew about the truce. No, that was a flat-out lie. I just wanted to see her. Period. For all I knew she was about to shoot me, and I couldn't really blame her if she did. Didn't change how bad I needed to be near her, even if it was just so she could hate me in person.

Not only that, I didn't trust Hayes to fill her in on the changing situation. She shouldn't have to live in fear for the next year, wondering if the Jacks were out for revenge. Not that Skid was her number one fan . . . But he wanted the truce as much as the rest of us, not to mention she'd kept her club from killing him. He'd been drifting in and out of consciousness at the time, but he remembered that part.

Unfortunately, the Jacks's leadership was still up in the air. Our current president, Mason, had rallied. Now the doctors said he had a few more months. I thought we should just get the elections over with while we had the votes, but Burke was holding off. He felt like he couldn't really count on the full support of the club while Toke was still alive.

He was probably right about that.

The good news about the situation was that Clutch was expected to make a full recovery—eventually—despite the fact that Toke had taken a baseball bat to his leg. In the end, it hadn't been either MC that found him. Some Good Samaritan heard him moaning through a hotel room wall and called the cops. They'd come bursting in to save Clutch and they'd caught Toke when he came back to the room with food.

"Liam?" Em called, her voice cool in the darkness. Christ, I loved the way she said my name. Nobody else called me Liam, it felt like something special, just from her. Went straight to my cock, which wasn't so good because tonight wasn't about getting her naked. Chances were, that'd never happen again.

"Over here," I called softly. She walked toward me, pulling out a small gun and pointing it at me. Of course she'd taken me up on my suggestion. The fucking thing looked like a toy.

I'd bet my bike it wasn't.

"Did you like the presents I got you?" I asked.

She looked blank.

"The shit you bought with my credit card," I continued, cocking a brow. I still couldn't believe she'd picked my pocket. Pissed me off, but I had to admire her for it. "I shut it down, by the way. No more shopping."

She smiled and a wave of lust smacked straight through me. Fuck, I'd forgotten how beautiful she was. I really, really wanted that beauty wrapped around my dick, screaming my name. How did she do that to me? A cunt was a cunt, but not Em . . . Christ. *Unsexy thoughts*, I told myself. *Slugs. Athlete's foot. Skid.*

"Sorry," she said lightly, in a tone that clearly wasn't sorry at all. "I suppose you could report me to the cops."

I had to smile. *Cops.* Yup, that was unsexy enough to do the trick.

"I guess you earned it," I admitted.

"Oh, I earned more than that," she said, the gun unwavering. "You kidnapped me, you fucked me over, and then you took pictures of me naked. Gonna take more than pretty panties to make that right."

"I'll concede the point," I said, considering the photos. I might regret everything else, but damned if I'd regret those. "Anything I can do to make it up to you? More shit from Victoria's Secret sounds perfect to me, but I'm open to suggestions."

"You know, I've given this quite a bit of thought over the past week, and I keep coming back to one idea . . . How about I shoot you in the balls? Payback seems only fair, right?"

My eyes widened. Em laughed, the sound delicate in the darkness. Then she shook the gun at me like a little finger "tsking" me for being too loud in a library.

"Hey, you asked," she said. "I'm going back inside now."

"No, stop," I said quickly, holding up a hand. "I have shit to tell you. About the situation between our clubs."

She frowned.

"Why should I trust you?"

I shrugged.

"You don't have to trust me," I said. "But I owe you my life. Thanks for that phone call, by the way."

She flinched.

"I don't know what you're talking about."

"Okay, well, assuming you *had* done something for me—

theoretically, of course—I'd want you to know how much I appreciated it," I said softly. "I'd also want to tell you what's happening
with the truce, maybe make sure you know you're safe now."

I reached toward my pocket. She straightened her arms into a
shooting stance.

"I'm just grabbing some weed," I told her. "Been a hell of a
week, could use a smoke. You want some?"

She shook her head, but when I pulled out the joint, I saw her
relax a little.

"Go ahead, sit down," I told her. "Keep your gun on me if it
makes you happy. But I'd rather you didn't. Knowing my luck,
a spider will fall on you or something and the fuckin' thing will
go off."

"Sexist much?" she asked, frowning. "Poor little Em, scared of
spiders. Can't handle her gun. Afraid I won't remember which end
goes bang?"

I started laughing. In fact, I laughed so hard that I couldn't talk
at first. She glared at me the whole time, but she also lowered the
pistol.

"Babe, I nearly shot Skid in the ass one time because a spider fell
on me while I was holding a gun," I finally managed to say. "Those
things freak me right the hell out. They got eight fuckin' legs, and
that ain't natural. That's some Dr. Seuss shit right there."

She cocked her head at me and a smile crept across her face.

"It's really hard to take you seriously when you're afraid of spiders and Dr. Seuss," she murmured. Damn, I loved the sound of her
voice. If I ever found myself alone with Toke, I'd be killing him with
my bare hands. Not because of what he did to Clutch—no, I owed
the bastard for ruining my chance to fuck this gorgeous girl.

"So, what's the proper, Devil's Jacks–approved policy regarding
scary spiders and children's books?" she asked lightly. "Do your
bylaws stipulate extra points for making more than one reference
in a conversation? 'Cause I'm not really a Dr. Seuss fan."

I stared at her, startled.

"Em, you gotta be a fuckin' communist, you don't like Dr. Seuss. Jesus."

She started laughing and relaxed her stance. The gun was still out, but she came over and sat down about six feet away from me, back to the bunkhouse wall. I lit up and took a hit, feeling the harsh smoke slide down my throat and into my lungs. I wasn't a huge stoner, but I figured I'd earned a little relaxation.

"So what did you want to tell me?" she asked. I took another hit, then let my arms rest on my knees.

"Well, the cops caught Toke," I said. "You probably knew that."

"Nope," she muttered. "I'd guessed things were settling down, seeing as we're not at war, but nobody confirmed it for me."

"You sound a little tense. Sure you don't want some?"

"No. I want to shoot you in the balls."

"That's the second time you've mentioned that," I said slowly. "I'm startin' to think it's not a joke?"

She smiled at me. Not a nice smile.

"Nope. Not a joke. Like I said, I've been thinking about this all week. Just because I'm not screaming and yelling doesn't mean I've forgiven you."

I studied her face, trying to decide how to play this out. I took another long drag, enjoying the cloudy feeling in my head.

To this day, that's the only explanation I've got for what I did next.

"Okay, let's compromise," I said, standing slowly. "No shooting, but you can kick me if it means you'll forgive me? I get that it's over between us, but I don't want you hating me. It's important."

The whites of her eyes grew huge in the moonlight.

"Are you serious?" she asked, scrambling to her feet.

I shrugged.

"I know I've earned it," I admitted. "Probably earned more. Just do it and get it over with. Before I change my mind."

I took one last inhale and then tossed the joint into the dirt. I think some part of me didn't actually believe she'd follow through . . . I mean, in a movie she'd be overcome by the gesture and fling herself into my arms.

But Em? Not so much.

She straight-up kicked me in the balls, her pink Converse hitting me hard. *Damn* fucking hard. Agony erupted in my crotch, and I fell to the ground, biting my lip to keep from whimpering like a baby. Christ, what a bitch. Then she made it worse, because she laughed at me.

"Wow, that felt really good."

"Jesus, I can't believe you did that," I grunted, stars still exploding behind my eyes. It was all I could do to keep breathing. Couldn't fucking believe she actually did it. And I let her. I should've just asked the nice asshole Reaper inside to shoot me and be done with it.

After a few minutes, I managed to pull myself up. Em was sitting against the wall, calmly smoking my joint, gun propped up on her knee. Would've been kind of sexy if I had even the slightest capacity for anything but excruciating pain in my groin.

On the bright side, I didn't have to worry about an inconvenient hard-on for once.

"Oh, I'm thinking about doing something even more fun," Em said sweetly. "It's so sweet to see you rolling around in pain that I'm reconsidering shooting you."

She lifted the pistol and pointed it straight at me.

Fuck. I had seriously misjudged this situation. She held my gaze for long seconds, taking another slow drag and blowing out a smoke ring. *A fucking smoke ring.* Somewhere in the back of my head, I heard the theme from *The Good, the Bad and the Ugly* playing.

Liam "Hunter" Blake was about to be shot dead by a cliche.

Then Em burst out laughing. "The look on your face right now is the most beautiful thing I've ever seen in my life. I'm never letting you scare me again."

I sagged in relief as she let her weapon drop, then held the joint out to me. I sucked it down, hoping to kill some of my adrenaline.

"You're a scary little bitch when you want to be," I muttered. "Christ, Em. You need to stop playing with guns."

"I'll take that as a compliment," she said. "So tell me whatever it was you came here to say."

I shook my head slowly, trying to think. Kind of hard to focus between the pain, the adrenaline, and the weird, surreal sense of pride I felt in her.

She'd make an amazingly unholy old lady.

"Toke's in protective custody in the Clackamas County Jail right now," I said slowly. "Nobody's talked to him. I guess if the Reapers made contact, they aren't telling us. They have a lot more to lose than we do."

"How about your friends?" she asked. "The ones he shot up?"

"All good. I mean, they definitely got hurt, and Clutch has some rehab ahead of him. Your guy did a number on him—"

"Not my guy," she broke in. "He sliced me open, remember?"

Oh, I remembered. I'd never forget the sight of her half naked, her fantastic tits right in front of me just begging to be touched. My dick twitched and I shifted, trying to find a more comfortable position. That was good news . . . Glad to know all the plumbing still worked.

"So what happened between the clubs?" she asked. "Truce in effect again?"

"Yup," I said. "Picnic and Burke hammered it out. I don't know what you told your dad, but he helped push it through. Good news for all of us. Means we can get back to riding and living instead of fighting with each other. You see a Jack, you don't need to be scared of him."

"Yeah, that is good news."

Silence fell between us, and Em scooted a little closer to pass me the joint. Slowly I relaxed, considering Em's little demonstration of force. I still felt the occasional twinge of pain, but the more I thought about it, the funnier the situation was.

"You fucking kicked me in the balls," I said, looking up at the sky.

"Yup. Enjoyed it, too."

"Maybe you don't realize this, but usually people try pretty hard not to piss me off. Bad things happen when I get pissed off."

"Bad things happen when I get pissed off, too. You might want to remember that."

I snorted, a reluctant smile crossing my face. We sat in silence for a while longer, the evening air just cool enough that I wished I had a blanket. Or Em's warm body up against mine. After a while I scooted down, lying back in the grass and looking up at the stars. For once I wasn't totally preoccupied with sex around her, which was kind of nice.

"It's really pretty out here," I said finally. "You're lucky you grew up in a place like this."

I heard her moving, and then she was lying in the grass next to me. Not too close—we weren't touching. But close enough I could smell that unique, flowery scent that seemed to follow her everywhere.

"Where did you grow up?" she asked.

"Hell," I said shortly.

Silence fell again.

"I miss you, Em."

She didn't answer. I yawned as something dark flew over us, followed by a second shadow.

"What are those?" I asked.

"Bats."

"No shit?"

She laughed.

"Yeah, I'm lying to you about the bats, Liam."

Christ, I loved hearing my name from her lips. Without thinking, I reached out and caught her, pulling her over and into me. She stiffened.

"Relax," I whispered. "You're safe."

She pulled away for an instant, then sighed and nestled her head against my shoulder, slowly relaxing. Just holding her in the darkness kicked ass.

"You know, you were wrong about something," she said after a while.

"What's that?"

"I'd make a shitty old lady."

"How do you figure?" I asked, genuinely curious.

"Well, among other things, I have a habit of warning my club's enemies so they can get away before they're killed," she said slowly. "You won't tell anyone about that, will you? Dad would never forgive me."

"Of course not," I said, my voice firm. "You saved my fuckin' life. I wouldn't do that to you. Hell, I don't want to do *anything* to hurt you. Should've stayed away tonight, but I wanted you to know it was all over."

Bullshit. I wanted to see her. Touch her. Smell her hair.

"It's hard to know what you'd do," Em said. "You taught me an important lesson—you can't trust guys you meet online, remember?"

I winced.

"Yeah, about that . . . I'm sorry. It was a dick move."

"But you were cool with romancing me and using me to manipulate my father in the first place?"

"Well, to be fair I did it to get laid, too. Wasn't all business."

She gave a little snort. Not an angry snort, more of a snuffly, surprised laugh that caught her off guard.

"Are you going to erase those pictures?" she asked, finally, her voice sobering. "I don't want them out there. You owe me—I saved your ass, I saved Skid, and I saved this precious truce of yours."

She made a good point. But there was no way I'd erase those pictures. Fuckin' crown jewels in my spank bank.

"I'll get rid of them," I lied. Shit, if that was the worst one I told today, it'd be a damned record.

"How do I know you're telling the truth? For all I know, you've emailed them to your whole club already."

"Naw, if I'd done that, it would've made the rounds of your club, too," I told her. "No way my brothers would be able to resist sending them to your dad. I'll take care of it. You never have to worry about seeing them again, okay?"

"Okay," she agreed, her voice drifting. She was falling asleep, I realized. I held perfectly still. After a few minutes I heard a very soft, very feminine little snore.

Note to self: Pot knocks Em on her ass.

I smirked, and then it faded because not like I'd have a chance to use that information. Pretty sure I wouldn't be seeing her again after tonight. Hell, best-case scenario, the peace would hold and I'd see her across a campfire in a few years at some kind of gathering between the clubs. She'd have an old man by then . . . I'd just have to deal.

Unless it was that cocksucker Painter. I didn't like that guy.

My last thought before I fell asleep was that if I ever saw him with Em, I'd have to kill him.

Just no escaping it.

EM

The birds woke me up. I was freezing cold on my right side, which seemed to be resting on . . . the ground? My back was warm, though, and a man's arm lay heavy over my body.

What the fuck?

Then it came to me.

Liam. Hunter. Whatever the hell his name was. He'd met me outside last night. I'd kicked him in the balls, and the memory warmed me immediately. Then we'd talked and smoked and it hadn't been bad at all. Shit. That'd probably been stupid. But even with the ground all cold and damp beneath me, I felt fantastic cradled in his arms. His bicep made a hell of a nice pillow.

Ewww. I'd drooled on him.

I felt carefully in my pocket and pulled out my phone. Five thirty in the morning. I needed to get back inside, I realized. Not that Painter was my boss or anything, but he was a damned good spy for my father. I slid out from under Hunter's arm carefully, then stood over him, taking him in one last time. Like so many people, sleep made him look young and innocent. Sure, he was still a big man made up of strong muscles and sharp angles, but his face had softened. Dark stubble covered his chin, and his near-black hair flopped forward over his eyes.

He wore his Devil's Jack cut, too—the first time I'd seen it.

It looked good on him, I decided. Of course, everything looked good on him. He was such a beautiful son of a bitch, I thought wistfully, and now I'd probably never see him again. I couldn't help but wonder what could've been.

Pulling out my phone, I took a couple quick pictures, figuring he'd done far worse to me. Then I walked carefully around the side of the bunkhouse and back to the house. I felt like a teenager sneaking inside after a date, a more accurate analogy than I'd realized because Dad's bike was parked in the driveway. Sometime in the night he'd come home, although how I'd missed the sound of his big black Harley I couldn't imagine.

Oh yeah. I'd been stoned off my ass. Oops.

I opened the door carefully. Then I snuck past Painter and climbed the stairs. I pulled out the phone and the gun, setting them on my bedside table before crawling under the covers. On Monday I'd give the folks at the aesthetician's program a call, I decided. Follow up, see what they'd think of me coming to Portland for classes when the next quarter started.

It was a city, after all. Not like I'd ever see Liam at all.

PART TWO

CHAPTER NINE

SIX WEEKS LATER
COEUR D'ALENE, IDAHO
EM

I considered the playlist I'd put together on my phone, and smiled.

Then I hit play on the stereo system's control app.

Bass filled the front of the house, rattling the windows. Dad's room was in the addition off the back, so it wouldn't be *too* loud in there. Just loud enough to make a hangover much, much worse, if you were unfortunate enough to have one.

Odds were whoever came home with him last night—giggling hysterically, because the endless sex noises weren't *quite* annoying enough—had a hangover and a half. It'd been the club's Halloween party. I'd gone for a classic, the Playboy Bunny (in honor of Bridget Jones), which had been rather satisfying. Painter was all over me, something I would've killed for six months ago. Now? Fuck him.

Fuck all of 'em.

Men, I mean. I was done with people who had penises, especially bikers. Liam (he'd disappeared off the face of the earth after his late-night visit, so far as I could tell). Painter (who only wanted me when he couldn't have me). My dad (ugghh).

I'd decided to start campaigning for a woman's right to marry her vibrator. So far I'd collected signatures from . . . well, mostly just Maggs. Her old man, Bolt, was coming up for parole soon, but she didn't think he'd get out. He wouldn't admit he'd done anything wrong. We all knew he was innocent. Hell, we even knew the DNA would exonerate him.

Convincing the state to actually get off their asses and test it, though? Good luck.

Maggs had dressed up like a prisoner in an orange jumpsuit, declaring it was her current version of slutty. Said she'd started associating prison jumpsuits with sex, seeing how the only time she got laid was during the very occasional conjugal visit.

I considered the music volume levels, then turned them up just a notch. I wasn't blasting the back bedroom *too* loud—but listening to perky dance songs is a great way to wake up and get moving, right? Not only that, it seemed only civil to make a nice brunch for them.

A new song started, and I heard stirrings from the back of the house. Guessing who would come out of Dad's bedroom any given morning was a real crapshoot. I kept fantasizing that he'd bring home someone over the age of thirty, but no joy so far. Knowing my luck, it was yet another chick I'd been in high school with.

I should start carding them to make sure they were legal.

It hadn't always been this way. When Mom died, my dad went dark on us for a while, an angry lion who prowled around the house and occasionally swatted at things that got in his way. That first year I hadn't seen him with a woman, not even once.

After that? It's like a switch went off, and now he screwed around more than Ruger did before Sophie, which was saying something. But I might as well make Dad's "friend" feel welcome, I told myself piously. After a long, hard night she would be hungry. I started whipping up pancakes, singing loudly as songs cycled through.

By the third song, the griddle was hot and the batter ready.

By the sixth I had a dozen pancakes cooked and ready. I'd also heard some thudding from the back of the house, and a high-pitched squeal. His latest party favor sounded just like a baby pig, I decided uncharitably.

Sure enough, when the girl marched into the kitchen, I recognized her. Yet another one I'd gone to school with. Officially icky. I eyed her as I took a sip of coffee. Then I raised my cup, wordlessly offering her some. She shook her head, wincing from the motion. I took another sip of sweet caffeine, hiding my smirk.

I set the cup down and poured a measuring bowl of whipped eggs into the frying pan. I heard a gagging noise behind me as she took off running for the bathroom. A few minutes later, Dad wandered into the kitchen. He wore nothing but flannel pajama pants, leaning against the counter as I passed him a cup of coffee without comment.

He took a sip, then spoke.

"You have plans for today?" he asked.

He didn't ask about the girl or complain about the loud music. He never did.

I had a secret theory that he liked how I chased off his women first thing in the morning. Sort of like letting out the dog, or hauling the trash to the curb. It was just one of the many small things I did to make his life more pleasant. In return he made it impossible for me to date and tried to micromanage my life.

Didn't seem quite fair, something I needed to discuss with him. I took a deep breath, figuring there was no time like the present.

"Actually, I've got a project today," I told him.

"What's that?" he asked. A loud barfing noise came from the bathroom, and we both winced.

"Classy, Dad."

A pained look crossed his face.

"Yeah, you got me there. So what's this project?"

"Well, you know I've been looking into getting my aesthetician's certification? I found a program and they've accepted me. You

know I love doing nails, but I think this would be a great step forward."

"That's nice," he said, then smiled. "I got no idea what that is,
but if it makes you happy, go for it."

"Here's the thing," I said, taking a deep breath. "The program's
in Portland."

I braced myself, expecting him to explode. He didn't disappoint.

"What the fuck are you thinking?"

"Cookie and I were talking at the wedding," I said. "She's got
space and could use a little rental income. She's lonely since Bagger
died. She loves Portland, but having a friend around would help."

"Don't bullshit me, little girl," he muttered. "This has to be
about Hunter. What the fuck did he do to you? You gotta talk
to me."

I shook my head. He'd been after me to give him details of
my time alone with Liam, but I wasn't ready for that. I might never
be ready. It seemed like my feelings changed daily, but I knew one
thing for sure.

Dad wasn't the person I'd be talking to when and if I felt the
need.

"No, this is about me," I told him firmly. "It's time for me to
strike out on my own. I love Portland, I love Cookie, and I need to
get out of Coeur d'Alene."

He looked away, face hardening.

"If it's not Hunter, is it Painter? You need to get away from him?
I know he was all over you last night, but I can make him back the
fuck off, baby."

"No," I repeated. "That's part of the problem. Everyone thinks
it's about the men in my life, or the club. It's not. This is about *me*.
I love you, but I'm almost twenty-three years old. I want my own
space—it's time."

"I want you to be happy," he said slowly. "And I can even understand moving out on your own. But Portland is the wrong city."

"Don't give me that," I told him. "The truce with the Devil's

Jacks is solid. Deke and the brothers will be there for me. You have to accept the fact that I'm an adult and I can take care of myself. I promise you—if I need help, I'll ask for it. But you can't just tie me up in bubble wrap and store me in the basement. Kit's on her own and she's doing fine. It's my turn."

"Well, if that's what you really want . . ." he said finally. He shook his head. "I don't like it. For the record, I don't like her being out there, either."

I smiled, because I knew I had him.

"I'll be fine, Dad. I love—"

"Oh, I can't believe how much my head hurts," moaned my former classmate as she stumbled into the kitchen, her face faintly green.

Kind of like the inside of a cucumber.

The wave of warmth I'd been feeling toward Dad chilled. Why the hell did he keep fucking around with women like this? Mom would kill him dead if she saw him pulling this shit. Not out of jealousy. Nope. Straight-up mercy shot.

"You think you could turn that music down?" she whimpered.

I shook my head in mock sorrow, then shouted, "Can't find the remote!"

Her entire body shuddered and then I felt sort of guilty. I might be disgusted by the situation, but now she was turning all pitiful on me, ruining a perfectly good self-righteous snit.

"Oh, here it is," I muttered. I grabbed the phone and turned the music off, wishing I could remember her name.

"Do I know you from somewhere?" she asked, and I bit back a sigh. At least I wasn't the only one with a shitty memory.

"We went to school together," I said. "Unfortunately, you fucked my dad last night, so I thought I'd make you breakfast. Consider it your consolation prize."

Confusion filled her face, and I let the last of my snit go. Who cared if Dad screwed twenty-year-olds? At least he wasn't marrying them.

"You want some coffee?"

"No thanks," she said. She looked over at the silent man watching us and frowned. "She really your kid?"

He nodded, and I saw a hint of humor in his eyes.

"That's kind of creepy," she said, glancing between us. He shrugged.

"You ready for a ride home?"

She pondered, the wheels in her head obviously a little rusty.

"Um, yeah," she said. "That's probably a good idea."

"Vanessa!" I blurted out, feeling proud I remembered her name. She winced, and I realized I'd shouted. "Sorry—I couldn't remember what it was, and then when I did . . ."

She just looked at me with big, postparty raccoon eyes. That's when I noticed her "costume." It was a super short, super tight little dress that had something weird and orange on the front. There was a fluff of green covering each boob.

"What the hell is that?" I asked. "I mean, what are you supposed to be dressed like?"

"I'm a sexy carrot."

I looked at Dad and shook my head slowly. He wouldn't meet my eyes.

"I'm just gonna go get my things," Vanessa said nervously. "This is too weird for me."

"Good idea," Dad told her. "We'll leave in five."

She stumbled back out of the room.

"Seriously? *Sexy carrot?*"

He shrugged.

"I didn't realize how young she was. She looked older last night."

"Keep telling yourself that."

"Are you sure about this Portland shit?" he asked, clearly uninterested in discussing his carrot fetish, which wasn't a huge surprise. He didn't take women too seriously. In fact, that was his excuse every time he ran off one of my boyfriends.

He didn't want me hooking up with someone like him. Too late for that. *Fucking Liam.*

"I'm sure. I've made all the arrangements. I'll finish out my notice this week at the salon, and I'm moving on Saturday. I'd like it if you'd drive down with the truck, help me get my things settled."

He sighed, reaching up and rubbing the back of his neck.

"You're an adult," he said finally. "You can do what you want. But what about Painter? You totally sure that's over? Boy's got it bad for you."

I raised an eyebrow.

"Painter turned me down and then screwed some slut in the bathroom not five minutes later," I said dryly. "I'm done with Painter. Been done with him for a while. This isn't a secret, no matter how much he's been following me around lately. He just wants what he can't have."

His eyes darkened.

"It wasn't the right night, baby girl."

"It never is," I snapped. "I think I can do better."

Dad nodded thoughtfully.

"Okay," he replied. "Hey, Emmy?"

"Yeah?"

"You're making the right choice," he told me. "About Painter, I mean."

I froze. Didn't see that coming.

"What? I thought you wanted me with a Reaper?"

"I do," he replied. "But Painter never fought for you. He never stood up to me, never asked if he could date you, nothing. You deserve a man who'll fight for you, baby girl. You remember that, all right?"

Wow. Didn't see that coming. I felt sudden tears well up, and I lurched forward into his arms. He wrapped them tight around me, resting his chin on my head and rubbing my back softly.

"Just remember," he said. "You and Kit—you can always come home. I don't want you to leave. It's perfect with you here, but I guess you'll do fine in Portland. Just don't sell yourself short. You find what your mom and I had, and don't settle for less."

"Painter is definitely less," I murmured.

"Yup," Dad said. "He's my brother now and I'll stand by him. But I never cheated on your mom. Never wanted to. You need a man who feels the same way, and don't stop until you find him."

"I love you, Daddy," I whispered.

"I know."

"Hey, you got any Febreze or air freshener?" Vanessa asked, her voice a shrill whine. "I got beer shits. Your bathroom reeks."

Damn. I wasn't the only one who could do better.

"This is a new low, Dad," I whispered. His chest rose in silent laughter.

"Yeah, I'll give you that. Shit. What the fuck was I thinking?"

"Something to consider . . ." I said, pulling away to look up into his face. He smiled down at me, the blue eyes he'd given me crinkling just a little around the edges. "Moving forward? There is no such thing as sexy produce. Words to live by."

"I'll keep that in mind."

TWO WEEKS LATER
PORTLAND, OREGON

"ID?" the bouncer asked. Kit rolled her eyes and pulled out the little plastic rectangle. He studied it carefully before handing it back. Then he checked mine and let us go down the stairs and into the bar.

This was my first full weekend in Portland, and Kit had driven down from Olympia to celebrate my new freedom with me. We'd started out by having dinner with Cookie and her daughter, Silvie, at the Kennedy School. Cookie headed home after that. We moved our party across the river to the Pearl District in search of the perfect dive bar.

Looking around the darkened, underground room, I was pretty sure we'd found it. The music was loud, the crowd was mixed, and the pool table was surrounded by a group of guys I'd rank at about a seven or eight on the "I'd hit that" scale, Liam being a perfect ten.

Bastard.

How dare he be all sweet and nice in the moonlight, and then take off and never talk to me again? Of course, I *did* kick him in the balls . . . The memory always gave me a smile.

"Dad know you have a fake ID?" I asked as we moved toward the bar. Kit smirked.

"Of course," Kit replied. "He gave it to me."

I stopped dead.

"No fucking way."

"Yup," she replied. "Right after I got caught with a bad fake during high school. Told me that he didn't want me getting arrested or in trouble, so I needed quality."

"That is so unfair," I muttered. "He never gave me one."

"Did you ask?"

I shook my head.

"No, I guess it never occurred to me that I could . . . I mean, after a certain point he let me drink sometimes at the club and home, but I just didn't think about bars."

"Well, that's the difference between you and me," she said. "I'm always looking for new ways to get in trouble. You're always looking to slide by without anyone noticing."

She had a point. Hell, you could even see it in our clothing. I wore a simple black top. It showed a little cleavage and outlined my curves, but in terms of club wear it was designed to blend in.

Kit, though . . . Not so much.

She'd gone full vintage for the night, a look she'd been developing for a while. Her hair was dyed dark black and arranged in an elaborate style that screamed Bettie Page. She wore a fitted, off-the-shoulder red blouse that matched her bright red lipstick and showed off her tattoos. She'd paired it with ultra tight capri pants that somehow looked old-fashioned and slutty at the same time. The entire outfit was eye-catching and unique, and completely above any particular fad or momentary fashion trend.

Kit had always been that—ruthlessly making her own path, oblivious to other opinions. I loved it.

I loved her, too.

"I love you," I told her, catching her up in a hug. She giggled.

"You're drunk."

"So are you!"

"Not drunk enough," she countered. "Get me a vodka Red Bull, okay? I'm going to hit the powder room."

I waited for our drinks, musing about my sister and her unique view of life. Powder room, for fuck's sake? Who says that? Somehow it was all part of that vintage persona, and on her it didn't seem artificial at all.

Quite the accomplishment, really.

I got the drinks and found a table in the back. The top was a little sticky, as was the padded bench against the wall. I couldn't see much in the dim light, though, and that was probably a good thing. When it comes to sticky in a bar, spilled drinks are sort of the best-case scenario.

My phone buzzed.

PAINTER: How's Portland?

Yeah, right. Like I wanted to talk to fucking Painter. I picked up my drink and chugged it down fast.

Kit slid in next to me, eyes wide.

"Are we not a happy camper?" she asked. I slid my phone over to her and she picked it up, studying the message. "Ah, the amazing Painter."

Then she started typing. It took me a minute to realize what she was doing. I lunged for the phone and she laughed, hitting send.

"You bitch!" I yelled. She laughed and gave it back to me.

ME: Figure it out, dumbass. You blew it, and now I'll never
    blow you.

"Wow, that's cold," I said, impressed. "He's gonna be really
pissed at me."

"You found him fucking a girl in the bathroom right after he
turned you down," she said bluntly. "He doesn't get to be pissed.
Ever. And what do you care? You're done with him."

"Yeah, but I still have to see him around when I go home."

"So what?" she asked. "It's like your head is still in Coeur
d'Alene. You live in Portland now, babe. Bottoms up!"

She passed her drink over to me, and I chugged that one, too.

"I think I'm drunk," I said after a couple minutes. She leaned
forward, looking deep into my eyes like a fortune-teller.

"Really drunk, or just mostly?"

"Mostly," I replied. "But definitely not sober."

"Excellent," she declared. "Now we're going to talk about
Liam."

I swayed.

"I never should have told you about him."

"Probably," she agreed. "But you did, so that's a done deal.
Have you heard from him at all since that night?"

"No," I said. "I don't know if that pisses me off or not. I mean,
it was all lies. I know that. But I still sort of miss him. How fucked
up is that?"

She cocked her head, thinking.

"Pretty fucked up. But that's how it is when you break up with
someone."

"You have to be with someone before you can break up with
them."

Kit started laughing.

"What?"

"You and Liam—Hunter—whatever we want to call him . . .
You guys *definitely* had a relationship. You talked every day for

weeks. You had phone sex with him and you pretty much had real sex with him, even if he didn't literally stick his dick in you. He screwed you over and then he came to visit you and let you know you were safe. That's more of a relationship than I had with that dumbass I got engaged to. Well, except for the sex part. We had more of that. But my point is, you broke up with someone. Of course you're gonna be thinking about him."

I considered her words. She had a good point.

"You know, that actually makes me feel a little better," I said. "Less like I'm crazy."

"So have you stalked him online since it happened?" she asked.

"Of course," I said. *Duh.* "I mean, I looked at his house and stuff on Google. Went through his wallet. I already told you about the panties and shit. But there's not much to find. His profile is gone and I can't find anything else on him. I have no idea how much of what I knew of him was real."

"This is going to take more alcohol," she said, surveying our empty glasses.

I considered her statement, then nodded gravely.

"I have to pee."

"You go do that," Kit said, equally serious. "Try not to get lost. I'm gonna go replace these drinks. It's my duty as a sister to make sure you don't sober up any time in the near future."

I stood, swaying, and realized there was no real danger of me sobering up any time soon. I made my way to the bathroom, passing the guys playing pool. One of them made eye contact, and I smiled. Yeah, being away from the club was pretty cool. I could flirt with him and not have to worry about him suddenly disappearing because some prospect started growling.

It took a long time to get to the bathroom and back. I can't quite remember why, but I think I might have gotten lost near the pool table. Kit sat waiting for me, my phone in front of her, fingers flying.

Shit, why hadn't I taken it with me?

Oh yeah. Drunk.

"Okay, two things," she said when I got back. "I changed his name from Liam to Hunter in your contacts. It's confusing me to keep track of both. Also, he said this."

She handed it over to me. I looked at her blankly.

"Read it already," she said. "Here, I got you a drink."

She pushed a glass toward me, then glanced at the phone pointedly.

I looked down.

ME: Hey. Wht r you doing?

HUNTER: Em? Holy shit. How are you? I'm not doing anything. Can't believe your messaging me

ME: I just wondred how you were, maybe if you think
about me?

I looked up and gave Kit a death glare. Why hadn't I drowned her when we were both still small, and I could've gotten away with it?

"What the hell were you doing?"

"Starting a conversation," she said brightly. "I feel like we've got unfinished business here. Let's get it out and over with, and then we'll find someone to punch your V Card and move on."

She said this last part way too loud, because the guy at the next table turned his head to eye us. He gave me a smile, and one of those chin lifts guys do.

"You need to stop talking," I hissed at her. My phone vibrated, and I glanced down.

HUNTER: I think about you all the time

My heart skipped a beat. Well. That was interesting.

Kit tried to grab the phone again, but I stuffed it down the front of my pants. Ha! I smirked at her triumphantly until she whipped out her own cell. She hit a button and suddenly mine started vibrating.

Oh, *wow.*

There was something really, really wrong about how good that felt.

"I've had way too much alcohol," I said. "I think I'm turning into a sex fiend."

"Can I buy you a drink?" asked the guy next to us.

"No!" I grabbed Kit's arm and started dragging her away.

"What are you doing?"

"We need to get the hell out of here," I muttered. "Go dancing or something."

This shit was out of control. Typical night out with my sister.

Two hours later I found myself in a cab headed toward Hunter's house.

How we got from me dragging Kit out of a bar to stalking my former kidnapper, I wasn't quite sure. I'm usually a pretty sensible person.

But in my defense, she bought me shots.

Anyway, because Kit is a sneaky bitch, she had the cabbie drop us not quite a block from Hunter's address, so we could creep up on him. (I swear, in the moment it made sense. *Shots!*) We tiptoed along the sidewalk like two cat burglars, which would've been far more effective if we hadn't been giggling hysterically and stumbling around. About two houses away we realized there was a party going on at his place.

Even during a party he took the time to answer "my" text!

Some part of me deep inside—the part that's too stupid to live— thought this was sweet. That's when I had to bitch-slap myself mentally, because seriously? Kidnapper. Naked photos.

Endless orgasms . . .

No. Don't think about those.

We stopped behind a giant rhododendron and peered through the leaves at the house. People flowed through the front door, and loud music filled the air. Hunter stood in the corner of the old-fashioned porch, leaning against the rail and looking down over the yard. It was one of those old houses that defines Portland—tall and skinny on a narrow lot. Almost Victorian, but just a little more raw, as if the builders couldn't quite afford the gingerbread. The porch slanted forward and steep stairs led to a narrow walk. Tree-sized shrubs surrounded it, many of them still flowering despite how late it was in the year.

Hunter watched impassively as a group of girls staggered up to the house. A tall chick with giant boobs tried to talk to him and I felt myself tense, but he ignored her and after a minute she followed the others inside.

"Wow, he's hot," Kit whispered. "No wonder you're obsessed with him."

"I'm not obsessed."

"Whatever," she said. "But damn . . . That chick looked like she was ready to drop to her knees on the spot if he gave the word. Not many guys would turn that down. Text him!"

"And say what?"

"Ask him what he's doing," she hissed.

"You already asked him that!"

"Oh yeah. I forgot. Ask him if he's got anything interesting planned."

I dug my phone out of my jeans and started typing, which was harder than you'd think, since my thumbs kept hitting the wrong spots.

ME: So you have anthing intrsting plnned? I'm out wth my sister

Seconds later Hunter reached into his pocket and pulled out his phone, glancing down at it. He smiled and I melted, because he really was gorgeous. He started to type something back, but then a beautiful girl with bright red hair came out and wrapped her arms around his waist.

I waited for him to push her away or freeze her out like he'd done with Big Boobs.

Instead he hugged her back. She said something to him and he laughed, the expression on his face so tender I could have thrown up. Bastard. *Motherfucking cocksucking bastard.* Hunter leaned over and whispered in her ear. She smacked his stomach playfully.

"I think we should kill him," Kit hissed. "He doesn't look nearly as cute with that bitch wrapped around him."

I nodded.

He kissed the top of the girl's head and she laughed again, then pulled away and went back into the house. Hunter turned back to his phone and I got a text from him.

HUNTER: Nope nothing planned. Just hanging out with the roommates. Shit it's good to hear from you Em. Miss you. How are you?

I showed the message to Kit, and she growled.

"That takes balls," she muttered. "You saw how they were together? That's not some new thing, they're a *couple*. He's fucking with you. Either that, or he's fucking her while *thinking* about you. Not sure which one sucks worse."

"I know," I said, my voice grim. God, why had I wasted so much energy on this guy? Why the hell was I surprised to see him hanging on some bitch right after he texted me?

Hunter wasn't a nice guy.

We'd covered this.

I should just slink away. Just go home before I embarrassed myself even more. Then I pictured him naked with that redheaded twat and my head exploded.

I stepped out from behind the shrub and started marching across the lawn. I'm sure he noticed me right away, because Hunter had been doing that same watching thing my dad always does. He liked to keep an eye on everyone, always looking for potential threats. Considering what a *giant dickhead* Hunter was, I'd bet tons of people wanted him dead.

I was the new queen of their special club.

Pushing through the group at the foot of the stairs, I headed straight toward him. The surprised shock on Hunter's face was satisfying as all fuck.

"Em, what the hell are you doing here?" he asked, glancing around the yard quickly. Maybe he expected an army of Reapers behind me? Well, I might not have the brothers with me, but I had Kit. Under the right circumstances, she could be scarier than a dozen angry bikers.

"So, you *miss* me?"

"Um, yeah," he said, studying me like I was some sort of alien creature. "Where did you come from? I thought you were in Coeur d'Alene."

"Just because you leave me somewhere doesn't mean I'll stay," I hissed. "I'm not a dog, Hunter. I don't do what I'm told."

He narrowed his eyes at me.

"You're pretty fuckin' drunk, aren't you?"

"And that would be your business because . . . ?"

"Shit, let's get out of here," he muttered. "Get you some water or something. Figure out the rest of this later."

"Why, are you trying to hide me?" I sniped. "Afraid I might run into someone, make things awkward for you?"

He shook his head slowly.

"No, I just figured tomorrow you'll wish there were fewer witnesses who saw this," he said. "I'll bet you're gonna have a hell of a headache, too. Let's get some water, maybe some Advil. Then we can talk, okay?"

"Fuck talking. I *saw* her, dickwad."

"Who?"

I cocked my head and sneered. Did he really think he could fool me?

"I saw you with your girlfriend like two minutes ago, Liam. You kissed her, for fuck's sake. Don't pretend you're trying to do anything more than use me."

"Jealous?" he asked, a slow, sexy grin stealing across his face.

"Don't smile at her, asshole," Kit said from behind me. Like always, she had my back and I felt a rush of love for her. At least one person would always be on my side.

"Babe, that girl was my *sister*," Liam said carefully, his voice almost gentle. "Kelsey. Trust me, she's not interested in me like that."

I froze.

"Your sister?" I asked, the fog in my head clearing enough to realize that I *might* have stepped over the line . . . "You told me you didn't have any family, that you grew up in foster care."

"She's my foster sister," he said. *Shit.* I felt like a complete bitch. "We've been together for more than ten years, I practically raised her."

"I saw how she looked at you," Kit snarled. "That's not a sisterly kind of look."

"You want to say that a little louder?" a new voice demanded, and I looked over to find the redhead in question glaring at us, hands on her hips. "Because it sounds like you were saying I want to fuck my brother. That's pretty nasty, even coming from a skank like you."

Kit bristled like a porcupine, and for a second I thought she might launch herself across the porch, hissing and spitting.

"Drop it, Kels," Hunter said, his voice cutting through the air like a whip. "This is Em, and that's her sister. Trust me, I'm happy she's jealous of you. Means she still gives a shit."

"I do not give a shit," I muttered, and Hunter laughed.

"This bitch tied you in knots—" Kelsey started to say, but Hunter cut her off.

"Drop it. Put away your claws, because I'm just thankful she's here."

Kit snarled, and I stepped quickly between her and Kelsey. Wait. Wasn't this supposed to be *my* dramatic scene? Ughh . . .

"This is between me and Hunter," I told Kit. "I appreciate the support, but you need to back off."

"Christ," Kit muttered, turning away and running a hand through her hair. "I need a beer."

Kelsey narrowed her eyes at her. Hunter put a hand on her shoulder and squeezed just a little tighter than what looked comfortable.

"Play. Nice."

"You can come out back, we have a keg," she choked after a long pause, her tone still hostile. "Let dumbass talk to his precious Em, maybe he'll stop moping around. I'm seriously tired of his shit."

She turned and stalked back into the house. Kit caught my eye.

You okay? she mouthed. I shrugged, which she took as a yes. I wasn't sure if I was okay or not, but I figured I wouldn't make any progress fighting on the porch with this Kelsey chick.

"Look, let's go get some coffee or something," Hunter said. "There's a diner a few blocks from here. Then I'll take you home."

"No, let's stay. I need another drink."

I turned toward the house, but he caught my arm.

"I don't want you inside."

"Why not?" I asked. "You can't tell me it isn't safe. You let your sister go inside."

"It's safe enough," he replied reasonably. "But there's shit in there I don't want you exposed to."

"My dad is the president of an MC," I snapped. "Or have you forgotten? Because if I remember correctly, it's why you got in touch with me in the first place. I've been exposed to plenty in my life."

Hunter sighed and ran a hand through his hair. It'd gotten longer since I'd seen him. Unfortunately, I remembered exactly what it felt like to run my fingers through that hair.

Lust hit me, and I bit the inside of my cheek. Goddammit. Why did he have to be so beautiful?

"Trust me, I haven't forgotten who you are," he said. "Would make my life a hell of a lot easier if you were nobody. I'd just fuck you and get it over with."

CHAPTER TEN

I stared at him, stunned.

"I know guys *think* things like that," I said slowly. "But you do realize you're not supposed to say them out loud, right?"

He sighed.

"Em, I really like you. We covered that. I like you enough not to play games, okay? That means I'm not gonna feed you any romantic bullshit."

Huh. Wasn't sure how to take that. On the one hand, I didn't want him lying to me. On the other, I didn't like the honesty, either. Made it too hard to pretend that this wasn't completely insane.

"So let's lay it all out," I said. "You want to fuck me, but you don't care about me. I want to fuck you, but trust me, every time you open your mouth, I care about you less."

"Pretty much," he muttered.

"We should do it."

"Excuse me?"

"Let's do it," I said, warming to the idea. "Fuck. Screw. Boink.

I know you're good at it, and it's about time I got it over with. Let's go in there and have at it. Like ripping off a Band-Aid."

I smiled up at him brightly, pleased with myself. It was a brilliant plan.

"You have got to be kidding me," he said, closing his eyes. "Un-fucking-real. Em, we need to get you home. Now."

"You're turning me down?" I asked, raising my brows. "Because you seemed pretty ready to go for it at the bar, and you sure as shit weren't faking it when you had me cuffed to the bed. Pretty certain I didn't imagine that part."

"Yeah, Em. I'm turning you down."

"Well, fuck you, asshole. Oh wait, we're not doing that, are we?" I said peevishly, looking past him. The front door had opened, and I could see girls dancing inside. Some of them weren't wearing much in the way of clothing. Interesting. "If you're gonna be boring, I'll just go check out the party."

I pushed past him and walked into the living room, looking around curiously. If Hunter wanted to be a dickwad, I'd find someone else to entertain me.

Now, I grew up in an MC, so it wasn't like the party totally shocked me. But Dad always kicked me out before things got too crazy at the Armory, because he's mean like that. I have a good imagination, though, and I've heard stories about wild club parties.

Stories that were apparently pretty accurate. *Sweet.*

Across the wall was a long banner that said "Welcome Home, Clutch." Right underneath it sat a big recliner, all covered with gold cloth like a throne. There was a mini fridge set next to it, and attached to one arm was an elaborate remote-control holster. I made careful note of each peripheral detail, because my eyes kept shying away every time I tried to look at the action taking place *in* the chair.

A man wearing a Devil's Jack cut lay back, a giant grin on his face. I couldn't tell if it was from watching the half-naked stripper working the pole in the center of the room, the two fully naked chicks on the couch sixty-nining each other, or the girl giving him a blow job. Whatever the cause, Clutch (I assumed it was Clutch) was in a very, very good mood.

Well, at least now I knew what the party was for.

I started wandering across the room, which was full of guys drinking beer, couples making out, and oh . . . look at that. There was a giant plasma TV playing porn.

"Em," Hunter called, his voice warning. I ignored him. This was far too interesting. Past the living room was a dining area. Big Boobs lay back on the table while a tall man with a hairy ass fucked her in front of the crowd. I cocked my head, studying him carefully. He needed a wax in a big way.

Then everything turned upside down.

Hunter had grabbed me and thrown me over his shoulder, which wasn't the most comfortable position for a woman who'd been drinking all night. It took everything I had not to barf down his back, so I started smacking him and demanding that he let me go.

"Jesus Christ," he muttered, passing through the kitchen and up a flight of stairs. He turned into a room at the top, flopping me down on an unmade bed. Everything started spinning. I tried to focus on the ceiling, where something faintly green shimmered. What *was* that up there?

Then I burst out laughing.

"The fuck?" Hunter asked, hands on his hips, exasperation written all over his face.

"There's a glowing unicorn on your ceiling," I said, awestruck. But was it real? I closed my eyes, rubbed them, then opened them again.

Nope. It was still there. Holy shit.

I sat up.

"Is there really a glowing unicorn watching us?" I asked, feeling a little panicky. "Because I see one. It's right there."

A smile crept across his face and he sat down on the bed, leaning back against the headboard.

"Yup, there's a unicorn up there all right," he said. "Must've been a kid's bedroom before we took the place over. Someone painted it for him, I guess."

Well, that was good news. I might be drunk, but at least I wasn't hallucinating.

"Why don't you paint over it?"

"Kelsey likes it," he said. "Actually, I kind of like it, too. We had some shitty foster homes, but there was one place we stayed that was pretty good. The woman there was way into unicorns. All over the place. They remind me of her."

"Are you still in touch with her."

"She's dead," he said shortly. "Died about a month after we moved into her house. Heart attack or something. We were damned lucky they kept us together after that—even real brothers and sisters get broken apart. Fuckin' miracle we weren't separated."

I thought about my mom and dad, and how happy I'd been with them as a kid. I missed her so much. And while Dad drove me crazy, I loved him. He was always there for me. Always.

I rolled to my side, curling into him and resting my head against his chest. Then I brought my hand up and rubbed up and down the plane of his muscles, almost restlessly.

"So, what do you think?" I asked.

"About what?"

"Fucking, of course. Remember? I'm not a little girl who needs protection, Hunter. I know what I want. Just lie back and relax, because it's not personal. I'm just going to borrow your dick for a while."

He stilled.

"You're really, really drunk, Em. I think we should talk about it tomorrow. If you're still interested then, I'm all over it."

I pushed myself up to lean on his chest, glaring at him.

"If you don't fuck me right now, I'm going downstairs to find someone who will," I threatened. "I'm serious. I'm done with this virgin princess bullshit."

His face hardened.

"Yeah, that ain't happening."

I tried to sit up, but he wrapped his arms around my waist, holding me tight. Then he rolled, taking me with him until I was settled underneath, one of his legs between mine. I felt his dick against my stomach and smiled. That was good—for a minute I'd been worried he'd lost interest. I tried to kiss him, but he pulled away, scowling.

"Oh, *seriously*?" I asked. "Let me get this straight. You've got a drunk girl who wants to have sex with you in your bed. You've made it clear you aren't interested in love or romance. The drunk girl is cool with that. Are you sure you're actually a real biker? Because something here isn't adding up, Liam."

His face softened.

"Say it again."

"Are you sure you're actually a real biker?" I asked. He shook his head and grinned.

"No, my name. Liam."

"Liam," I said, letting it roll around my tongue. "Liam. Liam. Fuck me, Leeeeam."

"Christ, I love how you say that. Nobody calls me that but you, Em."

"That sounded almost sweet," I said, narrowing my eyes. "But we aren't playing games. I know you aren't sweet, so stop pretending."

He dropped his forehead down, resting it against mine.

"Never thought I'd see you again," he said quietly. "Not gonna blow it now."

"Maybe I should blow you?"

His face twisted almost painfully, hips swiveling against mine. For a minute I thought I had him. Then he kissed the tip of my nose and rolled off me. He tucked me into his side again, and used his free arm to grab a remote control off the bedside table. The TV sitting on top of a battered dresser flickered to life.

"Tell you what. Let's hang out for a while. You sober up and still want to go at it, no problem. My dick's all yours," he said. "Until then, we'll watch some TV. You like *Top Gear*?"

"Sure," I said, trying not to yawn. I glanced up at the unicorn. It seemed to wink at me, sneaky bastard. I decided to rest my eyes for a minute, because they obviously weren't working right. Five minutes later I was sound asleep.

I was dead.

Only death and damnation to hell could explain suffering this terrible.

Horrible, unspeakably bright sunlight attacked me. I tried covering my eyes with my arm. Unfortunately, this brought it into contact with my head, which exploded into waves of painful throbbing.

I heard the door open.

"Morning," Hunter said cheerfully. "I brought you some coffee."

I wasn't dead, I realized. I tried to think back, remember the night before. Flashes hit me. Strippers. A glowing unicorn. British people talking about cars . . .

Oh God.

I'd thrown a jealous tantrum and demanded Hunter have sex with me. Then I'd fallen asleep on top of him. *Kit.* This was all Kit's fault. She bought the devil shots. She insisted we stalk Hunter. Hell, she'd texted him in the first place.

My sister would pay for this.

"You want some Advil?" Hunter asked. I slowly peeled my gummy eyelids open. He stood over me, his hair wet and his skin glowing with the fresh vigor of a newly showered man.

Damn him and his sobriety.

"Advil would be great," I said, unsteadily sitting upright. The covers fell down as I reached for the coffee.

Then I realized I was wearing only my bra and panties.

"Crap," I said, grabbing for the sheet.

"Not like I haven't seen it before," Hunter said reasonably. "I stripped you down last night, figured you'd be more comfortable. Also, I think you spilled booze on the shirt. It smelled funny."

Of course it did, I thought, mentally sighing. Because getting drunk and making an ass of myself wasn't enough. Nope. I had to stink, too. Wordlessly, I reached for the coffee. I took a sip of the dark, bitter liquid, feeling it flow down my throat like a miracle drug. I was already feeling more human—amazing what a little caffeine can do.

Hunter sat down on the bed next to me.

"Think you'll live?" he asked.

I considered the question carefully.

"Not sure," I admitted. "Physical suffering aside, I'm pretty sure I'll never live last night down. I'm sorry I was such a freak."

He gave a laugh.

"Yeah, because I've never seen someone get drunk and stupid before," he said. "Not that I didn't appreciate you climbing all over me. But what the hell was that all about? Wasn't like you."

"*Kit*," I said, her name a curse. "All her idea. For the record, she's the one who texted you, too. My sister is insane. I'm not entirely sure she's even human."

I took another drink, then had a horrible realization. I'd abandoned my sister—drunk—in the middle of a party where screwing women publicly on tables was socially acceptable.

"Is she okay?" I asked, full of sudden panic. "Have you seen Kit?"

"She's fine," he said. "Down in the kitchen with Kelsey. They're making breakfast for all the stragglers. I guess they hit it off last night—now they're building some kind of unholy alliance."

I shuddered.

"Just what the world needs. Did I really ask you to fu—have sex with me last night?"

"Yup," he said, looking smug. "I'm on board with that now, by

the way. You were just way too out of it last night for us to have
any fun."

"Wow, what a prince," I muttered. "You won't screw a drunk
girl. Were you class president, too?"

He laughed.

"Trust me, it wouldn't have been fun for either of us. I'm not
into necrophilia. You were so out of it I kept getting nervous and
checking to make sure you hadn't stopped breathing."

"Ewww."

"Hey, not my fault. I was sober, remember? You're the one who
poured those shots down your throat."

Oh, I remembered that part. Vividly.

"I feel like something died inside me."

"That would be your liver," he said helpfully, reaching down to
tuck a strand of hair behind my ear. "I'm gonna go check on Clutch,
and then we'll talk. Make yourself comfortable. Bathroom's across
the hall. Oh, and Em?"

"Yeah?"

"Last night was a game changer, so far as I'm concerned. I gave
you your space, let you go. But you came back, so now you're fair
game. I'm done being the nice guy."

I eyed him suspiciously, then pulled the covers up and over my
head. I wasn't ready to think about this. I heard him leave the
room. Damn it. Why didn't he have blackout curtains in here? After
a while, the door opened again.

"Sorry," I muttered. "I'll get up. I was just drifting . . ."

"Don't worry about it," a voice said. Not Hunter's, but one I
knew way too well. I peeked out and over the covers.

Skid.

"What are you doing?" I asked, eyes darting nervously. He
closed the door behind him and clicked the lock, loudly and deliberately. Then he leaned back against the door with his arms crossed
in front of his chest.

"We need to talk," he said, his voice cold.

"You can't hurt me," I said quickly, hoping it was true. "Hunter will be pissed as hell if you try to do anything."

He gave a harsh laugh.

"I don't care about you enough to hurt you," he said. "What happened before? That's behind us. You were defending yourself and I was trying to save my brother from a fucking Reaper lunatic. We'll call it even and let it go, at least as far as you're concerned. This is something else."

I cocked my head, not sure whether to believe him. Not that I had many options. I mean, I guess I could scream for Hunter. But Skid wasn't making a move at me and now I was curious.

"What?"

"You need to leave Hunter alone. You have no idea how much you're fucking up his life. I want you to get up, take your sister, and go away."

I narrowed my eyes.

"Why would I do that?" I asked, even though until that moment I'd half planned to take off anyway. But I really didn't like being told what to do.

"Do you give even the slightest shit about him?" Skid asked, meeting my gaze without a hint of trickery. "If you do, you need to end this. It's a game for you, but it's going to destroy him. You're like a virus in his head, eating him up and burning him out. How much do you know about his background?"

"I know he was in foster care . . ." I said, not wanting to admit how little he'd told me.

"He has *nobody*," Skid said with careful emphasis. "It's him, Kelsey, and the Devil's Jacks. We're his family, his work, his home. Everything. At this rate, he'll be running this club some day—a *functional* club, without all the bullshit we've been fighting our way through these past few years. A relationship with you ends all that. He'd have to step back. We'd let him stay in the club, but if he's with a Reaper, he won't be trusted."

I stared at him.

"That's totally unfair—and it doesn't make sense. You guys planned for him to get together with me in the first place. I'm the glue to hold the truce together or some such bullshit. How come it's all changed?"

Skid snorted.

"Yeah, that was fine when he didn't give a damn about you," he said. "But it's pretty obvious it's deeper than that now. He talked club business with you—I know he did, so don't bother denying it. And if he told you shit once, he'll do it again. We can't have our national sergeant at arms sharing secrets with Picnic Hayes's daughter. He starts sleeping with you, it's over for him and that's a fact."

I lay back, thinking. Wow.

"He's really going to be a national officer?" I asked. "That's . . . Isn't he too young?"

"Things are changing for the Jacks. He's one of the men behind those changes. We'll have elections soon and that's how it's gonna play out. Unless you fuck it up for him."

"Crap," I muttered. I sat up, carefully holding the sheet in place. "You do realize that I have no idea what's going on with him and me? I'm not even sure there's an *us* at this point."

"Exactly," Skid said. "So are you willing to destroy his life just so you can explore it? Because if you care about him, it's a shit thing to do. And don't try to tell me you don't care about him, either. I saw you last night. You're as fucked in the head as he is."

I stared at the wall, trying to process what he was saying. The hangover wasn't helping.

"Can I ask you one thing?" I said finally.

"Sure."

"Why are you so sure I can't be trusted?"

He just looked at me for long seconds, judging me with his eyes.

"Because you lied to your own club."

"I had no idea Hunter was a Devil's Jack—" I started to protest, but he held up a hand, stopping me.

"Not that," he said, his voice cold. "Later, at the house. You called and told him to get out, right in the middle of a meet with your dad. Don't bother trying to bullshit me. You used my fucking phone to do it."

My breath caught.

"I smashed your phone."

He offered a dark, cynical smile.

"Let me guess, your dad pays for your cell?"

I didn't reply. He did, but I'd be damned if I'd admit it now.

"I have an online record of calls," Skid said slowly and carefully, like he was talking to an idiot. Apparently he was. "I saw the number and the time stamp, Em. I know what you did. I can prove it."

Oh, fuck . . . He could destroy me. And he would, too. I saw it in his eyes. *Double fuck.*

"So you hate me because I saved his life and yours?" I asked, feeling like a cornered animal. "I protected the peace between our clubs, Skid. That wasn't a betrayal. That saved all of us."

"I don't hate you at all," he replied. "I'm thankful to you. I love Hunter—he's my brother, and he'd be dead right now if you hadn't done it. Why d'you think I've kept my mouth shut? But can you look me in the eye and tell me you wouldn't do the same for your dad? Say you were Hunter's old lady. Would you make a call to save your father's life, if you knew we might kill him? Because this truce may not last long term. You ready to make that choice?"

The thought stabbed through me. *Of course I would save my dad.* It must've been written all over my face. Skid gave a sad smile.

"You'll always have divided loyalties, Em," he said almost compassionately. "Our sergeant at arms shouldn't be with a woman who isn't a hundred percent behind the Jacks. Not if he's been stupid enough to fall in love with her."

"You think he's in love with me?" I asked, my heart hopeful and breaking all at once.

"I think he's something," he replied, shrugging. "I don't know if 'love' is the right word. Not sure he's capable of love the way you'd think of it. But he cares enough about you to compromise his judgment. I know he went to see you at your house, and I know he told you things you shouldn't have heard. That's enough to end it right there. If you care about Hunter—if you want him to have a future—you need to leave this house and never come back."

I wanted to argue, but I couldn't think of a damned thing to say. Skid was right.

"Go on," I told him, feeling sick to my stomach. "Distract Hunter or something. I'll grab my clothes, then Kit and I will take off. I don't want to see him, though. Not sure I can handle that."

"I'll take care of it," he said. "I'll ask him to help me in the back yard. We need to move the keg and clean up anyway. You've got fifteen minutes."

Eight minutes later, I was practically racing down the street, Kit trailing after me like a sad, spoiled little puppy.

"Why did we have to leave?" she whined. "I like Kelsey. We were having fun. She's a lot like me—I think we could be friends."

"I'll tell you when we get home," I muttered, keeping my eyes forward. I couldn't let myself think about Hunter, let alone explain it right now. I didn't want to start crying.

Sometimes doing the right thing sucks.

HUNTER

I stared down at my empty bed, jaw clenching.

I'd known something was wrong the instant Skid and I walked into the kitchen. Kelsey stood at the stove by herself, flipping pancakes and muttering soft curses.

"You," she said, turning to glare at us. She pointed her bright red spatula menacingly, waving it back and forth, apparently unable to decide on a target. "You scared them off."

"Who?" I asked.

Skid sighed.

"It's my fault," he said. "I told Em she should get out of here and leave you alone."

"What?" I asked, stunned. I glanced over at Kelsey, who shrugged. *"Fuck."*

I took the stairs two at a time, which was a complete waste of effort. Em wasn't up there. I found a piece of paper on the bed, though.

Liam—I'm so sorry, but this whole thing was a big mistake. I want you to know there's no hard feelings and I hope things go great for you and your club.

Take care, Em

I dropped the note and strode over to the window, pushing it open and looking outside.

Nothing.

Fuck. FUCK.

Then I clenched the windowsill until my knuckles turned white, trying to decide the best way to kill Skid. It came to me. I'd beat him to death. Immediately. I found him down in the kitchen, locked in a glaring match with Kelsey. Without a word, I spun him around and punched him in the face.

He staggered and I punched him again, sending him into the fridge with a crash. The top was lined with bottles of hard liquor, and they started falling like dominoes. Some bounced on the painted wooden floorboards and others shattered.

The raw stench of alcohol filled the kitchen.

"What the hell did you do?" I yelled at him. "Who I screw is my business! Not yours. Not the club's. You stay the fuck out of my life, *brother.*"

He held up his hands, clearly not wanting a fight. Tough shit. I jerked him to his feet and hit him again. Blood spurted from his nose, and I saw—reflected in his eyes—the instant he decided to start fighting back.

I'm not sure how long it lasted.

What I do know is that we tumbled off the back porch, through the shrubs, and onto the lawn all without losing a beat. By the time it ended, Clutch, Grass, Kelsey, and several random women left over from the party were all standing on the back porch watching.

Pretty sure Clutch and Grass were taking bets.

I decided the winner owed me drinks, because I'd kicked Skid's ass . . . But by the time I had him knocked out and helpless in the dirt, my brain had started working again. I glanced up at our audience and frowned, staggering slightly. He'd gotten in some pretty good hits. My head was spinning—I figured there was a decent chance I had a concussion.

"Go away," I growled. "This is private."

Grass herded them back in, although Kelsey tried to insist on staying outside. He ended the argument by picking her up and carrying her while she rewarded him with a flurry of head smacks from the spatula.

I collapsed to the ground, staring blankly up at the clouded sky.

"You okay?" I asked Skid. He rolled over, moaning.

"Yeah," he muttered. "I had to do it, bro."

"You didn't have to do shit."

"She's no good for you," he said. "She's not some little puppet you can control. She lied for you to her own club, which is fuckin' romantic until you consider that same loyalty is attached to the Reapers, too. You'd never be able to trust her, brother. And if you did, we'd never be able to trust you."

"Still not your decision to make," I said slowly. "So you figured it out, I guess?"

"Phone records," he said shortly. "Don't worry. Won't show 'em to anyone. Figure I owe her that much, given that she saved your sorry ass. But seriously—elections are coming, and unless you want to pull out, you can't be with her."

"That's my problem," I told him.

"No, it's a club problem," Skid said seriously. "Burke needs a right-hand man he can trust, and we all know it's you. But I'm *your* right hand, bro. It's my job to make sure your head's in the game. Right now it isn't."

I flipped him off, draping my arm over my eyes.

"Nobody knows about that phone call," I said. "It's not an issue."

"*I* know about the phone call," Skid replied, his voice quiet without compromise. "And the day it puts our club in danger is the day I'll stop guarding her secret. It's not personal, brother. I don't actually dislike the chick, despite what you might think. But I can't let her get too close to you."

I sighed. Fuck.

"This isn't over," I told him. "I'm not giving up on her."

"You giving up the national office?" Skid asked. "Think carefully, bro. You can only have one or the other."

I didn't reply—I'd spent the last eight years working to prove myself, to show Burke I was the man he could count on in a fight. I wasn't ready to give up all I'd earned.

Shit. Skid was right.

I had a problem.

CHAPTER ELEVEN

ONE WEEK LATER
EM

I couldn't breathe.

Something heavy crushed my chest, pressing down on my lungs. Something evil, I realized. A demon hungry for my soul? I hovered in that dark space between sleep and wakefulness, terrified as my worst dreams came to life.

"There's ghost monkeys in the closet . . ." a soft, weirdly high-pitched voice whispered in my ear. Adrenaline spiked and I sat up, tumbling a four-year-old devil child off my chest.

"Ouch!" Silvie squawked, looking up at me from the end of the bed with an air of betrayal. "Ghost monkeys are scary! I want you to get them."

Oh, fuck. Was it morning already? I glanced at the clock. Sure enough, seven a.m. Already. Pisser. Well, at least Silvie was in here pestering me and not Cookie. That woman worked way too hard—she deserved a morning to sleep in.

"Sorry, baby," I said, opening my arms. Silvie scampered up the covers and crawled into them, snuggling into me tight. "What's this about ghost monkeys?"

"In my closet," she said, eyes wide. "Wanna eat me."

"There are no ghost monkeys," I told her firmly. "Where'd you get that idea?"

"Cody," she whispered. I should've known. I'd only lived here two weeks, but I already hated Cody Weathers, a five-year-old brat who went to daycare with Silvie. His parents let him watch anything and everything on TV, which meant he was constantly filling Silvie's little head with bullshit and scary stories.

The worst part? He wasn't even doing it to be mean. So far as I could tell, little Cody had a serious crush on our Silvie girl.

"Cody doesn't know what he's talking about," I said. "Would I lie to you about ghost monkeys?"

She cocked her head at me, then shook it gravely.

"Let's go look in the closet together," I said. "I'll show you it's safe, and then I'll use some of my monster spray just to be sure."

We crawled out of bed. She held my hand while I grabbed a spray can of vanilla-scented air freshener I'd bought for just this purpose. Then we stepped across the hall. I heard murmuring voices from the kitchen—apparently Cookie had company. We were coming up on the one-year anniversary of the death of her husband, Bagger, in Afghanistan. She was doing pretty well all things considered, which meant she wasn't doing that great at all, but she hadn't rolled over and died, either.

Cookie impressed the hell out of me.

"The monkeys were there," Silvie said, pointing to the closet fearfully. I flipped on the bedroom light and walked over to the door, opening it.

"No ghost monkeys," I declared, taking a few seconds to examine every inch, knowing it would make a difference to her. I even checked behind the hanging clothes.

Wasn't the first time I'd had to inspect Silvie's closet for monsters.

"Spray," she demanded.

I coated the small space thoroughly with air freshener.

"There we go," I said. "No way ghost monkeys or any other creatures will get in there now."

"Thank you," Silvie whispered, wrapping her arms around my legs.

"Any time," I muttered, fighting back a yawn. Shit, I needed some coffee. "Let's go find something to eat."

"Mommy's in the kitchen talking to Uncle Deke."

Interesting.

So much for Cookie sleeping in.

"Uncle Deke" came to visit a lot. He was the president of the Portland Reapers chapter, and he'd been looking out for Cookie since she moved down from Coeur d'Alene. I couldn't tell whether he was just taking good care of a brother's widow or there was more going on.

If so, I was pretty sure Cookie hadn't noticed him.

I walked in to find them sitting at the kitchen table, coffee cups between them. A box of doughnuts sat on the counter.

I didn't know Deke very well. He was probably around thirty years old, although hard to tell for sure. I knew he'd been in the Marines before joining the club, so I figured he understood what Cookie was going through better than most. He was a big guy, powerfully built, and one of his arms had been burned pretty bad. Now scars roped it, although it'd missed his hand. Some guys would keep that covered up.

I'd never seen Deke in a long-sleeved shirt.

"These doughnuts for anyone?" I asked, drifting toward the counter.

"Help yourself," Deke answered. He and Cookie had fallen silent, and I wondered what they'd been talking about.

"Silvie, baby, let's go get you dressed," Cookie said. She smiled at me, the hint of sadness she always wore these days firmly in place. Even her hair seemed different since Bagger's death. The wild, red corkscrew curls were somehow flatter.

She took Silvie's hand and walked her out, leaving me alone with Deke.

"How's shit with you?" he asked. I shrugged and smiled.

"Is that you asking or my dad?"

"More me bein' polite than anything," he said, his face unreadable. "You know we're here if you need us, but I got better things to do than babysit. Glad someone's in the house with Cookie, though."

"Yeah, I'm happy to be here," I said. "She's doing me a huge favor. I won't be able to work much once my program gets started, so keeping costs down is pretty important. Win-win for both of us."

My phone buzzed in my pocket, and I pulled it out, offering him a quick look of apology.

"Tell Cookie I said good-bye," he said, standing. I nodded, then looked at my phone.

HUNTER: How you doing?

Shit. I glanced at Deke, but he wasn't paying attention to me at all. Good, because I was pretty sure my guilty vibes were strong enough for him to sense if he bothered.

ME: Good. I thought we weren't going to do this anymore.

I'd told Hunter to stop contacting me at least once a day since the party at his house. I suppose it made me a horrible person, but each time he got back in touch anyway, I felt the thrill all the way through my body.

HUNTER: Yeah . . . about that. I need to see you
ME: Skid was right. I wont be part of ruining you
HUNTER: Skid doesn't know everything. Its more complicated.
  Thats my problem to deal with.
ME: No
HUNTER: Tonight

ME: I'm babysitting Silvie tonight
HUNTER: Then call when she's asleep
ME: I'll think about it

I thought about it, all right. I thought about it all day as I filled in at Cookie's coffee shop. I continued to think about it while I made Silvie dinner (Kraft macaroni, because that shit is good) and while we had a bath (because that shit is messy). We checked for ghost monkeys and I monster-proofed the bedroom before tucking her in for the night. Then I went out into the living room and turned on the TV, still wondering if I should call Hunter.

Probably not.

Absolutely not.

I called Kit instead.

She didn't answer. Not a huge surprise, considering it was a Friday night. Kit wasn't really a stay-at-home-on-the-weekend kind of girl, and apparently she'd met some new man in one of her classes last Tuesday. Kit also wasn't a wait-and-see kind of girl, so I'd be willing to bet she was putting him through his paces right now.

At ten thirty I turned off the TV and changed into a tank and some boxer shorts before slipping into bed. I considered my Kindle. Then I grabbed my phone and texted Hunter.

ME: What's up?
HUNTER: At the house, hanging out. Clutch has a few girls
    over. Says its important to celebrate life or some such shit.
    Think he just wants to get laid as many times as possible
    while the pity fuck thing still works for him
ME: Poor guy
HUNTER: Heh. How about you?
ME: In bed. Silvie is sleeping and Cookie is at a friends house.
    She doesnt get out much so I told her she needed a night off
HUNTER: Hows she doing?

ME: Good I think. I like it here. Feels good to be treated like an
   adult
HUNTER: I'll treat you like an adult . . . Call me?

HUNTER

I stared down at the phone, wondering if she'd do it. I'd promised
myself I'd let her call first. Of course, I'd also promised myself I'd
let her text first, and look at how long that'd lasted.

My phone rang.

Fuckin' beautiful.

"Hunter?"

Her voice was soft and questioning, a whisper in the darkness.
Holy shit, she sounded soft and pretty. Just texting with her was
enough to get my dick up, but hearing her voice?

Made me so hard it hurt.

"Hey," I said, falling back down on my bed. Outside my door
I heard voices and the faint sound of music. Not too loud—the
phone wouldn't pick any of it up. Last thing I needed was her hearing whatever bullshit might be going on downstairs. "Call me
Liam."

"Hi, Liam," she said. Damn. What was it about this girl?

"Fuck, Em. I missed talking to you. So you're in bed?"

"Yeah," she said, and I felt my balls tighten. I reached down and
pushed on my denim-covered cock with the heel of my hand, the
pressure sweet and painful all at once. Those pictures of hers did
me in every time, but they had nothin' on her voice. Husky and
sweet, just for me.

Jesus, I wanted to drive over there and just pound her 'til she
screamed. No, scratch that. I wanted her here, with me. In *my* bed.
Riding my cock. Shouldn't be so goddamned complicated to make
that happen. I'd given almost a decade of my life to the club. Never

complained, never held back. I'd done terrible things for the Devil's Jacks. I'd keep doing them, too.

All I wanted in return was one thing. One girl. Of course it had to be the girl who could start a fucking war with a phone call . . .

I still wouldn't give her up.

"This is bullshit," I muttered. "Let me see you tomorrow. I'll pick you up, we'll go for a ride. Hell, it can be like a date or something."

She laughed.

"Do people still date?"

"Fuck if I know," I admitted. "Not my thing."

"So you're a love-'em-and-leave-'em kind of guy?" she asked, her voice teasing.

"Yeah, but I leave my women happy," I replied, rubbing my hand up and down my dick again. I imagined her lips wrapped around it and my hips arched a little. It took everything I had not to groan. Damn. I couldn't think.

"I don't know what to say to that," she replied softly. "I don't know, Liam. I want to . . . But is it a good idea?"

I gave a short laugh—she had no clue how bad an idea it was.

"No, probably not," I said. "So why don't you tell me what you're wearing instead? No harm in that."

I heard her breath catch. Would she answer?

"I've got a pink camisole, with pink and gray jammie shorts," she said. "It feels weird talking about this. Should I have said I was wearing something sexy from Victoria's Secret?"

"I can't imagine anything sexier than what you just described," I replied, and I meant every word. I'd jacked off to the pictures of her naked a hundred times—and yeah, I get how creepy that is, and no, I don't give a shit—but hearing her talk about her little pink cami was fuckin' hot. Em wasn't some cover model or anything— nice curves without being super stacked. But those tits of hers were perfect for me in every way. Now I pictured them, spread out a little as she lay back in her bed, the nipples making little peaks in the soft fabric of her top.

I wanted to suck them into my mouth and roll them around until she screamed. Maybe bite them when I finally came after fucking her tight cunt for an hour. I slid the zipper on my jeans down, letting my cock pop out. Then I wrapped my hand around it.

"What are *you* wearing?"

"Jeans, an old T-shirt. Nothin' special."

"You look pretty special in jeans," she whispered. Then she gave an awkward giggle. "That was so cheesy. I can't believe I said that."

"I'll take it," I replied, smiling.

"I'm just not real good at this. I mean, I know we've talked at night, but that was before . . . You know."

She didn't want to say it and I sure as shit didn't need her remembering what I'd put her through.

"We're not doing anything," I said, slowly rubbing my cock up and down. I squeezed it hard, watching as fluid beaded up on the tip. "This is just two friends talking, okay?"

"Okay," she said. "But there's something I need to know first."

"Ask," I told her, hoping to hell it was a question I could answer.

"Liam, do you have an old lady tucked away somewhere? I mean, I know I don't have any right to ask, but . . ."

That caught me off guard. What the hell? This was what I got for giving her space, I realized. Was someone filling her head with shit?

"No. Fuck no—where'd that come from?"

"Well, you say you're not into relationships, but a lot of guys say that when they want to get laid," she replied, sounding nervous. "Then it turns out they're already with someone, just looking for something extra on the side. For all I know you're married with ten kids. You've already lied to me about other stuff, and I know some of the brothers keep more than one woman."

I coughed.

"If I was married with ten kids, I wouldn't be talking on the phone with you. I'd be shooting myself in the fucking head."

She laughed.

"So the answer is no?"

"The answer is definitely no," I said. "I've slept around—I'm not ashamed of that. And I lied to you for my club. But I don't have to trick girls to get laid."

"So no more surprises?" she asked.

"No, straight up," I answered, hoping she'd believe me. My phone beeped—another call—but I ignored it.

"Where are we going with this?" she asked. "Has anything changed? Or should we just hang up and end it before things get worse?"

I considered carefully before I answered.

"I don't know," I replied, and for once it was the truth. "You want me to be honest, so I'll be honest. I don't know what's between us because it's not like we've had a chance to explore it. You're different than any other woman I've been with. I actually like talking to you about shit that's not sex, but I won't pretend that fucking you isn't what I think about the most. Just your voice makes my dick stand on end, so I'll take whatever I can get. If that's just a phone call, don't spoil it for me yet, okay?"

She didn't say anything for a moment.

"I just slid my hand down into my boxers," she whispered, and I swear a pint of blood left my brain. "I'm remembering what it felt like when you sucked my nipples. I want to lick your stomach."

My entire body clenched. My fingers slid up my straining cock to find the beads of precome. I palmed my cockhead, then started jacking myself slow and hard.

Yeah, this was what I needed.

"Find your clit," I told her, my voice going low. "Are you wet yet?"

"Yes," she said. "I feel really weird doing this . . . Like I'm a whore or something, because the club—"

"You're not a whore. And don't think about the club. I don't want you thinking about anyone else at all when you're touching yourself, got me? Think about me and what I'm going to do to you the first chance I get."

"What's that?"

"I'll start by sliding my fingers deep inside your pussy, get them nice and wet. Then I might play with your clit."

I heard her breath catch.

"I'm doing that right now," she said. "What about you?"

"I've got my cock out and I'm jerking off while I listen to your voice," I told her bluntly. "My balls are so fucking tight they feel like they're in a vise, and I keep imagining how hot and slick you'd be around me right now."

"Oh," she whispered. Her breath caught again. "You're better than my vibrator, you know that?"

The image of her using that vibrator filled my brain and I lost the power to speak. I felt my balls drawing up, my hand gripping my dick so hard it almost hurt.

Almost.

"How are you doing?" I asked, trying to slow myself down.

"Good," she whispered.

"Tell me about it."

"I'm rubbing my clit, one finger on each side," she told me. "First up and down, and then I sort of wiggle them against each other. I'm using my other hand to play with my nipples. Your turn."

I gave myself another hard tug, hips lifting. Hell, I was getting damned close. Usually I could last for hours, but something about Em fucked with me on every level.

"Jesus, wish I was better with words," I muttered. "Honest to fuck, Em. I'm pretty close to blowing my load. Picturing you getting yourself off makes me feel like I'm gonna have a heart attack."

"You want me to stop?" she asked, her voice almost playful. My dick spasmed and my balls drew up tight. Shit shit *shit*.

"If you stop—" I started to say, and then the door to my room burst open.

"The fuck?" I yelled, sitting up and dropping the phone with a crash.

"Get your ass out here," Skid said, his voice grim.

I decided to shoot him.

I let my cock go and reached for the gun sitting on the bedside table, but he held up a hand.

"You gonna get off the phone?" he asked, giving me a pointed look. I couldn't think—all the blood in my body was currently concentrated in my dick. My balls seized up and I realized I was in for some serious pain.

"Liam, are you okay?" I heard Em's voice, high-pitched and tinny. I reached down and grabbed the phone, pulling myself together.

"It's fine, babe," I said, glaring at Skid. He shook his head and made a slashing motion across his throat. "I have to go, though. Skid needs help with something. I'll talk to you later."

"Wait—" she started to say, but I hung up.

"This had better be really, really fucking important," I told my club brother. "You got shit timing."

"It is," he said. "Put away your joystick and get your ass downstairs. We got serious trouble."

I walked painfully down the narrow stairwell to the living room. Damn house was a hundred years old and it showed. Zipping up my jeans hurt like a bitch and I decided the next time I needed information from someone, I'd torture the fucker by making him talk to Em, then turn off the call and force him to put on my pants.

Like most Friday nights, we'd had company. It hadn't been a formal party, but Skid and the other guys had invited a group of slutty girls over. Not quite a real clubhouse, but better than nothing. Now two of those girls were naked and making out on the couch. Another had passed out cold on the floor and I heard more laughing in the kitchen.

Typical night for us.

It wasn't normal for the girls to be playing alone, though. They were putting on a hell of a show, and it went against everything my club brothers believed in to miss live girl-on-girl action.

"Down here," Skid yelled. I followed his voice to the basement stairs. It was a dankish pit kind of a place, but it had its uses. Smoking out, storing product, laundry, and even one memorable night when this hippie chick did some kind of weird talking-to-spirits thing . . .

It was also where we had church. Not that we were a real chapter or anything, but we essentially functioned as one, complete with formal meetings and the occasional vote.

"This better be fuckin' good," I muttered as I climbed down. Clutch lay back on the ratty couch next to the semifunctional washer and dryer, his bum leg propped up on the armrest. Grass paced back and forth, muttering, while Skid leaned against the washer, fingers tapping a rhythm restlessly against the ancient metal.

"Got news," Grass said, eye twitching. Fuck, was he tweaking? I'd told him no more, but it'd been a rough couple of weeks. He stopped pacing and rubbed his chin mindlessly, the motion spasmodic.

Yup, he was. Great, because we needed one more thing to worry about.

"Toke is dead," Skid said. I glanced at him sharply.

"How?"

"They found him this morning," he replied. "Still in protective custody, but his throat was slit. No explanation. Word just filtered down—I guess Picnic called Burke."

I raised my brows.

"No shit?"

"Gets weirder," he continued. "Reapers want to know how we

pulled it off. Burke bullshitted them, bought us some time to inves-
tigate. He wants to know if you arranged something. You been
playin' games without tellin' the rest of us?"

I cocked my head, feeling something dark building inside me.

"Don't care for your tone, brother," I said slowly and carefully.
"One, I didn't do shit—but if I had, that'd be between me and
Burke. Two, why is Burke talkin' to you and not me?"

Skid offered a twisted smile.

"He called you first, asshole. You didn't answer. What were you
doin' that's more important than takin' a call from your VP? Seein'
as I found you on the phone with your dick hangin' out, you might
wanna consider what you plan to tell him very carefully."

Shit. I shut my eyes and shook my head, rubbing my temples.

"Jesus, Skid," Grass snapped, his voice high-pitched and trembling. "Stop being such a little bitch. What are you, jealous?"

We both looked at him, startled. Grass threw up his hands,
clearly frustrated and even twitchier than before. He wasn't done
yet, either.

"What does Burke want from us?" Grass demanded. "I'll bet it's
the Reapers that took him out. He fucked them over, and now
they're tryin' to blame us. Use it as an excuse to end the truce."

"That doesn't make any sense," Skid snarled. "Jesus, Grass. You
need to lay off that shit, it's makin' you paranoid. Reapers want
peace, too. They don't *need* an excuse to go to war. They wanna
fight, they'll just start shooting. It's entirely possible they killed
Toke—fucker betrayed his club, no surprise there. But I don't think
they'd come callin' if that was the case."

"Don't talk to me like I'm an idiot!"

"Shut the fuck up!" I roared. The two men jumped. "Christ,
what are we, fucking children? Skid—did Burke have anything he
wanted us to do?"

Skid scowled.

"No," he admitted. "Although he said to watch out. Until we

know who killed Toke and why, we need to assume there's a new player."

"Cartel?" Clutch asked. "You think they have the contacts this far north to pull off a hit in protective custody?"

We all stilled. Shit. Not a comforting thought.

"Okay, we need to assume there's someone local we don't know about, someone with that kind of power," I said slowly. "Time for more security. Make sure you check in with each other, and we all start carrying. Grass, when you stop seein' shit that isn't real, I want you to make sure Clutch has a place in his truck that's safe from a search, okay? Can't risk a parole violation. Anyone else need help rigging up something for their bikes?"

"It's covered," Skid said, sighing. "Sorry, Hunter. Didn't mean to be such a dick."

"Fair enough," I muttered, running a hand through my hair. Christ, what a night.

"I fucking hate Portland," Grass announced suddenly. "This town is like hell, only cold. It rains all the time, like we're living underwater, and now we have to worry about the cartel, too? Getting away from them was the only good part about moving north."

"We're doing our jobs," I reminded him, my voice cooling as I moved into enforcer mode. Enough of this shit. "Burke needs us here—we all agreed to it—so stop whining. He wants active intel, and that means we're in Portland until he says otherwise."

Skid crossed his arms, silently backing me up. God, I wanted to kill him sometimes, but I had to give him credit—he always put the club first, and that meant keeping discipline. He never let it get personal.

Grass glared at me, but he closed his mouth. He knew damned well I was right. He also knew I'd make an example of him in a heartbeat if I had to. We couldn't afford kindness, not with the club divided and elections coming.

"We have a problem?" I asked Grass bluntly. He held my gaze a moment longer, then shook his head. I glanced down at Clutch, deciding I was way too sober for this shit.

"You okay?"

"Yeah," he replied. "Leg hurts like a motherfucker, but I'll pop some pills so it's all good."

"Pussy," Skid taunted, rolling his eyes. "Been a full two months since Toke tortured you. You still whining?"

Clutch let out a choked snort and shook his head. The tension broke and just like that, it was all good. Thank fuck for Skid— it'd been a long stretch in this water-logged city without allies, but every time we found ourselves at each other's throats, he'd step in and somehow make it better. The guy had a gift when he chose to use it.

I flipped the guys off and climbed back upstairs.

The chicks on the couch had passed out, and I didn't see anyone in the kitchen. I used my foot to roll the girl on the floor out of my way, grabbed a beer, then flopped down in a chair and clicked on the TV.

Porn. Of course.

Naturally, that made me think of Em fingering herself, and I wondered if I should call her back. I decided not to—it was late and the mood wasn't right. Not only that, I wasn't sure I could handle hearing her husky, sexy little voice calling me Liam again. My balls fucking hurt, and not in a good way.

A few minutes later, Clutch hobbled in and sat down on the couch next to the girls. Together we watched some redhead with giant implants get fucked up the ass on the big screen.

"Shit," Clutch said after a few minutes. "The high-def has totally ruined porn. Are those ingrown hairs?"

I choked on my beer, and he grinned at me.

"Jackass."

CHAPTER TWELVE

Em filled my dreams.

Her ice-blue eyes—surrounded by thick, dark lashes—peeked up at me as she thoughtfully licked the tip of my hard-on, then slowly sucked it into her mouth. I knew she didn't have a hell of a lot of experience, but damn she sucked dick like a pro.

Her hand wrapped around my shaft and I bucked up.

Fuck, that was worth the wait.

Then she drew me even deeper, taking me into her throat, catching me off guard.

How the hell did she know how to do that?

I felt a sudden desire to kill the owner of whatever cock she'd been practicing on. Her tongue flicked the underside of my dickhead, fluttering, and I forgot all about my upcoming murder plans. I stiffened, my balls tight and ready to blow, but my brain was starting to question the whole situation.

What was wrong here?

Em sucked hard, humming deep in her throat as she bobbed

faster and faster. Her other hand reached down between my legs, rolling my balls with her fingers as she sped up. I was close, so I reached down to touch her head, give her a warning.

Wait. Em's hair wasn't this short.

But her mouth was so goddamned hot and wet. Shit. I couldn't think. I'd never dreamed she'd know so many tricks, and some small part of me started to consider murder again. My Em wasn't so innocent anymore, and whoever taught her would answer—

I lost the thought as my load exploded, blowing the world apart. Holy shit, I needed that.

Wait. Those weren't dream lips on my cock.

Adrenaline hit and my eyes opened.

"The fuck?" I demanded, looking down to find one of the carpet munchers from last night slowly licking my come off her lips. I jackknifed up and backhanded her, knocking her off the bed with a crash.

"What the hell is wrong with you? Fucking cunt!"

She clutched her cheek and looked up at me, eyes filling with tears.

"You didn't like it?" she whispered, looking confused. Her pupils were tiny, tiny pinpricks and I saw tracks on her arm. I was lucky she'd sucked me off instead of stealing my wallet or stabbing me. Wait. No. Stealing the wallet would definitely be better . . .

I pulled that shit on a girl, they'd call me a fuckin' rapist.

Goddamned junkie.

"I'm supposed to like some random stranger sneaking into my room and putting her mouth on my dick without asking?" I demanded. "You don't fucking touch me without permission, bitch. Some guy did that to you, you'd be screaming rape. *Christ.*"

I swung my legs out of the bed. She fell backward, scuttling away from me like a crab. I rubbed a hand through my hair, trying to focus.

Shit, but Em had me all twisted up and making stupid mistakes. Men like me don't sleep with the door unlocked. I didn't normally sleep heavy, either—breaking into my room was an invitation to meet my gun, no apologies.

Yet this junkie not only got in, she invaded my dream about Em. *Fuck*.

The bitch pushed to her feet and darted out of the room, which was a damned good thing. If I had to look at her again, I'd throw her through a fucking wall.

Then it hit me.

Since when did a surprise blow job piss me off?

My phone dinged somewhere in the covers. I dug through them, trying to find it. Was it even morning yet?

I found it and saw the time—six a.m. I'd been asleep for two whole hours before Princess Sucky Fucky came in to kiss me awake. I checked my messages, wondering who the hell would be texting me this early. Hell. Burke. His words were short and sweet.

BURKE: We have a situation. Call me

Wasn't that just perfect—exactly what I needed to start my day. But there was a message from Em, too. Sent while I was downstairs drinking beer and watching porn with Clutch.

EM: Hey—thinking of you. Hope everything is okay. I'm sorry you had to go. Also sorry I had to finish by myself . . .

And there went my dick again—so much for the morning head. I pulled on my pants and took a quick piss across the hall. Then I dug out a burner phone and called Burke.

"What's up?" I asked him, hoping to hell it wasn't war with the Reapers. "This about Toke? Was that us?"

"Nope," Burke said. "That's a mystery hit. I wish we had that kind of pull up there. Not that I was upset to get the news . . . But we got a bigger problem. Someone took a couple potshots at Mason last night, at his old lady's house."

"Fuck," I muttered. This was serious. "He okay?"

"Yeah, he's fine," Burke said. "But it's the tipping point—he's done. Says he's held on as long as he can, but that he wants to die with his family, not in the middle of a war."

"Shit." Mason stepping down meant that Burke—as VP— would take over as national president. But not an elected president. Throw in the fact that the club was divided about the Reaper truce and what direction we should be moving . . .

"I wonder if it's an inside job," I mused. "Puts you in a tough spot. Things are already weird with the Toke situation, Reapers are trigger happy. Now you have to take over right as we're lookin' at a war. No vote means you're weak."

"Could be," Burke said. "Hate to think of one of our own doing this. Unfortunately, some of our brothers aren't worth much these days."

"Yup," I said. Damn club was falling apart around our ears. "Of course, it could be the cartel."

"Or the Reapers."

Silence fell for a minute.

"Drake will step up as VP," Burke said. "That means I'll need a sergeant at arms. I know we wanted to wait for elections, but consider this your call, son. I'll need you in Salem tomorrow. Officers are gathering, we'll put you in place then."

I felt myself sway.

I'd been waiting for this a hell of a long time . . . but shit. Things were so up in the air with Em right now, on top of everything else.

"Okay," I said slowly. "And after that?"

"You're with me," he said. "We'll keep Skid and the boys in Portland for now. I still want a presence there, even more important now. Pack your shit, we'll be traveling light. I figure the next few weeks'll get interesting. Bring Skid with you when you come down, got me?"

"Yeah," I said, trying to wrap my head around it. I hung up the burner and sighed, flopping back down on my bed. I needed more sleep. Sleep, and then I'd figure out what the hell I was doing.

I didn't text Em back.

No idea what I'd say to her anyway.

EM

Water hit me in the face.

I screamed, falling out of bed to find my witch of a sister standing over me, laughing her ass off.

Note to self: Tell Cookie to never let Kit in the house again.

"You're a bitch," I muttered, wiping off my face with the sheet.

"True," she said thoughtfully. "But I'm the bitch who's here to take you shopping. I need a new purse."

"They don't have stores in Olympia?"

"They have stores," she said. "But they don't have my sister. I'm so excited to have you close—it's like we're back in high school again!"

"You were a bitch then, too."

She picked up my phone.

"Oohhh," she said. "What happened last night? I see a long phone call to Hunter and then a text saying you finished alone? You want to tell me what that's all about?"

I climbed out of bed and pulled off my cami, flinging it at her. It landed on her head and dripped water into her hair, but she didn't even seem to notice.

"We talked for a while," I said. "Then he had to go. What time is it?"

"Almost noon," she said absently. "So you can't really blame me for throwing water on you. How else would I wake you up?"

"Some people use words."

"Boring people. You want to shower before we go? I really do need a purse. We'll go shopping, then come back here and fix dinner for Cookie. Then Kelsey and I are taking you dancing."

"Kelsey?"

"Hunter's sister," she said. "We've been in touch. No offense, but I think me and her have way more in common than me and you. She's in touch with her inner bitch, and she's not afraid to go after what she wants."

"I'm not afraid."

"I see that," she said, holding up the phone with a wicked grin. "I'm really proud of you. You should try calling him now."

She hit a button and handed me the phone already ringing. I glared at her, but it was too late to hang up. He'd know I called, so might as well play it through. Unfortunately, he didn't answer.

"Hey, it's me," I said, glaring at Kit. "Just wanted to make sure you're okay. I'll talk to you later."

I hung up.

"Good," Kit said. "You've made a move. Now you're going to leave your phone here while we shop, so you can't answer if he calls back."

"Why?"

"Don't want to sound too eager," she said thoughtfully. "You not only talked to him last night, but you've already texted and called, too."

"I didn't call," I said pointedly.

"He doesn't know that. You want to shower before we go? No offense, but you look like shit."

"I'm not sure I like living closer to you."

"You love me and you know it."

Unfortunately, I did.

Six hours later we pulled back into Cookie's driveway, the car full of Chinese carryout and three new purses. Two for Kit and one for me. Not that I needed a new bag, but it would've been rude not to buy anything at all, right?

"Sorry we aren't cooking," I apologized as I walked in the door. "We sort of lost track of time. Hope takeaway is all right?"

Cookie glanced up from the couch, where she sat reading with Silvie.

"If I don't have to cook it, I don't care where it comes from," she said. "Silvie, help me clear off the coffee table. Let's have a picnic out here, sound good?"

Silvie loved that idea, and after another five minutes we were opening boxes of hot, steaming food.

"Where are you girls going tonight?" Cookie asked.

"Just downtown," Kit said. "Meeting up with a friend, doing some dancing. That kind of thing."

"Be careful," Cookie said. "Deke tells me things are a little unsettled."

"He give any details?" I asked.

"No," she said. "But if it was serious, they'd let us know. Just don't get too drunk, okay?"

We promised, finishing our dinner. Then we got slutted up in my room and I realized I'd gone all afternoon without my phone. I searched through my covers, turning it on hopefully.

Hunter hadn't called, though.

Nope, just a quick text.

HUNTER: Sorry I had to go last night. I'll catch up with you later. Lot going on

"That's not very exciting," Kit said, biting her lip thoughtfully. "He should be all over you by now."

"Well, he said he was busy."

"No man is too busy to get laid," she replied, her voice knowing. "Speaking of, that's what you'll be doing tonight. I've made up my mind."

"What?"

"Getting laid. Before we leave the club tonight, we're finding someone for you to sleep with. Hunter wants a piece of your ass, he'll have to stand in line."

"Do I get a vote in this?" I asked, rolling my eyes.

"Do you ever?"

Kit made good on her threat. Ten minutes after we walked into the club, she'd scoped out six different guys she'd decided might be worthy of my bed. I flipped her off and bought myself a beer. I wasn't interested in sleeping with some random asshole in a bar.

Still, as the night progressed and no word from Hunter, I got a little annoyed. I'd had phone sex with him just the night before, and now nothing? Not that he owed me anything. I knew that. But the fact that I didn't have the right to be annoyed was even more annoying.

I drank another beer.

An hour later Kelsey joined us at the club. She was definitely a little rough around the edges, but I decided I liked her. She and Kit really were alike in so many ways it was scary. Put them together on the dance floor and the men didn't have a chance.

Not that I did too poorly myself.

I had no intention of bringing anyone home, but after a while I found a cute guy to hang out with. His name was Devon, he was tall and somewhat built, and he smelled pretty good when he wrapped his arms around me. He had clean-cut looks, the total opposite of Hunter in every way. Kit gave me a silent thumbs-up in approval. Kelsey told me pointedly that her brother could kick his ass without even noticing.

I told Kelsey that Hunter wasn't around, so he couldn't kick anyone's ass. She flipped me off and I decided she could go screw herself, along with her stupid brother who couldn't call me back after hanging up mid-phone-sex. Fortunately, Devon was a great distraction. We alternated dancing, talking, and drinking, and gradually I learned that he was in as fucked-up a nonrelationship as mine.

Well, maybe not *quite* as fucked-up. I didn't ask, but so far as I could tell, he hadn't actually been involved in a kidnapping.

But other than that, things were about the same.

It made him the perfect partner for the evening, and it got Kit off my back, too. Of course, Kelsey continued to scowl at me, but I didn't give a shit about her. I might like her all right, but I wasn't looking for a new best friend. Anyway, once I established Devon as "safe," I let myself go and enjoyed his company, leaving Ms. Grumpy scowling behind me. We danced to almost every song, and nothing I did was too dorky for Devon.

To be fair, he was kind of dorky himself, and so funny I got to the point where I couldn't stop laughing. Seriously. I had this giant laughing fit and I couldn't stop and he kept doing weirder dance moves and it was insane.

"Make it end," I gasped, clutching my stomach. "I'm gonna puke if you don't stop."

He stopped. Abruptly.

"Oh my God, I can't believe how weird you are," I giggled, but he didn't laugh back or smile or anything. I cocked my head.

"What's wrong?" I asked.

"Your friend is going home now," a deep, familiar voice said behind me. "Right?"

Devon nodded, then took off without even saying good-bye. *Rude.* I turned slowly to find Hunter behind me, his sister standing next to him, smirking.

"What the hell are you doing here?"

"I've been looking for you," he said. "I tried calling but you never answered. Then I happened to talk to Kelsey and she mentioned you were here."

I narrowed my eyes at Kelsey, who didn't even bother trying to look innocent.

"You had all day to get in touch with me," I told Hunter, bracing my hands on my hips. "Now I've made other plans. I'm hanging out with my sister tonight. Family first."

"Kit took off with some guy half an hour ago," Kelsey said smugly. "She texted you a heads-up and made me promise to make sure you got home safe."

My eyes widened, and I whipped out my phone. Sure enough, there was a missed call and a text from Kit. There were also three missed calls and two texts from Hunter.

Oops.

Guess I'd silenced it completely, instead of just putting it on vibrate.

"What the hell is she thinking?" I muttered. "Kit's lost her mind. And I'm sorry I didn't get your messages, Hunter, but I do have the right to go out and enjoy myself. You had no business running off Devon, either."

"He was pretty easy to run off," Hunter said, his tone dry. Then his face grew serious. "Em, I really need to talk to you. Think we can get out of here?"

I wanted to tell him no, to take himself right to hell. He'd left me hanging and then he hadn't gotten back in touch all day . . . But his face said this was important, so indulging myself in a snit was probably off the table.

Deke said things were unsettled.

Fuck.

"Yeah, let's get out of here," I said. We grabbed our stuff and walked Kelsey to her car. I'd be having words with Kit later, I decided, thumb-typing her a quick update. I knew it wasn't the first time she'd taken off with a random pickup, but she really needed to be more careful. I loved my sister so much, but for all her personality and spark, she had a pretty strong self-destructive streak.

It scared me sometimes.

"Bike's this way," Hunter said, catching my hand as Kelsey drove off. He tugged me toward an alley and I followed.

"What's going on?" I asked, feeling awkward. "Obviously something is wrong. Is it us? Club drama? I swear to God, if you kidnap me again, I'll let them kill you this time."

I said it like a joke, but I wasn't entirely kidding. That shit was *not* going to be my new way of life.

"I have to leave tomorrow," Hunter said, starting down the alley. It was dark and while I could hear people, I couldn't see anything but the narrow path between the buildings. I started to get that uncomfortable feeling again. I tried to tug my hand loose, but he wouldn't let me go.

Fuck.

I stopped, digging in my heels.

"I'm not going anywhere with you unless you tell me what's happening," I said, eyes darting as I scoped out my options. It wasn't particularly promising. The narrow passage was dark, and a big Dumpster blocked the street view.

Great. Was I walking into another trap?

"Club business," Hunter said, tugging on my hand again. I refused to move. "Em, I'm not trying to do anything. My bike's on the other side of the block. I just figured this would be faster than walking all the way around."

I studied his face, trying to decide if he was fucking with me. Shadows covered his face, making him look like some kind of comic-book villain.

"I'm calling a cab," I said abruptly, reaching for my phone.

"Fuck it," Hunter muttered, and then he grabbed my waist, lifting me and carrying me two steps to the wall. He shoved me up against it. Then his hand was in my hair, twisting to hold me captive for his kiss.

He took my mouth hard, forcing me to open for his tongue. Then he was inside and I thought I might die because it felt so good. His other hand pushed up my shirt, shoving the cup of my bra up and over my boob, palming me as his hips pushed into my stomach.

Whatever other bullshit Hunter might have going on in his life, one thing was for sure.

He hadn't lost interest in having sex with me.

Of course, *that* had never been our problem. His mouth tore loose as we both took deep, gasping breaths and stared at each other. Then his hands came down under my ass, hoisting me and wrapping my legs around his waist. My short skirt pushed up around the tops of my thighs, but I didn't give a shit.

Nope.

All I cared about was the unreal, amazing sensation of his denim-covered cock against my panties. He started that slow thrust that'd destroyed me last time. My head fell back against the brick wall. I'd probably have some scrapes there in the morning.

I didn't give a shit.

I wrapped my arms around his neck and thrust against him, desperate to feel him inside me. God. Oh God, I wanted this man. More than sex, too. I knew in that moment I was well and truly screwed, because nothing had ever felt more right in my life than his arms around me, and it had nothing to do with sex.

Well, maybe a little . . .

"You have a condom?" I gasped. Hunter didn't stop the hard, spasmodic thrust of his hips, but I swear he growled.

"Yeah, but it shouldn't be like this. Fuck, Em. You deserve so much better than what I have to offer you."

"Just screw me already."

He froze against me, panting, then set me down with a groan. I reached down to pull off my panties and stuffed them into the little purse hanging from my shoulder. Hunter ripped his pants open, and I watched in panting fascination as he rolled on a condom.

Then his hands reached for my thighs, shoving up the skirt as he lifted me again. Jesus, he was so strong, it was like I weighed nothing. I felt his cock against my bare skin as I wrapped my legs around him, his length silky steel against my opening. Then my back hit the wall and he shoved into me.

I screamed.

Holy shit. I'd expected Hunter to go slow for the first time . . . (Although I'd expected to be in a bed, too, not some nasty alley.) Instead, he slammed home and I felt it all the way in the back of my throat. I cried out again, then leaned forward and bit the side of his neck. His cock jerked inside me as he groaned. Then he started moving.

I don't even know how to describe what I felt. Hunter didn't hold back at all, nothing. I took all of him and I knew I'd be sore as hell in the morning, but I didn't give a shit. The stretch of his cock deep inside, the pain of his fingers digging into my ass cheeks?

I loved it.

My body was a mess of lust and longing and desire, all trapped inside for way too long. I didn't care that people were walking up and down the street not ten yards away. I could smell the trash from the Dumpster, I could see the strip of stars shining above us through the tops of the buildings, and it all just added to the intensity of the moment. I felt encapsulated, caught up in a moment that would last forever.

Objectively, we didn't hold on for very long.

Hunter's cock dragged along my clit with every thrust, and he paused to grind himself against me in a way that pushed me right up to the edge of sanity. Then he pulled back and slammed into me again. I swear the tip of his cock tried to push through my cervix, he went so deep.

That did it.

I cried as I blew up, clenching down on him deep inside while my fingernails tried to dig through the leather of his cut.

Holy shit . . .

Hunter grunted and thrust four more times, and then he came, too, cursing. I couldn't believe nobody heard us or tried to see what we were doing. If they had, I wouldn't have given a shit.

I'd done it.

I've finally done it, I realized with a thrill, tears rolling down my face. I didn't even care that my back was raw, or that I'd be walking funny for a week. I didn't regret any of it, not for an instant.

"Well, that was pretty good," I said after a minute, sniffling.

Hunter grunted, lowering me to my feet.

"Glad it was adequate," he said wryly, leaning down to kiss the tip of my nose. I pulled away from him, straightening my skirt and digging for my panties. Now I felt weirdly embarrassed.

"Um, can you turn around and give me some privacy?" I asked.

Hunter just looked at me, a strange expression on his face.

"No."

Well, that was direct. I decided getting out of the alley was more important than exploring our postcoital boundaries, so I pulled up my panties with as much dignity as I could under the circumstances. Hunter caught my hand, tugging me back into his body. His hand slid into my hair again, this time the fingers gentle, and he kissed my bruised lips softly.

"That was fuckin' incredible, babe."

"Yeah. I know," I said, smirking through my still-watery eyes. I must've looked like a clown.

Hunter smacked my ass.

"Don't get cocky on me yet," he muttered. "I'm not finished with you."

Unfortunately, he *was* finished, because that's when everything fell to shit.

CHAPTER THIRTEEN

HUNTER

Em's phone blew up first.

We'd just reached the bike when the first call came through. She dug it out of her purse and frowned down at the number.

"It's Dad," she muttered. "I wonder if he has radar that tells him I just did something he'd hate?"

She sent the call to voice mail, laughing up at me like we shared a secret, which I guess we did. But then the cell went off again. This time it was Cookie.

"Shit," Em swore. "Do you think he called her?"

"Answer," I told her, feeling uncomfortable. Things had gone way too well this evening—we were due for disaster. She nodded and took the call, and I knew it was bad by the way she gasped and swayed. That was when my own phone went off. Burke.

"Yeah?" I answered.

"We got a serious problem," he said. "Mason is dead."

"Fuck," I said, keeping a close eye on Em. She'd started pacing with short, jerky strides. "I didn't realize we were quite so close to the end."

"It wasn't the cancer that got him," Burke replied, his voice grim. "Someone shot him execution-style in his own bedroom. His old lady found him. She was out of the house when it happened, thank fuck."

"He was alone?" I asked, startled. Mason shouldn't have been alone, retirement plans or not.

"No," Burke said. He paused, and my stomach sank, because nothing good happens after pauses like that one. "He had two brothers with him, Tucker and Dob. They think Tucker's gonna pull through. Dob was DOA."

"Fuck," I muttered. I glanced over at Em, who was dialing frantically. Whatever was going on there, it wasn't good, either. "What do you need from me?"

"Get back to the house and lock everything down," he said. "We've got three more reports of shots fired at different clubhouses, although no more injuries. This wasn't just a hit. This is a declaration of war."

"War with who?"

"Reapers or cartel," he said. Em seemed to be arguing with someone over the phone. So fuckin' pretty, I'd take her again right on the spot If I could. Damn. I hoped to hell I wouldn't have to face off against her dad. "We figure it out, we hit them back hard. Plan on coming down tomorrow like we talked about, but take extra precautions to stay safe."

"Got it," I said, hanging up the phone. Em was still talking.

"Dad, I don't know where Kit is," she said. "If I knew, I'd tell you. For fuck's sake, I realize this isn't a game. Keep trying to call her and I'll do the same, sooner or later she'll have to look at her phone. She wouldn't make us worry on purpose, but she's probably busy right now."

She paused again, giving me a quick look.

"She's busy having sex, Dad," she muttered. "No, I'm going home right now. And don't send someone to get me—I have a ride."

She fell silent again, and my stomach churned. If the Reapers were behind this, wouldn't they have gotten her safe before it went down? Picnic wouldn't risk his girls, I decided. And I couldn't see them pulling off something this big without him on board.

Had to be the cartel.

"I'm with someone," Em was saying. "He can give me a ride. Honest, it's safe. He'll protect me."

Her eyes met mine. Then she took a deep breath and answered the question I couldn't hear but I could sure as shit guess at.

"I'm with Hunter, Dad," she said. Fire didn't explode out of the phone, which kind of surprised me. I did hear yelling, and then Em's face tightened.

"Deal with it," she snapped. "He'll keep me safe and give me a ride. But only if you promise the guys at Cookie's house won't do anything to him. Otherwise I'll go to a hotel . . . I'll get myself safe, but I won't tell you where I am. I won't let you use me to find him or hurt him."

Something tightened in my chest and I couldn't breathe for a second. I felt a surge of possessive pride in my girl. I wanted to grab her, kiss her hard, and then fuck her up against another wall. Or pretty much anywhere else, for that matter—the list of places I'd fantasized about doing her was nearly endless. She gave a frustrated growl, hanging up the phone.

"Things aren't so good at home," she said with quiet understatement. "I don't want to be a hassle, but I think we need to find a hotel room."

Normally I'd consider that was a great fuckin' idea, but tonight was anything but the usual. She needed to be under guard. Much as I hated to admit it, right now the Reapers were her best bet for protection.

"Give me the phone."

She shook her head.

"Em, give me the fuckin' phone," I growled. "I don't know what's happening on your end, but a bunch of my brothers got shot up in the last hour and two of them are dead. I don't have time to argue with you or find you a goddamned hotel when you should be with your club. I want you safe so I don't have to worry about you."

"We lost a brother in Boise tonight," she said slowly. "Dad wants me locked down. They think it was Jacks, Liam . . ."

My name on her lips twisted something up inside my chest. Looking back, I think that's the instant I made my decision. I wasn't going to give her up. Ever. I'd die first.

"It wasn't the Jacks," I told her. We'd have to talk about "us" later. I needed time to think, and I wanted her ass off the street. For once, I agreed with Hayes. "Please, Em. Let me talk to him."

She shook her head slowly, but she handed over the phone and I hit the callback button.

"Baby, we don't have time to argue," Picnic said.

"It's Hunter."

Silence.

"What are you doing with my daughter?" he demanded, his voice like ice. He didn't give anything away, but he had to be scared for his children. Last time we'd talked like this, I'd threatened to kill her. Hell, I completely understood why he hated me after that. Sometimes I hated me, too.

"I'm trying to take her somewhere safe," I said, my voice steady. Unthreatening, but not showing any weakness, either. "I think the best place—at least for tonight—is with the Reapers, but I need more information. We've got two men dead. If that wasn't you, now would be a good time to tell me. My brothers will want blood."

More silence. Then he spoke.

"It wasn't us. We've got our own casualties. One dead, two in the ER. Someone took potshots at four clubhouses, including Portland. Care to tell me what you and your brothers were doin' earlier tonight?"

Your daughter, up against a wall in a dirty alley.

Yeah, probably best not to mention that.

"The Jacks aren't behind this. It's the cartel. Has to be. Unless you know another crew we've both pissed off? Because someone executed our national president tonight, and fingers are already pointing your direction."

"Fuck me . . ." Picnic said slowly. Silence fell between us as we processed the situation. "You playin' games with me?"

"I wish to hell this was a game," I said. I reached out and pulled Em into my side, eyes sweeping the street for danger. I wanted her behind walls. "I want to take her home, Pic. Only way that happens is if you give me safe passage. No fuckin' way I'm letting her go to a hotel without protection, so if I can't take her to her people, she'll be staying with me."

"She with you voluntarily?"

"Yup," I replied.

"Shit," he muttered. Then he sighed. "Daughters are a curse. The other one isn't even answering her phone . . . At least Em's safe right now, although I hate to give you credit for that. Can't say the same about Kit."

"We're in the open here," I told him, losing patience. "No reason they'd know where I am, but I'm not comfortable just standing on the street. Tell me where to take her."

"Bring her to Cookie," Picnic said. "I'll call Deke, he'll make sure you get in and back out without trouble."

About fuckin' time.

"Hunter?"

"Yeah?"

"Thank you for protecting her. You get her home safe, I'll consider it a personal favor."

I felt a grim smile steal across my face. He wouldn't thank me if he had any clue what I'd been doing to his baby girl fifteen minutes ago . . . Or what I had every intention of doing to her again as soon as I got her alone in a room with a bed. Little Emmy had a trip around the world in her future.

I shook my head, trying to clear the mental image. Damn.

"I don't need your favors," I told Picnic. "Tell me about Kit. You can't get hold of her?"

"She's not answering her phone," he muttered. "Em says she took off with some guy, but she doesn't know what he looks like. Fuck, Kit drives me crazy. Odds are good this prick's got nothin' to do with our situation, but I'm not gonna breathe easy until we find her."

"My sister saw the guy," I said. "Want me to have her call you?"

"I'd appreciate that."

I hung up and handed the phone back to Em. Her eyes were haunted.

"How'd it go?" she asked. I shrugged.

"Hard to tell. Not as bad as it could've—he says it's safe to take you home, and I believe him. He wants you behind walls more than he wants me dead. Let's go."

I swung a leg over my bike and she hopped up behind me. A true child of the MC, she didn't think twice about climbing on in her little skirt. I kicked the scoot to life and we took off.

EM

Cookie's small front yard was full of motorcycles. Like, *full* of motorcycles. Half the Portland brothers must've been there, which wasn't a good sign.

Hunter still insisted on walking me to the door, despite the fact that two prospects stood in the yard eyeing him. In theory this was safe. Dad should've called ahead, made sure they knew he was coming . . . But walking into a Reaper stronghold with a Devil's Jack felt like tempting fate.

Deke himself opened the door. He and Hunter were about the same height, although Deke's build was heavier. Seeing them together, I was struck by how similar they were. Not in appearance . . . No, more in the way they held themselves, casually poised for violence, faces blank. I'd heard rumors about Deke over the years. They said he made people who caused trouble for the club go away. I glanced at Hunter with new eyes, realizing he'd never actually told me what he did for the Jacks.

Did he make people go away, too?

"Thanks for bringing her home," Deke said, reaching for my arm. Hunter met his gaze, then took my chin and turned my head toward him. He leaned over and kissed me, slow and deliberate.

That kiss had nothing to do with sex. Nope, this was all about marking territory.

Dad's head was going to *explode*.

"She's here because you'll keep her safe," Hunter said. "Don't know if Picnic told you, but we have our own problems tonight. I'm assuming we all got hit by the same crew."

"Maybe," Deke said, his eyes cold. "I find out you're behind this, I won't kill you fast, boy."

Holy shit. Deke was *scary*.

"Night, Em," Hunter said, ignoring the Portland president's threat. He leaned forward and whispered in my ear. "I'll call you later. Might not be right away, but don't worry."

Then he turned his back on us and walked back down to his bike. There was something almost cocky about the way he moved. Like he was taunting Deke. The Portland president pulled me into the house, shutting the door behind us. I tried to pass through to the kitchen, but he blocked me.

"Your dad know you're fuckin' the enemy?"

I swallowed, but I held firm.

"I'm an adult, Deke. What I do is my business."

He crossed his arms and eyed me, something almost like disgust in his face.

"You're a spoiled brat," he said bluntly. "You and your sister both. I've never given a shit about that because you're not my kid and you're not my old lady."

I gasped.

"Here's the thing, though," he continued. "You do anything— *anything at all*—that puts Cookie and Silvie in danger, I'll kill you myself. We clear?"

I'd never had anyone talk to me like that. I knew my eyes must be wide and I had no idea what the hell I should say to him.

"Em!" Cookie called, running into the living room. Her face was red, like she'd been crying. She pushed past Deke to catch me in her arms, hugging me tight. "I can't believe what's happening. When Picnic called because he couldn't get hold of you . . . I was terrified."

"It's all right," I said, watching Deke over her shoulder. His face was still blank. Had I imagined what just happened? "I'm safe now. No word from Kit, though."

Cookie pulled away.

"Shit," she muttered. "I hoped she'd be in touch by now. You know anything about the guy she took off with? Your dad is nervous. He's thinking it might be one of them . . . whoever they are. The shooters hit a pipe at the clubhouse, flooded the whole place. That's why the guys are all here tonight."

"It wasn't the Devil's Jacks," I said firmly, and I believed it. The look of shock on Hunter's face had been too real.

"We don't know who it was," Deke said. "And you don't need to worry about that right now, anyway. Jumping to conclusions gets people killed. We'll figure it out and then we'll take care of business. Em, you keep trying to get hold of your sister, okay? Cookie, you might as well go to bed. Doesn't matter how much drama we have tonight, Silvie'll still be up at the crack of dawn and she'll need her mama."

"What about work?" Cookie asked him. "I'm supposed to open the shop tomorrow morning. I have a sitter coming over."

Deke shook his head slowly.

"Either call someone in to cover for you or I'll have one of the boys put a note on the door."

Cookie got a funny look on her face.

"I'm a business owner, Deke," she said. "I can't just close up for the day."

"You can tomorrow," he said. "Until I know what's goin' on, you're staying where it's safe and I can have my guys watching you."

Cookie crossed her arms, her face growing wary.

"I'm not an old lady anymore," she said slowly. "In fact, I'm not attached to the club at all. Just because you guys check in on me doesn't mean I'm a target. Or I wasn't, until everyone parked their bikes on my lawn and made this your new headquarters."

"Listen to me very carefully," Deke said softly. "You're one of ours, and you always will be. But I can't afford to keep too many men on you. That means I need you and Silvie in one place, where I know you're safe, so I can focus on what needs to be done. Either find someone to cover for you or the shop stays closed. Your call."

He turned and walked away, leaving both of us staring at him.

"Fucked-up night," Cookie muttered.

"No shit," I answered, my voice subdued. "I think I'll try calling Kit again. You going to do what he says?"

She nodded slowly, her eyes thoughtful.

"For now. They shot Swinger in Boise. He was a friend of Bagger's, you know. Best man at our wedding."

I looked over to find her twisting her wedding ring around her finger absently.

"I'm going to bed," she said suddenly. "But come and get me if you hear from Kit, okay?"

"Okay."

HUNTER

The ride down to Salem the next morning was fucking cold. It'd
started raining right on the edge of Portland. Not bad. Just enough
to make the trip utterly miserable. Some asshole in a Hummer
nearly took out Skid on the freeway, which almost got ugly, seeing
as we were both trigger happy and paranoid as hell.

Dickwad came damned close to getting shot.

When we pulled up to the Salem clubhouse, I saw a good fifty
bikes parked outside. I'd known officers would be coming, but this
was a bigger turnout than I'd expected.

Guess war will do that.

Skid and I backed our bikes into the line. He glanced over at
the prospects standing guard, then gestured at me to wait before
going in.

"Kelsey says you were with Em last night?" he asked. I bristled.

"I put Kelsey on a plane at six this morning. Picked her up at her
place, and she won't land for another hour. When the fuck did you
talk to her?"

He just looked at me, and I clenched my teeth.

"I knew it," I muttered. "She deserves better than you."

"It's none of your business," he said.

"What I do with Em is none of your business, either."

"Different situation. Fuckin' Kelsey doesn't put anyone in danger but me, and I'm pretty sure you won't kill me outright unless I
knock her up or something . . . But this shit with Em hurts the
whole club, bro. You need to go in there and tell Burke."

"Don't lecture me, asshole. I know that. Or are you saying I
can't handle myself?"

"So long as you put the club first," Skid said. "Burke needs us.
Remember that."

"Trust me, I never forget," I snapped. "And don't hurt my
sister."

Skid snorted.

"I wouldn't worry about that if I was you."

"What the hell is that supposed to mean?"

"Ask her," Skid muttered. "Trust me, she's not the victim here."

The atmosphere in the clubhouse was darker than I'd ever seen it. Burke sat in the back, talking to several of the chapter presidents. His eyes caught mine as I walked in, and he gestured me over. I realized this was it—decision time.

Might as well get it over with.

"I need a moment, Burke."

He tilted his head, considering. Then he nodded.

"In my office," he said. He stood and I followed him down the hallway, wondering how the next ten minutes would play out. You never knew with Burke. He'd been like a father to me . . . But he'd also taught me to kill.

He couldn't afford to show mercy, especially not right now.

"Shut the door," he said, sitting back in his chair. "What is it?"

"It's Emmy Hayes," I said, figuring it didn't make sense to be anything less than direct. "I fucked her last night and I'm pretty sure I'll be doing it again in the near future. Hopefully on a regular basis."

He studied me, eyes cold like a snake's. Sometimes I wondered why Burke helped me kill Jim all those years ago. At the time I thought he was saving us, that he didn't like seeing two kids suffer. In retrospect, I wasn't so sure.

Burke was always ten moves ahead of the rest of us. Had he seen an angry teenager and decided I might suit his purposes some day? The chance to shape a valuable asset for the club? I'd probably never know.

"You with her last night?"

"Yup," I said, holding his gaze. "That's why I'm convinced it was the cartel that hit us. I talked to Picnic right after it happened. He had no idea I was with her and no time to put together a story.

He played tough, but the man was scared shitless for his kids—scared enough to give me safe passage to take her home. Her dumbass sister was still missing, by the way."

"Interesting," he said, betraying nothing. "I know when we started this, you thought keeping her around would work out for you . . . That was under very specific conditions. Apparently those conditions have changed—you're obviously emotionally invested—and that's not so convenient for my plans. How serious are you about this?"

"Pretty serious," I admitted. "I'm not sure where we're going, but I won't give her up without a fight."

Silence fell between us. I held his eyes steadily, refusing to soften what I'd just said or back down.

"I'll need you to talk to the others," he said finally. "Explain your relationship with her, including your plans and how they differ from the original arrangement. I won't have this used against me. Of course, that kills any hope you have for leadership, at least for now."

"I understand."

Yeah, I understood. But it hurt.

"There's some good that can come of this, though," Burke said thoughtfully. "I'll have you talk about Hayes's reaction, explain why it reinforces the cartel theory. We've got hotheads pushing for retaliation against the Reapers. They don't want to believe the cartel has the reach to pull off an attack like this."

"So you think it was the cartel?"

"I'm certain of it," he said, his voice grim. "I've met the Reapers' president, Shade. He's a good man. This isn't his style. The others don't want to accept that, though. They'd rather blame another MC than admit we're really at war with the cartel."

I nodded, because he was right. Fighting the Reapers was weirdly safe, almost comfortable in a strange way. We all knew the rules and what to expect from each other.

"Like I said, this pretty much kills any chance you have to go

higher in the Jacks," Burke continued. "So you'll stay in Portland.
At some point I'd like to see a true chapter started there, assuming
we can get the Reapers to sign off on it. Deke's still pretty pissed at
us over his niece, and I'm sure the Toke situation didn't help things.
That happens, you'll have another shot at leadership. Until then, I'll
still expect you to be available for delicate assignments. You'll have
to get a regular job, though. I'll make sure you still get a bounty
when it's warranted, but the others won't tolerate a man on payroll
who's sleeping with the enemy. And they're still the enemy, at least
in most minds. We clear?"

I thought about Em and nodded. She was worth the sacrifice—
assuming things worked out. Shit . . . This was happening too fast.
Something must have crossed my face, because Burke paused.

"How sure are you of this girl?" he asked.

I considered the question, reluctant to answer. Would've been
nice to pin Em down, spend a little more time together first . . .

"Not as sure as I'd like," I admitted finally. "I mean, we don't
have anything arranged formally, and her dad hates me. All her
people do. But she stood up for me last night, so that's something—
even told her father we were together. That means I've got a shot,
and God hates a coward."

Burke snorted.

"You're an idiot," he said flatly. "Believe it or not, I can understand giving things up for a woman. I really can. But giving away
everything for a girl you barely know? I'm saying this as someone
who cares about you—you're a fuckwit. You're lucky I need you to
convince the others the Reapers aren't behind this attack. We don't
save this truce, the cartel's already won."

"Hope they listen," I murmured.

"Won't hurt that you're throwing everything away to tell them,"
Burke said offhandedly. "Of course, your judgment is obviously
fucked, so it balances out."

I shrugged.

"Can I ask a question?" I said. Burke was the closest thing I had to a father, but I was all too aware that I didn't really know him at all.

"You can ask," he said.

"If it wasn't for what happened last night—if you didn't need me to convince the club it wasn't the Reapers—would you still let me have her?"

Burke laughed, but there wasn't any humor in his voice.

"Romeo and Juliet died, son. Consider that all the answer you need."

CHAPTER FOURTEEN

EM

Kit finally called at four in the morning.

"What the hell is going on?" she demanded, and for once there wasn't a hint of playfulness or laughter in her voice. "I just saw my phone—there's about a hundred messages here. I want to know what I'm getting into before I get hold of Dad. Do you think I should wait a couple hours to make the call, when he's awake?"

"Definitely don't wait until later," I told her, keeping my voice low. The house was crawling with people, and I didn't want to wake anyone up if I didn't have to. We were all exhausted. "Someone tried to shoot Shade last night in Boise. Swinger is dead. Not only that, they shot up some of the clubhouses, including Portland. Everyone's been scared you were kidnapped or murdered or something."

"Oh my God. I'm calling Dad right now."

She hung up on me, and I flopped back down on my bed, throwing an arm over my eyes. What a clusterfuck. Ten minutes later my phone rang again.

"*You were with Hunter last night!?*" Kit demanded, her voice incredulous. "Dad says he brought you home. What the hell is going on? It's like the world turned upside down while I was getting laid."

"Yeah, I was with Hunter."

"You want to give me the details on that?"

"I'm not sure even I know the details. We had sex, but before we could talk about anything our phones blew up and everything fell apart. He took me home and then left. Hopefully I'll hear from him today."

"I hate to say this, but have you considered he might be playing you again?" she asked quietly. "I know I'm the one who dragged you over to his place last weekend . . . But I didn't think there was any danger then. Now people are dying. This is bad shit, Em, and Dad says the Devil's Jacks could be behind it. He wants us to come home."

"Hunter's not playing me," I said firmly. "You didn't see how he reacted last night—totally shocked. Someone tried to kill their president, too. He's dead now, along with another Jack. They got hit worse than we did."

"Sweet baby Jesus on a stick. That's fucked up."

Hard to argue.

"Where are you?" I asked. "I'm assuming Dad told you to come to Cookie's place? I guess this is where we're holing up for now. The Portland clubhouse had some water damage. Nobody got hurt, but one of the bullets burst a pipe, of all things. Weird."

"Deke's sending someone for me right now. Not sure whether I'll make it back up to school tomorrow or not. Dad wants to arrange some kind of family emergency leave or something. Next week is Thanksgiving break, so that'll give me a little breathing room. I was planning on driving over on the Wednesday before, but even if I head back to school, I'll leave the minute classes end. I know it isn't like me, but I want to be with Dad, Em. This is scary shit, and I don't like the idea of him alone."

I snorted.

"Dad is never alone."

"You know what I mean," she replied. "He's always had you to keep an eye on him. I know he's a big bad MC president, but we both know how lonely he gets. Why do you think he drags home all those losers to sleep with?"

"Because he's horny," I said, my tone flat. Sometimes the truth isn't pretty. "I'm not going back. I just got away from him for the first time in years, and he'll use this as an excuse to try and keep us there. You know he will."

"You're not a slave, you know. You can leave whenever you want."

"Or I can just stay here. They weren't shooting at women, and if it's safe enough for Cookie, it's safe enough for me. I'd rather stay in Portland and keep moving forward. I'm not going to take stupid risks, but I'm not getting locked away forever, either."

"You're letting hormones cloud your brain," she said bluntly. "This is about Hunter. But he's just a guy, Em, and there are millions more all over the country. A dick is a dick."

"It isn't just about Hunter, Kit. Okay, I'll admit, maybe it's a little about him. But I also fought hard to get out. I'm not like you—I'm not independent and strong . . . If I go home, I might just stay, and I don't want that."

"We'll talk more when I get there," Kit said, sighing. "I see them pulling up right now. I feel kind of bad for this guy I picked up. He was talking about making me breakfast, but I'm just gonna leave him a note. No point in waking him up."

I snorted.

"You're a slut."

"Probably," she replied with a hint of her old spirit. "But he's shit in bed. It's better this way. See you in a few."

By nine that morning, the kitchen was warm and full of good smells. Cookie and I were making a king-sized batch of pancakes while Kit sliced fruit. Deke and the brothers had a council of war going in the living room, so we'd closed the sliders that separated the kitchen and dining room to give them privacy. Silvie sat at the table coloring and singing some weird, unending little song about pizza fairies.

I couldn't seem to stop checking my phone. No word from Hunter. I wasn't particularly surprised—I assumed he was in his own council of war right now. I just hoped he stayed safe.

"I think Kit is right," Cookie was saying. "You should go home to Coeur d'Alene with her. If this thing with Hunter is real, it'll still be real in a couple weeks, when we've had a chance to wrap our heads around what's happening."

"I'm not going home," I said, my voice firm. "Moving out was hard. Really hard . . . I don't want to slip back into old habits. I'm too comfortable in Coeur d'Alene and the club was smothering me. I'm happier here and I don't think it would be any safer back home. In fact, I haven't even decided if I'm going for Thanksgiving. Maybe I'll have other plans."

Cookie and Kit exchanged looks.

"You know I'm all about getting laid," Kit started carefully. Cookie snapped her with a towel.

"Little ears."

"Sorry. I think it's great that you and Hunter made a *connection*," Kit started again. "But you're building castles in your head and that's not too smart, sis."

"I'm gonna live in a castle when I'm a grown-up," Silvie declared.

"Good luck," Cookie muttered. "I leave the shop closed another day and we won't be able to afford a house."

"Are things really that tight?" I asked, startled. She shook her head, frowning.

"No, but you get what I mean. I'm just frustrated because Deke seems to think he's my boss. No thanks—I'm a sole proprietor."

I snickered.

"Bikers are crazy," Kit said, rolling her eyes. "All caveman and bullshit. You'll never catch me with one of them, I promise you. Life is too short to let a man call the shots."

"And yet you're the one trying to convince me to go home to Coeur d'Alene. You do realize it's infested with them, right?"

She opened her mouth to argue, but Cookie's phone rang and we all froze. What now? Cookie grabbed it.

"It's Maggs," she told us, her face nervous as she answered. "Hey, hon . . . What's up?"

She listened for a minute, her eyes growing wide. Then she screamed and started jumping up and down. Seconds later the kitchen door burst open and Deke ran through, gun in hand. Cookie burst into tears, a huge smile transforming her face.

"Bolt's coming home!" she yelled "He got parole. It's a fucking miracle. They're actually letting him come home!"

Kit and I burst out screaming and hugging each other. Deke collapsed back against the door frame, and for the first time in my life I saw him smile.

"About time we got some good news," he said. "Fuck. Didn't see that coming. Idaho never paroles 'em if they won't confess to the charges."

"Let me talk to Maggs," I demanded, reaching for the phone. Cookie laughed and handed it over. "Maggs! I can't believe it! When did you find out?"

"He called Friday afternoon but made me sit on it," she said. "It killed me not to tell you ladies, but I got the go-ahead this morning. I guess he had some business he wanted tied up before word got out? I dunno. The parole hearing was two weeks ago, but you don't get a decision right away . . . We didn't think it would happen. He won't admit he did anything wrong, and you know how that goes. They aren't supposed to consider anything but his behavior inside, but the parole board does whatever the hell they want."

"How?" I asked, stunned. "How did he pull it off?"

"I don't know," she said, obviously crying. "I just don't know. I don't care. All I know is he'll be coming home. *Finally.* I have to go. I have phone calls to make, and so much to do. We'll have a big party for him, of course. You'll come back for it, won't you?"

"Of course," I said. "Oh my God, of course I will!"

Then Kit was demanding the phone. I saw Cookie hugging Deke out of the corner of my eye as more brothers crowded into the kitchen.

Thank God.

We needed this. We needed it in a big way.

Later that night, Hunter finally got in touch. I hadn't realized how nervous I was until his text popped up. Kit's words had been eating at me, making me doubt him.

HUNTER: How are you doing? Can't call, no privacy

ME: Good. Still at home. Kit got in touch early this morning. She's fine. Dad wants me back in CDA, of course. Kit is trying to get leave from school

HUNTER: You planning to go?

ME: Do I have a good reason to stay? We decided to stay away from each other but then last night happened . . . I don't know what's going on between us.

I waited for his response, holding my breath. We hadn't discussed the future or anything between us. It'd never been a secret that he wanted to have sex with me, but I wasn't stupid enough to think that meant anything serious.

I had hope, though. Before everything fell to shit and he'd kidnapped me, we'd talked every day. We shared jokes and laughed and I'd felt like I could tell him anything. So we hadn't spent much time together in person, but that didn't mean we hadn't spent time together . . . That had to count for something, right?

Hunter still hadn't answered. Shit. Had I pissed off everyone I knew over a one-night stand? For one horrible minute I thought I might throw up.

The phone buzzed again.

HUNTER: Sorry. Lot of shit all around me. I hope to hell you have a reason to stay in Portland . . . I just told my whole club about you, that I plan to make you my old lady. Skid can go fuck himself, along with his bullshit reasons for us to stay apart. Hoping I didn't do it for nothing?

I sighed, feeling the tension drain out of me. Okay, I hadn't imagined whatever it was between us. Then what he'd said hit me—he'd told his club he wanted me for his old lady.

Holy hell . . . that was practically a proposal!

ME: You almost gave me a heart attack. For a minute I thought maybe that was just a one night stand. Old lady? That's a big step . . . but I like the sound of it . . .
HUNTER: Def not a one night stand. We need some time together, time to talk. This is insane.
ME: No shit . . . Ha. My old man. wow
HUNTER: Damn straight. Where did you think this was going? No offense, Em, but us being together is way too dangerous and crazy to risk for just sex. Fuck that. I want to do this right. Are you with me?

I took a minute, wondering if I'd lost my mind. Probably. Definitely. I didn't care.

ME: I'm with you. My dad might kill you
HUNTER: He can try. We'll figure it out.
ME: You sure your club is good with this? It seems so unreal
HUNTER: They're not thrilled but they'll get over it. FYI—I won't be home for a couple days. I need to go now, but I'll

try to call when I can. Don't freak out if you don't hear from
me tho. Fucked up shit all the time right now
ME: Don't worry about me. You stay safe.
HUNTER: You too. A lots up in the air, but I'm with you Em.
Don't doubt that, okay? No matter what happens or what
you hear . . . Promise?
ME: I promise. xoxo

I set down the phone, feeling a little giddy. Hunter's old lady.
Wow. I knew my friends Marie and Sophie had struggled with the
term, not quite understanding how important it was. But I'd grown
up in the MC—I knew exactly what Hunter was asking me. Calling
me his old lady meant more than offering me a ring, it meant he'd
taken responsibility for me and all my actions to his own club.
     The daughter of a Reapers MC president, despite the fact that
his brothers and my father had been enemies since before I was
born.
     Hunter had handed me his life.
     Literally.

Monday afternoon Cookie and I sat at the kitchen table playing
rummy. Hunter hadn't been in touch again and I'd gotten over my
initial giddy excitement. Now I was just bored.
     "I'm tired of coloring," Silvie declared. "I wanna go to the
park."
     "Me, too," Cookie murmured. "But we need to stay inside to-
day, baby. Why don't you go to your room and pick out a book? I'll
come back and read it to you in a little bit. I want to talk to Em for
a minute."
     "Okay."
     Silvie hopped down and ran out of the room. Cookie leaned
toward me across the table.

"I'm losing my mind," she confessed in a low voice.

"At least the shop is open again," I replied, trying to sound cheerful. It wasn't a particularly successful attempt. I was losing my mind, too.

"For now," she muttered. "But they can't handle taking stock or ordering, even if the counter's covered. I'm thinking about telling Deke to leave. They may have water damage at the clubhouse, but that's their problem, not mine. I think it's time for this operation to move out."

I opened my eyes wide.

"Seriously?"

"Yes," Cookie said, glancing toward the living room. "I'm a prisoner in my own home. You know what makes it worse, though? This isn't my fight. I'm not even part of the club anymore. Bagger is dead and I've been on my own for nearly a year. Deke has no fucking right to show up here and treat me like club property. I may have been Bagger's property, but that's over. Not like he's coming back."

"I don't know what to say . . . I didn't know you felt that way about the club."

She sighed, and shook her head, tossing her cards down.

"I don't," she said, running a hand through her curls. "Or maybe I do. I don't know. I'm just tired of being stuck in my house when I have a business that needs running. I'm not getting laid and I'm not getting any younger. You know, it's only been eleven months since Bagger died, but he was deployed for ten months before that. I've been alone forever, Em. Or at least it feels that way . . . I'm tired of being a good old lady, staying strong in memory of a man who cared more about his fucking war than his family."

I stared at her, eyes wide. I had no idea what to say. None. I heard a throat clearing and looked up to find Deke standing in the doorway.

"Um, hi, Deke?" I asked.

"Fuck it," Cookie said, turning her head to glare at him. She stood and walked out, pushing past the big biker without another word.

Awkward.

Deke walked slowly to the table, then leaned across it on his hands, his face about a foot from mine.

"What the hell was that about?" he asked, his voice like ice. God, did he have any settings that weren't scary?

"I have no idea," I whispered, eyes wide. "Seriously. We were just sitting here playing cards and she started talking. I've never heard her say anything like that before. I had no idea . . ."

My voice trailed off. Deke nodded, then sat down across from me. He folded his arms across his chest and studied me like a bug. I hoped very sincerely I wouldn't pee my pants, because that's how terrifying he was. No joke.

"We need to talk."

"Okay?"

"Your dad wants you home," he said. "You should've gone with Kit yesterday."

"I'm not going home. Coeur d'Alene isn't a good place for me anymore."

"Listen up, little girl," Deke told me, his voice cold and matter of fact. "Hunter is using you. I know you don't like that idea. It probably hurts your feelings or some such shit. But these are the facts. This club—*your* club—is under attack. We don't know for sure that the Jacks are behind it, but we do know one thing—when they needed a weak link last time, they went after you. You already fell for Hunter's shit once. He's a proven liar who's not afraid to use a woman to get what he wants. Don't you think it's a pretty big coincidence that he just happened to be with you the night every-thing went down? The Jacks could be trying to pit us against the cartel for their own reasons. For all you know, he's using you to convince us they're victims, too. Take us off guard for another sneak attack."

"What about their president?" I demanded. "Two men are *dead*, Deke."

"So they say," he replied, leaning back in his chair. "But all the cops are saying is that two men were shot. We know their club is tearing apart at the seams. Their VP—Burke—has stepped up, but there's no guarantee he can hold them together. At least that's how I read it. For all we know, the Jacks took them out for their own reasons. Power struggle."

I shook my head.

"You didn't see his face," I said. "It was real, Deke. He had no idea."

"Says the girl who talked to a Devil's Jack online for almost three months without a fuckin' clue she was being set up. Use your brain, Em. Don't make a fool of yourself again. Just go home and forget you ever met him."

I stood carefully, blinking back tears, and walked out of the kitchen with as much dignity as I could manage. I agreed with Cookie—Deke needed to go away.

I didn't like him one little bit.

TUESDAY

ME: I'm sick of being stuck in this house. They won't let us do anything. Not even Kit is this trapped in Coeur d'Alene!!!

HUNTER: They didn't shoot up the clubhouse in CDA and it's farther north. Not the same thing. But I hear you—I'll be back to town tomorrow. See you then?

ME: Definitely

HUNTER: Think I can call tonight. I never have any privacy, but I fucking miss you. Want to hear your voice. Keep thinking of that sexy mouth of yours and what it will look like wrapped around my dick.

ME: Um . . .

HUNTER: Don't worry. I'll take care of you first, babe . . . And after. I can't wait to strip off all your clothes and get you naked in my bed. Might not let you out for a month.

ME: Well, when you put it like that . . . Ok :)

My phone rang at ten p.m. I'd almost given up on him calling, so when he did, I was so excited I nearly fell off my bed.

"Hey," I said, trying not to sound too eager. "How are you?"

"Exhausted," he said. "I've been down to California and back a couple times now. I hate to admit it, but I think it might be time to park the bike and break out the cage. I hate winter in Oregon."

I laughed.

"It's not even winter yet, and at least it's warmer here than Coeur d'Alene," I said. "They had the first snow last night, according to Kit. She wants to know if I'm coming home for Thanksgiving."

"What did you say?"

"I haven't made any plans yet," I said carefully. There were so many things we hadn't had time to talk about. It wasn't like either of us had our own place. Did he want to spend the holiday together? I kept looking back over our texts to make sure I hadn't hallucinated the whole thing. "Figured I'd see how things play out. I can't wait to be with you again."

"The feeling is mutual, trust me," he muttered. "Christ, I've been thinking about talking to you all day, and now that I've finally got some privacy to do it, I'm fuckin' exhausted. Sorry, babe."

"Don't worry about it," I said. "Why don't I talk and you can listen?"

"Sounds good."

"I've been thinking about you a lot," I said hesitantly. "About what I plan to do to you when we finally get together again. I want it to be special, so I decided to do a little research."

"Oh really?" he asked, and while he still sounded tired, I caught a hint of something else, too. "You do this 'research' on another guy?"

I burst out laughing.

"Yeah, because there are so many available men in this house. Reapers don't count, especially annoying ones. No, I decided to download a book, get some ideas."

"Sounds interesting," he murmured. "What kind of ideas?"

"Well, you know I don't have tons of experience," I said. "So I figured if I wanted to do this right—sex, I mean—it might be a good idea to read a manual. I bought the *Guide to Getting It On.* Interesting stuff. For example, did you know that most men are far more sensitive on the top half of their penises than the bottom half?"

"I haven't researched the wider population, but I'm not surprised," he said, sounding amused.

"Well, that's why it's so important that when I do finally get you alone, I make sure I spend a lot of time exploring the head first. I think it's the . . . hmm, let me check my notes. The frenulum? You know, the little—"

He started laughing.

"Babe, two things. Don't use the word 'little' when you talk about my dick, okay? And two, don't use the word 'frenulum.' Ever. Not that anything said in that voice of yours isn't sexy, but it's sort of blocking the visual I'm trying to paint in my head."

I frowned. Last time we'd had phone sex he took the lead. This was harder than I'd thought.

"Okay, well, it says I should take my time and explore that little notch on the bottom side. For example, I thought I might start by running my tongue all the way around, make sure I have a feel for the layout before doing anything else."

"That'll work," he said, his voice lowering.

"I have a theory," I said. "According to my book, some men prefer it when a woman sort of points her tongue and just uses the tip. Others like it when you really spread the tongue out, and rub the cock's underside as you pull the head into your mouth."

He cleared his throat roughly.

"Yeah, that'd be okay."

I thought I heard the sound of his pants unzipping. I hoped to hell I was right, because otherwise I might feel sheepish about the way my hand was sliding down into my sleep shorts.

"So here's my theory," I continued. "The book says the best way to find out is to just ask, and I can appreciate the efficiency in that. But I also think it would be really fun to experiment and decide for myself. You know, like a randomized series of tests so I can gather lots of data?"

"You're going to kill me," he grunted. "Less data, babe. More licking."

"Just a sec. I'm gonna grab my vibrator before I keep going."

"Fuck."

"Yeah, that's the general idea."

I rolled over and dug out my trusty magic bullet, turning it on low. Not too much . . . not at first.

"So I'm a little worried about how big you are," I said. "The book tells me I might want to consider licking you all over, until you're good and wet. Then I'll wrap my hand around the bottom so you can't accidentally go too deep. Think that might work?"

"Can't hurt to give it a shot," he muttered. "Fuck. I love your voice, babe. You using that vibrator yet?"

"Uh-huh . . ." I whispered. "I'm just laying it against my clit right now, letting it sort of warm me up. I'm imagining what it'll feel like the first time I taste you. I'm a little nervous, so before I take you in my mouth, I'm going to explore that little slit at the top, okay? You know, try out some of your precome? I figure a little taste is just what I need to get a sense of how it'll be. Not sure if I want to swallow or not."

"Babe, I don't give a shit if you swallow," he said, his voice strained. "Just don't stop talking."

I laughed, feeling powerful.

"I think I'll turn up my vibrator a little now. I'm rubbing it up and down, first on my clit and then along my labia. I feel really empty, though. I wish you were here, Hunter. I'll never forget how it felt when you first pushed into me. It hurt a little, but it was great, too. You know I'm still a little sore?"

"I've never felt anything as good as your cunt around my dick, and that is the fuckin' truth."

"The good news is you'll feel it again soon. In fact, I wish you were feeling it right now."

"Why don't you slide a finger inside, check and see how things are going?" he asked. I propped the phone on my pillow next to my ear and then reached down to follow his instructions.

"Well, for one thing, I'm pretty wet already," I murmured, closing my eyes. "I guess the thought of sucking you off turns me on. Does that make me a slut?"

"Only in the nicest possible sense of the word. Can you hear me jacking off? Because I swear, I'm pumping so hard it sounds like a freight train in here."

Oh shit. That went straight to my center. I stuck another finger in, reaching for my G-spot. As usual, I couldn't quite get there.

Fortunately, my vibrator was available to compensate.

"I feel tingles and pressure running all down my body," I said. "I'm not there yet, but I will be there soon. I want your weight on top of me—"

I gasped, because the vibrator found a particularly sensitive spot. I felt my muscles tighten and my hips jerked.

"I'm getting close, Hunter."

"Liam," he muttered. "Call me Liam. Fuck, I want to be inside you. Shit. Oh, *fuck* . . ."

"Liam," I gasped as my back arched. "Holy shit. I can't wait to do this in person."

He groaned in my ear, the sound harsh and tight.

"I'm coming," he said. "Fuck. *Fuck.*"

He grunted into the phone. I imagined his hand on his cock,

the sight of his come squirting out. I started pumping my fingers in and out harder, pretending they were his. My clit tightened, every muscle clenched, and then my hips lifted off the bed as I exploded.

"Ahhh . . ." I lay still, panting into the phone.

It took a couple minutes to recover.

"You're pretty good at phone sex," he said after a while, his voice low and growly.

"Thanks," I whispered. "I miss you."

"Miss you, too. I'm sorry, babe, but I'm really fuckin' tired, and blowing my wad just now didn't help."

"Go to sleep. I'll still be in Portland when you get back. Promise."

WEDNESDAY MORNING

HUNTER: I feel like shit telling you this, but I'm down in Cali
   again. Thought I'd make it today but had some business
   come up
ME: Its okay. I understand :(

That evening I watched nervously as Cookie slammed dishes around the kitchen. I wanted to offer to help, but I was a little scared of her. She'd been muttering about men, control, and how much she needed to get back to work.

I understood her frustration.

So far as I could tell, there was a whole lot of nothing going on. Deke wouldn't tell us anything, but Kit had been listening at doors back home. According to her, the Reapers were divided over who to blame for the shootings. Quite a few thought it was the cartel down south, but they couldn't rule out the Jacks, either.

So far they hadn't found any real evidence to prove who was behind the attacks. Until they could, a lot of questions would remain unanswered, and the Jacks would be suspect. Had Hunter's club broke the truce? Should we start hitting back?

Nobody knew.

In the meantime, Deke wouldn't let Cookie go to her shop. He wouldn't let me go to work, either, which wasn't such a big deal because I'd just been picking up shifts as needed. But she could tell things were falling apart without her, and Deke didn't even seem to care.

On the bright side, the guys were back in their clubhouse, which meant the house wasn't full of bikers anymore. The water damage still needed to be fixed, but apparently it was workable. That was a big relief. Cookie didn't want her house to be a target, and even Deke had to acknowledge she had a point.

He still left guards with us, though, and he'd spent almost every night at her place. Silvie had moved into Cookie's room, so at least he had a bed. Of course, that bed was pink and covered with stuffed kittens.

Apparently, Deke was above worrying about such things.

Around six, the front door opened and Deke walked in . . . home from work just like a 1950s sitcom, only with guns and cartels and lives at stake. Cookie came out of the kitchen, a determined look on her face and a plastic bag in her hand.

"Deke, we need to talk," she said, her tone ominous, thrusting the bag at me. "Em, would you keep an eye on Silvie? I have a Lunchable in here, and some fruit in case she's hungry. Not sure how long it'll take."

I nodded quickly.

"Out here or back in her room?" I asked, wondering what was the safest distance. I had a bad feeling about this . . .

"Room might be best," Cookie said. Deke glanced over at the prospect he'd left with us that morning, who was watching uncomfortably.

"You can head out," he said, jerking his chin toward the door. "I've got it from here."

The prospect and I met eyes, and I'm pretty sure we were thinking the same thing. World War III was about to break out in that kitchen. I wished I could leave with him. Instead I grabbed Silvie and took her to my room.

Outside the house, I heard the prospect driving away. Coward.

"I'm hungry," Silvie declared. "Mom lets me eat the treat first."

Yeah, right.

"Start with the meat and crackers," I told her, peeling off the plastic and handing her the food. Then I wondered why I bothered—the chocolate was probably healthier than the waxy, fake cheese in the little carton. I dug a granola bar out of my purse for myself, wishing I'd thought to grab a Diet Coke or something.

During the next hour, I read Silvie four books before starting a movie for her on my laptop. Then I crept out into the living room to scope out the situation.

I heard yelling in the kitchen, and then I heard something hit the wall and shatter.

I crept back into the bedroom.

Around eight Cookie knocked on the door.

"Sorry about that," she murmured. Her hair was all messed up and her cheeks were flushed.

"Deke still here?" I asked quietly.

She shook her head.

"Nope," she said. "He called someone else to come over. I think he's got some stuff to sort out . . ."

"Everything okay?" I asked hesitantly.

She shrugged.

"Not sure," she admitted. "But he's gone for the night. I guess we'll see what happens tomorrow. I'm planning on going to work. If he's smart, he won't try to stop me."

CHAPTER FIFTEEN

My phone rang at eleven that night.

"Yeah?" I asked, not quite asleep but not entirely awake, either.

"I just got back to town," Hunter said. "I know it's last minute, but can I come and pick you up?"

"Of course!" I said, a wave of excitement perking me up. "When?"

"I'm just down the street."

"Um, I need to grab some stuff," I said, glancing around frantically. "Give me fifteen minutes? Or at least ten?"

"Ten," he replied, his voice low and sexy. "Fuck, I can't wait to get my hands on you, babe. The shit I'm gonna do to your body . . . Don't forget to grab that dirty book of yours. You don't need clothes, but the book sounds like my kind of reading."

I giggled, feeling all silly and happy.

"See you soon, babe," I said, hanging up the phone. I started grabbing things quickly and throwing them into my backpack.

Then I caught a glimpse of myself in the mirror and nearly screamed. My hair was all lank and flattened, I'd already washed off my makeup, and even my teeth felt grimy.

Like something out of a horror movie.

I darted across the hallway to the bathroom and brushed my teeth, then sprayed some dry shampoo into my hair and slapped on some lip gloss. Full makeup wasn't really an option at this point, but it was better than nothing. I dashed off a quick note for Cookie and crept quietly out of my room to the kitchen, where I propped it up on the table. I figured I'd email her, too, that should cover things well enough. Then I walked out into the living room to find one of the prospects, Gordie, on the couch watching TV.

Pisser. I'd been hoping he'd be asleep.

"What's up?" he asked, taking in my backpack and shoes.

"I'm going out," I told him brightly. *Nothing to see here.* "Don't worry about it."

He stood up immediately, fully alert.

"I have orders to keep all of you safe in the house."

"You don't get to make that decision," I told him, sounding far more confident than I felt. "I appreciate the concern, but I'm not a prisoner."

"I'm calling Deke."

"Fine, call him," I said, moving toward the door. Unfortunately, he was bigger than me and he blocked it. "Are we really going to do this? Like, are you actually planning to hold me prisoner in this living room?"

"If I have to," he told me, his voice grim. "Deke can decide."

Double pisser.

I whipped out my phone and called Hunter.

"I have a situation," I told him. "They aren't gonna let me leave. Maybe we should just do this tomorrow . . ."

Hunter growled through the phone.

"I'll be there in a minute," he said,

"Wait! What do you mean?"

"I'm coming to get you. How many guys are in the house?"

"Just one," I said frantically. "But seriously, this could get ugly. Why don't I—"

There was a pounding on the door.

I locked eyes with Gordie.

"That's Hunter, and I don't think he's going away," I told him quietly. "Is this really worth a fight? Just let me head out, okay? You don't have a right to keep me away from him."

"Not my call to make," he said, shaking his head. "Deke's on his way. You sit tight and he'll decide how to handle this."

Hunter pounded the door again. Shit. I texted him.

ME: Deke is coming so I think you should just go home. We don't want a fight over this. Not now, when everyone is so touchy

HUNTER: No fucking way. You're my old lady and you're coming home with me. They have a problem with it, I'll call in my brothers to help me

I froze. That didn't sound good. Not at all.

ME: What about the truce? Wasn't that our first priority?

HUNTER: I've already claimed you in front of my club, you're my property now. If the Reapers won't let my old lady come with me, that's an act of war

I read the words and felt sick. Had he lost his mind? Yes, I decided. He had. Apparently he was so tired and worn out he'd forgotten what really mattered here.

Keeping the peace for all our sakes.

ME: It's just one night babe. We'll get it sorted out tomorrow. You have too much to lose here

HUNTER: No fucking way. I back down now it shows weak-

ness. I'm not the one being unreasonable here Em. I just
want to pick up my girl friend

More pounding on the door. Gordie looked nervous, but he
stood his ground, blocking me.
"Open up!" Hunter shouted outside.

ME: Is this really about us, or about you making some kind of
point with Deke?
HUNTER: It started out about us. But him saying I can't see my
woman? Thats a problem. Deke is pulling up now. We'll
figure it out

Sure enough, I heard a truck engine. Cookie wandered out into
the living room wearing a man's bathrobe, rubbing her eyes.
"What's going on?" she asked, sleepily. "I have to be up at four.
This better be important."
"I think we're having a contest to see who has the biggest dick,"
I muttered, frustrated. "Hunter came to pick me up, but Gordie
won't let me out and now Deke's here. I'm just waiting for them to
start whipping out their rulers."
"Ridiculous," Cookie said. "Come with me."
I raised a brow.
"Kind of in the middle of something," I muttered. I heard Deke's
voice out front, yelling at Hunter. Shit. If we didn't shut this down,
someone was going to get seriously hurt.
"Come. With. Me." Cookie said, her voice harsher than I'd ever
heard it. Damn. She looked almost scarier than Deke.
"Okay," I said, eyes darting toward Gordie. I followed her back
to her bedroom, where Silvie lay sound asleep with her favorite
stuffed animal tucked in next to her. Cookie made a "ta-dah!" kind
of gesture, showing me the French doors next to her bed.
"You can go out there and sneak around the front," she said.
"Just bypass them entirely."

I gaped at her and she shrugged.

"Why didn't I think of that?"

"Because hormones impair thinking," she said, rolling her eyes. "Go on. Get outside before they start shooting or something."

"Why are you helping me?"

"Because I'm sick of this shit," she said, her voice blunt. "The Reapers don't own either of us. Deke has no right to keep you here and neither does your dad. Make your own decisions, Em. I miss Bagger every day of my life and I wish I'd spent more time with him. We just never know when it's all going to end, and life is too short to sit around waiting for a man. I still think it's a mistake to hook up with Hunter, but it's your mistake to make."

"Thank you," I whispered, giving her a quick hug. "I'll call you tomorrow."

"Good," she said. Then an evil smile crossed her face. "I know it's wrong of me, but I'm really looking forward to Deke losing for once. About time someone stands up to him."

I stifled a giggle as she turned off the alarm and opened the door. Then I ran quickly across the wet grass, feeling the cold seep into my pink Chucks. I crept carefully around the house to find Hunter and Deke in a standoff on the sidewalk.

Gordie watched from the porch, mesmerized.

"You can leave on your own or we'll make you, but you aren't taking Em with you," Deke was saying. "Not gonna happen."

Hunter bristled.

"She's my old lady now. She belongs with me."

God, it would be *so much faster* if they just did a side-by-side penis comparison. I ran my eyes over Hunter, torn between wanting to lick his entire body and punch him in the face. Instead of doing either, I walked quietly to my car. I needed to time things perfectly. I took a deep breath and counted to three before opening the door, hopping into my seat, and sliding the key into the ignition, all in one smooth move. The car started right up (thank God!) and I slammed it into reverse, backing out into the street with a jolt.

Both men turned to stare at me, the surprise on their faces priceless.

I rolled down my window, foot poised on the accelerator.

"I'm leaving," I yelled at them. "Hunter, call me if you'd rather sleep with me than fight with Deke."

With that, I slammed my foot down and took off into the night.

Damn, that felt good.

"I'll strangle you if you ever pull something like that again," Hunter said, pacing back and forth across the hotel room we'd gotten. Under the circumstances, neutral ground seemed like a good idea.

Someone was grumpy.

"You could've gotten shot. *I* could've shot you. What were you thinking, sneaking around outside a house under guard?"

I leaned against the bathroom door frame, my arms crossed, and sighed heavily. This reunion had been nowhere near as fun as I'd pictured it. Sweet baby Jesus, but the man could pout.

"Maybe if everyone wasn't so trigger happy, this wouldn't be such an issue," I said, my voice tart. "Don't give me this shit, Hunter. You caused a big scene because you weren't willing to wait a few hours to get things sorted out. Someone could've gotten hurt. *Silvie* could've gotten hurt. Don't we have enough to worry about from the cartel? I thought you wanted peace?"

He stopped pacing to snarl at me.

"Goddamn, Em—whose side are you on? I've been going hard for four fucking days. I drove for six hours to get here and claim my woman, and I wasn't going to let some pissant Reaper prospect keep her from me. You're mine now. I don't fucking share."

I took a deep breath, poised to rip him a new asshole. Then it struck me—something was really wrong here. Hunter was usually so cool, always calculating. This was nothing like him, something else was going on here.

"You're overreacting," I said slowly and deliberately. "I hear what you're saying, but it's not making sense. This isn't like you. What happened?"

His face twisted, and he turned away from me, running a hand through his hair.

"Bad shit, Em," he said finally. "I saw some bad shit today. Did some bad shit. I just needed to be near you, around someone clean and whole. He wouldn't let me have you."

Well, fuck. Now he looked all broken, and seeing this big, strong man so close to the edge made my insides twist. I still wanted to kick him, but I wanted to make him feel better even more. Hunter turned away, so I walked up behind him and wrapped my arms around his waist, pulling him back into me. My cheek rubbed against the red devil on the back of his cut, reminding me that I'd left my club behind for this man.

"You have me," I said into his back, letting go of my anger. I started running my hands up and down his stomach. I loved the feel of his hard muscles, but this was about more than sensation. He needed to realize how much I wanted him, how special he was to me. I tugged his shirt slowly out of his pants, trailing my fingers along his bare skin. Those amazing muscles of his tightened and he groaned.

"You don't have to tell me about it," I whispered, knowing he couldn't. "Just relax, okay? Let's just finish fighting tomorrow."

"Do we really have to fight?" he asked, sounding exhausted. "God, Em. You have no idea. No fucking idea at all . . ."

Shit. What the hell had happened?

I slid my hands lower and caught his fly, pulling apart the button and sliding down the zipper. His cock was still soft, something I'd never felt from him before, but instead of being disappointed I was curious.

I wanted to explore. Seeing as he clearly had something he needed to forget, now was the perfect time to satisfy my curiosity and distract him in the process. I rubbed his length gently through the soft fabric of his boxer briefs with one hand, using the other to lower his pants. He sighed, and I felt him stir to life. I continued my exploration, finding the head as it slowly hardened, running my fingers around the ridge ringing it.

"That's really good, babe."

"Then I must be doing it right," I murmured, wishing I were tall enough to kiss the back of his neck. "Let me make you feel good again, Liam. I want you to feel clean."

He reached down and caught my hand in his, pulling it away long enough to shove down his briefs. Then he was putting my hand around his cock again, wrapping the fingers around his erection and using me to squeeze himself tighter than I would've dared on my own.

I moved my hand up and down, his length growing harder with every stroke. Then I slid my other hand up and under his shirt, savoring the ridges of his abdominals once more before finding his chest. His nipple.

I pinched it and Hunter inhaled sharply.

"Good?" I asked, the question a whisper.

"Very," he said. "Very fucking good."

"Just relax and enjoy. Let me help you."

He sighed heavily. Something had obviously gone terribly wrong, something I might never know the details of. But whatever it was, when he needed peace, he'd come to me.

I liked that idea very much.

Hunter's cock was fully erect now. I kept playing with his nipple, working his cock slow and fast alternately, exploring what seemed to give him the most pleasure.

After a few minutes he gasped, his hand catching mine again, jerking it up and down. Now it seemed almost as if he was using my touch to punish himself. I couldn't imagine something so rough could be anything but painful, but the groans coming from his mouth weren't unhappy.

"Christ," he muttered, reaching around with his free arm to grab me, pulling me hard into his body. The embroidery of his patches rubbed against my cheek. Would I ever have sex with him fully naked?

Not at this rate.

His hips started pulsing forward involuntarily, and his hand around my back tightened. My arm was growing tired but I didn't care. I didn't really care about anything—all I wanted was to bring him some kind of relief.

Well, that's a lie.

I very much wanted his dick in my body, but this was clearly working for him. He needed my touch more than I needed his, at least for the moment. Hunter gave a long, low groan and then I felt it hit. He came in a series of pulses that seemed to run along the bottom of his cock. I slowed my hand, thinking I should stop, but he grasped me and kept moving.

All righty then.

I kept stroking him for another minute as his body shuddered and then relaxed against mine. Finally his hand dropped away and I let him go, wrapping both arms around his waist.

"You know, I'd planned for something a little more mutual," he said slowly. "Sorry. Just a shit night. I'll get you off—"

"Don't worry about that right now," I said, still hugging him. "You're tired and I want you to rest. You'll need your strength for later, I think. Right?"

He gave a little laugh, turning around to face me, raising a hand to catch my hair in that way he seemed to like so much. His lips took mine, slow and sweet. Then he pulled away, rubbing his nose gently against mine.

"I hate to say it, but I'm about a minute away from passing out, babe. Can we go to sleep? I need you all soft and sweet and wrapped around me."

"Sure," I murmured. I pulled away, then considered the mess we'd just made. "Um . . ."

"I'll clean it up," he said quickly. "Just get ready for bed. I want to hold you—remember that night out behind the bunkhouse at your dad's place? Aside from the part where you nearly killed me, that was one of the best nights of my life."

"You also held me the night you kidnapped me," I said, my voice dry. He shrugged.

"That was pretty good, too," he admitted. "At least for me. But I figured you might have a different perspective . . ."

"You'll make it up to me," I told him, and I had no doubt of it. But not tonight.

My beautiful man needed rest, and he'd damned well get it.

HUNTER

I woke up to an empty bed.

Em had been so cute last night . . . First she jerked me off like a pro, and then she'd come to bed wearing one of my T-shirts, which I'd confiscated. Guess she didn't have time to find any of those pretty presents I'd "given" her. Not that it mattered—I didn't want anything between her skin and mine anyway. I slept surrounded by her warmth and smell and her hair all over my face, which should've been annoying but in reality kicked ass.

Her face wasn't waiting for me when I closed my eyes, though. Nope, I saw the faces of my brothers right before I'd shot them. One of them had cried, begging for his life. The other sneered and flipped me off.

Two of our own, selling us out to the cartel.

It wasn't the first time I'd killed for the club—but I'd never had to put down a brother like a dog before. I'd known there was dissension in the ranks and fully realized that there were men who'd do anything to keep us from making peace with the Reapers. I even understood their perspective, to a degree. We'd been in a cold war with the other club for close to twenty years. That made for a lot of bad blood.

But they'd gone beyond betrayal—this was treason.

Good men died because of what they'd done.

On the long drive up from Redding, I focused on Em. How much I wanted to hold her and smell her and absolutely not think of anything but her gorgeous body and the flash of her ice-blue eyes.

Then Deke and his pet prospect got in the way and I'd lost it.

Fuck.

I couldn't believe how stupid I'd been. I hated to admit it, but Em had been right. What the hell was I thinking, risking the peace for one night? With any luck we'd have years together, something that definitely wouldn't be happening if I started a new war with her dad's club.

So *fucking stupid* . . . but at least one of us had kept her shit together. A reluctant smile crossed my face, because Em had saved my ass yet again. I heard the shower running in the bathroom, and I realized she must be in there, all slippery and wet. Ten seconds later I was on my feet, sliding back the curtain and stepping in behind her.

"Hey, baby," I whispered in her ear. "I forgot to give you something last night."

She gave a sexy little squeak as I slid my hands around her body, grasping her breast and reaching for her clit at the same time. Then she leaned into me and for the first time I got to explore her body without rushing.

Beautiful.

Of course, I knew every curve she had. I'd studied her pictures a thousand times, memorizing every inch of her skin and fantasizing about what I'd do to her, given the chance. The reality was better than my dreams. Way better. She was soft, but I felt the strong muscles underneath her curves. I knew she'd have endurance, and despite what she'd said to me that night in Coeur d'Alene, she'd already proven herself one hell of an old lady.

She said she didn't want to follow orders.

Fine by me—I didn't need to control her . . . I just wanted to sit

back and watch her, try to figure out what made her tick and hold
on for the ride. I knew she'd support me, but I also knew she'd protect me from myself. She'd already protected our clubs. Last night
she'd done a better job than I had. I promised myself that I'd never
pull that kind of bullshit on her again.

Hell, I should be following her lead, because she'd been smarter
than me and Deke put together. Now that I'd cooled off, I could see
the humor in the situation. Somehow she'd managed to bypass all
of us, not exactly defusing the situation, but definitely ending it
without violence.

So what if Deke was pissed? So far as I could tell, the man was
permanently pissed. He hated the Jacks and had threatened to
kill me more than once, so I wasn't exactly crying over his hurt feelings. As for Em, she was under my protection now, so it didn't really
matter how frustrated he got. He'd be dealing with me from now on.

Em squirmed in my arms, pulling me out of my thoughts.

I reached down and slipped my fingers into her hot warmth, and
she squeaked in my arms. Why the fuck was I thinking about Deke
when I had a naked woman in my arms?

I swiveled Em in my arms, finding her mouth and sucking her
lower lip into mine. Then I lifted her, carrying her out of the tub
and setting her on the bathroom counter. My hand slipped between
us, dipping into that sweet pussy of hers.

So fucking hot and tight . . .

Em gasped against my mouth, giving me the opportunity to slip
my tongue inside. Down below, I had two fingers up inside her now.
She clenched around me, bringing back some mighty fine memories
of her wrapped around my cock the other night, when we visited
my very favorite alley in the history of time.

She reached down and grabbed my dick, squeezing it hard like
I'd taught her the night before.

Very nice.

Then she tried to guide me into her.

"Condom," I managed to get out. "They're out in the room."

"Let's go find them," Em whispered, her blue eyes bright and hungry. Like I'd argue with that? She hopped down and tried to push past me, but I caught her, jerking her into my body for a long, hard kiss that left both of us gasping.

"Holy crap," she muttered as I let her lips go. "How do you do that? Seriously, that was like a movie kiss or something."

"Chemistry," I told her. "Technique doesn't even start to explain something this good."

She gave me a wicked smile.

"Ooohh, I love chemistry. How 'bout you be the science teacher, and I'll be the dirty girl who needs detention?"

EM

I tripped out of the bathroom, giggling as Hunter lunged after me. He caught me, lifting me high and throwing me down on the bed. Before I could catch my breath, he had me over his lap, one hand in the center of my back, the other sliding down between the cheeks of my ass.

I screamed, wiggling wildly.

"You said you needed detention," he told me, his voice stern. "I'm just trying to be a good teacher."

With this his fingers slid into me, deep. I stiffened at the invasion, then relaxed and sighed as he found my G-spot.

"That good?" he asked, rubbing my back up and down.

"Sure," I muttered, letting my head fall forward on the bed. It felt more than fine, actually. His fingers kept working me, and then his second hand lifted and smacked my ass abruptly.

I squealed and tried to sit up, but he held me down tight. His thumb had found my clit, and now he worked me inside and out. I felt tension spiraling up, and I squirmed awkwardly. I wanted him inside me, damn it. Hunter had other ideas. His clever fingers kept going, pushing me closer to an orgasm.

Holy hell, that was nice.

"You like that?"

"Yeah," I whimpered, twisting on his lap. "Like" wasn't really the right word. I wanted him to go faster, harder. Instead he slowed down, teasing me with a low, satisfied laugh.

"Please," I muttered, closing my eyes. "I need . . ."

Hunter smacked my ass again. I was so close now, something he must've sensed because he sped up again. My orgasm hovered, taunting me. I felt myself reaching for it, my legs stiffening. Hunter's cock was rock hard beneath me, and I realized with a thrill that after I came, I had another whole ride ahead of me.

That pushed me over the edge.

When I came, it hit so hard I clawed the bed, completely focused on the sensations taking over my body. Holy shit, that was incredible. I drifted through the aftershocks as he lifted me, laying me down on my stomach across the bed. I stretched out my arms, enjoying the feel of cool sheets beneath me as he stretched over me.

Hunter kissed his way slowly down my back, fingers trailing along the lines of my body until they reached my rear. My flesh knew the touch of his hands now, and when he slid his fingers back in, I sighed happily. Then his thumb edged up, lightly touching my asshole, and I stiffened.

"Trust me, babe?"

I considered the question. I trusted him not to hurt me, but this? I wasn't sure I was ready for this.

"It's okay," he murmured, kissing the small of my back. "Christ, I'll never run out of ways I want to fuck you, believe me. If you don't like one, we'll move on."

I sighed, then rolled over. Hunter nudged my knees apart, settling himself over my body as he smoothed a condom down over the length of his erection. I watched, mesmerized that something so large could fit inside me.

Then he kissed me, tongue probing deep as my arms came up around his shoulders. The kiss went on forever, alternating between deep, openmouthed tongue-play and him pulling back to suck and nibble on my lips. The whole time I shifted restlessly beneath him, his dick sliding back and forth along my clit.

Perfect.

Hunter lifted his head, eyes dark with need.

"You ready?" he asked me, positioning the tip of his cock against my opening. I nodded, more than ready. I felt his broad, rounded head push against me, slowly sliding deep inside. This was different than that first time. He was gentle this morning, and while the pain I'd felt in the alley had been sheer pleasure, this was something different entirely.

This was fantastic.

He spread me wide, opening me up as I watched us come together. There was something incredibly sexy about the sight of his cock entering my body.

I reached down between us, rubbing my clit gently.

"That's fucking hot," Hunter said, looking up at my face with a smile that literally took my breath away. "I think you should have to touch yourself every time we're alone together, even if we're just watching a movie or something."

"That might get awkward," I murmured, trying not to giggle.

"I don't care," he said, his tone urgent. "Fuck awkward. I want this."

"Ahh . . ." I gasped as he hit bottom. I let my hand drop, savoring the feeling of being pinned down.

"I like those little gasping noises you make, too," he said. "In fact, I like almost everything you do when you're naked."

This time I did giggle, although I stopped as he pulled out, then started sliding in a rhythm that had clearly been invented by Satan for the express purpose of driving me crazy. I tilted up my hips just a little, which was just enough to make his cock drag along my clit with each stroke. Then I let my arms flop to the side, because everything felt so good I couldn't imagine doing anything but just lying back and drinking it in.

"Sorry," I murmured. "I think I've lost the ability to move."

"Your moves last night were pretty good," he told me. "I'll give you a freebie?"

"Perfect," I whimpered, then closed my eyes to focus on the sensations running through me. Damn. Hunter was just really good at sex.

My orgasm built slowly this time.

Not because it wasn't perfect, the way he moved inside me. But I was more relaxed than I'd been in the alley, able to simply enjoy the feeling of his hard cock filling me and then retreating, brushing my clit and bumping my G-spot with every stroke. And even though his movements stayed slow and steady, each one built me up just a little higher until I felt an electrical tension winding tight.

"You getting close?" he asked, dropping his head to kiss the side of my neck.

"Uh-huh," I managed to say. "Very close. Oh God. Just a little more."

He sped up then, clearly reading my desire. Now his strokes hit harder, pushing up against my cervix with every thrust. It should've been painful, but it felt fantastic.

Just what I needed to push me over the edge.

When I finally came, it was almost a surprise. He'd created such a slow, steady buildup that I hadn't realized just how close I'd gotten until it hit. I spasmed around him, setting him off because he started moving faster, pounding me into the bed for long seconds before he came, too.

I felt his pulsing release with deep satisfaction, loving the press of his weight across my body. My arms wrapped around him, fingers tracing the lines of his back gently.

"I've decided we're staying here in the hotel," he muttered, nuzzling my hair. "We'll have food delivered and I'll just keep you naked."

Food?

My stomach woke up, growling suddenly. My cheeks heated with a blush. Could I ever—even for a day—be smooth and fabulous? Apparently not.

"Or I can take you out and we can talk," Hunter said, winking at me. "I don't want you fainting from exhaustion, and I have a feeling that if we stay in, you're not gonna get a chance to actually eat."

"Waffles?" I asked hopefully. He lifted up on his arms and smiled.

"Honey, seeing as my dick's still in your body, you can have whatever the hell you want."

HUNTER

I glanced over at Em, then reached down to catch her hand and put it on my thigh. It wasn't as good as having her arms around me on the bike, but her sitting next to me in my truck kicked ass in a big way.

God.

I still couldn't believe I was lucky enough to have this woman, despite everything I'd put her through. Emmy Hayes was either a saint or an idiot. Seeing as we'd already established she was smarter than me, I was hoping for saint.

"So, any place you want to go special?" I asked. She smiled at me, those brilliant blue eyes flashing.

"Anywhere they have food. I can't believe we're up already. You'd think we'd be exhausted after last night . . ."

"Don't worry, sweetheart. I promise I won't faint on you," I said with a smirk. She giggled. Then her face sobered.

"Hunter—"

"Liam."

"Liam, I don't want to get all weird and serious on you," she said. "But I'm pretty sure I'll be getting a pissed-off phone call from my dad in the next hour or so. Things got a little out of control last night . . . I'm not sure what I should tell him."

"You'll tell him you belong to me now," I said, turning into a Denny's parking lot. Not the world's greatest food, but they'd have waffles. Damn, I'd learn to cook them myself if it made her happy.

"What do you mean, exactly?"

I put the truck into park, then glanced over at her. Uh-oh. Em's face was shadowed and worried. I reached out and caught her chin, turning her to face me.

"You're my old lady," I said, catching and holding her eyes. "I respect that he's your dad and I don't want to get between you two. But he needs to know you're mine now. If he has a problem with that, you hand him off to me. I'm serious, babe. Nobody gets between us. Never again."

She blinked, her eyes bright.

"Okay," she whispered. "But—"

"No," I said. "That's all there is. We'll have shit come up, fight, whatever. But you're mine now. I won't be sharing you, I won't be leaving you, and I sure as fuck won't let the Reapers take you away from me."

"I hear what you're saying," she said slowly. "But I think I should make something clear, too."

"What's that?"

"I don't share, either. I know guys in clubs who have two or three old ladies. Or they have a citizen wife and a club girlfriend. You should be aware that this is an exclusive relationship, and that's nonnegotiable."

I shrugged.

"Okay," I said, reaching for the door. "Let's get food."

She grabbed my arm.

"No, I'm serious," she said. "You can't just blow this off."

"Baby, I'm not blowing it off," I said, smiling. I kind of liked jealous Em. "But seriously—I don't give a shit about anyone else anyway. We're fine."

She rolled her eyes.

"You're a little too good at this," she said. "Got all the right answers."

"It's hard to be perfect, but I have lots of practice."

She hit my arm and laughed. Then her face sobered.

"I have another serious question for you," she said. "I don't want the right answer, though. I want the truth, even if it hurts."

Shit. That didn't sound good.

"Do you love me?"

I studied her, considering my answer.

"No," I said finally. Her face fell, but I pushed forward. "My life has been pretty fucked up, Em. I'm not even sure I believe in love. But here's what I can tell you—I've never given a shit about any woman except you and Kelsey. That's it. Hell, I don't even remember their names half the time, and until I saw you I never even saw a problem with that."

She blinked rapidly. Christ, telling the truth sucked. But she asked for it and I'd already done enough lying.

"I remember the first time I laid eyes on you," I said. "It was at that little mini mall across from Costco, back in Coeur d'Alene. You'd just gotten your toes painted at the Vietnamese pedicure place. You had those funny, girly things between your toes and you fell off the damned sidewalk because instead of watching where you walked, you were looking at your phone."

"That never happened. I've never fallen down after a pedicure—I'd remember. That would totally ruin the nails."

"Well, you missed the curb but still managed to catch yourself," I told her, smiling at the memory. "Your phone fell down and broke, I think. I remember you looked up, right at me in my truck, and started laughing at yourself. Then you waved at me, grabbed the phone, and got in your car."

She frowned.

"I actually remember that," she murmured thoughtfully. "That was you?"

"Yup, that was me."

"That's . . . creepy. And weird, because why didn't I recognize you when we met again?"

"I had a full beard, my hair was shorter, and I was wearing sunglasses," I said. "Not only that, the window was tinted. I guess my point is this—I've spent days fucking women whose names I couldn't remember if my life depended on it. But you? I remember everything about the first time I saw you, even though we didn't even talk to each other. That's when it started, whatever this is between us. 'Love' is a word that doesn't mean a damned thing to me. 'Em,' though? That's a word that means everything. I'd die for you, babe. Kill for you, too. I stood up to my club for you and I don't regret any of it, not for a minute. So, you wanted to know how I feel? I don't even have a word for what I feel, sweetheart. I just know it's really fuckin' good."

Em sniffed, leaning forward and wrapping her arms around me. She squeezed me tight, then pulled back and took my face in both of her hands, studying me intently.

"I love you, Liam."

I closed my eyes, savoring the sound of the words. Then I said the only thing I could think of, even though I knew it was fucking pathetic.

"Thanks."

Her face fell, although she caught it, smiling at me a little too brightly.

Telling the truth sucks ass.

CHAPTER SIXTEEN

FIVE DAYS LATER
EM

On the Tuesday before Thanksgiving, I walked into the upstairs bathroom to find black beard hairs all over the sink. Ugh. Boy cooties.

"I really need to get an apartment," I muttered.

"No shit."

I jumped as Skid spoke behind me. I swung around to face him, glaring. God, the man was like a fucking cat—always sneaking up and freaking me out. I think he got off on it.

I'd been staying with Hunter since he'd liberated me from Cookie's house, which started out fun. I'd gone back a few times, of course, and still kept most of my stuff there. I couldn't live at her place long term, though, not if I wanted to have Hunter sleeping with me. Cookie didn't want me bringing guys home, and the last thing we needed was another confrontation between Deke and my boyfriend. Somewhere Hunter could stay over had become a very high priority.

God, this house was a cesspit.

I'd made excuses for the guys at first. It's hard to keep up with housework, especially if you're not used to it. Clutch still couldn't get around very easily, and they had so much to worry about with all the drama.

Yeah, after five nights here I could officially call bullshit on the excuses. Sure, they had to worry about the cartel. That consisted of keeping their eyes open for anything suspicious (nothing) and bitching (endlessly). I knew Hunter and Skid ran errands for Burke, and I knew that Grass held down a job of some sort . . . But so far as I could tell, their other primary activity was watching porn.

Oh, did I mention the extensive porn collection?

And I do mean *extensive*.

Kelsey and I got drunk together Sunday night and she filled me in. She was sleeping with Skid, something I couldn't quite understand a woman doing voluntarily, but she assured me she was just using him for sex. According to her, the place was a clubhouse in every way but name, seeing as Portland wasn't an official charter. Unofficially, Hunter was acting as president, with Skid as his VP/sergeant at arms. Grass and Clutch were muscle.

All of them were pigs.

I turned to look at Skid, who stood in the doorway behind me.

"Got any suggestions?" I asked. "I need somewhere cheap that doesn't smell like feet."

He sniffed, then gave me a puzzled look.

"It doesn't smell like feet in here."

"No, in here it smells like mildew."

He shook his head, frowning.

"Did Kelsey talk to you?"

"About what?" I asked.

"Her place," he said. "She's got a spare room and she's having trouble making rent. I had to buy her groceries this month. She was going to see if you wanted to move in."

"She didn't say anything."

"I wonder if Hunter told her not to," he said slowly. "He's worried she'll be a bad influence on you. He might've mentioned something to her about backing off and leaving you alone. If you ask about the room, I bet she'll say yes."

"What the hell is up with you two, anyway?"

"Me and Hunter?"

"No, you and Kelsey."

"Fuck if I know. When she's horny, she comes to see me. Sometimes. Pretty sure she has at least one other guy on the side."

"And you're cool with that?"

He shrugged.

"I can get laid other ways, too," he said. "No shortage of pussy. But I don't like seeing her struggle—sharing a place would be a good solution for both of you. You should talk."

"I will, thanks."

Huh . . . That was almost . . . nice?

Skid nodded and took off down the hallway. Weird guy. I wasn't nearly as scared of him these days, but I wouldn't mind seeing less of him. I closed the toilet seat, setting my stuff on it while I grabbed a chunk of toilet paper to wipe down the counter. That's when my phone started ringing. I glanced at the Caller ID.

Dad.

I swallowed, trying to decide if I should answer. Things were a little awkward between us, although he kept tabs on me through Kit. To say our initial conversation about Hunter hadn't gone well was an understatement. A big understatement.

Fortunately, nothing new had happened in the whole Reapers/Devil's Jacks/cartel triangle since the original shootings, but people weren't exactly breathing easy these days. I think we all assumed it was just a matter of time.

I sighed and grabbed the phone. I didn't want him worrying about me, and I knew he would if he couldn't track me down.

"Hi, Dad."

"Hey, Emmy," he said. Thankfully, I could tell from the tone of his voice that there wasn't an emergency. Lately my default assumption was disaster. "I'm just calling to find out if you're coming home for Thanksgiving. There's supposed to be a snowstorm tonight, figured I'd check in. You'll want to drive during daylight tomorrow, if you plan to be here . . ."

I smiled despite myself. No matter how weird life got, some things about Dad never changed.

"It's killing you that you're not here to check the tire pressure on my winter tires, isn't it?"

He stayed silent for a minute.

"Not gonna answer that," he said finally. "But since we're talking vehicles, when's the last time you changed your oil? I think it's just a matter of time before that car starts burning it. You should really be thinking about getting something newer."

"My car is fine, Dad," I said, feeling a little squishy inside. Sure, he drove me crazy. But I also loved the way he was always watching out for me. I missed him, I realized. I wanted to go home for the holiday.

"I need to talk to Hunter about Thanksgiving," I said slowly. "We'd discussed cooking something here, with his brothers."

Silence fell.

"You could bring him to Coeur d'Alene," Dad said.

I almost dropped the phone.

"Can you repeat that? I think I heard you wrong. Did you just invite Hunter for Thanksgiving?"

"Yeah," he said. "Not to the Armory, of course. I know you're convinced he's all innocent and shit, but a lot of the guys don't buy it. But I'll let him into the house if you come home."

I tried to process this.

"Where would he sleep?"

I heard a strangled noise on the other end of the line.

"He could stay in your room with you."

"Dad?" I asked carefully. "Are you dying?"

"What the fuck is that supposed to mean?"

"Like, do you have cancer or something? This isn't you. You're being . . . nice."

"I want my daughter home for fucking Thanksgiving," he snapped. "If that means I have to put up with her douchebag boyfriend, I will."

"He's my old man, and he's not a douchebag."

"Talk to your sister," he said suddenly, and then Kit was on the phone.

"I think Dad's about to have a stroke," she told me, her voice excited, the words tripping out almost too fast to follow. "Seriously. He's clenching his fists and his face is all red."

"He just told me Hunter could sleep in my room for Thanksgiving."

Dead silence.

"That is so fucking unfair," she burst out. "You know how many guys I've tried to bring home? He never lets any of them stay with us."

"That's the problem," I heard Dad say in the background. "Guys. Plural. I don't agree with Em's choice, but at least she made one. You're just using them up like tissues."

"Like you should talk?" she demanded. "You're worse than a fucking alley cat!"

Great. Once they started, they could go on like this for hours. I hung up, knowing Kit wouldn't even notice. I'd talk to Hunter after my shower, I decided. I wasn't quite sure what to think. I wanted to be with my family for the holiday, but I didn't entirely trust Dad not to shoot Hunter. He'd nearly killed at least two of my boyfriends in the past, and they hadn't even done anything to piss him off.

I shut the door and locked it, then stripped down and stepped into the shower with a shudder. I'd bleached the hell out of it the first morning I'd stayed there, but whatever lived in there was vigorous and fighting back. Nasty black crap was already creeping in along the seams.

Kelsey, I thought. *Talk to Kelsey, see if she has room. No mat-ter how much you love him, you can't live in a house where the shower is hostile and sentient.*

And to think, all this time I'd been afraid of the Devil's Jacks and their guns—it'd never occurred to me that the real danger was their disgusting, moldy bathroom.

Chemical warfare.

Hopefully Hunter would go to Dad's house with me. At least there, I knew the bathroom would be clean*ish*. I'd only been gone from Coeur d'Alene a month, nowhere near enough time for this kind of damage, even if Dad deliberately sprayed the mold with magic mold-food every day.

HUNTER

Em sat on my lap, her legs on either side of my hips, facing me. She was a smart girl—it's pretty damned hard for a man to say no to a woman when her pussy's snuggling up to his cock. Would've been perfect if it weren't for her clothes. I really needed to steal those, maybe set them on fire . . .

"So you'll come with me?" she asked. "I won't leave without you, but I really want to go. You can even bring Kelsey."

I snorted.

"Kelsey hates holidays. Says they make her think of kittens vomiting, too much nice family crap."

Em frowned and cocked her head.

"That makes me sad," she said softly. "You guys deserved so much better."

"It's better now, babe." I leaned up and kissed her, sucking her lower lip into my mouth. She wiggled against my dick, with pre-dictable results. Would I ever get tired of holding this woman? Couldn't imagine it happening, that's for damned sure.

Then she pulled away and I groaned.

"You didn't answer my question," she said, smiling at me eagerly. "Will you come for Thanksgiving?"

"You're not being particularly subtle," I told her, raising a brow.

"I'm all about direct communication. What's the verdict?"

"I need to talk to Burke about it," I said, considering. "I know it's about seeing your family, but there could be larger implications. But if Burke's okay with it, I can't imagine anything more fun than spending a holiday in the home of the man who wants me dead. Like our own fuckin' Hallmark movie, but with live ammo."

Em squealed, wrapping her arms around my neck and squeezing tight. This crushed her boobs against my chest, which I approved of completely. Did Hallmark movies have sex scenes?

"You're the best," she whispered. "I can't wait to show you everything. And I promise, I'll protect you from Dad."

I burst out laughing.

"I don't need protection."

She pulled away and gave me a look.

"Yeah, right," she muttered. "You're a big bad biker and everyone is afraid of you. Unfortunately, so are the Reapers, and there's a whole lot of them all concentrated in one place. We're going to play it safe the whole time, I promise. This means so much to me, Liam—when will you talk to Burke?"

"He's supposed to call sometime this evening," I said, running my hands down her back to cup her ass. "I'll ask him then."

"Sounds good," she murmured as I pulled her up tight into my hips. Then I rolled until she lay flat under me, all soft and open and gorgeous.

"I love seeing you like this," I said. "Love it when your hair is all over my pillow. I want a picture."

"What do you mean?"

I reached for my phone, unlocking it and opening the camera app. Then I sat up, straddling her, and held it over her head.

"I want a picture of you like this. Smile for me."

She rolled her eyes.

"Way to put me on the spot," she muttered, but she smiled. Then right as I took the shot, she stuck out her tongue.

"You're a very naughty girl," I said, frowning at her. "Now smile for real this time or I'm giving you a spanking."

I snapped another shot as the disposable cell on my bedside table started ringing.

"That'll be Burke," I said. I dropped my phone on the covers and reached for the burner. "I'll be right back, okay? Don't move."

She laughed and nodded. I took the cell and stepped out of the room, answering it in the hallway.

"Hey," I said. "What's up?"

"The sky and hard dicks," Burke said. "What the hell do you think?"

I snorted.

"God, you're a ray of sunshine in my life."

"I do my best. We've got news," he said. "Not good news. I guess there's a guy up in Coeur d'Alene pretending to be a Devil's Jack. Got a call from a bar owner, says he's been in a couple times, talking shit about the Reapers, making threats."

"You're fucking kidding me."

"Nope."

"Any chance he's one of ours?" I asked. Shit. I really, really didn't want to put another brother in the ground.

"He's not ours," Burke said. "But he's sneaky as hell. I guess the Reapers know about him, but they haven't caught up to him yet. He must've been sent by the cartel, kind of like waving a red flag in front of a bull. They're desperate for us to turn on each other. I think there's something deeper going on down south than just a territorial expansion. This isn't their usual M.O."

"You want me to look into it?" I asked, leaning back against the wall. "I've got the perfect excuse. You'll never guess who called today and invited me to his place for Thanksgiving."

"Hayes?"

"Got it in one," I answered. "You think it's related?"

"Possible," Burke said. "I can think of several reasons he might do it. He wants his kid back, probably sees inviting you as the best way to get her there. Not only that, you walk right into his house, easy as hell to ambush you. Or I suppose—and this is a hell of a long shot—that it's possible he's just being a decent human being, opening his home to his daughter's old man. If we can open communications, that'd be a real win-win here."

"So basically I'm bait?" I asked.

"I prefer the word 'chum.'"

"You have no idea how inspiring it is for a man to get a personal pep talk like this from his president. I'm assuming finding this faker is a high priority while I'm there?"

"You got it."

"And if I find him?"

"I'll want to talk to him," Burke said. "If he's connected to the cartel, we'll share him with the Reapers. Maybe that'll convince them we're for real. After that, accidents happen. Now go tell your girl you're going home with her for the holiday. Maybe get a special 'thank you' blow job. I think you should enjoy your dick while you still can—Reese Hayes is probably planning to cut it off when you get there."

He hung up on me, and I snorted. Always a joy.

I turned off the phone and opened my bedroom door.

"Hey, babe . . ."

I froze, taking in the sight of Em kneeling in the center of my bed, staring at me with tearstained eyes. Her hand trembled as she held up my phone. Fuck. Something was very, very wrong.

"I wanted to surprise you," she said softly. "Put that new picture with my contact info, so you'd see it whenever I call. I went to grab the one you just took."

Oh, double fuck. I knew exactly where this was going.

"Em—"

"Don't you fucking talk to me!" she screamed suddenly, throwing the phone across the room at me like a missile. I ducked and it hit the wall, faceplate shattering.

Okay. She'd found the pictures I was supposed to erase. Time for damage control.

"Let me explain."

"I. Said. Don't. Talk. To. Me." she said, her voice like ice. That was when it hit me. I'd screwed up bad. Real bad. "You know, I wasn't even trying to snoop. You took that picture less than five minutes ago, your goddamned phone was still turned on when you dropped it. *It was in a fucking album with my name on it.* Christ, Hunter. Do you ever tell the truth? You promised me you'd delete those photos. You *promised* me. I shouldn't be afraid to look at something that has my fucking name written on it!"

Her voice had been rising steadily through the whole little speech, and I winced by the end because she'd gotten so shrill it actually hurt my ears. To my horror, Em climbed out of the bed and started grabbing things, stuffing them into her backpack.

"I suppose it's too much to ask whether you shared them with the other guys?" she muttered. "Let me guess, did you give them to the whole club, or just the guys here at the house? I know how much you all enjoy your porn. I suppose I should feel honored you felt I could compete."

"Nobody has ever seen those but me," I told her, holding up my hands defensively. Shit. I'd had girls mad at me before, but I'd never really cared. Jesus—no wonder women hated me, if I made them feel this way. "I swear to you, Em. I kept them for myself . . ."

"Like that makes it better?"

She leaned over and grabbed my phone off the floor, stuffing it into her pocket. Then she swung her backpack over her shoulder and came to stand in front of me, arms crossed over her chest protectively.

Em wouldn't even look me in the eye. Nope, she just stared at my chest coldly.

"Move out of my way," she said. "I'm leaving. I can't stand to be around your lying ass right now."

"We need to talk—"

She held up a hand.

"You will move out of the way," she said, every word slow and distinct.

"This isn't over," I said carefully. "You go and calm down. Then we'll talk."

"I can't think about that right now," she muttered, pushing through the door. She started toward the stairs, then turned back to look at me. "You've lied to me all along. Makes me wonder . . . What else have you been lying to me about?"

I shook my head.

"Nothing," I said quietly. Em shrugged.

"I don't believe you."

EM

Deke's bike was parked outside Cookie's house when I pulled up in the darkness.

Just what I needed.

I punched in the code and crept inside, not wanting to wake her up. It wasn't that late—only eleven—but she went to bed early because her shop opened at five every morning.

Knowing my luck, Deke would still be up.

I stepped inside, closing the door carefully. No sign of Deke in the living room. He must be sleeping in Silvie's room. Lucky me. I started down the hallway, but halfway down, Silvie's door opened, and Cookie stepped out. She froze with a guilty, deer-in-the-headlights look on her face.

"I had a fight with Hunter," I said quickly. "I don't want Deke or anyone else to know about it."

Cookie nodded, then glanced back at Silvie's door.

"Let's just say tonight's a don't-ask, don't-tell situation?"

"It's all about plausible deniability," I answered, desperate to get away and pretend I hadn't seen anything. She nodded, then darted down the hall to her own room. I followed her lead, closing my door and locking it behind me. Deke? Ugh. I pulled off my clothes and climbed into bed, staring at the ceiling, my mind spinning. It felt like everything was going horribly wrong.

Hunter had lied to me, keeping my pictures.

Cookie and Deke were . . . doing things I didn't want to think about.

At least Kit and Dad were still fighting. Not everyone in the world had lost their minds. It would be good to see them tomorrow. I'd leave Portland around ten, and enjoy the holidays Hunter-free. It would give me time to think and decide what I should do about the situation.

I was pretty sure I'd made a terrible mistake. I just wasn't sure whether that mistake was falling for him in the first place or walking out on him after our fight.

CHAPTER SEVENTEEN

"Wake up!" someone yelled, pounding on my door. I rolled over, trying to figure out what was going on. The spot next to me in bed was empty, and I frowned.

Where was Hunter?

Then it came back. The pictures. Lying bastard.

"Fucking wake up," Deke shouted at me, his voice grumpy. I stumbled to my feet, thankful I'd pulled on sweats to sleep in last night. I managed to open the door a crack and look out at him.

"What is it?"

"You left something disgusting in the driveway," he said. "Go clean it up or I will."

I raised my brows.

"What are you talking about?"

"Go see for yourself," he muttered. "Oh, and Em?"

"Yes?"

"I don't want to hear any rumors about Cookie. Got me?"

Seriously?

"Cookie is my friend," I said, trying not to yawn as I rubbed my eyes. "She opened her home to me, she gave me a job, and she treats me like a sister. No matter what I might think about you, I wouldn't do anything to hurt her."

He studied me, eyes narrowed. Then he nodded.

"Okay," he said. "Good to know."

I rolled my eyes and shut the door. God. I had no idea what she saw in him. None.

Five minutes later I stood on the porch, looking out across the lawn to the driveway. My little car was tucked up next to the garage. Boxing it in neatly was Hunter's truck. I couldn't see that well, but he seemed to be asleep in the front seat.

Fucking great.

I marched over to the truck, slamming my hand down on the hood with a crash. Hunter sat up quickly, and I saw him reach for something. Probably a gun. Good—he might need it if he fucked with me any more this morning.

He opened his door and stepped out. His face was drawn and tired, his hair messy and tangled, like he'd been running his hands through it. I'm probably a horrible person, but it made me happy to see him suffer a little.

"Hey, Em," he said, his voice low. "I know you don't want to see me, but I had to catch you before you took off. I assume you're still planning to go to Coeur d'Alene?"

"Yes," I replied, folding my arms. "Probably leaving in a couple of hours. We can talk when I get back, Hunter. I'm still too pissed right now."

He shook his head slowly.

"Sorry, babe. Can't let you do that."

"Do what?"

"Drive to Coeur d'Alene by yourself."

I raised my brows.

"Have you lost your mind? Consider yourself uninvited to Thanksgiving, asshole."

"I don't have to be at your house with you," he said quietly. "But with all that's happening, there's no way I want you driving across the state by yourself. If you don't let me go with you, they'll make some prospect do it. Do you really want some poor kid to miss the holiday with his family just so you don't have to look at me during a car ride?"

When he put it that way, I felt like a bitch. Of course I didn't.

"Okay, you can drive with me," I said. "But you're on your own once we get there.

"I'll be driving," he said. "We'll leave your car here. I'll stay with friends or in a hotel, but I'm delivering you safe to your family."

"Controlling much? What's wrong with my car?"

"Babe, think it through. If I'm in Coeur d'Alene for the weekend, I'll need some way to get around. You'll have your sister and dad to ride with."

I glared at him a moment longer, because he was making sense and that was frustrating as all hell.

"I hate it when you're right," I finally muttered. He gave me a crooked smile, so sexy I actually felt a twinge down below.

Bad girl!

"Well, lately I'm not right very much," Hunter said. "Don't know if it makes a difference, but I'm really damned sorry for what I did to you."

"About that," I said, glancing away. "You're going to need a new phone. Yours may have gotten smashed up a little more after I left last night. . . maybe run over a couple times."

"Kinda figured there might be a tragic accident," he said with a straight face. "I'll pick one up."

"What about the pictures?" I asked. "Where else do you have them?"

"They were backed up on my laptop," Hunter said. He caught and held my gaze. "I erased all but one last night. Secure erased, overwritten on the hard drive. Nobody will be able to get to them now."

I considered, wondering if he was telling the truth.

"I don't know whether to believe you. And what's this 'all but one' bullshit?"

Hunter glanced down at the pavement.

"I kept it," he admitted. "My favorite. I figured if you're dumping my ass, I wanted something to remember you by. As for believing me, I guess the only way to get there is for you to give me another chance. Give me a shot, Em. No more lies. We both know there's shit I can't tell you—"

I cut him off, holding up a hand.

"Club stuff wasn't part of this," I said. "And *you* know that *I* know better, so don't try to use it as an excuse."

He sighed, leaning back against his truck, hands in his pockets. I tried to think, figure out what to do.

"You can drive me home," I said slowly. "But you're not staying with me, and this isn't me saying we're back together. I need time to think things through, decide if you're worth the risk. I won't be with someone I can't trust."

"I understand," he said. "If nothing else, I'm relieved you'll let me see you home. We all want you safe—me and your dad both. He and I aren't on the same side very much, but I respect the hell out of him. He raised a daughter who won't take my shit."

I turned away, my eyes suddenly full of tears.

"Deke says you need to leave," I said. "Come pick me up at ten."

"Will you actually be here?"

Swinging back around, I narrowed my eyes at him.

"I guess you'll just have to *trust me*, Hunter. Don't worry, I'm not the liar in this relationship. I'll be here."

"Guess I earned that," he muttered.

"Damned straight. Now get out of here before Deke has a temper tantrum."

HUNTER

I watched Em out of the corner of my eye as I drove. She was staring out the window at the desert, apparently fascinated by the vast expanse of nothing. Either that or she just wouldn't look at or talk to me because she was pissed off.

Still pissed off, that was.

We'd been on the road for three hours, and the only time she'd said a word was when she needed a pit stop. It'd felt like a huge victory this morning when she'd agreed to ride with me—like getting a second chance. Now I was starting to worry it was just a ride, that she'd never talk to me again. That fucking hurt. Hurt in a way I'd never experienced before. Like real pain, physical pain.

I was starting to hate this romance shit. Life is just so much damned easier when you don't feel anything.

I had to make it end.

Spotting an exit up ahead, I flipped on my turn signal.

"What's up?" she asked, turning to me and frowning.

"You'll see," I murmured. We pulled off the freeway and I turned onto the small, lonely road and started driving. A few minutes later we passed behind a big hill littered with exposed rock formations and tumbleweeds. I slowed and shifted the truck into park, swiveling to face her. She stared straight ahead.

"Em," I started.

"I'm not ready to talk to you," she said. "Just keep driving. I don't know how I'll feel after the weekend, but I just want a break from you right now."

"You want to kick me in the balls again?"

Christ, did those words just come out of my mouth?

Em looked at me. Finally.

"What is this, some kind of joke?" she demanded. "You think me kicking you will change what you did?"

I shook my head slowly.

"Nope, I know it won't change a thing," I said. "But it might make you feel a little better, at least it seemed to last time. If it does, that's good enough for me."

"I won't promise to forgive you."

"That's okay."

She narrowed her eyes.

"You're insane," she muttered, but I could see her softening, her mouth twitching. Thank fuck for that. "Kicking you in the nuts won't fix anything."

My balls agreed one hundred percent.

"But you know what? Last time it really did make me feel better. Let's do it."

I swallowed, then opened the truck door and stepped outside slowly. Em climbed out, and we met in front of the truck. I spread my legs, crossed my arms, and waited.

"Close your eyes," Em said, her voice cold. Somehow that was worse, but I did it anyway. "And pull down your pants. Briefs, too."

"That's not part of the deal."

"Fine," she said. "I'll get back in the truck. Let's go."

I looked up at the sky and swallowed, wondering how I could care about someone so much and want to strangle her so badly at the same time. Then I unbuckled my pants and dropped them, closing my eyes. Nothing. She walked back to the truck and I heard her digging around.

"Do it," I growled. "I can't just stand here forever, waiting."

"If you insist. Are you ready?" she asked, her voice soft.

"Fucking do it already, Em."

"Okay, get ready."

I heard a strange, popping noise, and then icy cold liquid sprayed my balls and cock.

"*The fuck!*" I yelled, jumping back and opening my eyes. Em stood in front of me, spraying me with a can of Diet Coke in one hand. The other held her phone.

Pictures . . . Fucking karma, biting me on the ass.

"Jesus Christ, you're a bitch!"

"And you're a dick," she said sweetly, starting to laugh. The pop ran out, but that didn't stop her giggles. I grabbed my pants, jerking them back up as I stuffed my wet dick back inside.

"What the fuck was that all about?"

"Payback," she said, eyes bright. "You got bested by a girl, and I have the video to prove it. C'mon, you have to admit that was better than what you had planned?"

I scowled.

"I don't know," I muttered. "Are you going to show the pictures to Skid?"

"What, don't like naked pictures floating around that you can't control? Wow, that must really suck. I wonder what that feels like?"

"You know damned well I'll lose face if they think I can't control my woman. It's not the same thing."

The instant I said it, I knew I'd fucked up. Again. Christ, I should just crawl into a cave and die, it'd be more efficient.

"You want to try saying that a different way?" she asked, putting her hands on her hips. "Only this time, listen to your words very carefully in your head first. Then ask yourself whether you *ever* want me touching your penis again."

"I'm a dick," I said, raising a hand to run it through my hair. "This is not a secret. But I don't want to control you, Em. You know that. Fuck."

"And I don't want to humiliate you in front of your brothers," she said seriously. "I just wanted you to feel a little of what I felt. At least I didn't lie to you about it."

"You're right," I said, shaking my head slowly. "I don't know what else to say, babe. You were right, I was wrong."

"That came out a lot better this time," she said, offering me a smile. Then her face grew serious. "You know, when I kicked you before, it felt damned good, but it's not like it changed anything. Am I supposed to torture you—just because I can—every time you screw up? I fucking love you, asshole. I don't like seeing you in pain. That's why lying to me was so horrible in the first place."

I took a deep breath, overwhelmed. Fuck, I hated shit like this.

"I don't deserve you, babe. But this last night? It's like I died. If you forgive me, I swear to you—*I swear*—I will never knowingly do anything to hurt you again."

"Knowingly?" she asked, cocking a brow. "That's a pretty big loophole."

"Let's be honest here," I said, throwing it all out. "We both know I'm gonna fuck up. But I'm pretty sure I love you, Em."

Her breath caught.

"What did you just say?"

"I love you," I repeated, the words tasting strange in my mouth. "At least, I think I love you. I've never felt this way before, but I can't imagine caring about anyone more than this. I want to be with you, Emmy. Hell, I offered to let you kick my balls just so you'd feel better. Doesn't that count for something?"

She stepped forward and wrapped her arms tight around my neck. I reached around her hesitantly, then pulled her close. Shallow man that I am, my cock immediately hardened, despite the cold Diet Coke shower.

"I love you, too," she whispered. "But I need to know one more thing."

"What?"

"Which picture did you keep?"

I stilled. Now there was a trick question. All of them were damning, but I had a feeling she'd hate the one I kept the most.

"The one of your ass all covered with my jizz," I muttered, feeling like a bigger prick than ever before in my life. "It's really hot, babe."

She started laughing into my shoulder, or at least I hoped to hell she was laughing and not crying.

"Will you erase it?"

"Yes."

"Okay," she whispered. "I'll forgive you. This time. But you don't get another pass. No more lies. It's a deal breaker for me, Liam."

"Fuckin' love my name comin' out of your mouth."

"I know," she said. "I have a present for you."

"Really?" I asked, pulling back to study her face. "What? Crap, that's the wrong question. Why?"

"Maybe because I love you. Or maybe because you shouldn't get out of this totally free and clear. So you have a choice . . . reunion sex—right here, right now—or you can keep that one special picture, so long as you never show it to anyone."

Hellfire. And I thought the last one was a trick question.

"Can we got back to the getting-kicked-in-the-balls option instead?"

EM

"I still can't believe you picked the photo," I grumbled.

"Maturity is all about delaying pleasure to improve your situation long term," Hunter said, grinning at me. "Love you, Em."

I rolled my eyes. He'd said it something like ten times now, and as much as I enjoyed hearing the words, I was starting to feel like maybe we needed a new topic of conversation.

It was getting dark outside, and we'd just passed through Post Falls. A nasty, freezing rain had started as we drove through Spokane, slowing traffic. I saw at least four cars in the ditch along the way—I'd never admit it, but I was actually kind of glad Hunter was driving.

I was kind of glad we weren't fighting anymore, too.

Not only that, Kit had texted a couple times, talking about all the different foods she'd bought for our dinner tomorrow. We loved cooking together, and while it wasn't the same without Mom, I never felt closer to her than in the kitchen with my sister.

"You're sure you're okay with this?" I asked Hunter yet again. "I know it sounds like a joke, but Dad seriously has a history of shooting my boyfriends. He says it's an accident, but after the second attempt you start to wonder."

"Your other boyfriends weren't like me," he replied without a hint of concern. "The fact is, I'm with you and that's not gonna change. Picnic and I will come to an understanding. Don't worry about it."

I tried to picture how that might play out.

"If he asks you for six goats in exchange for me, you don't have to actually buy real goats. He'd probably take kegs instead."

Hunter snorted, then reached over, putting his hand on my knee.

"Don't worry about it, Em. You said you'd give me another shot, so trust me on this one. I've got it covered."

My phone rang. Dad.

"I swear to God, he can hear when I'm talking about him," I said, rolling my eyes as I answered the phone. "What's up?"

"Where are you?" he asked, voice tight. Well, crap. This wasn't a friendly call to check up on us.

"We just passed through Post Falls," I replied. "What's going on?"

"I need you to come straight to the Armory. We've got a situation. There's been another shooting, right here in Coeur d'Alene. We don't have proof, but one of the Jacks has been in town for the past week."

"Oh fuck . . ."

"What is it?" Hunter asked.

"Shooting," I said, my voice terse.

"Give me the phone," he demanded.

"Stop talking," my dad ordered in my ear. "I'll explain things to him in a minute. You will *not* tell him what I'm about to say to you, though. This is important."

Oh my God. It was happening. Right here, right now . . . Things were falling apart between the clubs. Was I going to have to choose? I peeked at Hunter out of the corner of my eyes and swallowed.

"Give me the phone," he said again. I shook my head.

"Let me finish talking to Dad," I told him. "Then I'll hand it over."

Hunter nodded tightly, but I saw the muscles in his jaw clench.

"Like I said, come straight to the Armory," Dad continued. "We don't know that it's the Devil's Jacks, but if it is, you're a valuable hostage. We've been through this before. I love you, Em. I loved your mother, too, so I know what it's like to care about someone so much it hurts—I think that's how you feel about Hunter. I hope to fuck he feels the same about you. But I need to get you away from him, get you somewhere safe until we figure things out."

"Dad . . ." I whispered. I glanced at Hunter again and tried to think of how to say what needed to be said without kicking off the damned war all by myself.

"I'll protect him, Em," my father told me, apparently reading my mind. "I know you might not believe it, but I'll make sure he gets through this alive, so long as he brings you home. If he gets hurt, it'll be because of something he does, not because of who he is. I swear this, baby."

"I'm giving the phone to Hunter now," I said slowly.

"Promise me, you'll come to the Armory?"

"I'll let you know where we're headed once we figure that out," I replied, feeling my eyes tear up. Shit. This was happening so fast.

"Okay, pass me off to him."

I handed over the phone, then watched as my man's face slid into that horrible blankness I'd seen when he faced off against Deke.

"I understand," he said. "We're coming, don't worry. I want her safe as much as you do."

Then he hung up the phone.

"We're going to the Armory," he said, his voice almost expressionless. "There's at least one shooter. I'm sure they suspect the

Jacks—we know someone's trying to start trouble in Coeur d'Alene. He's not one of ours, Em. Part of my job this weekend was to hunt him down."

My heart clenched.

"So this is actually a business trip for you?" I asked, feeling small.

"No," he replied. "This shit came up after I asked Burke about visiting your family. If something happens to me, you need to convince your dad to at least talk to Burke before they do anything. Someone's working very hard to turn us against each other. Don't let them play you, okay?"

I swallowed.

"Okay," I said. "Are you sure you want to go to the Armory? Dad says he'll protect you, but he's just one person."

Hunter gave a short, harsh laugh, then looked over at me. He reached over and touched my cheek.

"The Armory is the safest place I can think of right now," he said. "This isn't the army we're up against. It's one or two shooters, and that place was built to withstand a hell of a lot worse. Your sister is already there, and I guess most of the other women are, too. Fuck of a way to start the holiday."

I reached down and grabbed my purse, pulling out my little black semiautomatic. I checked the magazine before setting it in my lap.

Then I glanced back over at Hunter. To my surprise, he was smiling.

"Best fuckin' old lady ever," he muttered, shaking his head.

"No, that was my mom."

"Love you, babe."

"I love you, too."

Guess we didn't need another conversation topic after all.

Things fell to shit about three miles after we turned off the main highway headed north. The sun had just set, and the frozen rain had covered everything, leaving a sheen of ice across the road. God, I hated driving on ice.

I knew there were probably guys stationed at the turnoff to the Armory, but I didn't see any of them. I'd texted Dad with our ETA and Hunter's license plate number, so hopefully they were just letting us pass through because they recognized us. I knew they'd call it in, though, which meant we'd hit the point of no return.

"Slide your seat forward, Em," Hunter said as we started up the winding road. I slid forward, and then he reached around behind my seat. I heard the sound of Velcro tearing open, and then I felt his hand against my back, inside the cushions.

He pulled out a large handgun.

"Hold this for a sec," he said. Then he reached over again and dug around some more, this time bringing up two spare magazines.

"Okay, you're good to scoot back. Take a look for me?"

I dropped the magazine and examined it. Fully loaded, all good. I popped it back in and chambered a round. He tucked it down between the seats after I handed it to him.

"You know, Dad would never trust me to check his gun."

"He sees you as a little girl," Hunter replied, his eyes darting back and forth across the road. "I see you as a competent adult, one I trust. Big difference. Something feels off here."

I shivered, thinking he was right. The weather was forcing us to drive way too slow. Fucking ice.

Suddenly there was a loud bang and the truck careened to the right.

"Crap," Hunter grunted, fighting the wheel as the truck lurched to the side. At first I thought we'd just blown a tire. Never a good thing, but not the end of the world. Then there was another loud bang, and the front end collapsed. Two tires out, I realized. We slid abruptly toward the edge of the road, Hunter cursing steadily, but there was just too much ice. I braced myself as the truck skidded off the embankment, rolling down the side of the hill and smashing into a tree. Air bags exploded as the truck flipped over onto its side, passenger window pointing toward the sky.

Sudden horrible silence filled the cab.

It all happened so fucking fast. I couldn't quite breathe and my heart was exploding with adrenaline.

"Shit," I muttered, pushing the bag away from my face. God, something smelled horrible. Like burning. "What happened?"

Hunter didn't answer. I blinked, trying to get my bearings. My eyes were watering and I couldn't quite see. The seat belt held me suspended on my side, the position painfully uncomfortable. I reached up and rubbed my eyes, which didn't help, and realized that the air itself was hurting my lungs.

Flopping my hand around, I found the window control and pushed it, the battery miraculously still working. The window rolled down into the door and a rush of cold air came in. I took a deep breath. Thank God, I could breathe again. Unfortunately, with the fresh air came cold, freezing rain.

"Hunter?" I whispered. Nothing. I looked down at him and gasped. A shattered tree stump had smashed up through the driver-side window, the remains splintered into sharp spikes of wood. It was less than an inch from the front of Hunter's face, and I saw blood trickling out of his nose. Branches and pine needles were everywhere, so many I could hardly see him. They filled his entire half of the cab.

"Babe?" I asked slowly. I reached down and touched his shoulder. He shifted his head and moaned. *Alive.* Thank God, because if that thing had been one inch closer, it would've gone right through his skull. I reached down and felt his neck, finding a strong pulse. Okay.

Now what?

I shook my own head, forcing myself to focus. I needed to call for help, but my purse had gone flying. Where the hell was my phone? I couldn't see it anywhere, and I'd smashed his last night.

Damn it. That's what I got for having a temper tantrum. Then I spotted my purse down in the footwell.

But how to get it? I reached down with my left hand and braced my body against the side of Hunter's seat, then unclicked my seat belt with my right, holding on to the strap like a jungle vine for balance. Slowly I slid down into my footwell, kneeling on the side by the center console.

Hunter stirred again.

"Em?" he asked, his voice rough.

"I'm fine, babe," I said, looking down at him. His eyes were open now, and I tried to see his pupils. Were they the same size? That's when I realized the radio was still playing . . . I reached up and turned on the light, and we both flinched from the sudden brightness.

"Look at me," I said. His head turned, and I breathed a sigh of relief. Pupils were fine, and he seemed to be getting more alert every second. Must've hit just enough to knock him out, but hopefully nothing serious.

"We had an accident," I explained, my voice shaking. "I don't know what happened—I think we lost a couple tires, maybe? Then we hit ice."

"Someone shot out the tires," Hunter said. He started squirming in his seat, trying to move his arms, but the stump and branches held him completely trapped. "One tire blowing, I can see. But two? That's someone who knows their shit. We need to assume they're outside, Em. Have to get ready for them. Start by turning off the light. No reason to give them an easier target than we have to."

I froze, eyes wide. I hadn't quite processed the whole shooting thing, but of course this wasn't an accident. Not good. Not good at all.

"This really sucks," I whispered, then realized how ridiculously inadequate that was, given the situation. *Shit.* I turned off the light and started fumbling in the darkness for my purse. It fell open and

I nearly lost the phone. I caught it right before it fell, but unfortunately I dropped the purse in the process.

Hunter watched the whole time, frustration written all over his face.

"Call your dad. The club can get here faster than anyone else, and they'll have the best shot of dealing with whoever's out there, too."

"What about an ambulance?" I asked.

"I'm fine," he said, twisting in his seat uncomfortably.

"That's what people usually say right before the brain hemorrhage kills them. You need a hospital."

"Em," he said, his voice firm. "Stop talking to me and call your dad. Now. Then I want you to find my gun and get ready to protect yourself while I try to work myself loose. Fuckin' tree."

My hands shook a little as I dialed my father's number, but I forced myself to stay calm. Our lives depended on me not falling apart, no matter how scary the situation had gotten.

"Yeah?"

"Dad, it's Em," I said. "We're about four miles from the Armory, and we're in trouble. Hunter's truck went off the embankment by the railroad tracks, on the south side of the road. I need you to get here fast."

"Ambulance?"

"Hunter says no," I said, glancing down at him again. His color was good, so that was something. "Someone shot our tires. That means they're out there right now, they're close, and they know what they're doing. I need to hang up and grab my gun now."

I shoved the phone into the console. Now what? My gun was in the purse, which had disappeared into the mass of branches and pine needles.

"My gun should still be down between the seat and the console. I have a holster built in."

I started digging around, and sure enough, the gun I'd checked for him before was still there. I pulled it out carefully, checking the magazine one more time out of habit before I cocked it. Then I pulled myself up and tried looking out through the windshield.

More branches, everywhere.

That was a good thing, I realized. We had decent cover.

"Should I climb out my window, you think? Look around?"

"No," Hunter muttered. "Just stay down in the footwell. Our best bet is to hide and wait for the cavalry."

"I'm a good shot," I told him, refusing to acknowledge the panic I felt welling up into the back of my throat. *Calm down*, I told myself firmly. *You can lose it later, once we're safe.*

"It's dark, there's freezing rain, and all you have is a handgun," Hunter replied, his voice dry. "Nobody's a good shot under those conditions. Just stay low, sweetheart. I'm gonna try and get loose, but I'm thinkin' they'll have to cut me out of this one. If I die in this truck, don't tell Skid I got my ass kicked by a tree, okay?"

I snorted, then giggled. Obviously he'd lost his mind. I tried to stay quiet but another giggle broke free. Then Hunter stuck out his tongue at me, and I laughed out loud, tears rolling down my face.

"You're crazy," I said, wiping my face with the back of my hand.

"Maybe," he said, giving me his crooked smile. "But nothing burns off tension like a laugh. You think you can reach my seat belt?"

I leaned out of the footwell and dug around through the pine needles, ducking my head down to get a better look. In that instant, a bullet punched through the windshield into the passenger seat, passing through right where I'd been just seconds before.

I froze.

"Goddammit," Hunter said, suddenly thrashing to get free. "Holy fuck, I cannot believe this."

I fumbled for his seat belt urgently. *Crap. CRAP.* Just because I knew how to shoot a gun didn't mean I was ready for a fucking firefight. Another shot tore through the glass, this time closer to Hunter's head. So much for all that cover . . . Or were they just shooting randomly? I couldn't figure out how they could possibly see us.

"Back in the footwell," Hunter ordered, and his voice didn't leave any room for negotiation. "Keep the gun handy. I don't know if you'll get a chance to shoot, but if you do, I want you ready."

"What do you mean?"

"Well, a sniper's not gonna come in close unless he has to," Hunter said. "Which means ideally—from his perspective—you're dead without ever making eye contact. Right now this one doesn't have a clear target, so that's in our favor. We just need to hold on for a couple minutes, until the Reapers get here."

Another bullet came through, winging Hunter's ear.

"Fuck," he muttered as blood started pouring out.

I gave a sobbing gasp.

"Emmy, you have to hold your shit together," he said, his voice sharp. "I love you, babe. I can't hide or defend myself, so I need you safe in that footwell. Then if he hits me you're alive to save me. Hold your shit together for me, sweetheart. I need you to hold it together."

I took a deep breath and nodded, although I knew he was lying again. If the sniper hit him, it would be a headshot—Hunter wouldn't have a chance. He was just trying to protect me. *Ridiculous*. Like a footwell would stop a bullet, anyway? I racked my brain, trying to think of some way to protect us.

This was insane—I had to do something or we'd die out here. I looked up through the rain at the open passenger window. We needed a distraction. I eased out of my hidey-hole.

"Stay down, Em," Hunter said, his voice cracking like a whip. I ignored him, checking the gun to make sure it was ready. All good. I slid into position expecting another shot to hit any second, crouching with one foot on the side of Hunter's seat and the other on the inside wall of the well. I counted to three, then popped up and shot four times into the darkness.

I dropped back down, gasping.

Hunter blew up.

"What the fuck was that about?"

"I want him to know we're armed," I said. "Playing possum only works if they don't know what they're doing. I'll bet a hundred dollars his orders are to make damned sure we're dead, and I'm not just going to sit and wait for some asshole to put a bullet in my brain."

"He could've shot you, Em."

I stared at him, trying not to let out the hysterical laughter I felt bubbling up deep inside.

"Seriously, babe? That's your argument? That's a fucking bullet hole about an inch from your face, and let's not mention the ear. Getting shot is almost a given at this point, more of a *when* than an *if*. We need to hold out for Dad, and now that our sniper knows we can fight back, he'll have to be more cautious about approaching the truck. That'll slow him down, which might make the difference for us."

"So your solution is to play Whac-a-Mole with a murderer?"

"Hunter?"

"Yeah?"

"It's done."

"Fuck, but you piss me off," he muttered. His body twisted, and then he kicked out, hard. "Fuck!"

Long seconds passed, and I started shivering as the icy rain soaked my shirt. Maybe I should shut the window? No . . . At least this way maybe we'd hear something if they got too close.

Hunter kicked the truck again, rocking it slightly.

"Well, let's look on the bright side," I said, deciding he needed a distraction.

"Don't."

"The good news is that we'll probably be either rescued or dead before we have to worry about serious hypothermia. There's always a silver lining, Hunter."

He growled at me again.

Men.

CHAPTER EIGHTEEN

HUNTER

I don't think I've ever been so pissed off in my life.

Em frustrated me so much I wanted to strangle her, maybe save our sniper the trouble. I was angry with myself, too, because I should've been able to control the fucking truck. Now instead of protecting my woman, I was stuck watching her crouch over me with a gun, ice building up in her hair as her lips turned blue.

All because I'd been captured by a fucking *tree*.

Another shot rang out, although this time it didn't hit the truck. At least that was something . . . Although if I died tonight without protecting her, I hoped to hell I'd find a way to come back and haunt Picnic Hayes. I'd use my ghostly powers to make him desecrate my useless fucking corpse.

More shots. Then shouting.

"Em!" I heard someone yell. She rose slightly.

"No," I said, voice cracking. "Stay down until they find the shooter. Just call out. Let them know we're okay, but under fire. Safer that way."

"We're safe!" she bellowed, so loud it hurt my ears. "The sniper hit the truck at least three times, so be really fucking careful. Also, I have a gun. Identify yourselves before coming too close, or I'll shoot you myself."

"Hang tight, kiddo," I heard a deep voice yell back. "We're comin' for you."

He sounded familiar . . . Then I placed him. Duck. Old guy I'd met when I negotiated with the Reapers for Em's release.

"Do you think they'll be able to find him?" Em asked. Her teeth started chattering. Shit, at least I had my pine needle blanket . . .

"No idea," I told her. "If he's smart, he's already taken off. He could stay out there and try picking them off, but weather like this sucks for everyone."

Then I noticed her hands had started trembling. From the cold or adrenaline—didn't matter which.

"I think you should set down the gun."

"Nope."

"Don't shoot me by accident, please."

Em looked down and smiled, still gorgeous despite the icicles building up in her hair. In the faint light from the dashboard, I could see that her lips were blue, her nose was red, and her shirt was soaked through. Not the best time for a wet T-shirt contest, but her tits looked outstanding.

"I promise," she said softly, biting her lip. "I will never shoot you by accident."

I considered her response.

"That's less comforting than you'd think."

Several more shots rang out, and then we heard a high-pitched, agonized scream.

"Holy shit," Em whispered, smile gone. Her eyes were huge, and she brought the gun back up, finger moving to the trigger. Then someone shouted through the darkness. Someone close.

"Em, it's Painter."

Seriously? Fucking *Painter* was going to rescue us?

And right there I had it—proof that God's a twisty bastard.

"Did you get him?" Em yelled back.

"We got one of them," Painter said. "No way to know if there's more. But we're searching. Prez says to get you out, take you back to the Armory while we look for a second sniper."

"We're going to need a chainsaw or something," she yelled. "Hunter's trapped."

"He alive?"

He sounded a little too cheerful when he asked the question.

"Yes, he's fine," she replied.

"I'm fuckin' great," I yelled out. "Get Em out of here!"

"Okay, I'm right by the truck now," Painter called back. "I'm gonna climb up and look inside. Put down your gun, Em."

Em lowered the gun, but I noticed she didn't let it go. She gave me a quick glance, offering a smile that didn't quite meet her eyes.

"What's that about?" I asked quietly.

"Painter isn't my dad," she replied. "He hasn't made any promises about your safety."

"You're going to hold a gun on *Painter* while he's trying to rescue you?"

"No, I'm going to protect my old man while he's stuck under a tree. Consider me your life insurance, babe. If I leave, Painter's got no reason to keep you alive and nobody to witness what he does to you. I'm staying put until my dad gets here."

The truck lurched and Painter leaned over the open passenger-side window, taking in the situation. First he gave Em a quick once-over, probably checking for blood or obvious wounds. Then his gaze turned to me, eyes predatory. I stared him down, wordlessly telling him that I saw right through his shit. He gave me a chin lift, then turned his attention back to Em.

"Take my hand," Painter said, reaching toward her. "We'll get you to the Armory. Ruger can go back and grab the tools we'll need to cut out your *boyfriend*, but you need to get warm."

She shook her head.

"I want Dad."

"He's kind of busy right now."

"Nope," she said, lifting the gun from her side and balancing it carefully on her knee with both hands. She wasn't pointing it at anyone, but it wasn't the friendliest of stances, either. "I'm staying with my *old man* until Dad gets here."

Painter flinched. Heh.

I hated that cocksucker. I really did.

"Will you please go get him?" Em asked, her voice like very polite granite. She might be scared as hell, but she wasn't showing any weakness. "I'm not going anywhere without my dad."

"Screw this," Painter muttered, shaking his head. "I'll be back in a few. Enjoy the fuckin' cold while you wait, Em."

She relaxed visibly as he jumped down off the truck.

"You okay?" I asked. "I really wish you'd go with him."

Em rolled her eyes, waving off my concern with one bluish hand.

"No fucking way," she said. "I leave, you got no witnesses. Painter hates you. Ruger's not too fond of you, either, and he's the one with the chainsaw. Anyone decides to kill you, they'll be going through me first."

"Babe, I say this with all due respect. You scare the shit out of me."

She reached down and touched my cheek, and I turned my head to kiss her fingers.

"Emmy, it's Dad," I heard Hayes call out. Then I felt the truck shift as he climbed up to look through the window. "Painter said you won't put down your gun and go to the Armory."

"Thank God," she said, her voice full of relief. She'd been closer to the edge than I realized. "I'm so glad you're here. I won't leave Hunter with anyone but you. But I'm really cold . . . Not sure how much longer I can last out here."

I couldn't see his face well in the darkness, but I had a feeling I'd recognize the expression—the same mixture of love and frustration I'd seen in the mirror a hundred times since I'd met her.

"Emmy, nobody is going to hurt Hunter," the Reapers president said. "I gave my word."

"Would Mom have left you behind?" she asked, her voice a challenge.

He sighed heavily, then reached down to take her hand.

"Nope," he said. "That's why I wanted you with a Reaper, honey. We really can't afford not to have you on our side. You remind me more of her every day."

EM

It felt good to be back in the Armory again. Better than I expected. Of course, it probably didn't hurt that I'd been met at the door by Dancer, Marie, Kit, and Maggs. Sophie was upstairs with the kids, who were constructing a mighty campsite in the game room on the second floor.

Horse had given me a ride home, stepping inside long enough to catch Marie and stick his cold hands on her stomach. She'd shrieked and swatted at him until he caught her close for a long, hard kiss. Then he'd headed back out into the rain, leaving me dripping in the center of the kitchen. Dancer wrapped a blanket around me, and Marie handed me a cup of hot coffee. I found myself shivering so hard my jaw hurt.

"So what the hell happened?" Dancer asked, settling me on a stool. "The guys ran out of here like the world was ending."

"Someone shot out our tires," I told her. Wow, saying it out loud made it sound so . . . insane. "Hunter was driving, and the truck started sliding on the ice. We went off the road. A tree pinned him inside the truck—he's still there—and I called for help. That's when whoever shot the tires started shooting at us."

The women all stared at me, eyes wide.

"That's some serious shit," Kit said slowly. "But you're okay? And Hunter, too?"

I nodded.

"Yeah, but they'll have to cut him out."

Kit tapped her fingers against the counter nervously.

"Did you know a Devil's Jack has been seen around town?" she asked. "And I guess they spotted him earlier tonight, right after someone took potshots at Dancer and Bam Bam's house."

My eyes widened.

"They shot at your house?" I asked Dancer, stunned. *"With the kids there?"*

"Yes," Dancer said, her face more serious than I'd ever seen it. "Em, I love you, but I don't understand how you could be with a man who's part of that club."

I stiffened.

"The man who shot at your house wasn't a Devil's Jack," I said firmly. "Hunter told me he wasn't. He says that someone else is trying to set us all up for a war. They want peace—they *need* peace, or their club won't survive."

The women exchanged looks, and Marie coughed nervously. Great. Now they all thought I was a gullible idiot.

"Anyone want a drink?" Maggs asked brightly. "I could use a shot."

"Grab the bottle," Kit said, reaching out to take my hand. I tugged it away from her, frustrated.

"Just don't make any judgments until we have the full story," I told them. "You don't know what happened out there. Remember, the sniper tried to kill Hunter, too."

"I guess we'll see," Marie said. "It's good to have you back, Em. The good news is we all brought food with us—whatever else happens, we can celebrate the holiday together instead of just canceling everything."

Perfect, I thought. Just what I needed. Now everyone could

spend tomorrow glaring at me and Hunter, blaming him for everything that'd gone wrong for the Reapers during the last twenty
years. And with his truck all busted up, it wasn't like we could
leave. Maybe I could rent a car . . .

"Drink?" Maggs asked again, her tone forced. I shook my head.
I already had a headache. The last thing I needed was to throw a
hangover into the mix.

Grown-up life was complicated.

HUNTER

By the time they pulled me out of the truck, my nuts were the size
of raisins. Fuckin' cold out there. Despite that, I remembered to
grab our bags from behind the truck's seats. I also grabbed my
Devil's Jacks cut, folding it carefully over my arm before climbing
up the bank. Hayes had an SUV waiting for me. At least, I hoped
the SUV was for me. A black cargo van had been parked there, too,
reminding me of the one we'd used to kidnap Em and Sophie.

Not the most encouraging of sights.

When I reached the top, I found Hayes. He eyed my colors but
didn't say anything. He also didn't tell me which vehicle would be
carrying me to the Armory. I knew he'd promised Em that he'd keep
me alive, but it seemed likely that my comfort wasn't part of the
deal.

"You catch the shooter?" I asked him.

"Shooter's in the van," he said. "But you'll ride with me.
C'mon."

I followed him to the SUV—score one for me. Hopefully it was
a good sign. Horse and Painter joined us in the backseat. Nobody
spoke to me on the short, tense drive to the Armory, which was just
fine. The night was far from over, but I'd had plenty of time in the
truck to consider my strategy. I'd been in situations like this before,

although usually on the other side. I knew better than to show weakness or volunteer information.

On the bright side, at least I wouldn't have to waste any time looking for the asshole pretending to be one of my brothers. He was in the van, I was almost certain of it. Smart money said once they took him into the Armory, he wouldn't be coming back out, which saved me even more time.

We passed through a gate in the building's courtyard wall. Em was somewhere inside, hopefully snug and warm, surrounded by her girls. Just the thought of her exposed in that truck, the way those shots had blasted through the windshield, chilled my blood.

This love shit sucked.

Now it wasn't enough I had to watch out for Kelsey, I had to keep Em covered, too. *This* was why I'd never had pets. Too much work. Hayes stopped the rig, turning it off and looking at me.

"Come inside?" he asked, as if I had a choice.

"Sounds good," I replied, opening my door. I stepped out to find us parked next to a sunken stairwell leading under the building.

Nothing ominous about that, right?

They'd packed our bags away in the back of the vehicle, which meant I didn't have access to my spare sidearm. At least they hadn't searched me. I considered that a good sign, seeing as the hunting knife on my hip wasn't exactly subtle.

I guess technically I was still a guest.

Hayes started walking toward the stairwell, but I paused to pull on my cut. Painter stopped cold, glancing back and forth between me and his president.

"You aren't letting him wear his colors inside, are you?" he demanded. Christ, this guy was a drama queen.

"You'll get them off my dead body," I told him, my voice matter-of-fact.

At least five or six Reapers gathered to watch as Painter and I faced off. I unstrapped my knife, wrapping my fingers around the hilt loosely. Shitty way to go out, but with any luck I'd take the asshole with me. Then Picnic stepped in.

"We still have a truce, brother," he announced. "At least until we prove they're behind the attack. I don't know if you got a close look at the cut our sniper friend was wearing, but it didn't look quite right to me. Until we know better, Hunter is a guest of the club paying us a friendly visit."

Yeah, 'cause all friendly visits happen in darkened basements.

Still, the look of frustration on Painter's face was nice. I winked at him, then followed Em's dad down the stairs. He unlocked the metal door, which scraped open onto a barren concrete hallway lighted by naked bulbs screwed into the ceiling.

"Nice place," I murmured, and Picnic snorted back a laugh.

"We try," he said. "I've got a room here that'll work for you to wait in."

He unlocked one of the doors lining the hallway. I peeked in. Room, my ass. This was a straight-up prison cell. I cocked an eyebrow at him.

"Thought I was a guest?"

"We'll leave the door open, don't worry," he said, smiling pleasantly. "And I wouldn't want you getting bored, so I asked Horse to keep you company."

Horse. Could be worse, I decided. I'd met the man several times in the past few months. Seemed to be a straight shooter. Thorough, too. There'd been an incident with one of our guys back in Seattle around the end of August. Fucker was out bad and on the run. When Horse and Ruger came across him, they'd been sweet enough to call us for a pickup. They'd even wrapped him up as pretty as a Christmas present, all ready for delivery back to his old chapter.

The big Reaper stepped forward, offering me a cold smile.

"Why don't you fill me in on what's been happening in Portland while we wait?" he said. "I always love catching up on gossip."

"Yeah, I'll get right on that," I told him, resisting the urge to flip him off. He gestured toward the room graciously enough, so I walked in, flopping down on the low cot. I might not have any serious injuries from the accident, but I figured I'd be plenty sore in the morning, assuming I lived that long. Might as well make myself comfortable for now. Horse followed me in, carrying a rusted metal chair from the hallway. He set it down facing away from me, then straddled it, leaning forward against the backrest.

"So what's your story?" he asked. "I hear rumors about you and Em. You know she's like a little sister to all of us. I'm real protective of my sisters."

"Yeah, I've gotten that vibe from several of your brothers," I said, folding my arms behind my head. "She tells me Daddy doesn't like it when she and Kit bring home their boyfriends."

"You could say that."

"Well, I'm not her boyfriend. I'm her old man and I'm not gonna let anyone get between us. You could get around that by killing me, but until then, consider Em taken. How's that for gossip from Portland?"

He raised a brow and nodded thoughtfully.

"To be honest, it's more interesting than what we usually hear from Deke," he said. "He likes to talk about pesky little Devil's Jacks moving in like they have a right to exist on our territory."

"Don't you ever get tired of this?" I asked, considering how many different versions of this conversation I'd heard over the years. "You insult the Jacks, we insult the Reapers, someone gets shot and then we all pout for the next decade?"

I'd caught him off guard, and he laughed.

"Can't believe I'm sayin' this, but I kind of like you. Hope I don't have to bury your body tomorrow."

"Well, I have to admit," I said, sitting up and leaning forward on my knees. "I'm kinda hoping you don't have to bury my body tomorrow, too."

A scream cut the air, and Horse cocked his head.

"Think that might be your club brother," he said, studying my reaction.

I shook my head.

"Not one of ours," I said flatly. "Let me lay it out for you . . . If that was my brother, I'd be fighting for him right now. I'd rather die than let a Reaper torture a Jack. But him? That's the cocksucker who tried to kill my woman. One of his bullets missed her head by a couple of inches at most. Hell, he grazed my ear. The only problem I've got with this situation is I'm in the wrong room. I should be in there with him, making sure your boys don't kill him too fast."

Another scream wailed out.

"Mind if I take a nap?" I asked, catching and holding Horse's gaze. "Sounds like it could take a while."

Horse laughed again.

"Make yourself comfortable."

CHAPTER NINETEEN

I actually managed to drift off for a while, which says something about how tired I was. I guess it shouldn't have surprised me so much—I hadn't gotten much rest the night before, most of which I'd spent in Em's driveway. I woke up when someone kicked the cot, instantly alert. Horse stood at the foot of the bed.

"Apparently our friend has finally decided to talk," he said. "Oh, and good news. He's not a Devil's Jack."

"No shit," I muttered, rubbing my face. Felt like a cheese grater. *When was the last time I shaved?* "I told you he wasn't."

"Glad it was the truth. Get up, Pic wants you in on the interrogation. Says you need to hear what this asshole has been saying. Some pretty serious shit coming to light."

I followed Horse into a room significantly larger than the one we'd just left. A hint of bleach hung in the air, along with the acrid scent of urine mixed with the copper of blood. Work lights hung from the ceiling from extension cords, and the floor sloped downward toward a drain in the center.

Convenient.

Right over the drain sat a bloodied, dark-haired man in a metal chair, arms and legs tied down tight. His face was a mass of bruised flesh, eyes swelling shut, and his lips were both split wide open. His shoes were off, showing the smashed remains of his toes. Blood dripped from his fingernails, too—or rather, from where his fingernails used to be.

Someone had had a long night.

"This our guy?" I asked, taking a quick glance around. The room held Ruger, Duck, Horse, and three men I didn't recognize. One seemed to be the designated bad guy, because blood still covered his hands. I shot a quick look at his name patch. Bam Bam.

Picnic came over to stand next to me, his face grim.

"Yup," he said. "He's not one of yours."

It took everything I had not to roll my eyes.

"Yeah, we covered that before," I said politely. "So whose is he?"

"Cartel," Pic replied. "Of course, this one's not important or valuable. They sent him up here to parade around in fake colors, set things up. Cut's over there, you can take a look in a few . . . But that's not the interesting part."

I cocked a brow in question. I found someone wearing fake Devil's Jacks colors pretty damned interesting.

Pic walked over to the chair and kicked it. The man moaned.

"Tell my friend here what you just told me," he ordered.

The man lifted his head, although I had no idea if he could see me through the swelling.

"I'm just a *halcone*," he whispered, his English faintly accented. Mexican, I figured. Of course, not a huge leap, given where the cartel was headquartered. Men like this—poor and desperate—made up most of their cannon fodder.

"I follow orders. They told me to go with some *gringo* boss, come up north. Wear that vest, go to bars, talk to people. Do whatever the boss says. Tonight he said to shoot at people, so that's what we did."

"We?" I asked.

"Soldier," he muttered, his words slurred. "Called himself Sam, don't know who he really is. He came with the boss, maybe."

"White?"

"*Sí.* American."

"Who was shooting at the truck?"

"Sam shot the tires," he said. "Then he told me to kill the people in the truck and he disappeared. I don't know where he went."

"Do you know anything about the other shootings?"

"I was down south until last week, when they sent me here," he said. "Nothing to do with any of this. Are you going to kill me?"

I glanced at Picnic. His face was blank.

"Burke will want to talk to him, if you're willing," I said. "This isn't just about your club—the Jacks need all the information we can get, too."

"Holding him for a couple days is no problem," Ruger said. He pinned me with a hard stare. "We have plenty of room down here, could keep someone prisoner forever, if we wanted to."

I had a feeling he wasn't talking about the bloody pawn sitting in the chair.

"Take him out and get him cleaned up," Picnic said to Horse. The big man stepped forward, nodding to one of the others I didn't know. Together they lifted the man—chair and all—and carried him out of the room. I looked down at the blood on the concrete, considering my own situation.

Fuck it. Now was as good a time as any to play this through.

"I'd appreciate it if you could give Burke a call," I said to Picnic. "I'm fresh out of phones."

"I'll take care of it," he said. He turned to leave, but I caught his arm. Ruger stepped forward, cracking his knuckles. I resisted the urge to roll my eyes again. *Yeah, I get it. You're gonna protect the prez, kill me with your bare hands, et cetera* . . . So fucking predictable.

"We need to talk," I said. "Might as well get it over with. Can't do it in front of Em."

"No offense, but you're not my favorite person," Pic replied, narrowing his eyes. "Just because we called you in to witness for your club doesn't mean I feel like chatting. Better be damned important."

"I think it is. I figure you've spent a fair amount of time and energy considering different ways to kill me over the past couple months?"

Pic gave a harsh laugh, nodding.

"You would, too, in my shoes."

"Can't argue with that," I said. "Here's the thing . . . I don't want to spend the next twenty years waiting for you to shoot me in the back. I love your daughter and I won't give up on her, so if that's a deal breaker, you should kill me now. Otherwise you need to back the fuck off me and my old lady."

That caught his attention.

Picnic studied me. I waited for him to say something, but Ruger stepped forward, his face cold and tight.

"Let's put him in the ground," he said. "Sophie went through hell because of this asshole. I nearly lost her."

I held Hayes's eyes, ignoring the other man. This was about me and Pic, about determining—once and for all—whether he could tolerate me as Em's man. I raised my hands, palms empty, and turned around so my back was to him.

"I'm ready," I said. "Go ahead and do it. Good timing, too— you can say the cartel got me. She'll never know the truth, and neither will my club."

"Why?" Pic asked.

"Because she deserves a man with a future," I said, stretching my neck to one side. Already getting sore from the accident. "I want that man to be me. I love her and I'll do everything I can to keep her safe and happy. But I'm a realist, too. If the Reapers are determined to kill me, I'm dead already. Might take you a while to make your move, which means it'll hurt her even more when it finally happens. I'd rather end it now than set her up for something worse down the line."

They stayed silent behind me. I wasn't stupid—the timing wasn't perfect. A smarter man wouldn't have pushed, but if Pic planned to do it, he might as well get it over with. We needed to get out from under this shadow or it would eat us alive.

"I should shoot you," Pic said slowly. "Because you know what? I think you're gonna hurt her. You won't mean to do it, but it'll happen and then I'll have to pick up the pieces."

That wasn't promising. I braced myself, waiting for a bullet. Would he do it fast, or drag it out?

"Turn around."

I swiveled to find him closing in on me, fists clenched. I tried to force myself to relax as the first punch caught my face, to roll with it. Pain exploded through me, radiating out from my cheekbone. A second hit came from another direction, and I realized Ruger had joined in on the action.

Just what I needed . . .

I lost all sense of time after that. At some point I fell to the ground, which made it easier for them to kick me. I handled it pretty well, I think, considering my entire body had turned into one great raging wave of agonized torture. I managed not to scream, although I couldn't stop myself from moaning when someone got in a particularly good shot. By this point I hurt so much I figured it couldn't get much worse.

Then I felt a rib snap . . .

It was worse. *Motherfucker.*

"Enough," I heard Hayes say, his voice sounding distant. Someone rolled me onto my back, and I squinted against the bright lights on the ceiling. Then a face looked down into mine.

My least favorite face on earth. Fucking Painter.

He was saying something, but I couldn't quite make it out through the ringing in my ears. I shook my head, focusing my eyes on his lips. He said it again.

"Can I take his cut?"

Jesus fucking Christ.

Did this man not learn? I rolled to the side, pushing up slowly with my arms until I was on my knees. I took a few seconds to recover, vaguely aware that more men had filtered into the room. They were talking but I couldn't quite make out the words.

I pushed to my feet—swaying—every breath a slice of hell as my broken ribs shifted and grated in my chest. Painter stood right in front of me, smirking like a playground bully. I spat out a tooth and offered him a hate-filled smile.

Then I grabbed his shoulders and slammed my forehead into his nose.

He dropped like a stone, blood flowing freely. I swayed again, stepping back. It took everything I had to stay on my feet, although the beating I'd just had gave me a bit of an advantage. I already hurt so damned much that the pain in my forehead blended right in.

I took a deep breath and answered Painter's question.

"I already told you. You'll take my fucking cut off my dead body and you'll leave my woman alone. Fuck with me again and I'll put you in the ground."

I staggered back, raising my head to find Picnic.

"We done here?" I asked, reaching up to test my ribs cautiously. Jesus, the pain was incredible. "Because this is your last shot. Kill me now or leave us alone."

"We'll put you and Em in a room upstairs," Pic said, his face grim. "I don't like it, but I'll accept it. I can respect a man who'll fight for my girl."

He glanced down at Painter one more time, then turned and walked out of the room. I staggered after him, hoping to hell someone in this place had some fucking Vicodin.

"So what story do you want to tell Em?" Hayes asked as we

walked slowly down the hallway. He didn't push me, which I appreciated. Just staying upright was a goddamned miracle at this point.

"No story," I said. "My balls are the one place that hasn't been kicked tonight, and I'd like to keep it that way. I'll tell her it's business, so we can't talk about it."

"You've never been in a real relationship before, have you?" he asked. I shook my head. We stopped in front of the steps and I looked up. Fuck. I didn't want to climb those.

"How did you know?" I asked him, pausing to catch my breath. He gave a sharp laugh.

"You'll find out."

EM

It was after two in the morning when Dad walked into the darkened kitchen. I'd been getting more and more nervous about Hunter's safety, especially when I'd seen several of the guys going back and forth to the basement.

I wasn't an idiot.

I knew what was down there—hell, Kit and I practically grew up in this building. There weren't a lot of secrets left, although I'm sure my father was clueless about how much we'd seen and heard over the years.

Hours ago, I'd listened as the vehicles pulled into the courtyard, so I knew Hunter had to be down there with them. Horse even came in to tell us they'd found the shooter, and that we could stop worrying.

That scared me more, because if they'd found the shooter, why wasn't Hunter back with me already? Around eleven, I considered a rescue mission, then decided the odds of that backfiring on Hunter were way too high. As much as I hated to admit it, interference from me wouldn't help him. Not under these circumstances . . . It was one thing for me to protect him in the truck, when he'd been pinned down. But barging in on him now? That'd make him look weak in front of my dad and his brothers, and Hunter couldn't afford to look weak.

I should've stayed in the pickup truck.

Now Dad stood in front of me, his face wearing an expression I couldn't even begin to understand.

"Well?" I demanded. "Where is he? Is he all right?"

"Nice to see you, too, baby girl."

"Hey, Em," I heard Hunter say. He stepped out of the shadow of the stairwell, leaning against the door frame as if just standing was almost more than he could handle.

Holy shit.

I brought a hand to my mouth, horrified.

"What the hell happened to you?" I whispered, feeling tears building. I ran over to him, but when I tried to touch him, he flinched away.

"Sorry, babe," he muttered. "Feeling a little low. Why don't you grab some ice and maybe help me up to bed?"

"You can use the room on the second floor," Dad said. "I'll find some painkillers."

I looked back and forth between them, trying to figure out if we'd somehow stumbled into an alternate universe where people showed up randomly beaten and nobody seemed to find it noteworthy.

"Do either of you want to tell me what the hell happened here? He wasn't like this when I left him, Dad. I trusted you!"

My voice rose as I spoke, my hands fluttering. I felt like I should be doing something, but I had no idea what.

"Babe, you know I promised never to lie to you again, right?" Hunter said. I nodded, stunned by the damage to his face. It was all mottled and bruised. Blood dripped sluggishly out of his mouth, trailing down his chin. He held a hand to his ribs, and his breathing didn't sound quite right to me. "Well, this is one of those times that

I'm not gonna lie, which means no matter how much you ask, you won't hear a story to make you feel better. You want the truth, you need to accept that. Just help me get clean and patched up, and let's go to sleep."

I glanced back over toward Dad. He was crouched down, digging in one of the cupboards. Then he pulled out a large first-aid kit.

"I'll meet you upstairs," he said. "There's a bed waiting on the second floor, Hunter. They saved it for you. Bathroom across the hall has a shower. Just try to keep it quiet—don't want to wake up all the kids. I guess they're camped out in the game room, which is just down from where you'll be staying."

"Thanks," Hunter said. "Appreciate the hospitality."

"Am I the only one who's not crazy here?" I demanded suddenly. "What is *wrong* with you? What did you do to Hunter?"

They exchanged glances, and Picnic shrugged.

"I'm starting to get what you meant earlier," Hunter murmured to him. "I'm not used to this."

"Used to what? Having the only not-insane person in the room demand answers from you?"

"Having someone care this much about me," he said quietly. "Em, I really, really love you. I think I've finally convinced your dad of that. Whatever you're imagining this is"—he gestured down at himself—"you're wrong. But believe me when I say I can't explain it. Just know it all ended right, the good guys won, and I really fucking want to crawl into bed with you and sleep. Pic, you got any Vicodin?"

My dad nodded, then stepped out of the room.

"You're really not going to tell me?"

"Nope," he said. "I guess you'll just have to trust me when I say it was necessary, and you don't need to worry about it happening again. And Em?"

"Yes?" I whispered.

"I didn't lie to you. Remember that. I could've told you all kinds of stories to explain this, but I didn't. Would've made my life a lot easier. I hope that means something to you."

I shivered, trying to process his words. Nothing made sense.

"Baby, can we please go upstairs?" he asked quietly. "I can see you have lots to think about, but I'm not sure I can stay upright much longer."

I nodded, forcing myself to snap out of my fog.

"This isn't over," I told him. "But let's take care of you first. I think you need the ER. If Dad won't loan me his car, I'll borrow Kit's."

"There's an inch of ice covering the road," he said, and I think he smiled, or at least tried to. Hard to tell under the circumstances. "We already crashed once tonight. I'll be fine—this isn't the first beating I've taken, and it's not like they'd do much for me anyway. Tape up my ribs, maybe give me a few stitches. Painkillers. We can do all that here, although I think I'll take a pass on the stitches. I could use a few more scars, it'll enhance my reputation with the brothers. They're always sayin' I'm too pretty."

This time I knew he was smiling.

"You're insane," I said, shaking my head. "What if you have a head injury or something?"

He sobered.

"It's not worth the risk to go back out, babe. There was at least one shooter we didn't find tonight."

I froze.

"Horse said we didn't need to worry anymore."

"Well, that was probably before we had all the details," Hunter said, sighing. "Thought it was one guy at first. I'm sure they'll gather everyone tomorrow and fill them in on what they need to know. I'll even bet the second guy disappears after this—they weren't after us in particular, just trying to stir up shit between the clubs. But we have proof now that the cartel was behind this at-tack, which should be enough to convince the Reapers and the

Jacks that we have to work together. Tonight backfired on them in a big way."

"Damn," I whispered. "I guess that's something. But I get your point. Between the ice and the cartel, I guess staying put is smarter. I suppose we should go upstairs?"

"What a great idea. Wish I'd thought of that," he murmured, although I thought I caught a hint of humor in his eyes. Maybe. Like I said, hard to tell with all the swelling. I took his arm and led him carefully across the room, through the fire door, and into the main stairwell.

"You want to wait for my dad to give you a hand?" I asked, considering the climb ahead of us. I could steady him, but that was about it.

"No," Hunter said, his voice wry. "I'd just as soon not get any more help from your father. I've had about as much as I can handle."

An hour later I crept downstairs. Hunter was out and I doubted anything short of the zombie apocalypse would wake him up. I knew I'd find Dad in the Armory office. He had a couch in there, and with so many people sleeping over, he wouldn't take up a bed some kid could be using.

I knocked on the door softly, not wanting to wake up whoever else might be camped out nearby.

"Give me a minute," Dad said, and I heard him moving around. Then the door opened and he looked down at me.

I didn't smile.

"I need to talk to you."

He sighed. "Come on in."

I pushed through as he turned on a lamp, shutting the door behind me and leaning against it. He sat back on the couch. We stared at each other for long seconds.

"I really miss your mom," he said finally. "She knew how to handle you girls. I never figured it out."

The words caught me off guard and I felt the sudden prickle of tears. I shoved them back ruthlessly.

"This isn't about Mom. It's about us."

"What happened between me and Hunter is none of your business. You know that. It's not your problem and you shouldn't be worrying about it."

I shook my head slowly, wondering if he'd ever get it.

"No, Dad. It's definitely my problem when the man I love gets beaten half to death because my father hates the idea of me growing up."

He opened his mouth to reply, but I held up a hand, cutting him off. His eyes widened.

"I understand club business," I continued. "I get that you're the president and we all have to do what you say. I've never disrespected you in front of your brothers. But this isn't about the club, it's about our family and you need to listen up, because I am not fucking around right now. If you ever touch my man again, you're dead to me. *Dead.* I won't talk to you, I won't look at you, and I sure as shit won't let you see any grandchildren down the road. We clear?"

He sighed again.

"We're clear."

I turned to leave, but he stood up and caught me, tugging me into a hug. I held out for a second, then let the familiar sense of safety and belonging I felt in his arms surround me.

"I'll always be your father," he said quietly, resting his chin on my head. "Me and Hunter, we worked things out. He understands me and I think I'm startin' to understand him. But no matter how much you love him or where you end up, you'll never stop being my little girl. I love you, Em."

This time I let the tears come.

"I love you, too, Daddy."

A moment later I pulled away and looked up, studying his face. "I need to get back to Hunter now."

He nodded at me, running a hand through his hair, looking almost wistful.

"I know, baby. Go take care of him."

Thanksgiving morning dawned bright and sunny.

I woke up and crawled out of bed carefully, trying not to jostle Hunter too much.

Walking over to the window, I peered out to find everything covered in a thick layer of ice. And I mean *everything*. Cars, evergreens, the power lines. Yikes. Those cables looked about ready to collapse. As far as I could see, ice caught the sunlight and reflected it like millions of tiny prisms. Almost like we'd gone to bed on earth and woken up in a fairy tale.

Of course, there was one big downside to the whole frozen wonderland thing . . . No fucking way we'd be able to leave today, which meant Hunter and I would be stuck sharing our first holiday together with my entire Reaper family. On the bright side, only about half of them wanted him dead. Unfortunately, several of those who did would be cooking today, so I figured I should taste anything they offered him before letting him touch it.

Maybe we should just do Christmas in Portland . . .

I heard a noise from the bed. Hunter looked much, much worse today. His bruises had ripened and his face made me think of a smashed tomato. Make that a smashed tomato with eyes.

"Come back to bed," he muttered. "And bring the drugs with you. I feel like shit."

I walked back over and found the bottle, carefully spilling out a couple pills into my hand. Hunter managed to pull himself up long enough to swallow them, with the help of some water. Then he lowered his head painfully back into the pillow, clearly spent from even that small effort.

I settled on the bed next to him.

"I've been thinking things over," I said quietly. "And I want you to know how much I appreciate the fact that you didn't lie to me. I also realize you're not going to tell me anything, and I know why. He did this to you because we're sleeping together, although the kidnapping thing probably didn't help, either. And I'm sure you just stood there and took it because of some kind of macho, bullshit pact you made with him."

Hunter closed his eyes.

"I'm too tired for this, babe. You need to let it go. We'll have a nice holiday dinner together and then tomorrow we'll get the truck situation figured out. It's all good."

I crawled under the covers, leaning up on my elbow to study his pulped face.

"Promise me it's over."

"What's over?" he asked, his voice sleepy.

"Your shit with my dad. Or do we have to go out and buy him a herd of goats, too?"

"Naw," he whispered. "Pic said kegs were just as good. He's a practical man."

"You're going to drive me crazy. This isn't okay."

"I know. Love you, babe."

"Love you, too."

"Can we please go back to sleep now?"

I snorted, then rolled onto my back.

"Sure, why the hell not," I said. "Not like we can have sex, which sucks for you. I've been studying that book. Did you know there's a whole chapter on erotic massage? Apparently a man's penile tissues actually extend way down into the scrotum, and if you press gently—"

"Em?"

"Yes?" I asked innocently.

"You're an evil, evil woman."

I smiled, savoring my small victory. Then I decided I might as well go back to sleep—I'd need my strength to make it through the afternoon. Knowing my luck, Uncle Duck would decide to tell Hunter the story about when I'd been six years old and sang "Jingle Bells, Batman Smells" in a surprise solo at the school holiday program.

Uggh.

We were definitely spending Christmas in Portland.

EPILOGUE

SIX WEEKS LATER
PORTLAND, OREGON

The coffee shop was supposed to close at four that afternoon, but of course I had a couple of customers lingering. That wasn't usually a problem. I just flipped the "Closed" sign and cleaned up while they finished.

Unfortunately, these two guys were camped out for the long haul. They'd each bought a small cup of tea two hours ago and had been arguing ever since about whether God was dead or simply never existed. Cookie didn't like to kick people out, but she was also willing to draw the line in situations like this. I hated to ask them to leave, though. We couldn't afford to lose customers.

Unfortunately, the shop wasn't doing that great and I was worried about her. I felt guilty over moving to Kelsey's apartment, too, although realistically Cookie hadn't been charging me enough to make much of a difference in her monthly budget. I still tried to babysit for her whenever I could, and I'd even gone over last week and cleaned the house.

That single-parenting shit was exhausting just to watch. I couldn't imagine actually being in her shoes.

The door jingled as it opened.

"I'm sorry, we're close—" I started to say, then broke out in a smile when I saw it was Hunter. I supposed eventually I'd get to the point when I didn't feel totally giddy every time I saw him, but we weren't there yet.

"You get off work early?" I asked. He'd started a regular job at a mechanic's shop two weeks ago, although they seemed to be unusually flexible with his hours. I figured there was a story there. I also figured I'd probably never hear it. So far as I could tell, the shop was heavily financed by the Devil's Jacks. At least he didn't lie about it—Hunter had been painfully truthful with me ever since our fight over the pictures. This was a double-edged sword, something I discovered the first time I asked him whether an old sweater of Kit's made me look fat.

(Apparently it did.)

"Burke's in town," he said shortly. Then he jerked his chin toward the two hipsters hoarding their tepid tea dregs in the corner. "Why are they still here? You closed half an hour ago."

I shrugged.

"Chasing out customers feels wrong to me."

Hunter's mouth tightened, and he walked across the room, grabbing a chair from their table and sitting down across from them. Their eyes widened as he leaned back in the seat. He reached down and pulled out the large Buck knife he kept strapped to his leg, starting to clean his oil-stained fingernails.

"See that fuckin' gorgeous babe over there?" he asked Hipster One, jerking his chin toward me. "That's my woman. I'd love some time alone with her right now, but she's stuck waiting for you little posers to leave, even though the shop closed thirty minutes ago and you're probably not even going to leave a tip. Seems wrong to me, somehow. What do you think?"

Hipster Two spoke hesitantly.

"I think we were just leaving."

"Good to know," Hunter replied politely. "Don't forget the tip."

Hipster Two nodded, standing and digging in his pocket as Hipster One grabbed his gratuitously ironic leather briefcase, swallowing. They started toward the door, but Hunter cleared his throat pointedly.

"Seems like a pretty small tip," he said. "Those shoes you're wearing cost close to two hundred bucks, so I think you can afford to do better. Or were they a present from Mommy and Daddy?"

I frowned as they dug in their pockets again, then decided I should put a stop to this. God help poor Cookie if they got mad enough to start trolling us—they certainly had enough spare time.

"You're fine," I said, opening the door for them. "I'm sure whatever you left is great, and I hope you'll come back again when we're open."

"Um, right," Hipster One said as they scuttled out the door, leaving me alone with Hunter. I slid the bolt closed and lowered the shade, turning to face him.

"Was that really necessary?"

He stood and started stalking toward me.

"Absolutely," he muttered, eyes darkening. I knew that look.

"Hunter, this is my work," I protested. He reached out and caught my hair in one hand, twisting it in his fingers as he jerked me into his kiss. I tried to hold back, but his tongue attacked my lips and then he was inside. It was all over and we both knew it.

God, I loved the taste of him.

He kept kissing me as he backed me toward a table against the inner wall. I'd shut all the big window shades already, so we had total privacy, but this still felt very wrong. My ass bumped into the table, waking me to the reality of the situation.

If I didn't do something, Hunter was going to fuck me right here in the middle of Cookie's shop.

I needed to stop him.

But then his hand found my breast, and he started kneading it roughly. Damn, but that felt good. Tingling arousal started swirling through my body. Hunter pulled away abruptly to frown at me.

"What?"

"Burke wants to meet you."

"Burke, your national president?" I asked, eyes widening. "Why?"

"Hell if I know. He's a cagey old bastard."

His hands slid down my side, catching my skirt and tugging it upward.

"When are we meeting him?" I asked, trying to focus. It was almost impossible, because the skirt was bunching around my waist and he'd found the bare skin of my ass, exposed by my thong. Hunter's hands tightened on me, and he tugged me forward into his hips. His cock was hard and ready to go, which made it almost impossible to breathe, let alone pay attention to his words.

"He's in town already, at the Panther, right down the street," he murmured, massaging my ass. A finger slid toward my crease and worked its way under the thong. He'd been doing that more and more lately.

"The strip club?" I asked, trying to focus.

"Yeah," he said. "We're supposed to pick him up when we're done here. Says he wants to show me something. You up for that?"

I reached down between us to find his erection, squeezing it tightly. His breath hissed, fingers tightening.

"I'm up for anything," I whispered with a smile.

He gave a low groan, then spun me around and pushed me flat across the table. I heard the sound of his zipper going down and he caught my thong, wrenching it hard enough to snap the elastic.

Bummer. I went through more panties that way . . .

Hunter's fingers slid into me abruptly and I cried out. Holy *shit*, that felt good, he always found the target. *Always*. Then he pulled back out, rubbing my own moisture along my crease. I felt his finger press against my rear opening, pushing slowly inside. It was a strange sensation, but he'd done it a few times now, and I knew he wouldn't hurt me.

"Someday I want to fuck you here," he said, and I shivered.

Someday I'd let him. But now I felt the head of his cock tracing my pussy as he lined himself up with my opening. His free hand caressed the small of my back, soothing me.

"You ready?" he asked, his voice ragged. I nodded and braced my legs. Sex with Hunter was fantastic, but rarely gentle. Sure enough, he slammed into me, filling me in one hard stroke. My back arched and I moaned, tender tissues stretched to their limits.

"Christ, you're a good lay," he muttered, giving a few hard thrusts. Then he started hammering into me, all but attacking my pussy with his cock. The finger made my ass feel impossibly full, impaled and at his mercy.

Holy hell. I'd never been so turned on in my life, which was a good thing. I didn't see how he—or anyone—could keep up this pace for long. Not that I needed much more time. Every stroke took me a little higher, and my legs started trembling from the mixture of physical strain and building desire.

"I'm close," I warned him, reaching out and catching the sides of the table. "Really, really close, babe."

He pulled out of my rear, then gripped my cheeks with wide fingers, digging deep enough that I'd probably have bruises later. I didn't care. All that mattered was the sensation of his cock splitting me wide. He invaded again and again, until my entire body convulsed, the orgasm hitting me hard and fast. I whimpered, collapsing even as he kept going. Then I felt his cock start pulsing, hot come shooting deep into my body.

The sound of panting filled the shop. Probably shouldn't tell Cookie about this one, I decided.

"It's a lot better without the condom," I managed to say after a few minutes.

"Thank fuck for birth control," he muttered, leaning down to kiss the back of my neck. He pulled out, then stepped back. I pushed up shakily, catching my skirt with one hand and tugging it down. My shredded thong had caught around one leg, and I kicked it off.

"So when are we supposed to meet Burke?"

"About fifteen minutes," he said. "Just enough time to clean up and walk down."

"You want to bleach the table while I hit the bathroom?" I asked, feeling guilty. What would the health department make of *that* one? "Everything else is ready to go. Bleach is under the sink."

"Sure," he said, giving me a quick smile. "Gotta say, the idea of you out in public, wearing that little skirt and nothing else? It's turning me on again."

I snorted.

"Everything turns you on."

"Nope, just everything about you. Trust me, I don't feel this way at all when I see that fat chick at the DMV. Now get cleaned up. Or don't—hell if I care. I like the idea of my jizz running down your legs for everyone to see."

"You're disgusting."

"Yup."

I turned to leave, but he caught my hand, pulling me back for another quick kiss.

"Thanks," he said, resting his forehead against mine. "I was wound pretty tight. Usually when Burke shows up without warning, it's not a good sign. You helped a lot just now."

"I'm a very helpful girl," I said, waggling my eyebrows. I pulled away, turning toward the bathroom. Hunter smacked my ass and I jumped, laughing.

"Hurry up," he said. "Burke's waiting."

"Will I like him?"

"No," Hunter said, shaking his head slowly. "He's usually a complete asshole, so don't be surprised if he says something rude.

But he saved me and Kelsey as kids. That should count for something. I'd probably be dead if it wasn't for him. Dead or in prison."

"Then I'll love him," I said. "I don't care if he's an asshole. I still
owe him, big-time."

"Kinda how I feel about your dad," he said. "Go get clean,
woman."

I flipped him off and headed for the bathroom.

Hunter parked his new truck right in front of the strip club. Nothing fancy. In addition to everything else that sucked about the accident, he hadn't been able to collect on his insurance. Bullet holes
tend to draw cops, and the last thing either club wanted was law
enforcement poking around. I'd offered to help pay for the new rig,
but Hunter had blown me off, making it clear he could afford to
buy his own ride. I wondered about that . . . Working part time as
a mechanic wasn't exactly lucrative, but if the Jacks were anything
like the Reapers, his income stream was probably creative.

Hunter texted Burke, who stepped outside about five minutes
later. I don't know what I expected, but Burke wasn't it. He was
old—way older than my dad or our national president, Shade.
More like Duck's age. His hair was long and gray, and he kept it
pulled back in a ponytail. He had a full beard, and it was long, too.

Skid followed him, and we eyed each other warily.

Me and Skid had an uncomfortable truce these days. Kelsey and
I shared a place now, thanks to him. I still slept over at the house a
lot, but nothing like before. I guess that was a winning solution for
all of us. Well, all of us but Hunter. The idea of me and Kelsey living together seemed to scare him a little, and I guess I could understand that. It certainly made it easier to gang up on him.

"I'm Burke," the Devil's Jacks president said, stepping forward.
"You must be Em?"

I smiled and nodded.

"It's very nice to meet you," I said.

"You're not much, for a girl who causes so much trouble," he said bluntly. "I pictured you with bigger tits."

My smile didn't falter for a minute.

"I'm still saving up for my boob job," I told him politely. "Until then, I'm afraid Hunter's stuck with me like this. On the bright side, I give excellent head. He had to pay my father six whole goats for me, you know."

Hunter choked, but Burke burst out laughing. Skid's eyes widened, and he gave me a sly nod of approval.

"Well, she's not shy."

"Not even a little," Hunter said, wrapping his arm around my neck and pulling me close. "You said you wanted to show us something?"

"Yeah," Burke said. "I'll ride with Skid. You follow."

Hunter tugged me toward his truck and we climbed in.

"You nearly gave me a heart attack back there," he said. "And I think you gave him the wrong impression—it wasn't goats, it was kegs."

"My bad," I murmured. "It's so hard for me to hold all that information in my little female head. I get all confused."

"It's okay, sweetheart," he said blandly. "I can tell you what to do. We have to keep that feeble little brain of yours from getting tired."

I smacked his leg hard and he pretended to whimper as Skid pulled out ahead of us. Hunter followed, reaching over to lay a hand on my bare leg, running his fingers up and down my thigh as we drove.

God, how could I want him again so soon?

We didn't actually drive that far, but traffic was slow enough that it took a good twenty minutes before Skid pulled off into a residential neighborhood. The houses were all old, built in the typical Portland style. Narrow lots, high porches, trees everywhere. The house he pulled up to looked solid enough, but the paint was peeling and the lawn was practically a jungle. Interesting . . .

"What's this?" I asked Hunter. He shrugged.

"No idea."

I opened the passenger-side door, then tried to figure out how to get out of the truck without showing my goodies off to the entire world. Hunter smirked, but he came around and lifted me down, setting me on the sidewalk like a perfect gentleman. Skid and Burke were already up on the porch, watching us with interest.

We climbed up the stairs to join them.

Burke stuck a key in the door and opened it, gesturing for us to go inside. The place was completely empty, and while you could tell it had gorgeous lines, the house clearly needed work. The floors were all wood, but they were scratched to hell and back. It had a shotgun layout—living room, dining room, and kitchen all in a straight line. I assumed bedrooms were upstairs.

"What do you think?" Burke asked Hunter. "In addition to this, there's an old carriage house out back. You'd never know it, but it's a double lot. Spans the block."

"It's solid construction," he said. "But not quite sure why we're here."

"I'm buying it," Burke said. "Figured you and Em might like a house of your own. What do you think?"

HUNTER

I stared at Burke, wary. Em's eyes were wide, but she didn't say anything—proof positive that she was her father's daughter. She'd drill me later, but she wouldn't give away shit in front of witnesses. Good thing, too, because Burke was a twisty fucker, and for all I knew this was some kind of elaborate test of some kind.

"Skid, why don't you take Em upstairs, show her the rest of the house?"

"Sure," Skid said, his tone neutral, but I saw a hint of something dark in his eyes. Whatever was happening here, Skid was already in on it. We'd have words about that later. He led Em away, and I turned to Burke.

"What's this all about?" I asked bluntly.

"Investment property," Burke said, offering a fatherly smile. "The market's still recovering, and it's a good value. Plenty of room out back. I might want to store some things there at some point. You kids do the work to fix this place up, you live here for free. In a few years, you can buy it from me. Hell, maybe I'll just give it to you. You're the closest thing I have to a son, Hunter. If you're really ready to settle down, I want you in a good place."

I stilled, not buying it for an instant.

"What's the game?"

Burke dropped the pretense, eyes hardening.

"That's why I like you so much, always have. No bullshit. It's a fucking shame you can't go higher in the club, at least not for now. Until then, I like the idea of you playing house here in Portland. We've got a decent presence started, but it's touch and go. I set you up here with Princess Emmy, the Reapers will think twice about shooting up the place if things go south. Instant safe house."

I shook my head.

"I won't risk Em," I said, and I meant it. "Deal breaker."

"It's not a risk," Burke said. "She'll be safer here than anywhere else. We won't hurt her, and they sure as shit won't, either. That girl is walking, talking neutral territory, and putting her in this house brings us one step closer to establishing a real chapter in Portland. The only place she'd be safer is in her daddy's house, but I'm willing to bet you won't be moving in with him."

"She's a person, you know. Not just a pawn for you to play with."

"We're all pawns," he replied softly. If I didn't know better, I'd have said he looked almost human. "And the cartel will keep coming. This game doesn't end and we both know it. But that doesn't mean I'm not happy for you. Proud, too. You know, back when we first cooked this whole Em plan up, we figured she'd be a good old lady."

"Best ever," I agreed warily. God damn, but he was a wily old bastard.

"Then treat her right. You know, I used to be married. Didn't work out too well . . ." he said, looking away. "I regret that, I honestly do. You got something good with that girl, so don't fuck it up. Now go upstairs and look around, see if Em's on board. If she is, I'll call the real estate agent."

Em stood by the window in the front bedroom, overlooking the street. There were two smaller rooms and a bathroom, too. I came to stand behind her, wrapping my arms around her small figure and dropping my chin to her shoulder. Burke wanted me to use this beautiful girl again, and I fucking hated him for it. I'd hurt her once already on his orders. It had to stop here . . . although he'd been right about a couple of things. The first was the game—it wouldn't end. And the second was that I had something real good with Em.

Too good to lose for anything. Even the Jacks.

"Thoughts?" I asked, her small body tucked against mine, the feel of her completing me in a way even my club couldn't. It reinforced my decision and I felt a sense of something like peace about what I had to do. Sure, the thought of it still sickened me, but the thought of losing her sickened me more.

"I don't know," she replied. "Was he serious?"

"Yup. He wants to buy it and have us fix it up. In exchange, he'll let us live here for free."

"That seems a little . . . out of character? I mean, based on what you've told me about him."

"You could say that," I answered. "He's not doing it out of the goodness of his heart, that's for sure. He wants neutral territory, and figures putting you in a house with me will help keep the peace."

I felt her stiffen, but then she nodded. "I can see that. What do you think?"

"I don't like the idea of using you again," I told her honestly. "I love you and I realized something down there, listening to him."

"What's that?"

I paused, taking a deep breath, my heart suddenly pounding. The club had been my life. My family. My brothers. Everything.

Jacks first.

I'd lived by those words for eight years.

"Maybe I should leave the club, Em. We can pull free of all this."

She stilled. Some women wouldn't get what I'd just offered, but Em was a child of the Reapers. She *knew*. Then I felt her body relax and her hands came up and covered mine where they lay across her belly.

"But would letting him use me really be that bad, if it's for peace?" she asked softly. "My club doesn't want to hurt me, and if I'm helping you create neutral ground, that'll make me even more valuable to yours. Isn't that about as safe as we get in this life? This could be good for all of us, Liam."

Something in me unclenched, and I felt such incredible relief I could hardly stand. I loved my club so much . . . it was just that I loved Em more.

"Are you sure?" I asked her. Em tugged away from me and turned in my arms, looking up as she cupped my face between her hands. Her eyes met mine and she held my gaze, her expression utterly serious.

"I'm sure," she said. "There are things I don't like about your club, but they also helped make you who you are. They're your family, and now they're my family, too. I'm not a civilian and I didn't fall in love with a stockbroker. I fell in love with a Devil's Jack. I know what it means to wear a cut."

Then she gave me that same beautiful, goofy smile that'd made me fall in love with her in an instant so many months ago in that parking lot. Fuckin' punch to the gut. Every. Time.

"Now do you want to move in with me?" she asked lightly.

"Maybe create a little safe patch of peace here in Portland? The house has potential—I could be happy living here. But only with you. Skid and the boys can come visit, but they have to keep their own place. I don't want to live in a frat house."

"Easy call," I said, wondering what the fuck I'd done to get this lucky. "He doesn't smell nice like you."

"Well, I guess if smell is the criteria, I probably do win," she said, leaning forward, arms tightening around my waist. I could hold her like this forever. "I like the idea of keeping the peace. And we're practically living together already. I guess if things get bad, I could always go back to Cookie's house."

I clenched up again.

"No," I said firmly. "If things get bad, you'll stay right here with me and we'll work through it."

"Okay," she whispered, reaching up to tuck some hair behind my ear. Then she popped up on her toes and kissed me gently. "Want to get started right now?"

"Started on what?"

"Working through things. Because I think you need some clarification on the whole lying issue . . ."

I froze. What had I done now? I searched my memory, wondering if I'd lied without even noticing? Fuck.

"I know I said to only tell me the truth," she whispered. "But for future reference, when a woman asks a man if something makes her look fat, the answer is always no. Always. Think you can remember that?"

Oh, thank Christ.

"You're fucked up."

"But can you remember it?"

"Yeah," I said, trying not to laugh.

"Then I guess I'll move in with you. But I'm serious about Skid. He has to stay at the other house with the guys."

"That's fine, so long as your dad stays at the clubhouse when he comes to visit."

"No problem," she said, giggling. She squeezed me tighter. "Love you, babe."

"I love you, too."

It wasn't a lie.

JANUARY
COEUR D'ALENE, IDAHO
PICNIC

"Pic, check this out."

Picnic glanced up from his desk toward Gage. The club's enforcer sat in front of four screens streaming security footage.

"What?"

"New cleaning bitch," Gage said. "Marie's out, says she can't handle it and her homework. Nobody else is available, so Bolt hired a civilian. She runs a service or something, got a good rep."

"And I should care because?"

"Look at her ass, then rethink the question."

Picnic pushed up slowly and walked around his cluttered workspace in the pawn shop office. He'd spent the last hour trying to figure out what the hell he'd done with the ticket for the red and gold Harley out back in the yard. Some dumbass rich kid had pawned it, probably to buy pot or something equally stupid. He'd had his eye on it ever since. Spoiled little shit had defaulted that morning.

Gage leaned back in his chair, folding his hands across his stomach.

"Nice, hmm?"

Pic leaned forward and took her in, then gave a low whistle.

"She know there's a camera on her?"

"Probably not," Gage replied, smirking. "They're not hidden, but they don't jump out at you, either."

The new cleaner was down on her hands and knees, ass pointing toward the camera mounted in the corner. And what an ass it was . . . Her faded jeans had ridden down, exposing the very top of her rear. No crack, but damned close. It was shaped like a heart, nice and bouncy and curved exactly how he liked 'em.

She leaned forward a little more, and he realized she was using a knife to scrape something up off the floor, under the overhanging lip of the display cabinet. She wiggled again and Pic shifted, reaching down to adjust his pants. Fuck that was hot.

"Her face as pretty as her ass?"

"Yeah," Gage said, leaning forward to fiddle with the controls. The camera zoomed in on her crotch as she spread her legs slightly. Pic bit back a groan.

"This her first night?"

"Yup."

"Anyone tap that yet?"

"Nope."

"No fuckin' the help allowed. Make sure it's known."

Gage glanced up at him and smirked.

"Since when is that a rule? You've slept with half the girls at The Line. Hell, you took one home last night."

Pic grunted, eyes glued to the screen. "New dancers are easy to find. A good cleaner isn't."

Gage shook his head, then zoomed back out. The cleaner stood up, stretching her arms high over her head. She turned and said something to another woman working across the showroom. The reply made her smile and Picnic caught his breath. Damn, she was stunning, despite the fact that her dirty blonde hair was pulled back in a messy ponytail and her jeans and sweatshirt had seen better days. Thick, dark eyelashes. Deep brown eyes that sparkled. Big, pouty lips.

Lips that belonged around his cock.

Then she pulled off her sweatshirt, revealing a blue spaghetti-strap tank top. It showed off her tits just right—good size, and he'd bet his life the nipples hiding underneath would fit his mouth perfectly. Tossing the sweatshirt lightly on the counter, she leaned over, grabbed a spray bottle of blue window cleaner, and started attacking the display case.

"Jesus, I wanna fuck those tits," Gage muttered. "You sure she's off-limits?"

Pic growled. "Yeah. I'm sure. Anyone who touches her will answer to me. D'you think she's puttin' on a show for us? I don't need that kind of trouble."

"No idea," Gage replied. "She's missed her calling. Bitch should be doin' porn."

Couldn't argue with that.

"Fire her," he said suddenly. "Find someone else."

"We've had the prospects cleaning for a week now. We need them on other things, and I guess Bolt had a hell of a time finding her in the first place."

She stood, then leaned back against the counter, cocking her head as she said something to her co-worker. The fact that the counter was the perfect height to shove her down and fuck her on didn't escape his notice.

"We got a file on her?"

Gage leaned over and opened a drawer, pulling out a folder. Pic flipped it open. Not much there. London Armstrong, owner of London's Cleaning Service. Thirty-eight years old, which surprised him. She looked younger. A lot younger. Not that the security cam had the best resolution, but still . . . She'd been in business six years, solid reputation. Total civilian. And she might be single, but she had custody of a kid—some high school girl. Not hers. A cousin.

Shit.

London didn't sound like the kind of woman who'd be down for a one-night stand. Nope, despite her sexy little dance, she had a clean, wholesome look, which killed him, because he didn't do clean. He liked his girls filthy dirty and without strings . . . not to mention young enough to follow his orders without too many questions. Women her age were old enough to know better.

"Tell Bolt to find someone else ASAP," he muttered. "And until then, hands off. I'm serious."

Gage laughed.

"Just fuck her and get it over with. It's obvious you want to."

"Eat shit," Pic muttered, rubbing a hand across his stubbled chin, because Gage was right. He did want to fuck her.

He wanted to fuck her a lot.